BERENICE'S HAIR

Guy Ottewell

state 2015 Nov

ISBN 0-934546-66-5

Universal Workshop

Raynham, Massachusetts, and Lyme Regis, England

www.UniversalWorkshop.com

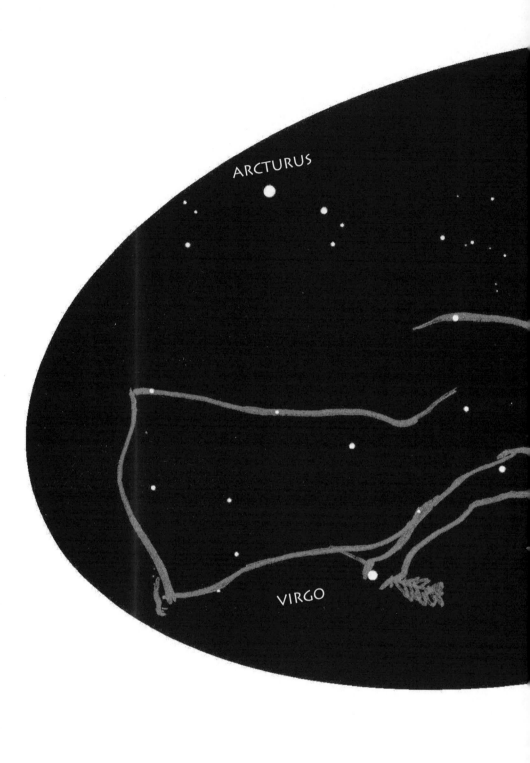

COMA BERENICES

LEO

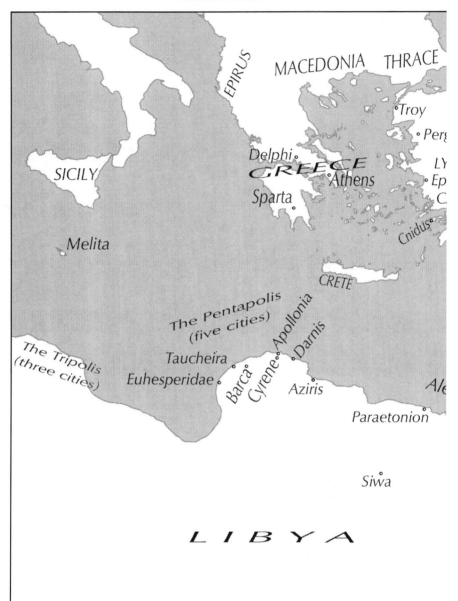

Prelude: How the Lion Lost His Tail

I was a newcomer to South Carolina, after two years in the high desert of Arizona, in whose clear air I had lain out watching the stars and absorbing skylore both European and Navajo. When I came to a moister and greener region, I put astronomy behind me—feeling I knew the universe well enough!—and turned to learning another side of nature: plants, insects, and gardening.

But Bill Brantley, professor of physics in a Baptist university, teaching an astronomy course to attract non-science majors into his department, had me take his students out and show them the stars. I took them out to the apple orchard behind his house, and pointed at stars and recited their mysterious names. This, rather than gravity and celestial coördinates, was what the students had been hoping for when they signed up. They wanted to be able to stroll with their girlfriends at night and wave aloft and say: "See that star? It's called Arcturus!"

"And there," I said, "is Leo, the Lion—"

("I'm a Leo!" at least one of the students will have interjected.)

"He does look quite like a lion, doesn't he? The bright star is his heart, and the curve of stars that goes up from there, like a backwards question-mark, is his mane and head. Then over to the left, that triangle is his hindquarters."

"So the star at the end of the triangle is his tail?" an eager student asks.

"Yes, it is, and it's called Denebola, which means 'tail of the Lion' in Arabic. (Roughly . . .)"

We rest with that, letting Leo burn his great shape into the memory. Then hoping that a bit more will not be too much, I add:

"But really that star is only the stub of the lion's tail, because he once had a longer tail, ending with a tuft. There it is, that dim patch higher up to the left, can you see it?—a little cluster of stars. But the lion lost the tuft of his tail, this is the story.

"There once was a queen of Egypt, called Berenice—"

"Sounds like Very-Nicey!" chimes a student.

"Yes, she was beautiful, and she had long golden hair. Her husband, King Ptolemy—" ("Can we just call him Tommy?") "Her husband, King Ptolemy, went off to a war, and Berenice vowed to sacrifice her hair if he came home safe. He did, and Berenice, with gratitude though some regret, cut off her gorgeous hair; and it was hung up in the temple of Aphrodite, the goddess of love.

"The king and his courtiers went to view it. But it was gone! Someone had stolen it!—some trophy-hunter or perhaps some secret lover of the queen. The king turned on the trembling priests, the guardians of the temple. 'Off with their heads!'

"But one, with quick wits, pointed into the sky: 'Sire, behold!'" and here I, though not normally a person from whom wide gestures are expected, have the chance to fling my arm skyward. "'The gods have transported the sacred tress to heaven, for all to see! It has become a new constellation!' The king looked up and saw that it was so! There was his wife's hair, a little cascade of stars just where the priest's trembling finger pointed! Evidently the dear king hadn't spent much time skygazing and didn't realize that the little mist of stars had been there all along. And so it has been known ever since as the constellation of Coma Berenices, Berenice's Lock of Hair."

"This is great!" exclaimed one of the girls. "This is the kind of thing I wanted to hear!" And they were able to memorize huge Leo, little Coma Berenices (which is a more important constellation than it looks, being the capital of our part of the universe), and maybe one or two others that evening. One and a half of them afterwards went on to become professional scientists.

The little story of Berenice and her hair is one of the easiest tricks in the repertory of the star-talker—it is as Fool's Mate is to chess or the Disappearing Saltshaker to the amateur magician. But as with all stories, the deeper you go into it the less simple it it becomes. The clever fellow who pointed was not a priest but an early astronomer, and he had a name: Conon. And the temple was not quite in the town; and there was more than one Ptolemy and more than one Berenice, and our Berenice wasn't exactly Egyptian. Nor was she entirely well behaved.

And, come on!—what really became of her hair?

Harmanaxa

A great *harmanaxa*, a curtained wagon, trundles from the palace door and down through Cyrene, the high city. The wagon lurches on the cobbles, and the heavy golden tassels fringing the curtains bob and swing annoyingly. Berenice jerks them aside and glances out at the huge view, which never fails—though she has known it all her life—to deepen the breath in her chest: the city tumbling down its rocky cleft, the Temple of the Spring, the gate in the city wall, and below it the country sweeping to the sea. Berenice, seventeen years old, is being carried down to the port to meet the man who is arriving to marry her.

But Berenice is in a mood. She would rather be going by herself to greet this unknown prince, Demetrius, of whom it is said that he is called Demetrius the Fair. Her mother has insisted on coming along. The wagon is a harmanaxa, a Persian women's wagon, because of Queen Apama's Persian descent; it was brought with her, quite a number of years ago, on the ship by which she herself was brought to marry Berenice's father. Apama, in contrast with her daughter, has black hair.

Apama's Persian chamberlain, Phravartes, walks in front, holding the bridle of the right-hand horse to steady the pair and damp the lurching. But a wagon, even with four stout wheels, must always lurch, and Berenice grips the seat, so as to stay stiff and not allow her hip to bump her mother's. The road eases onto the lower slopes, the horses and the chamberlain and the ladies' attendants plod on, the ladies doze. The wagon tips forward as the way again winds steeply downward, through the lower scarp. Under an overhanging cliff, dogs from a village snap at the ankles of the attendants, and the chamberlain hands back to them his whip, which he doesn't need, to drive the curs off. Berenice's eyes remain shut, until after eight miles the sea air tells her senses they are coming into Apollonia.

"Mother, I say to you again, we did not need to descend to meet this man. He should have been allowed to ascend to us."

"And I say again to you that I wish us to meet him before Apion and Charicles meet him. They still hanker for the earlier arrangement."

"Yes, the arrangement intended by my father before he died."

"The Egyptian boy is a monster. Not a monster—a monster would be interesting; he is a pitiful thing, a tadpole. What can be expected when a man marries his—"

"The Egyptian boy has a brother."

"Yes. Not in line for the succession, being the son of a discarded wife. A sister too. With the same name as yourself, being your cousin. Perhaps you would like to marry her. That would be not unlike the other habits of the Egyptians."

Berenice would like to strike her mother, but she has to content herself with turning her face sharply away.

What they refer to is that Berenice was betrothed three years ago, when she was only fourteen and her hair was more like silver than gold and had hardly grown past her shoulders, to one of the sons of the most powerful of all kings, the king of Egypt—a younger son, but heir, because son of the favored queen. A party among the courtiers still argues that any chance for alliance with Egypt should not be thrown away. But Apama, now that her own husband has died, has revoked the betrothal, on the ground that the son-and-heir is the inbred product of an incestuous marriage; and because she has been offered an alternative that she likes better, for political as well as genetic reasons. Her daughter will never marry a Ptolemy.

"Well, now, mother, instead of awaiting this—man—at home we must await him here in the port."

"I am surprised you don't welcome the excursion. It's true that our residence down here is even less superb than our hovel up in our little city, but I'm the one who cares about that. I should have expected you to delight in a change of bedrooms."

"What if his ship doesn't come in for two days?"

"Then we'll while away the time by swimming in the sea and collecting cockles," replies Apama impatiently. It is a reply designed to sting, since swimming in the sea is just what the girl would love to be allowed to do.

But, to their relief, the ships from Macedon are already in the harbor—not one ship but four: an impressive bodyguard has been sent along with the Macedonian prince. You can never be sure, even of your allies.

Demetrius's own ship is warped to the dock and he has strolled around the few streets of Apollonia, accepting a beaker of wine from a taverner, chatting with a few of the men—the Greeks and, if they are able to speak Greek, the Libyan natives—and returning the smiles of the women. But he is now politely back on the deck in order to be invited ashore by the queens.

He bows to them and sets his foot on the gangplank. At this moment he sees Apama give a start. Yes, she was certainly seized by a slight convulsion! His eyes are on her only, since she is a striking woman and has stridden to the edge of the quay, in front of her daughter; so he has not noticed that the same convulsion gripped everyone else ashore. Some of them, such as Berenice, merely quivered; some re-steadied their feet, some lurched, and one or two along the quay or back in the town even fell over. Demetrius the Vain, if he had noticed these, would have been even more complimented, but he is complimented enough by his effect on the black-haired queen. Though the gangplank has slightly shifted he balances elegantly along it, with his gold-trimmed blue cloak swinging behind his broad shoulders, kneels and declares his name and lineage ("Demetrius, son of Demetrius, son of Antigonus"), and is formally granted protection and offered hospitality in Cyrenaica—the land and its five cities. He is introduced to Berenice, but she barely has a chance to say a word to him, even supposing she were in a mood to.

As they walk toward the *harmanaxa* and the horse that is being held for Demetrius, Berenice imagines herself running ahead and leaping onto the horse (even though it is two hands taller than her own Draco) and leaving the man to go in the carriage with her mother, as he would clearly prefer. She controls her impulse, but—irritated by their slow pace—walks somewhat apart and ahead, so that Demetrius (even while his experienced eye strokes the maiden's outline) has a chance to murmur to her mother:

"Madam, I have to confess that I—felt a strange tremor in the moment I saw you."

Apama instantly understands and takes advantage of his mistake. "Indeed! Then I'll confess: I too—felt that tremor." She does not lie, in fact she is more truthful than he. She has not mentioned the inauspicious event, and has kept him at a distance from bystanders, and thus he has not heard their chatter. They are uneasy lest the little earthquake be followed by a greater, since there is an old tale that Apollonia was once struck by such a tremor and a prophecy that it will one day split and disappear under the sea.

(Some centuries later, it did, and I have swum over the sea-weedy masonry of its wharves and warehouses.)

Demetrius, as he rides up to Cyrene, reflects: "This Apama—who trembled when she saw me—promises passion; whereas the sulky girl—and what does a virgin know of the skills of love? Besides, it's the mother who holds the power here. I can marry the girl but keep myself from boredom with the widow." And Apama in the carriage is thinking something of the same.

Floor, Step, and Top

Cyrene's gate stands open and the span is wide enough for Demetrius to ride—right hand on hip, blue cloak swinging— beside the horses that pull the ladies' wagon; thus he enters the city, and harvests the admiration of new crowds. He gazes above their heads, displaying his own appreciation of the prosperous houses, the theatre scooped like a great shell into the left-hand cliff, and the soaring front of the temple set on a ledge.

"A fine temple!" he exclaims to Calliphron, the escort who has been deputed to ride beside him and point out the sights. "To which of the gods is it dedicated?"

"To Apollo. It stands over the spring, which was the reason for the city's founding. The Libyans led our ancestors to this place, promising them it was the best in the land. They said it has a 'hole in the sky', meaning it has plenty of water."

"So does it rain here very much?"

"As much as anywhere east and west along the mountain;

there is enough rain, in season, all along Cyrenaica, which is why they call it the Green Mountain. But there's an all-year spring here—"

"A hole in the rock, then!"

"Yes, and it was sacred to some nymph of theirs, whom they called something like Kurana, so to us she is the huntress *Kurênê*, a bride of Apollo, to whom we built the temple. For it's he who guides all explorers and colonists."

"He guided me too," confides Demetrius. "Frankly, it was my brother, King Antigonus, who negotiated all this. I was enjoying myself as I was, and didn't see any need to tie myself in marriage yet, so after a while he suggested that I send to Delphi and take whichever course the oracle advised. The question I sent was: 'Will I be lucky or unlucky if I go to Libya?' And I was favored with Apollo's answer in the usual style:

> The weapons of Eros are all you need fear
> If you sail to the south and you climb the third tier.

"That was encouraging, was it not? Did you understand it?"

"At once."

"I can say that I have already felt the arrows of Eros quite keenly! I didn't know how the 'third tier' applies to Cyrenaica, but when I asked I was told that this land is composed of three levels."

"Yes," says the Cyrenaican, "we call them the Floor, the Step, and the Top. That is the Top up there." And along the cliff to the right, and partly pouring down it, can be seen the outline of the palace. The horses climb on, and through another portal into the lower palace yard.

At the supper table Demetrius makes some effort to bestow proper courtesy upon his intended bride, but his head is mostly turned in conversation toward her mother.

"How often I have heard it said, Queen Apama—"

"I have to correct you: I am not a queen. My late husband was viceroy of this province, never a king, although he did for a while pretend to the title."

"Nevertheless, you appear a queen to me and deserve to be one. As I was about to remark, it is said that all the princesses of our Macedonian stock are tigresses."

"Macedonian! There are no tigers or tigresses in Europe. Have you ever seen a tigress?"

"Never, other than yourself."

"Tigresses live only in the lands beyond the River Tigris. That is where I come from."

"But your father—king of Syria—surely the Macedonian stream in your blood is as strong as any the rest of us can claim."

"I take after my Persian grandmother Apama, to whom my grandfather was married by Alexander."

"Yes, you are one of those who combine Europe and Asia, as Alexander intended—the highest blood of Macedon and the highest blood of Persia."

"And you wonder why I am not as proud of the conquering side as of the conquered? Tigresses, as we have said, live in the east. If the men, too, had been tigers, Alexander would not have conquered Asia."

Demetrius pauses to digest this view of the world's recent history. Berenice, who has been listlessly listening to such of these words as she could catch, yawns without hiding her yawn and takes her departure. Usually she asks her mother's permission before rising from the table, but now she wonders why she needs to. Is she not to be, by her father's will, ruler of Cyrenaica? She passes through the garden, climbs the stair into the upper palace, and seeks out her tutor, Callimachus the son of Stasenor.

He will not be expecting her at this time, but will be as usual in the library. She finds him outside its door: he has brought a scroll to read in the better light of the colonnaded gallery, whose long stone bench overlooks the darkening garden.

She sits down beside him, and he lets the scroll roll itself back to its beginning. It is a short scroll and a tight one, not often read, or newly acquired.

"What are you reading, Callimachus?"

"Eudoxus, on stars."

"Rolled up, he reminds me of a leek. —I would like you to tell me again the story of that monstrous wedding. It was at least a year ago—I mean it was at least a year ago you told me the story, and I've forgotten who the three wives were."

The marriage of Europe and Asia

"Well, it was not monstrous" (Callimachus flinches; the word the girl used makes it sound like the mating of Pasiphae with the bull, or of Penelope with the hundred suitors, but he doesn't care to explain the difference to her)— "it was, not monstrous, but it was certainly vast, there were nine thousand guests."

"You don't have to tell me who they all were!"

"No, just how it came about. Alexander—you know of the course of his campaign, and I went over it with you more fully for several weeks. How he marched out of Macedon and conquered his way through the whole Persian empire—Anatolia, Syria, into Egypt (he founded Alexandria, came as far west as Siwa, didn't come quite as far west as here); and back into Syria, Assyria, Persia itself, and all the way into Bactria and Sogdia in the middle of Asia, and even into India, which is toward the end of the world. I outlined to you the tactics of the major battles—"

"But as for the marriage?"

"The marriage was an incident of the homeward march (though as you know he never reached home)."

"I want to hear again about it." A woman wishes to hear about marriages, not about military history. (But of course, it concerns her mother. She is wondering about her mother.)

"It was an incident of the return through the middle of the empire. You will remember that the Persian empire had four capitals: Ecbatana and Persepolis, Babylon and Susa—and it was as soon as he came to Susa that he staged the wedding. It was Alexander's policy to reconcile the conquered peoples to their Macedonian conquerors by intermarriage, and he had already led the way by marrying Roxane. The Persians sound her name *roshan* and it means 'bright' and she was the daughter of a lord of Sogdia. And now he married Stateira, daughter of Dareius the dead Persian king; and at the same time he married Parysatis, daughter of the previous Persian king." "Roxane—Stateira—Parysatis," Berenice intones. She is still accustomed to reciting her lessons.

"And he made eighty of his officers join in his Persian wedding, by taking wives from among the Persian nobility."

"Eighty."

"Yes, some of them against their will."

"And others quite willingly?"

"Very likely. (Though some, I'm afraid, including Ptolemy, had already taken—wives—in India or elsewhere.) I cannot recite to you all of the eighty great Macedonians and the names of the

Persian ladies they married; I could list a good fifteen of the most important who ranked as the Companions of Alexander. But certainly the two of most interest to us, to you, were Ptolemy, to whom was assigned a lady named Artacama daughter of Artabazus; and Seleucus, who took Apama, of Bactria—your mother's grandmother.

"And then they all marched onward and got as far as Babylon, and there Alexander suddenly died, a month before his thirty-third birthday, and his empire—unlike the three-centuries empire of the Persians—fell apart. And its pieces were seized by his Macedonian generals, each striving to seize the other pieces and put back together the empire of the Persians and of Alexander, each frustrated by the others . . ."

Berenice had hoped for more about that wedding. Susa, "Shushan the Palace," the city of lilies, where black people had once lived. Was the wedding in a columned Persian hall lit by ten thousand candles? On what did they feast?—what music?—what did Roxane and Stateira and Parysatis wear and what did they say to each other?—and why did no more than one of them bear Alexander a child, and he a poor imperfect one? And among all those other eighty brides, what more about Artacama, wife (at least second wife) for Ptolemy, and Apama, wife for Seleucus? And was this the time when Alexander drank too much and killed the man who had saved his life or the time when the whole Persian palace went up in flames or is she conflating these other riotous nights into the night of the marriage? But Callimachus has about it no such further details as he has about the great debate in Babylon, after Alexander's death, as to the management of his empire, settled by one side trampling the other with elephants, or about the preserving of his sacred body in honey and its diversion, on its way home to Macedon, by clever Ptolemy so that it rests in Egypt.

Callimachus is still re-narrating (she knows it all, but he is not sure she does, and it is important for it to be established in a future queen's head) how the world came gradually to be divided, as it is now, between Ptolemy in Egypt and Seleucus in Syria. "That is, the first Ptolemy, father of the present one, and grandfather of that unfortunate young Ptolemy who was to have married you. And the first Seleucus, father of Antiochus, the father of your mother."

"Yes," says Berenice. Shifting her position a little on the stone bench, flicking from her lap a caddis fly that perched on it, but not yet getting up. "The world is divided between them."

"The world as we know it, or most of the world. There are barbarians beyond, but no great kingdoms."

"And back in Macedon there was still a kingdom."

"Yes," says Callimachus, hoping not to have appeared to have forgotten Macedon, "there remain some other smaller states between, Thrace, Pergamum, Epirus; but Macedon still counts as the third power."

"Seized in turn, as you told me, by several men, mostly ruffians."

"I don't think I described them that way. Macedon could claim, of course, to be the only legitimate kingdom, as long as that poor brother and that poor child of Alexander were alive, but since then it has indeed changed hands irregularly. But now the house of Antigonus seems to be well enough established in it, and to have regained control of Greece."

"The Ptolemies in Egypt, and the Seleucids in Syria, with Macedon holding the balance by allying sometimes with Syria and sometimes with Egypt." Callimachus's pupil can put it that way, though he would hardly presume to do so; it is well enough that she understands the political position in which she is a pawn. "And those of Macedonian family like me are the top peacocks everywhere, though we have mostly come to speak something like proper Greek; and along with us go you real Greeks to be our teachers and traders; and under us swarm the same Libyan and Egyptian and Syrian and Persian priests and peasants as ever."

"That summary is broadly correct. Though many of us Greeks have long lived in these countries. But this is how it is in this age."

"Now what is my position? What is my status? My father in his latter days said nothing very clearly, and my mother has a way of not making it possible for me to ask questions. Am I a princess, a queen, an heiress, or a statue?"

"I think you must ask this of someone higher, of Charicles or—"

"No, they won't answer. You may answer. You have a duty to answer, being my teacher, and you will be safe in answering, since I enjoy your company, Callimachus—I like you."

Callimachus looks down at his lap, and after a moment picks out of it the scroll that is like a "leek." "This is not actually

Eudoxus," he says, "it is my uncle's history of Cyrenaica. He has just sent it to me. I have the same name as him, though I am only his maternal nephew. He is Callimachus son of Battus—he believes that he and his sister, my mother, are actually descended from the old kings Battus of Cyrene, though I have my doubts. He left here a long time ago and lives in Egypt. I have thought of compiling such a history myself, but my uncle has beaten me to it. As you can see, his history is short. Most of his books are. It's too short."

"May I have it and read it?"

"Certainly, please take it. Now as to your question, the first Ptolemy, after establishing himself in Egypt, annexed our little country and sent here your father Magas, his stepson, to be viceroy over it. So that was your father's rank. After a dozen years he declared his independence."

"He made his rebellion, and marched against Egypt."

"Yes, though he had to turn back, perhaps fortunately for himself. At any rate he became, from being viceroy, king. And to strengthen himself against Egypt he made his alliance with Syria instead, and married Antiochus's daughter, your mother. Then, after you were born, he was reconciled with the second Ptolemy. And so you were betrothed to the young man who may yet live to become the third Ptolemy. Unfortunately last year your father died, and so, soon, may that ailing boy."

"But you have told me the things I know. Tell me of what is happening now, and let me see if I know that too."

"Do you mean the intentions of your mother?"

"Her intentions certainly seem to play a part. Yes, talk to me of them."

"I think I am still telling you what you are aware of. She, being the daughter of the Seleucid, would still prefer Cyrene to be in partnership with Syria against—for security against Egypt. But that is now not possible, because it is now Egypt and Syria that are to be united by marriage—Ptolemy, we learn, is to marry his daughter to the second Antiochus. So instead you are to marry the brother—"

"Half-brother."

"Of the king of Macedon, and Cyrenaica and Macedon will be somewhat safer against Syria and Egypt."

"Yes, it's as I thought. You've told me nothing I don't know."

"You are disappointed in me. I suppose your mother's intention is that just possibly you will become queen of a new Macedonian empire that will coalesce with Syria, and overwhelm Egypt, and resurrect the world-realm of Alexander."

"Or that she will. Well stated, Callimachus," says Berenice, tapping his knee with the scroll he handed to her.

"Thank you. We have rather simplified it all."

"Shall you explain it more deeply in your *History of Islands?*"

"Why, no. I had better not. I have to be careful what I write, even about the kings of ancient history. Anyway, neither Egypt nor Syria nor Macedon is an island, nor Cyrenaica."

The green mountain

But he is contradicted by his uncle, as Berenice finds when she reads the little scroll:

> Cyrenaica—where and what is it? I say it is a kind of island.
>
> West from Egypt stretches an ocean of sand, in which are scattered the islands of the oases; and six hundred miles west lies another and larger island, an island in that it is hemmed between the oceans of water and desert. It owes its greenness not to being sunk toward underground water like the oases but to being uplifted into the moist winds that come along the sea.
>
> It lies much nearer to the parallel island of Crete than it does to Egypt, and four hundred years ago there came two shiploads of Greeks, starving refugees from the volcano island of Thera beyond Crete. They were led by a man called Battus . . .

It was an abbreviated and rather whimsical retelling of the history that Berenice already knew—the old kings of Cyrenaica (all called either Battus or Arcesilaus), the Egyptian and Persian invaders, the throwing-out of kings and Egyptians and Persians by the people, and the republic that lasted more than a hundred years, until the annexation by Ptolemy. But, said Uncle Callimachus,

> the Battiads surely left cousins here, and the cousins left descendants, and among them was my father (your mother's father) Battus.
>
> When the Athenians made a doomed attempt to help

Egypt free itself of its Persian overlords, Cyrene gave refuge to
the survivors; and while Alexander was pursuing the Persian
king into the east, there was a famine in Greece, and Cyrenaicans aided the mother country with their plentiful corn.
For Cyrenaica is not such a humble little island of a country. It
is two hundred miles long, and grows much food (besides silphium, the healing plant that grows nowhere else). It has the
good fortune of three harvest seasons a year: the first along
the coast, the second on the step between the two scarps, the
third on the top—for eight months there is always harvesting
somewhere. And this island of a land is nearer to Europe than
Egypt is. And the Ptolemies do not confine themselves to
Egypt: their policy is to control a ring of coasts around the
eastern end of the sea—Greek islands, the coasts of Anatolia
and Syria—as an outwork to protect Egypt against enemies,
and they want to keep Cyrene as a link in this ring . . .

Next afternoon she returned the treatise to the librarian.
"Your uncle uses quite plain language," she said.

"He usually uses the most ornamented language—he calls it
modern—even though his works are short; in other words I
think he says even less than he seems to say. I believe this is not
a book: it is notes, intended to egg me into writing the proper
history myself. He wants to provoke me to expand his careless
statements—presumably in verse. That's why he tries to suggest
to me that Cyrenaica may be counted as an island."

"I think you're right. When I said he uses plain language, I
meant that toward the end of his essay he becomes personal,
addressing himself to you and saying things he might not put into
a book—as about the policies of kings."

"Yes, that is presumptuous of him."

"No, I appreciate it. He gets at the political situation I am supposed to cope with. Perhaps that's why you lent the scroll to
me."

Callimachus looked at her and thought: She's only seventeen.

"And you, Callimachus," she said, "to which tendency do you
incline? Are you Egyptophile, or do you favor the alliance with
Macedon, or with Syria? Or do you wish that republic back, or
the kingdom of your ancestor Battus?"

"If you would form a party yourself, daughter of Magas, my
heart would be with it."

Berenice and Demetrius were to be married at the spring

equinox, when greenery would return even to those slopes of Cyrenaica that the summer had made brown.

The morning after the betrothal, Demetrius found Berenice kneeling and weeping beside the body of Scylla, one of her pair of Molossian hounds. They had been allowed to roam the court-yards, playing with each other, and despite their fearsome size they were gentle toward most people, but Scylla had snapped at Demetrius and he had had her killed. He patted the girl's head, hoped she did not know who was responsible for the deed, and walked on. That night the other dog, Charybdis, still wailed inconsolably outside his window. Consulting with Apama, he agreed that it would now be best to have the second bitch killed also. This time Berenice found out, because it was a Cyrenaican servant who was sent to do it.

"Mother," said Berenice, "I hate this man. I cannot marry him."

Apama laughed. "'I hate and I love,' as the poet says. No real woman can hate him."

"Do you think I care for his pretty face and his yellow hank?" Demetrius was Fair not only in the sense of *kalos*, beautiful, but in the sense of *xanthos*, blond. Perhaps that was all people meant when they said he would be "a fine match" for her. Berenice's bright hair was kept tightly pinned in a shell at the back of her head (to let her ride, and to diminish her mother's envy), but Demetrius let his flow showily to his shoulders.

"Have you never heard," said Apama, "of charming rogues? He was born a charming rogue and that's the way he can't help being—born of a line of charming rogues. He is Demetrius the Fair, son of Demetrius the Besieger, son of Antigonus the One-Eyed. I'm not sure that Antigonus the One-Eyed was a charming rogue, but Demetrius Poliorcetes certainly was, Demetrius the City-Besieger. His famous siege of Rhodes is famous not for his taking it—he failed to take that upstart republic and reduce it to obedience to his father—but for his gallant and courteous behav-ior during it. And after he failed to take Rhodes, and his father lost his other eye and his life at Ipsus, he roamed the world, chased, adventuring, enchanting women (he was a better besieger of hearts than of cities—if it wasn't for that we wouldn't have our Demetrius), seizing Macedon for a while and then driven out, hunted and adventuring again, until he happened to fall into the hands of Seleucus, and he lived his last years at Seleu-

cus's court, an honored guest, still enjoying himself, still drinking without a care, still a favorite of the ladies." ("Of whom,"
Apama was inclined to add, "I was one.") "That's the way for a
man to live a life. A romantic skirmisher. At least, it's next best
if you can't quite be a Seleucus or a Ptolemy. Which is next best
if you can't be an Achilles or an Alexander."

"And so you think such a man would be faithful to me?"

Apama gazed analytically at her daughter and wondered, not
for the first time, whether this ninny could be her daughter. "She
would have sided," she suspected, "with the Rhodians."

Demetrius thought of going on a tour of the province that was to
be his, but postponed it. He was fully occupied in settling his
servants and belongings into his new home. Berenice, observing
the process—watching the carrying into the upper palace of
crates filled with furs, hats, armor, furniture, ornate washbowls
and mirrors, figurines, pictures, toiletries, keepsakes, a few
scrolls—wondered whether to be surprised by the quantity of
the household that was being grafted into their own. At any rate
it was clear that he expected to settle in Cyrene, not to carry her
back to Macedon. Should she be flattered by his assumption that
she would meet his expectations as a bride? She set herself—
since she would have to live with him—to like him.

He did not spend his time exclusively with her mother but
favored the girl with conversations, mainly about other and
greater cities that he had visited. When he had finished describing the delights of Sardis in Lydia, or it may have been Syracuse
in Sicily, she asked him whether he was interested in learning the
history of the country of which he was to be lord. He replied:

"Certainly, if you were to teach me!"

She did not care to do that, nor to have him share her lessons
with Callimachus, but she said: "My teacher has a little book,
written by his uncle—I could get it for you."

He deemed that hardly necessary; he had read, like every edu-
cated person, the *Histories* of Herodotus, which dealt with every
country in the world, even Cyrenaica.

In that case he already knew (no doubt) how the first Greeks
came, led by Battus whose name meant "stutterer" in Greek but
"king" in the language of the Libyans; how they found no good
place to settle until the natives offered to show them a spot they
would like; and led them (cunningly passing in the night the

fairest place of all) to this lovely cleft, midway along the upper scarp: Cyrene.

"Don't you like," said Berenice, "the story about Irasa? I want to find it some day."

"I'm afraid I have forgotten that part," admitted the prince.

"The place the natives led the Greeks past in the night—the place even fairer than Cyrene. Still no one seems to know where it is."

The red hollow

Before winter put an end to the sailing season, ten more fifty-oared ships came over to Apollonia, not only with yet more of Demetrius's belongings but with a larger complement of Macedonian men-at-arms. They were seconded to him by his half-brother the king Antigonus Gonatas. Macedonia, Syria, and Egypt could afford standing armies; Cyrene, like other smaller powers, could raise armies only for wars. It had a chiliarch, "commander of a thousand," but in times between wars he commanded only twenty fellows, who were enough to police Cyrene. And it was the same in the other four towns—except in Barca, where there was a larger barrack. It was only partly full now, but Magas had sometimes had to fill it. Apama advised Demetrius to station his troops there, where they were less likely to fraternize with the natives.

Cyrenaica rose from its curving coast in two concentric scarps. The scarps were such clear mountain fronts, especially where they were covered only with dry scrub, that children born here thought this was how the world was built: a base, a platform, a second platform set on top. But other parts were chiselled by ravines and cloaked in forest. From the upper scarp the land sloped slowly back into the infinite desert. The Greeks, after founding Cyrene at its commanding notch in the upper scarp, had built a port down on the shore (and though they called it Apollonia, Apollo's own oracle warned that it must one day sink beneath the sea); then other towns along the route to the west, Barca, Taucheira, and far western Euhesperides where the coastal plain, the Floor, widened. Hence the Pentapolis, the Five Cities of Cyrenaica.

Barca, seventy miles west of Cyrene, was the only other of the five that lay inland, though not so high; it lay on the Step, the level of the land between the lower scarp and the upper. The Libyans called it "The Meadow"; Greeks sometimes called it "The Marsh." It lay among fertile fields in a bowl of moist red ground. The farmers of Barca grew not only their share of Cyrenaica's corn but more than their share of fruit and vegetables and the unique herb *silphion*. More of its inhabitants were Libyan than Greek, and the people of the two races lived together co-operatively. They had been through some suffering together.

The winter was one of those with many "holes in the sky": the Green Mountain was wreathed in mists when it was not caressed by rains; there was even a day of snow, and the children could not be restrained from running out of their school and throwing up their hands among the falling flakes. So the spring was a spring when the anemones bloomed and the air was fresh. Berenice went riding on her stallion Draco in a rainshower. Coming home with her gown clinging to her, she hurried in before Demetrius should see her.

Demetrius was disposed to set out on his trip around his domains, and Apama would enjoy showing them to him; and first, westward to Barca.

Apama felt she had begun to live. She had borne decades of marriage to an unheroic man, relieved by no more than one furtive intrigue with a vagabond painter. This was her one life. She saw no reason why she and Demetrius should not enjoy the comfort of the traveling coach together, though he pretended to wonder whether he should have demurred, "out of respect toward your late husband Magas, for whom you are still in mourning."

"Magas," replied the lady, "was fat."

"Oh, surely—"

"*Fat.* He was a glutton. In his last years he was as broad as this coach. His belly would not have been able to accompany him into it. These horses would not have been able to pull him. It's a marvel that he managed to stay alive here for fifty years. He ate as much as he could, because—or so he said—in his childhood he ate little. He was a man of the stooping classes."

"Stooping classes?

"The common people, our laborers and servants. He was a brat of some mining town at the Thraceward end of Macedonia. His father happened to have the same name as the king—Philip— but was a miner. Magas owed his rise to the death of his father in a rock-fall, after which his mother Berenice had the luck to marry a soldier; and that soldier was one who had the ability to rise in the ranks. That soldier was Ptolemy the son of Lagus. And so it was that Magas's mother ended her days as queen of Egypt, and Magas as viceroy of Cyrenaica."

"Remarkable!" said Demetrius. "But I had heard—had I not?— that Ptolemy had married others—"

"You are right; she was not the first of Ptolemy's wives. She was the last and the favorite. I abbreviated the story of her rise. What she actually did, after losing her husband underground, was to find a place as lady-in-waiting to a noblewoman, who was younger than herself; and that noblewoman sailed to Egypt to marry Ptolemy; and Berenice went along with her, and seduced the king—which can't have been difficult—and displaced her patroness. And that was how she became Berenice Queen of Egypt and was able to find her son a well-fed place out here.

"And it was because of her that when I had a child I had to name her Berenice. I wanted proper Greek, Pherenice, but her father insisted on the 'good old Macedonian.'

"I'll tell you something else about Magas. He had risen from the people (by his mother's skill, not his own) and he gave the appearance of enjoying his rise above his origins, yet I saw that though he had plenty of gut he did not have the guts to be a ruler. He mentioned that he had heard his father screaming, and did not care to put anyone to a death like that. He even had some sympathy for that time before—the time before Ptolemy extended his victorious arms over Cyrenaica and sent Magas to hold it down for him—that time of the republic."

Demetrius held his well-shaved chin and thought about all she said. He was thankful for Apama, but she mastered him in talk as well as in bed.

Though most of the road from Cyrene to Barca lay along the Top, it was not all an easy road; it had to wind down into the beautiful gorges of several streams that crossed on their way to the sea. The streams, which in summer were dry pathways of pebbles, were now running full. Here beside the fords were the villages, each with a rest-house for wayfarers: a stoop where one could take wine and bread, a yard with sleeping-platforms around it. Apama and Demetrius did not eat and sleep in these, but in a pavilion that had been brought with them.

In what sense was he beautiful? His beardless jaw was large and smooth, but there was at least one of the serving-women (she had taken the Greek name of Polymela) to whom it seemed repellent. She was glad to have been detached from the court kitchen because she had been trying to stay out of Berenice's notice. There had been a moment when a spoon had dropped, and in picking it up and placing it on the table beside its companion knife Polymela had whispered: *"We'd kill him for you."* Berenice might or might not have heard, and Polymela found herself in fear for her own life, and her husband's, whom she had presumably included in the "we."

The journey required three days. On the second morning Demetrius gazed around at the passing meadows, rocks, and forests, and remarked: "I do see why they call their land the Green Mountain. It is not as green as Europe—still, it is quite a little garden of a country."

"If they would not let their goats eat everything, it would be greener," said Apama. "And you have only to go a few miles south to be out of it into the desert."

"And I have never known a land so riddled with earthquakes!" said the gallant, placing his hand on her knee. It had become their joke, a ready way of initiating intimacies: if, soon after they were alone in their pavilion, Demetrius did not say "I feel a tremor!" she would.

The third day of traveling unrolled. "Now this place Barca to which we are getting near." (The road had descended and the lowland of Barca lay ahead. Many of its fields were sheeted with water and glittered under the afternoon sky.) "It is the hotbed of the republican disaffection. It was the place that gave the most trouble to those old kings of Cyrene. It might be worth your knowing this. There was a line of old kings who called themselves Battus and Arcesilaus—four of each. The first Battus was a mere explorer—actually he was a mere outcast—but the first Arcesilaus learned to rule. The second Battus brought several times as many Greeks over from all of Greece and cleared enough Barbars" (by which she meant the jabbering Libyans) "out of land for them; the second Arcesilaus ruled even harder, so that a pack of his subjects ran away and set themselves up in this place, Barca. They went Libyan; they allied themselves—in more ways than one—with the tribes around here. The third Battus was weak—as a matter of fact, he was lame—and he tried to make everyone happy by bringing an arbitrator over from Greece and sharing out the land, and drawing up what they called a Constitution.

"That arbitrator is still looked up to by peasants as a sort of god; indeed I suspect he is a fictitious person; they say his name was Demonax, People's King, and he came from Mantinea, the city of prophets. Anyway the third King Arcesilaus did away with all that. When the rebels (there are always some who won't abide firm rule)—when the rebels took refuge in a tower, he had wood piled around it and burned them inside their tower. It was the Barceans who caught him and killed him, and for this his mother Pheretime got enough revenge to teach all rebels their lesson. There was a tigress, if you like! She brought in the Persian army from Egypt to help her. They gave Barca the chance to cough up the criminals, but the town replied that 'The act was the act of us all, because of the wrongs that he did to us all.' Barca held out for nine months and was only taken by an ingenious trick. Listen to this story. In the night the Persians dug a huge ditch in the soft soil of one of these plowed fields, and covered it with planks and earth and furrowed it again, and invited the Barceans out for a parley under oaths of truce."

"Aha! And they fell through?"

"No, it was subtler than that—Persians, no more than anyone, can break an oath without fear of the gods. Fair terms were agreed—Barca to pay a fine and be left in peace—and sworn on an oath that should last 'as long as the ground on which we stand.' Everyone was friends, and Barca opened its gates and the Persians walked in."

"Aha! And 'the ground on which we stood' didn't last much longer?"

"Minutes. Pheretime had enough citizens impaled to satisfy her, and by the time she had finished the city wall was festooned all around with the impaled men and the hacked-off breasts of the women." (Here Demetrius had the decency to vomit. He turned his face, and hid his vomit in one hand.) "But Pheretime died—so say the Barceans, anyway—of an unpleasant disease: her body festered and bred worms. It was seventy years later that the last

Arcesilaus was driven out and there was no rule in this land but
the infamous republic.   —Why, here is Galadeon riding to meet
us."

A small party of horsemen had appeared ahead, coming at a
brisk trot up the road (distant Barca silhouetted behind them),
and they halted in front of the coach.

"Is everything ready for our reception, Galadeon?"

"Yes. But, *despoina*, I think it might not be safe for you to
enter the town at this time."

"And why not?"

"The Barceans are out in the streets to meet you. They say
they have some grievance to present about their treatment by the
new garrison that has been posted with them. Their civic leaders
ask for an audience in the Stoa of the Lightning."

"They do, do they?—their ringleaders? They shall have their
audience. It will be their first chance to pay their respects to
Demetrius, son of Demetrius. —Is it their lord Demetrius they
crave to meet, or myself?"

"They have—as they have actually expressed it—they ask for
an audience with the lady Berenice, as being formally now their
ruler."

"Well, Berenice is not with us. Nor is she old enough to be
bothered with things of this sort. We are more than sufficient to
attend to their questions, as well as to receive their fealty.
Demetrius, you and I, and this force of yours that we had the fore-
sight to post to this place, shall give them their audience."

But Demetrius, after some moments of wise consideration,
said he thought he agreed with Galadeon that it would be cleverer to return to Cyrene and thus compel the Barceans to come
for their audience there. Fewer, probably, would come.

Apama gave him a hard look, told Galadeon exactly what was
to be done, and ordered her company to turn around. On the
journey back she at times gazed at the countryside and talked
only desultorily with Demetrius. But by the time they reached
Cyrene she was sitting up straight and was smiling.

Galadeon, returning to Barca and finding the people seething
around his stirrups, told them what he had to tell them, and then
going to the barracks, where the troops were keeping cautiously
inside, he rather reluctantly gave the Macedonian commander his
secret orders. These (which, he was led to understand, came
from Demetrius) were that he was to take half of his regiment out

at night and march them not along the direct road, but by the track down to the fishing village that was all that at this time existed on the coast directly below Barca; then all the way along the shore paths to Apollonia and thus up to Cyrene. They had already commandeered horses; they were to ride it in two and a half days, and would arrive before the slower-moving crowd of Barca's citizens, and at night.

The scream

"Berenice," said her mother, "I wish you to cease your lessons with this academic person, Callimachus the younger, whose hair is already thinning."

"Why?" demanded Berenice, bristling. As Apama knew she would. Sweet are the uses of perversity.

"He is a miserable influence for a girl of your status. It would be better if you had tutors in such subjects as archery, like the huntress Cyrene in the legend."

"It is for me to decide," replied Berenice. (She might have retorted that riding was as vigorous as archery, or archery as mannish as riding—but she kept the extent of her riding unknown to her mother, who disapproved of women's opening their thighs to clutch the horse.)

"Well, you may have one last lesson with him," conceded Apama. "He earns pennies by trying to be a teacher, but he is really only a researcher, a grubber among books and little facts. I am going to send him away on a small mission of research, which may take him a week or a year. Actually he has made a pilot journey, and will be back today to give me his preliminary report as to whether the matter is difficult or not. Perhaps he will have already found the answer and will not need to be sent again. After I have interviewed him, I'll let him go to you in the library, promptly at the first hour after noon."

"Research into what?"

"I have asked him to find out where this place Irasa may be, the place that is fairer even than Cyrene and that the Barbars led the settlers past in the night. Still nobody knows, or they won't say."

Irasa. As Berenice walked away to take her noontime meal, her mind was on scenes of meadows beside streams in unknown valleys, though she did hear the bustle of people down on the road in front of the lower palace.

The Barcean delegation had arrived in the late morning, having slept where they could at beerhouses along the way. There were as many as sixty of them, including women, but Apama and Demetrius were not surprised, having received word in advance. Nor were they surprised that these citizens and peasants had tucked what weapons they could—knives and slings— into their belts, or that they asked for a safe and open place in which to hold the parley.

"Certainly," said the chiliarch, "you are naturally concerned for your safety; the queen has anticipated your feelings and has decided to let you into her own courtyard—in through here." They were standing on the terrace-like roadway in front of the lower palace. "You've set her a problem, so many of you coming, but she's found a generous solution. And first you will have refreshment—it is already set out for you in the same place."

"Come on, Aondas!" said a Barcean—he was a rug-dealer and had been here before— "you don't mean the pool?"

"It is covered with planks, specially for the occasion," explained the chiliarch. A sarcastic laugh went up from the Barceans. "We had to do that, because this really is the best place. The only other such space is the garden, and you wouldn't want to trample on that. If you doubt the arrangement can bear your weight, peep in and look at the tables with the food waiting for you. You're hungry after all that tramping. If the planks can support those groaning boards, they can support you. One or two of you go in anyway and look around—test the whole setup, see whether there is any trickery in there. I swear there isn't." Then he told them what convinced them.

Cyrene's palace was double, neither part rivalling the many palaces of Seleucus or Ptolemy, but pleasantly situated. The King Palace was high, on the edge of the plateau, the Queen Palace (a Persian-style addition by Apama) was a little lower down the crag into the cleft of the city, and there was a garden between them. Magas and Apama had slept in their separate palaces, and Berenice preferred her apartment in what had been her father's dwelling.

Her mother's bedchamber was as far as it could be from hers

but most pleasantly situated of all. On one side it looked out over the city toward the sea; on the other it looked down on an internal courtyard, which contained a long pool and was surrounded on three sides—the near, the left, and the far—by a gallery, to which her room opened. Under her room was the wide entrance way. It was divided by two slender pillars; there were three doors, or grilles, made of bronze, that normally kept the populace out, but they had been lifted from their sockets and set against a wall inside the courtyard. Thus the courtyard of the pool was indeed wide open to the outside world.

On the planking across the pool were set four long tables, and the one at the innermost end was already occupied: by the twenty soldiers of Cyrene. They were already tucking in to their bread and onions. This was the security for the Barceans. The soldiers' swords were nearby, piled in a corner, but that was only to be expected since their guests, three times as numerous, were also armed. The mere twenty soldiers (who could have been used for a treacherous ambush only if they had been kept in hiding somewhere else) were shut in by the Barceans, not the other way around. There was no other ample but dead-end space like this, in which the Barceans could assemble and be sure that they had the only threat to themselves bottled up.

The rug-dealer was one of those who went in first to try to lift a plank (he couldn't, it was too stout and heavy) and say a friendly word to the munching Cyreneans. He looked around him, came out and asked a last question: "It is our lady Berenice we shall meet with, as we asked?"

"Yes, at the hour after noon, I am told to tell you. That is when she will come to give a fair hearing to your representations. She will no doubt appear in the gallery up there, and perhaps descend to talk with you. There is a water clock in the court-yard."

Berenice after drinking only a little soup felt drowsy, and thought of not going to her lesson with Callimachus. She had not slept well. She was confused. The evening before, climbing a stair and glancing down to a passage, she had observed Demetrius shaping his hand to the buttock of a laundry-room wench. *He's not even true to her.*

She laid her cheek on her arms on the table and dozed and, as it is with dozers, dozed longer than she thought. She rose weakly and went out into the garden, and on a stone bench warm in the sun she closed her eyes again. She was not asleep, but there are thoughts as silly as dreams that are exposed by being nearly asleep, and one of these was that there were servants passing on the other side of the wall and that one of them said: "They think they're going to meet with Berenice." "They" would be the Barceans, of whose demands she had heard Demetrius talking. The ghastly old story about Barca slipped back to her like a dagger, one of those that sometimes kept her from sleeping. She opened her eyes to let the thought be displaced by the green garden, and the images of Irasa. A cloud had moved over, so that there was no discernible shadow on the sun-dial. She rose and hurried to the library.

Callimachus was already there (either she was late or his interview with her mother had been short). The light inside the room was better at this time of day, though it seemed to become brownly absorbed by the piles of scrolls along the wooden shelves. Three scrolls lay near Callimachus on the table; two of them bore their labels ("The *Works and Days* of Hesiod," in two volumes) and were of the new leathery material called *pergamene*, parchment, because they had been borrowed, at great expense and with long delay, from the library of the king of Pergamum across the sea. The third was a clean papyrus scroll into which Callimachus had begun copying this dull book. He was always grumbling over the need for a copyist, the tedium of copying, the difficulty of holding one scroll open while writing in the other— "When, by Hermes, will someone devise some handier method of making books?"—the lack of so many standard works in this paltry library until they could be borrowed from some real library far off and he, Callimachus, author of the *History of Islands*, should have wasted his eyes and brain and life copying them! But at present he was reading another scroll, and was in the middle of it, its re-rolled and unrolled halves about equal in his left and right hands. (Actually he needed only his right hand to do the unrolling, using to stop the other half that curious book-end that he had, in the form of a model island.) It seemed he had been there some time.

"Have you found Irasa?" Berenice cried at once, gaily. "Have you already made your report?"

"My report?"

"Have you found Irasa or not?" she cried again, a shade less gaily.

The scholar's jaw retreated into the expression with which a scholar considers a crazy girl.

He had been sent on no mission to find Irasa. It was a lie. Why? To keep her out of the way.

She turned from him, and ran so wildly down the stairs that the heel of her left foot slipped off one of the steps and the sandal of her other foot came off and the sole, so inconveniently tender, fell on the next, and (a resolution "Never do that again!" flitting through her head and not quite obliterated by the yelp of her pain) she tumbled and lay on the paving slabs, her gown smirched and her left arm doubled under her and her right wrist shocked and her chin bleeding. At last she stumbled up and ran on, out of the King Palace, across the garden. A gong sounded— it was the *hapsis*, the *tocca*, the "touch" at the hour after noon, though the custom of sounding it from towers had never before been observed in Cyrene. She tore open the southern door to the Queen Palace, ran through its corridors, having to dodge women carrying trays and mopping floors and, most difficult, the star- tled face of her maid Polymela. She was fetching huge breaths, her limbs exhausted. The last corridor ran level to the southern end of the gallery.

She was too late. The wide way out to the sunshine on the road had darkened. The mass that filled it was a dozen Mace- donian soldiers abreast, swords drawn, others in rank upon rank behind them. The Barceans around the table had scram- bled to their feet and were staring both ways, their temples throbbing. Behind them Aondas the chiliarch had used his sword to wave his soldiers to their feet. It was not a histrionic sword-wave, it was a mere tight-lipped signal, and the men went to the pile of swords and took their turns picking them up, one burping, but they obeyed their orders. The gallery extended around the south, east, and north of the court: up to the middle side was the stair that gave access to the upper rooms, but there was no escape that way either. There had been one spear, placed under a table, and the man who picked it up had been sent up the stair and stood blocking the top. Across on the north side of the gallery, Apama had opened the door of her room and had stepped to the balustrade, to watch. She had a sleek, languid look. Seeing her daughter arrive to watch the slaughter also, she banished a fleeting frown and became even shinier.

From below, no one could see back past Apama into her bedroom, but Berenice, from the opposite end of the gallery, could.

"Stop, Kurênaioi!" she screamed.

It seemed to her that she glanced with amazement at some harpy crouching beside her who had let fly this tremendous yellow javelin of sound. She yelled again: "I see the traitor!"

Cyreneans and Macedonians paused. Berenice launched herself along the gallery. Her hair had loosened and streamed to her waist. The spearman turned to bar her way, his spear sideways across her path. She noticed that, though burly, he had a white fleck on the corner of his brown chin—it was a dab of sheep's wool, because he had shaved that morning and had nicked himself—a pathetic detail that gave one of the other Berenices inside her a twinge of motherliness toward him. He was acting under orders, she was the instrument of red passion. She wrenched the spear from his hands so sharply that he found himself turning like a wheel out of her way; like a cartwheel he turned down the stair and landed among the Barceans, and someone laughed. It was a damped little sound because the hall they were in was open to the sky. Apama was shouting too, but her shouts too seemed almost soundless: soldiers and Barceans scarcely heard them; Berenice heard them not at all. Apama blocked the way, but Apama's face was as white as if she had seen a tiger, and she backed into the room as if she had never smacked nor scolded this daughter. The spear brushed her aside, and there beside the bed was Demetrius. He was no longer naked; if he had been, her revulsion would have set in sooner and saved him. The spearpoint punctured his chest, then horribly slowed, and from the puncture onward it was difficult. She felt she was forcing it into her own screeching flesh. And the sound the man made as he felt himself killed . . . Berenice fainted.

Aondas had run up the stair, he looked in at the door of the bedroom, turned back to the balustrade. "Cyreneans, you have a queen!"

Cyreneans shouted to the Barceans: "Get back here with us, join us." Some confusedly stumbled in the wrong direction, seeking the open street, or fearing that they were being tricked by another layer of trickery; if Macedonian swords had begun to draw their blood, it would have seeded the battle, and the battle would have gone badly, blood would have dripped through the planks into the pool. But Aondas appeared again, bringing Berenice. He brought her to the head of the stair; her mind plucked at her limp shoulders. She did her best to stand up straight. Eurypho, chiliarch of the Macedonians, knelt.

Death in Life

"Is the lady Apama to live?"

"Ask me at the new moon," smoothly replied Berenice.

She was recovering from her deed. She didn't know what she wanted done about her mother. She had observed that her father Magas, though among his family he burbled, had in public the practice of pausing after he had been addressed—long enough to appear deliberate but not long enough to appear indecisive—and then saying something short and stately, even if it was no real answer. It was all that made him appear as that different kind of personage, a king. So she was training herself to the habit. Instead of saying "I've been trying to think about it . . . I don't know yet," she said: "Ask me at the new moon." And Apama had to wait through half of a cycle of the moon to know whether she was to die.

The moonlight flooded the terraces all night, and then it was seen only by those who rose early, and then came the nights of whole darkness. No one cared to hurry and tell Berenice when the thin moon first showed briefly in the west, and Apama had to wait two more evenings.

If she were to live, she would live as a slave, but how and where? Berenice's first thought was that her mother's head should be shaved, in mourning for her shameful lover. But the black hair would grow back, and then where should she live (if she were to live)? She should be sent to live out her days under guard at the deepest of the outposts. The Top of Cyrenaica sloped away into the desert: the juniper forests thinned to scrub and then to desert weeds and then to sand, and long before that there were the last forts, half abandoned; only Libyans wandered past, with their goats, and Apama there, as some Greeks had done, might mingle with them, might become a tent-dwelling burnt-faced woman of the Psyllian tribe or the Nasamones.

Or she might be housed in a hut on a bit of land at Barca and learn how to scratch a living growing onions, or be one of the women picking and crushing silphium for a farmer.

But no, she would have to be kept closer at hand. Left anywhere away among strangers, she would, unless her tongue were cut out, talk her way around them. Long before the evening of the new moon, Berenice had hit on the fate for her mother. She was to live in a small room behind the library, and copy scrolls.

The quest for Irasa

The room over the gateway to the Court of the Pool had a fine view but a cold floor, and so Apama had had it thickly laid with rugs. These remained, but the room was cleared of her robes and jewelry and some of the other fine textiles she had collected, and now it was Berenice's room.

Berenice had earned her name, "bearer of victory"; she had earned the respect even of the Macedonian troops, whose prince she had killed, by putting a spectacular end to the scandal at which everyone—troops, housewives, servant girls—had been sniggering. But there remained a problem. Would those troops sail quietly home?

The death of the foppish Demetrius had not left them leaderless, but their chiliarch Eurypho himself had a problem. (Eurypho ranked as a general, *stratêgos*, but had fewer than a thousand men here under him.) Was he to go back and present himself to king Antigonus Gonatas in Pella and report this lurid failure? Demetrius himself was no great loss to his half-brother the king, whose motive for sending him had been partly to get one of the royal bastards, his father's love-children, settled and out of the way. But tamely abandoning Cyrenaica—the western pincer in the Cyrenaica-Macedon-Syria crab that was to have been created around Egypt—was a graver matter.

The chiliarchs were negotiating with each other, and with Charicles, the chief counsellor, and Apion, the governor of the city. Berenice could only wait to be informed of what these men would advise. A girl could not be expected to apply her brain to such matters.

There were four hundred of the Macedonians here, still billeted on Cyrenean families, and as many back in the barracks at Barca. Berenice had (she couldn't help thinking about it, though ignorant of what the chiliarchs were discussing) only a score of soldiers in each of the five towns. And she—that is, Cyrene—could hardly go about calling the rest of its men to arms as if for a war. That would have started a war, a brief and one-sided one.

"Inform me when something has been thought of," she said to Charicles.

"Yes, *Basilissa*, it has: they are to return to Barca, except for twenty sent to each of the other cities."

Berenice observed her usual pause to form a response, or placeholder-for-a-response, which was: "I will decide tomorrow. Come to me with that and the alternatives."

"Oh, but they left for Barca this morning."

Swiftly, without any pause at all, spoke Berenice—the other Berenice, the inflammable one: "Send after them at once, bring them back!"

"But it has been—"

"How dare you decide without even consulting me?"

She and the counsellor stood for some moments, their eyes falling to the floor between them as they each thought a little more.

"What is it they are supposed to do in Barca?" she asked.

"They would be glad, as all soldiers are, to settle down and become owners of land. No doubt they will marry Barcean daughters." (Some of whom, Berenice remembered, they had come close to skewering.) "They have seen that Cyrenaica is a country less hard than Macedonia. They like what they have seen at Barca."

So it was a fine, a peaceable solution. But:

"Is there land enough for them there?"

"Oh, yes, there is plenty of land there. And more than half of the farmers there are Libyans. They can be moved out."

"And where will those Libyans go?"

"They can go back to herding goats through the mountains, as other Libyans do."

"Have the soldiers brought back. At once. Send a rider after them."

"But what shall we tell them?"

"Tell them we shall find them even better land elsewhere."

The party of riders, with the Libyan guide running ahead barefoot over stones and thorns, and cooks and other servants following leisurely behind, some leading donkeys and others riding
them, came up and over the rise of the ground. When Berenice
saw the view ahead and the meadow that enjoyed this view, she
reined her horse in and told them to pitch camp.

It was still forenoon, and they were surprised that she called
the halt so early. This was, what, a tenth of the way along the
coast from Apollonia to the bay of Aziris? It was a silly picnic
anyway (she knew they were thinking), and had she already forgotten that there was some urgency? No; but the land had to be
gone over slowly. If a coin has lain long in the grass unfound, you
don't find it by striding rapidly past.

She had asked Callimachus to tell her again the story of Battus
the Stutterer and his boatload of Greeks. They had been guided,
like all colonists, by the advice of Apollo's oracle at Delphi. They
had first settled on an offshore island that they called Platea. "I
suppose," said Callimachus, "that being islanders they were
uneasy about settling anywhere but on an island. We Greeks, in
my opinion, should not really live anywhere but on islands." Yet
Battus, finding that they still starved and he still stuttered, sent
one of them again to the Delphic oracle, to ask whether there
was some mistake— "You told us, god Apollo, to take ourselves
to Libya, but Libya seems no improvement on our famine-stricken
home." And Apollo through the mouth of his priestess gave
answer in his Doric dialect:

> ai tu emeu Libuên mêlotrophon oidas ameinon
> mê elthôn elthontos, agan agamai sophiên seu—

> If you know Libya, where you've never trod,
> Better than I who have—why, you're the god!

So they understood that they really had to land on the dry-looking
continent. They moved over to the shore, to a village called
Aziris—took it over from its Libyans. After a while the ousted
natives helpfully offered to lead these Greeks to somewhere they
would like better; and led them all the way along to glorious
Cyrene, but cleverly

"Measuring out the hours of dark and light
So that they passed the fairest place by night"

—said Callimachus, warming to his story and showing that he could improvise a couplet as well as any oracle.

"By what route," Berenice asked, "would they have traveled from Aziris to Cyrene?"

"The usual route, why not? that we all have to take if we go by land in the direction of Egypt."

"There are no other routes?"

"I suppose you could jag off the road to right or left, but why would you? The island Platea and the place Aziris are eighty miles east, where there is a large bay; the island is in the bay and Aziris is at the head of the bay; so of course the road goes straight east from Cyrene, overland along the Step (just dipping through a few valleys), until it descends to pass the head of the bay. That marks the end of our country of the Green Mountain, and then the road goes on, over the accursed dry stony region we call the Marmarica, the land of marble, and on and on and on, toward Egypt."

"So the route would not have gone along the sea at all?"

"Why should it? The Libyans were leading them to this place, up inland, and the straight way lay inland. And I can tell you that there are no notably fair spots along it."

"But would it be much farther or more difficult to go along the coast?"

"To go out along the side of the bay and then along the coast to Apollonia and then up?—three sides of a rectangle instead of one. But no, not a great deal farther, though I think more diffi-cult; the sea cliffs, they say, are rough in places."

"But what of the Greeks' ships?"

"What of them? They didn't travel up here to Cyrene by ship!" said Callimachus, allowing himself a smile. A scholar may not be sarcastic to a queen, but a teacher's mind need not forget its superiority over a pupil's.

"I know the Libyans led them by land, otherwise there would be no story about 'passing the fairest place by night'. But they had ships, they wouldn't have left them behind, and would the walking Greeks and the sailing Greeks not have wanted to stay in touch with each other?"

As Callimachus was silent, Berenice thought he had not quite understood what she meant, and added: "Until they reached

Apollonia? (And called it Apollonia because Apollo had led them there?)"

"I think they would," replied Callimachus, with his best imitation of the royal pause.

"And has anyone searched for Irasa along the coast?"

"I don't know that anyone has searched for Irasa at all. It's a mere story."

But Callimachus found himself on a horse for the first time in two years, and now camping on a rounded slope of soft grass that was still tawny from last summer, along with Berenice and the Macedonian general Eurypho and a small platoon of his, and an equal number of Cyreneans as bodyguard for Berenice, and the cooks and servants. They had started out from Apollonia, just now had crossed the hump of ground that ran out to Cyrenaica's northernmost cape, called by Libyans the Headland of the Crescent Moon, and were camped on the farther slope of the headland's base. The sun was kindly, the sky was blue, the sea was fuller blue; it tucked squarely into the cliff below them. Junipers and wild olives stood farther down the slope, and framed by them and over them the coast stretched away eastward mile after mile. Surf lay in white threads along the sea's edge; land of mottled greens and yellows curved upward, then wrinkled into the darker greens and coruscating whites of rock-crackled forests: the scarp here came even closer to the sea than it did at Apollonia, and was more riddled with canyons.

When the camp was settled, Berenice led them in a scramble down the cliffy slope below to explore the corner of the bay. At least as many of her bodyguard had to come along as of Macedonians, also the Libyan guide, who was anxious: he might be in trouble if she slipped on a rock, but he did not dare to touch her with a steadying hand. This however was done by one of the younger soldiers, all of whom were casting circumspectly admiring eyes on her—though all would have admitted to some nervous awe of her. The strap of her left sandal broke, but someone ran back for another—her dresser had brought four pairs.

As they came down over the steepest edge toward the water, they saw that a boat was sitting in it. A single small Libyan boat, at the end of a rope from a bush, with its paddle shipped, bobbing gently above its shadow on sunlit sand. No person was about. The fisherman must be off somewhere around a corner, perhaps setting pots for crabs.

"He's left his boat unguarded. How unpeopled this part of your country must be, though so pleasant!" remarked one of the Macedonians.

"Yes," said a Cyrenean, "it's fine, but it's drier than up on the Mountain, and we have plenty of choice."

When they reached the water's shingly edge, they found that the cliff to the left stuck out a bit, and into its base ran a wide dark cave, whose mouth therefore pointed back toward the mainland. Soldiers ran into it, and came back out.

"It goes down, not up! So after the first shingly bar it's full of water; we can't go any farther."

It is the abode of a sea god, thought some; one of the entrances to the underworld, said others. The Libyan had some explanation, which he stumbled unsuccessfully to translate into Greek. (It was a cave the Libyans had enlarged for hiding boats to escape their rulers' boat-tax.)

The soldiers threw off their clothes and swam, or at any rate splashed about. "They are not islanders; they are from up in Macedonia and can't swim," said Callimachus.

They climbed back up to the camp, now floodlit by the rising of the full moon. "But they call this the Headland of the Crescent Moon!" said Berenice. "Ask him why."

"The guide says, because from it you can see east and west along the sea."

"Well, and?"

"He says that, so, if you had been here a week ago, you could have seen the moon when it first appeared. Or if a week from now, you could have risen at dawn and seen it for the last time. It's important to them."

Next morning the party did rise early, but made even shorter progress, because of what Berenice found to be the intimate attractiveness of the country. They turned inland up the valley of a stream.

"Let's hope we get some hunting," said one of the Macedonians to another.

"Hmm! I'm not sure I want to see a spear in her hands again!"

"It should have been an arrow," said Calliphron. He, now a member of Berenice's bodyguard, had been the escort who rode beside Demetrius into the city.

They asked him what he meant, he told them about "the arrows of Eros," and they fell to discussing among themselves (at the back of the file, well out of Berenice's hearing) whether she would ever marry.

They followed the ravine upward; when it became too narrow, they climbed out and, scrambling on, discovered a circular flat lawn of rich green grass. Above it rose the theatre of higher cliffs, with glimpses between up to the very top of the scarp; around the other semicircular side, a vertical drop into the little world of the stream canyons. At the moment they came up and into view of this lawn on its ledge, Berenice said to herself: "This is Irasa. Here would I found a city."

But the lawn was barely large enough for their camp—it could only, if a city were founded here, be the queen's garden, and everything else would have to be in caves and on pinnacles of the rocks, a fairy city. Leaving the camp to be set up, some of the party explored downward until they found the stream again. It came out through a low arch in a rock, into a serene pool. Here Berenice very much desired to bathe. So the men retreated out of sight; the women stripped and dipped into the pool, shrieking at its first coldness. Berenice imagined herself Artemis, bathing with her companions and surprised by satyrs or the hunter Actaeon. She floated, her fingers reaching down to the sand, her chin just above the water, her hair still in its chignon but coming loose. She allowed the drift of the water to carry her to its outflow from the pool. In the curved sheet of the water as it shot over the ledge stood several small plump columns, bending slightly. "What are those?" she asked her maid Parysatis (whose name had been Pheretime until Berenice required her to change it). "Ook!—I don't know," squealed Parysatis, backing away—"What are they, Nasis?" "Leeches," said the Libyan pantrygirl.

Reluctant to leave the pool, they splashed each other, and Polymela, whose Libyan name was Jeshet, taught Berenice to swim. She supported her with hands under the waist and told her how to move her arms and legs. She removed her hands and Berenice sank spluttering; so now Polymela told her to rest her fingertips again on the sand below, and lay floating beside her, and they both thrashed their legs; and Polymela said close to her ear:

"I love you."

"Not as you love your husband, I hope!" sp;uttered Berenice laughing. Polymela's answer was lost in rustling water.

They stood up and waded—Berenice leading and now a little more aware of her body—to the pool's upper end and stooped their heads to venture through the rock arch, toward where they could see a glitter of sun-filled spray. They came into a kind of hall, filled by a smaller and deeper pool. The sky looked in from far above, and the space was backed by darkness, the overhang of the cliff. Down in front of the darkness hung a tongue of polished black stone, many fathoms long, widening slightly as it descended, ending abruptly a man-height above the pool. Vertically down this strap or tongue of rock the water slid, and off its end to plunge like a sword into the pool.

Water spoke, inserting into water. Berenice laughed with delight and waded forward to bathe her shoulders under the stinging silver cascade, which quickly untied her hair into a golden cascade. The other women shut their eyes, since this grotto had to be the shrine of some Libyan nymph.

When they clambered out and found their clothes and made their way back up to the lawn, they wanted to peer down and see where their pool and cascade were; but only one girl dared to crawl on her belly to the edge and peer over, and said she could not see it through the rock-tangle below. And now Eurypho ordered that some sort of fence be made around the edge, so that no soldier getting up in the night to relieve himself might accidentally walk over the precipice. Luckily among the hamper of clothes and accessories for Berenice there was found a spool of yellow ribbon; after stakes had been hammered into the turf at armlength intervals along the edge, the ribbon was long enough to be stretched all the way, with a hitch around each stake.

A fire was built and they sat around it into the night, all on the grass and clasping their knees except for Berenice for whom there was a stool. At first only a few officers spoke, to each other and formally, and Berenice gazed at the flames; but as they drank more wine there began to be stories and songs. They drank more wine, and fig-liquor; some liked even better a nasty-tasting liquid called ouzo, and at length a corporal of the Macedonians stood up and, after righting his balance, said: "I'm gonna do a Hip Hic Hippocleides!" In other words he proposed to do an imitation of Hippocleides, he who was chosen out of a dozen rich and noble suitors from all over the Greek world, after a year's testing of their athletic prowess, cultural polish, and social breeding, to win the hand of the daughter of rich Cleisthenes of Sicyon. Hippocleides won on all counts, but at the wedding feast he drank too much, stood up and showed his skill in dancing, both the Laconian and the Attic figures, then called for a table and danced on top of it, drank some more, finally stood on his head and danced with his legs in the air, the skirt of his robe falling around his ribs; whereupon the forbearance of daddy Cleisthenes reached its limit and he thundered: "Well danced, son of Tisander, but you have danced yourself out of your marriage." To which the upside-down dancer retorted in a merry slur: "Hipp'—hic—Hipp'cleides don't care!"

"No more ouzo, corporal," said Eurypho, "we all know the story of 'Hippocleides don't care', and it's time for bed."

But the corporal grabbed the flask, downed some more, threw the flask into space (it was heard some time later, bursting on a rock far below), and made a lunge toward Berenice, holding out his arms for her to dance with him.

A human fence sprang up to ward him off. He turned and swaggered out of the circle around the fire, to show how he could dance on his head.

"Grab him," said the chiliarch shortly, and all the men grappled themselves to the corporal. But ouzo is strong. Berenice looked on in horror. The grappling group lurched irregularly, in the figures of some ugly dance. The corporal could not even be seen, so that legs and shoulders that jerked outward seemed to be outer parts of what had become his extended body. Why could they not control him and tie him? They were all going to their deaths! She was ready to yell: "Let him go! Save yourselves!"

At least one foot had slipped over the edge, taking with it a sod of the turf, a stake was dislodged and the yellow ribbon tottered and sagged all around the glade—but at last they had him and were dousing his head with water. They sat him with his back to a small tree and lashed him to it tightly. Berenice did not care to sleep in her tent that night. She had her cot set out at the back of the glade, next to the rock. The stars were coldly clear. The Virgin was straight above. Why do the stars have their names?—Uncle Callimachus, author of the *Aetia*, the Causes, would know the stories that explained them. Berenice lay on her back, feet to the north; straight above her, the vast dim Virgin reclined on her side, feet to the east. Only one other was out to

see, but was not able to look up, nor trying to: the drunken corporal, ten yards to the right. Berenice had forgotten about him,
until he started cursing. And cajoling her to untie him. At last
his curses and droolings turned to snores. The early-summer
night, that had seemed at first as warm as the day, was by
morning cold.

Many shades of gold

"What shall be done with him, *basilissa?*" asked the chiliarch.

"Why—isn't he sober yet?"

"Yes. But he dared to try to touch you."

"Send him home." So the Macedonian corporal was told to
find his way back, and not be seen again. (He collected his pack
from Cyrene, and went on west and got work as a porter in
Euhesperides.)

They came down from among these rocks, found the road or
track that followed the coast, and rode on along the narrow plain.
The Cyrenaeans were used to seeing Berenice on horseback; the
young Macedonians were uncertain whether to ride behind her
so as to see her or in front so as to be seen by her. The plain
became somewhat wider, and they came to where two urns of
curious form stood by the wayside. They were hexagonal, and
each contained earth and a few shriveled sage plants. These urns
flanked the beginning of a straight avenue, wider than the road
itself, that pointed toward a group of plane trees near the base of
the mountain; and through the trees could be seen a house.
Curious, Berenice and her followers turned off toward it. There
were people, Libyans, moving about among the trees—some of
them up in the trees. Seeing the strangers, they did not come
nearer, but cautiously answered their question as to who lived in
the house: "Brito." The Greeks would have rapped at the door,
but Brito herself opened it and stood smiling to greet them.

She was (as she willingly explained, ushering them inside) a
Greek who had lived for seventy years (or thereabouts) among
the Libyans, teaching them to keep bees. She had come here
with a husband whose name and race she could no longer
remember, she had somehow found herself here alone, she

thought she had built this house with her own hands, she knew how to befriend bees and use honey for the preservation of life, and Libyans came from the tribes round about to learn her skills.

These apprentices lived outside her door, most of them up in the trees. They had made tree-houses, decks of planks that they had fixed among the branches. There they lay, sunning or fanning themselves, when they were not potting honey for Brito or helping her to catch a swarm in a tree and divide it and take it to another valley for the founding of a new colony.

Berenice's women looked sniffily at this woman: she had gone Libyan. Her dress was a single piece, yellowed and dirty, with holes for her neck and arms. She had bronze torques around her ankles but bare feet. And as she chattered she took lice from her head, bit them, and threw them aside. She soon had all her guests around a trestle table with bowls of honey and sticks to dip in them, and she returned from her kitchen with a special drink for Berenice. "What is it?" "Grasshoppers in milk," replied Brito— "sun-dried and ground, you know." Berenice set it away from herself on the table, what should she say?—but she was saved because the woman leapt to another idea and said: "Come and see my larder."

They stepped into a passage, lined with shelves, on which jars gleamed with honey of every color from red-black, gold, yellow, brown, amber, orange, cream, tan, to the white of the sun. "The color tells me—if I didn't know already—which valley every one comes from, and what flower the bees have been guzzling."

Berenice was distressed by the number of the colors; then becalmed by them; she gazed at them as she had gazed at the flames of the bonfire, one after another, then back at the one before, comparing them, wondering how such colors that would have been indistinguishably different were, alongside each other, as different as the notes in a tune. But the beekeeping woman pulled her away.

"Now come aside into the room I sleep in."

"I do not wish to—"

"Come and see, it's amusing! I don't often get a chance to show it to a Greek."

Berenice's retinue was out of earshot, her manner seemed not to have made clear that she was a queen, she could have said "I am your Basilissa, do not pluck me by the sleeve" but she did not, and found herself taken into a square room with a sack on the floor; she nearly tripped over this, and over a tall pair of boots. The boots were of leather, bright yellow, ornately chased. "I have to wear these when I go out to the bees!" said Brito— "like any Libyan woman; can't go barefoot into the hills."

The only light fell from a hole in a corner of the ceiling (with a basin under it to collect winter rains), but it was magnified by two mirrors, squares of rubbed iron pegged to the walls, so that there seemed to be four light-holes; and the room was bright because it was whitewashed. But one whitewashed wall was darkened, hugely blotched, with daubs of crude color. There were some letters, and catching what she thought was half a word Berenice flushed and tried to turn her eyes away. But, though she tried again—tried, that is, to read the words—they could not quite be read: they were swirls, compacted and over-laid, rather than words; no doubt they said appalling things, but the appalling things could not be read; they must have contained names too—surely the names, or initials, of the daubers—yet as in a dream no name or even initial could be quite surely read. Clearer, though entwined with the words, were the pictures, and the pictures too were appalling—or were they, what were they? They were human figures, somehow grappling, entwined.

"These graffiti," the woman chuckled, "were made by the sol-diers who were billeted on me here when the last war came through. Oh, twenty years ago. That's why they're fading, but I don't whitewash over them, I whitewash around them and touch them up with a bit of ochre and beetroot. See, that's the fat king of Cyrene, sitting on the kings of Egypt."

Her father Magas, exaggerated to a gross bladder. And the "kings" of Egypt he was flattening?—that made Berenice blush worse, because she knew what it meant: at one end stuck out in silhouette two side-by-side faces, both long-nosed but one male and the other female; at the other end sprawled their bodies, joined together like joined twins. The philadelphoi, Ptolemy the Second and his wife who was his full sister.

"They were rascals, weren't they, these soldiers, daring to poke fun at their masters? Political comments! They were sta-tioned here when the king of Cyrene's army went on toward Egypt, they were supposed to guard the supply line or watch out for Egyptian counter-attack or something. And see this comment they slapped on in a hurry just before they were pulled out." A goat, with lowered horns, charged toward Magas's bloated posterior. "Yes, that was our nomads of the Marmarica, who raised a rebellion behind him, so that he had to turn back and never got to Egypt. They could have balanced it with a crocodile or something biting the Egyptian in the rear, the mercenaries who rose against *him* so that *he* had to turn back, just as he was setting out to punish the king of Cyrene. But they were gone from here before that happened, my soldiers. I remember them, my soldiers," Brito said, smiling fondly. "But you don't know about all this old history."

Berenice did know, and she said she would like to go now.

Brito escorted her to the front of the house. Behind the creases of her smile there was a loneliness that Berenice didn't see. "Is there anything else you'd like to know?" she asked as they took their leave.

"Yes, where is Irasa?"

Berenice was about to explain her question, but the woman replied:

"Oh, yes, the empty place, it's on from here a piece. Ten miles, twenty?—where the Thestes comes out. It's been a while since I went. Why do you want to know?"

"We thought we might camp there."

"It's nice and you'll find plenty of space."

Water monster

There were other habitations along the way, but they pushed on more quickly, not stopping to ask again—there was some impatience to reach the place and be done with the inquiry. They encamped a second night, on the sea's margin. Next day the strip of level land narrowed to only a few hundred yards. To the right rose a bluff, its sandy rock exposed wherever gullies carved it; above, the slope could be seen rising and steepening toward the summits of the scarp. The last people they saw were some boys who had set up a target against the bluff for slingshot practice. But now just ahead the coastal lowland widened, because out of the hills came a river, the Thestes, in a sharp valley, and after cutting through the bluff it crossed to the sea through an apron of land, a small delta.

The river was what the Libyans called a *waad*, a wash, a water-course, but it was as great as any in Cyrenaica and flowed most of the year; it was certainly flowing now. The delta it had made was rich with trees and rushes—but not with date palms or corn. Indeed it seemed a solid grove: if there were fields among the trees, they could not be seen from the road. But this, half way between Apollonia and Aziris, was the place. The track, instead of leading into it, bent aside as if to avoid it. No, that was not the reason: the track had to go a little way inland up the valley to find a ford by which to cross the river. But why was there not a bridge over the river lower down, as there would have been if there was a village there?—where was the village?

They halted on the track to look down over the grove. Eurypho sent a man scrambling up the bluff to look across it from higher. He reported that he could see one tall white house at the far side, toward the sea. There was no visible path to it, so they blundered in through the trees. In places they stumbled on over-grown rocks, strange to find in the soft soil of a delta—realized that these were dressed stones, as if from buildings long gone. After a while they came across a thread-like path, and followed it to the house.

It was empty; no answer to shouts or knocks. No one felt willing to push inside, nor to spend the night in the delta; smiling though it appeared, it appeared to be an *abaton*, a place where no one went.

They returned to the roadway and went on, crossing the river by the ford. The delta, on its farther side, was scooped out by a small bay that could have been a harbor, opening toward the east. But it was shallow; the nearer water was silted up and turning into a reed marsh. Here, where the road almost touched the water, or rather the margin of the reedbeds, was a wayside stall.

A child, a Libyan boy of remarkable beauty and age about twelve, stood grinning behind it, ready to sell fruit to wayfarers, or to sponge divers whose boats sometimes put into the bay. His mother and two smaller children were behind him in a shade shelter among the reeds, but they only looked up and left the dealing to him. He was as cheerful as the abandoned delta appeared to be and was not. They laughed and bought pome-granates from him, and asked him about the place and the house.

"He says," said the Libyan guide, "that the man lives there and will have been out walking, he'll take us to him by the straight way."

"Not this evening," said Eurypho, forgetting himself in speaking before the queen. "We'll come in the morning."

From this point by the water the road bent rightward to climb inland onto the bluff, because the higher ground here came to the bay. Up here they camped. It was dry hard ground, and the Cyrenean soldiers told the Macedonians: "Kick the stones aside before you put your bedding down, there could be scorpions under them. Some times of the year around here, when the wind is from the southeast, it blows scorpions and scorpion spiders in through our windows."

In the morning they returned to find the boy, and he led them—not along the road, but by a path straight in among the trees and toward the midpoint of the delta. Where would they cross the river? To their surprise there was a bridge: a stone bridge, though so old and in need of repair that they crossed it one at a time. Beyond it the path threaded onward through the trees, to come out at the open space on the delta's nose.

Just as they came to the house, there began a sound, pouring small at first, like a thread of water finding its way over the lip of a jar. The rough Macedonians stopped and stood, their mouths open, their eyes jolting until they found the window from which it came. One whispered: "That's our music." Berenice heard tall cool forests; they heard cradle-songs.

The lute paused, fumbled among its strings, began something else. "That's *The March of Dionysus*. He must be a Thracian."

The boy called up, and a bald old man came down the stair. When he saw all these armed strangers, he showed no fear, perhaps because there were women among them. Indeed his gently melancholy face lighted.

Since no woman came out of the house, Berenice excused him of the duty of inviting them in for hospitality. All sat rather awkwardly, Berenice on the step of his house, everyone else in a ring on the ground, the child wandering about nearby and playing with a coconut.

"I and my men are Macedonians," said the chiliarch. "Of what race are you?"

"When you say you are Macedonians, do you mean you have only just come to this country?"

"Yes."

"Well, you have detected the barbarian edges to my speech," said the old man, though he spoke slowly and perfectly. "I was born in an island near Sicily called Melita. I was one of those who left it when the rule of the Carthaginians became too harsh; I was young and I went to Athens and got the name Xuthus. I studied at the Academy, philosophy under Polemon and music under—damn it, I can't even remember his name. I wasn't enough of a Sophist to make a living from philosophy, and the only musicians who get employed are slaves. I had to go to work for a barber, and I also pulled teeth, one of the things barbers are expected to do besides shaving beards and removing hair from ears and nostrils. (You'll think I have been many people, but that's because I've had a long life.) I had my own way with teeth, and I happened to earn the friendship of a rich customer by—to his immense surprise—pulling his tooth without hurting him. Being a philosopher of the Cyrenaic school, he knew how to make money from philosophy. In the end he adopted me as his son and married me to his daughter, and deeded to me a piece of rich land he said he owned in Cyrenaica—this piece of land. Being a philosopher, he was above knowing, or mentioning to me, its emptiness. I found that though it is on the sea no ship sailed to it, and we had to take ship to Apollonia, I and my wife and our servants, and come along here. We found that the place, though green as you see, had long lain uninhabited, because cursed. Its name, Irasa, had come to mean that.

"The story was that it had been the scene of an atrocious battle, and the dead lie thick. At first I thought this a mere legend, but historians write of it. It happened three hundred years ago. The second king Battus of Cyrene, called Battus Eudaemon, the Lucky, brought three times as many Greeks over to this country as there already were; they took so much land away from the Libyans that the Libyans rose, under a leader of their own, whose name was Adikran, and he called in the help of Apries, the pharaoh of Egypt, who no doubt expected to add Cyrenaica to his domain. Apries sent his army here—he sent it exactly here, because he sent it by sea, and this place was a port, with a harbor, and they didn't want to land farther along at Apollonia, under the Cyreneans' noses. Here these allies met, the Egyptian army and such bands as the Libyans could get together. Outside the village—for there was a Libyan village here—they met the charge of the Cyreneans. This was the first time Egyptians had seen Greek hoplites charge in armor. They were all killed—the Egyptians and the Libyans. They were shut up in the village, which had no wall, and the Cyreneans hunted them through it to the sea. A few Egyptians scrambled to their ships and got away, and when they got back to Egypt and told the story, Apries, who had lost his army, lost his throne. But of the Libyans, the last of them, with their backs to the sea, shouted out to the men of Battus, the Lucky: 'If you kill us all this place will be cursed to you too.'"

The old man stopped talking and let his hearers understand for themselves.

"So it is cursed for Libyans and Egyptians, whose bones lie here, and also for Greeks?"

"Not for all Greeks: for Cyreneans. It's a foolish superstition. It was three hundred years ago. I did not go far in philosophy. I can only use my reason.

"When we came here we had plenty of means and servants, and I built this house on the edge of the ruins. We cleared a field and had an orchard and livestock—if you look about among the bushes and trees you'll still find figs and lentils, and pigs that have gone wild. My servants have died or gone away and my wife died ten years ago. People from round about will come here and do a little work, but won't stay and live. About now I have no more means to pay them, so the time has come for me to starve. This boy, who is no relative of mine, picks the fruits that are still growing and feeds me with some of them. I would gladly give all this land away—to you, if you will farm it and keep me alive. It won't be for much longer."

He ended the long silence by adding:

"I humble myself, you are thinking. But I'm used to it, I've made the same plea to passers-by before, and in Apollonia and Aziris, with equally little hope."

The boy, who knew what the man had been talking about from the contours of his speech, though he didn't know the language, shuffled his feet.

"But this child is a Libyan!" Berenice suddenly said. "Isn't he?"

"Yes, and look at the health of him. This child and his family started living here because they had to, and they're living all right."

"They're living in the marsh," a soldier muttered. But Berenice turned to the chiliarch and said: "Would Macedonians

live here?" He asked permission to give his answer in the afternoon.

Eurypho with most of his men stood on the high ground where
they had camped. Here on the eastern bluff could be the place
to build a fort. There was a piece of flat ground near the top of
the bluff large enough for drill practice. The fort would look
down on the harbor, and was aloof but not too aloof from the
town—if there was to be a town—and would command and
protect the road out of the town toward Egypt. They discussed
where a town wall might run, so as to enclose some plowland but
not too much; and "That harbor—if you can call it a harbor—it
looks as if it needs a lot of dredging."

"You could build a mole out from that spit on the far side."

"Yes, it's quite well sheltered from the west and that would
shelter it from the north."

"I don't call the place well sheltered—the land's too low."

"Better a port than an inland place. We can sail back to
Macedon for wives!"

"You're going to build your mole that quickly, are you!"

It took the crumbling of a few more sentences for each man
to become aware that he was seeing what the others were seeing.
"What, in the name of Poseidon, is that?"

The water of the harbor, five hundred yards away, was disturbed. The disturbance, flat, goldish, was moving along, flut-
teringly, just in or under the water's surface, which crinkled and
sputtered above it. They were too far off to make it out. Could a
water monster be so vast? It was the size of a parade ground!
And the harbor was shallow; the hundred-yard long monster
could be no more than a few feet thick. They wanted to run
down the slope, get nearer, to see—and they didn't want to.

But the thing, the monster, the vision, the illusion, began to
dissolve. No, it wasn't dissolving, it was of the nature of dissolving and re-forming at the edges. — "Man!" burst out the corporal, "it's a shoal of fish!"

Mackerel, the sun glinting off their scales. The shoal fluttered
some more, changed direction, became harder to discern with
distance, dissolved away to sea.

"This place will do," said another soldier, "if there's fishing
like that."

"Your invitation," said Berenice, "is accepted by these men.
They, that is, their whole company which is back in Cyrene, as
well as their companions who are at present in Barca, are to
become subjects of mine, whereas they were formerly subjects
of Antigonus king of Macedon; and I, if you permit it, grant them
Irasa to live in and its lands to cultivate, for a worthy rent paid in
coin and kind to you."

The old man's effort to persuade them had so drained him of
power that he did not have much left for expressing gratitude.
He said:

"You should find another name to call it. Not Irasa."

Berenice asked, slightly flustered: "How—what other name
does it have? What should we call it?"

How does one choose an auspicious name? Was it hers to
choose or his? He helped her:

"Why not name it after this child?"

"What is his name?"

The boy shyly answered something like "Dzarrn." The man
told her it meant *idris*, "knowing."

How absurd, to name a whole town (even a whole town that
was yet to be) for a Libyan child! But that was what Berenice
gladly did. The town-to-be was named Darnis.

(It became quite a town, and some generations later it had
overtaken Apollonia in size, though not yet Cyrene. Its settlers
spread the word that it was only Libyan *men* whose bones
enriched the soil. It stood on both sides of the river, its halves
joined by a rebuilt bridge, its streets pleasantly shaded by vine
trellises; from it wafted a sweetish scent that derived from an oil
that its women and also its men liked to rub into their hair. The
high road eastward from Cyrene now changed course to take in
this new or refounded city. Instead of keeping on along the Step,
the road descended to the coast a few miles before Darnis; then,
on the other side, by the fort, went back up to make for Aziris.
In other parts of the world, a "pass" is a gateway through mountains, but in Cyrenaica it is the place where the road gets from
one of the three levels to another—the Taucheira Pass where it
climbs by many windings from the coastal plain near Taucheira
toward Barca on the Step, the Barca Pass where it climbs again to
the Top, the Cyrene Pass where it descends through the cleft, and
Darnis's West and East Passes: the West Pass where the road gets

down to the coast, the East Pass where it winds its way one last time up to the Step.)

"Irasa," said Berenice to Callimachus, "was hiding from us in plain view. And yet the story conflicts with yours. Yours was that the Libyans guided the Greeks past this fairest of places in the night—meaning that otherwise they would have settled in it. Why, then, did they not later, knowing of it, go back and settle in it instead? Indeed, how did they even know that a place had been hidden from them? The other story is that it was inhabited at the time they went by, that though fair it is no fairer than Cyrene—I like it but I think it not as fair as my high Cyrene—and that when Greeks did drive Libyans out of it they did not choose to settle in it."

"Both stories," replied Callimachus, "are told by Herodotus, the author of the great *Historiai* (of whose nine scrolls, titled after the nine Muses, we have only seven in our wretched library). At least, Herodotus tells the story of the passing in the night, and of the battle at Irasa, though not of its subsequent emptiness. But Herodotus was a collector of stories. This is an example. It's only too possible that when he came traveling here, with his notebook, asking questions, and they took him in a boat along this coast, and he noticed this green trapezoid where nobody seemed to be living, he bothered with his questions somebody who didn't know but at last said something like 'Oh, perhaps the Libyans led the colonists past it in the night.' And Herodotus wrote it down, as he wrote everything down."

So stories are not all true. Perhaps, then, thought Berenice to herself, that searing story about Barca was not true. Then why did people make up such stories?

They were for a last time in the Maltese dentist's upper room, level with the treetops. It was after dark, and a lamp on a shelf shone down on the bald brown top of his head. He had his lute in his lap. His wife had been used to sing as he played, and now Berenice, who had had as yet few lessons in music and whose voice was untrained, had accepted his request to sing with him. He remembered only the tunes, it had been his wife who knew the words. Callimachus was there to provide them from his well-stocked memory.

"I have much of Euripides by heart," he said; "I know choruses from the *Bacchae* and the *Ion*. Euripides was not popular in his time and his plays never won the prize, he was too free-thinking, they preferred the reliable Sophocles and grand old Aeschylus, but now it is accepted that his poetry is the most beautiful—any booklover will possess Homer and Euripides if he possesses nothing else. The Athenians captured by the Syracusans saved their lives by being able to recite Euripides, even though his dialect is the dialect of their enemies. I also know some songs of Alcaeus, Sappho, Simonides."

"Sappho," said Berenice.

So Callimachus searched Sappho in his head, found there was only one of hers he was certain of, coughed, and pronounced it several times until Berenice could repeat the words correctly in Sappho's Lesbian dialect; "Not *hê selênê*," he told her— "*a selanna*." Then the lutanist built a melody for it. The melody she instantly grasped, yet let him repeat it, it was so lovely. Then, when they were ready, she sang in her rough clear voice, the lute (though, as Callimachus remarked, it should have been a lyre) following her in perfect unison:

> *Deduke men a selanna*
> *kai Plêiades, mesai de*
> *nuktes, para d'erkhet' ôra,*
> *egô de mona kateudô.*

> The moon has set, and the Pleiades
> in midnight have gone down,
> and another hour goes crawling by
> and I lie down alone.

The eight-drachma piece

They returned the way they had come, and camped a last night on the Headland of the Crescent Moon. It was again time for that moon to appear in the west, but instead from the west there came driving along the sea the last cloudwrack of the early year.

For Berenice back in her palace there began a new kind of life, with a fullness to it and also a parentless hollowness. She had power, though what should she do with it, other than ask the men around her for advice on what to do with it? Coinage was minted in her name, but she had little contact with the working life of her government. She became surrounded by interesting men, though she could have wished some of them were younger. They were earnest men, statesmen---but statesmen less fawning, more candid, than they had been under the eyes of her father and mother. The Macedonian tendency and the Egyptian tendency—the possibility of alliance with those realms, or the threat of subordination to them—having been fended off, the old republican tendency of the Cyrenaican cities was free to lift its head. Cyrenaica was not alone in its aspirations: it considered itself a part of Greece—the five cities were Greek cities—and the way of the Greek cities had been to be stubbornly free, until Philip of Macedon, father of Alexander, came down from the north to swamp their freedom. They remembered their old freedoms, whether they had been democracies like Athens or oligarchies like Sparta; and they had begun to reassert themselves and (encouraged by Egypt) give trouble to Macedon. Recently there had been a rebellion led by those old rivals together, Athens and Sparta. It had turned into a disappointing war, but the Greeks had wrested back at least something of their independence. The name of Chremonides, the Athenian who started that war, was now associated with freedom restored. There were Cyrenaicans who imagined this kind of fame for their own names.

A citizen called Ecdelus came from Barca. At the daily audience, he proposed to the queen that the old Constitution of Cyrene be brought up again for consideration. She gave permission for it to be dug out from the library.

Drawn up back in the time of the third king Battus, it was reputed to be the work of one Demonax. Was he a myth?—his name, which would have meant "the people's king," suggested it; at any rate he lived on as an inspiration, a kind of demigod of democracy. But his Constitution had meekly imitated the customs of Athens, some of which, such as the extraordinary law of ostracism, were just a bit too democratic.

Another political consultant—this time his name was Demophanes—was brought over from Greece. Months passed in discussions of how the document should be revised. Berenice herself liked what she had read of the classic Athenian ways, and she made one useful suggestion—they called it Berenice's Rule. At last the thirty-eight long clauses were drafted, on a mess of separate bits of papyrus, and read out and approved by the assembly (which one of the clauses had created), and by Berenice. Fair papyrus copies would be needed—at least two for deposit in the palace library and one for each of the five cities; at least seven altogether, perhaps more for diplomatic exchange with other states.

"Yes," she said, "let them be made." It was her mother Apama who would have to write them.

With Demetrius out of the way, and Berenice sovereign in Cyrene, there began again to come from Egypt diplomatic approaches relating to King Ptolemy's son—the boy whom people unkindly called Ptolemy Phrissôn, the "trembler." But Berenice had no wish to give up her independence, her home, and her pleasant rural realm for a life with a sickly youth in a strange huge city. Nine years passed. And then it became known that the boy had died.

And that the elder children, by an earlier wife, had been brought back to prominence in the Alexandrian court, and the sister had already been sent to marry Antiochus of Syria.

Old Ptolemy Philadelphus summoned his elder son, now restored to the position of his heir. This son, being his first-born, had received the name that had become dynastic habit, *Ptolemaios*. When his mother had fallen from favor, he and his sister had not been sent along with her into internal exile, but had found themselves adopted by the new queen. But she adopted them in order to have control of them, and then she too had a son, and she insisted that he become the heir, and so this child too, though very far from "warlike," had had to be a *Ptolemaios*. So the father rather unwisely teased his firstborn by calling him Ptolemy Tryphon, the spoilt, the luxurious. It was sarcastic: not only was this youth not as pampered as he might have been, he was a bit of a rebel (of the sulky rather than the loudmouthed kind) against court etiquette and fine clothes.

Now that he was heir again, his father admonished him:

"You ought to become *Tryphôn* in fact, young man. People and especially Egyptians expect their kings to be magnificent, extravagant."

Tryphon might have been well treated of late, but he had suffered a teen-age of neglect, and he had not forgiven his father for the wrong done to his mother.

"I shall reform myself," he said. "I shall do my best to waste your money."

"Good! You are not without a surly kind of wit. And a Cynic streak, inherited from me, which will serve you in good stead. Now, listen to me. Our prospects have never been better—and especially yours. We are now, thanks to your sister, hand in hand with Syria, and Macedon is isolated. The way is clear for you to marry the *silph*" (by which he referred to the Cyrenaican princess). "When I am gone, you will rule the west, your nephew the east, and we may expect that in another generation a Ptolemy will rule the world. I have sent out new feelers to Cyrene."

Tryphon had guessed which way his father was driving. "Never!" he replied at once.

"Why not, my lad? There's nothing wrong with marrying a cousin, though it may be bad to keep marrying cousins."

"I've heard that she chased Demetrius three times around the palace before spearing him, like Achilles chasing Hector around the walls of Troy, and keeps her mother in a dungeon. Do you think I want such an Amazon in my bedroom?"

"You know well enough, I'm afraid, from my example, that marriage is an apparent, a political, a merely necessary matter, and hardly needs to concern the bedroom. You can keep her in a separate palace—"

"As you keep Didyme, don't you? And Myrtion, Mnesis, Stratonice . . . And Clino. And Pothine, for God's sake."

"Don't forget Bilistiche," said his father gently.

"Did you ever love my mother? You must have, since she produced us for you. Or are we, too, the children of some Bilistiche?"

"Go away, Tryphon, and think about it."

"I shall go to Coptos and visit my mother's tomb."

"Don't go incognito this time. It may suit old stories, it doesn't suit the modern world. You endanger yourself. Which matters, now that you are the heir to this throne. Go by the road and take the proper bodyguard."

"I find it interesting to go among the people. Nobody knows me, since you never made me a public figure, as you did with that misborn creature—"

The king rose from his place, and his son bit his lip and departed.

During the four weeks of the journey to Coptos, Ptolemy Tryphon and his Egyptian companion Iphthri, dressed in the simplest clothes they had been able to find in their wardrobes, went ashore at many a small riverside town, where their faces were certainly not known, to stroll around the market and find a tolerable hostelry. They did not care to sleep among the passengers on the deck, where even by day they had to mark out their own little territory and tell the peasants and Nubians aboard: "No spitting!"

They carried, well hidden in their bundles, pouches of the coins for which they had no need at home, to buy necessities, including the company of an occasional village girl. These coins were a joke between them: the first time Tryphon had seen a stater bearing the head of his adoptive mother he had brimmed with scorn: "That is no 'Goddess Philadelph'!—look at the beauty they have made of the hag!"

"Of course," Iphthri explained to him: "do you think a queen would sit halfway through the day while an artisan stares at her?—especially your 'mother', who disliked showing her right profile even more than her left. They get a harlot or a good-looking beggar woman to pose."

"Is that so?" replied Tryphon. "Then I want this one! Have her found for me," and Iphthri had arranged it.

Day by day along the broad road of the Nile labored the boat, its oars mildly scaring the crocodiles and hippopotami. The Egyptians' towns, unlike Alexandria, were compact, each tightly bounded by a canal, so as to consume as little as possible of the precious farmland; fronting each quayside stood the town god's temple, perhaps rebuilt by the generosity of Ptolemy the First or Ptolemy the Second but still in the Egyptian and not the Greek style. At Hermopolis, or Abydos, or maybe both, Tryphon stepping ashore missed his footing on the gangplank and emerged grimfaced from the mud while the peasants roared with laughter and Iphthri kept silence at his friend's clumsiness. At last they moored to the wharf at Coptos, four hundred miles up the river, though the barge itself had to toil on another two hundred, to Thebes, to Hieraconpolis the City of Falcons, to Syene where there is no need to roof houses against rain and where at midsummer the sun stands overhead; as far as a boat could reach, all the way to the First Cataract, where easy Egypt ends and stony Nubia begins.

After the crossing by ferry to Arsinoe's tomb and the offering in her small temple, the young men came back over to Coptos town, which the Egyptians called Qebti. Arsinoe Thrassa had been sent to Coptos because, though far away up the Nile, it was still far short of Thebes, the great city of Upper Egypt; there was little chance that a party of supporters could begin to form around her. Scarcely any Greeks yet lived at Coptos; among notable places (though it was not otherwise notable or very large) it remained so much the town of the Egyptians themselves that Greeks had started to call them "Copts." Here it was possible to visit the shrine of the Eleven Failing Gods, who accounted for Egypt's humiliations by invading races in the past. Coptos lay beside the river's great eastern bend. Here was where the land route came from the Red Sea to the Nile, bringing caravans with goods from Arabia to the east and Punt far to the south; so that Coptos market abounded with merchandise in a variety almost to rival the vast markets of Memphis and Alexandria. Tryphon stood fascinated by the non-stop gabble and deft motions of a stallholder as she dealt with her customers' money and outargued them and wrapped their purchases in twists of cloth. She seemed to be selling not only spices but dates, salt, birds' eggs, bulrush firelighters, amulets against the evil eye.

"Ask her how many kinds of weights she's using on all those scales. Aren't our Ptolemaic talents and minas and obols enough?"

Iphthri asked, and translated the woman's answer: "She says she has to use eight—there are people who still use Persian darics and Judaean and Tyrian shekels, besides the five old Egyptian kinds."

"And how many coins does she have to know the value of? Does she have to know the languages of all these foreigners who bring them and expect to pay with them?"

"She asks back whether you are a market inspector?—she's getting angry—she says she never never clips a coin or a weight."

"Buy something from her with a stater and get the change; I want to collect one of each kind of coin she has. I'll have a belt made from them."

"If you wish, but we have little more than a stater left for the whole journey home."

So they rationed their money, and the joke between them now was that they might have to sell their own bodies to pay their way. And as Tryphon stood on a street corner in Hermopolis a yellow-cloaked policeman took up position beside him and tried to pick him up, glancing down at his legs below the short Greek tunic and murmuring in fellaheen Greek: *"You very good for the zig-zig."* Narrating this afterward to Iphthri, he was careful to add that he had *not* followed the policeman to the old warehouse behind the harbor wall.

"You veree good for thee zig-zig!"—Iphthri found that hilarious. "You'd better take advantage of such offers while you can, Prince Tryphon: you're going to be bald before you're thirty."

"And you, buddy, may take advantage of your licence to talk to me like that while you can."

Iphthri felt a first small shock of fear, even hatred, toward his friend. He knew that his relationship with this son-of-a-king had begun to change when the other son died, and was certain to change more when the father died.

Tryphon was concerned only with the change in his hair. "It isn't really thinning, is it?"—clapping a hand to it.

"I'm afraid so. I see the sun glancing off your skull."

"And I off yours, between your curls. Is there anything we can do?—you know all about these village charms and so forth."

"You'll be able to pass for a shaven-headed scribe."

"No, thank you."

"You'll wear the pharaonic wig when you're crowned."

"That won't help me in the brothel or the bedchamber!"

"Well," said Iphthri, "that old barberess in Eleusis—barberesses not only shave you and see to your eyebrows and ears and nostrils but they know everything about the body—she told me that if you clip the hair as short as the fur on a cat's nose, it will grow back thicker, or coarser; anyway stiffer."

"Let's try it! We'll borrow shears from someone here and crop each other's noddles."

So that evening, in the Hermopolis hostelry, they set about it: Tryphon first gave Iphthri a crude version of what we would call a crew cut. A notably crude version, since it was far from simple to cut Iphthri's curls to an even stature, and Tryphon was neither delicate-handed nor patient. Iphthri cursed himself—silently because too late—for going like a lamb to the slaughter. But he took up the shears and, more skilfully, mowed the front upper circle of Tryphon's scalp. —At which stage Tryphon could endure to lose no more, and calling out "Stop!" pushed the shearing hands away. And remained, for the next weeks, with his hair in two provinces: a flat-top of short bristles, and a greasy glissade down back and sides.

The down-river journey was several days shorter; they passed Memphis and the three great pyramids, passed On, which the Greeks called Heliopolis, City of the Sun, with its forest of shining needles—pyramidions, "little pyramids," that is, obelisks, each made of a single piece of granite and sheathed with electrum to reflect the sun; Obeliskopolis, the place might have been called. They passed near, but did not visit, because it was along side-branches and canals of the mazy Delta, Bubastis, the city of Bast the cat goddess, popularly known as the city of the zig-zags. It was not until they were all the way back as far as Naucratis, the Greek port in the Delta, a day's stage before Alexandria, that Iphthri pulled from his pouch the last two substantial coins, a gold octadrachmon and a tetradrachmon made of electrum, "the child of gold and silver."

"Wait," said Tryphon, "let me look at those. The same face on both."

On the electrum coin, the head with the hair overdraped by a scarf, and on the reverse, a cornucopia.

On the gold, the hair flowing free, and on its reverse a representation of the heart-shaped seed of the silphium: the strange and useful plant known only from Cyrenaica.

The profile and the hair, and something about the sad set of the young eye above the cheek (whose rosiness could almost be seen in the soft burnished swell of the metal), caused the man to be silent.

The portrait "without the veil" meant she was a virgin. Or at any rate unmarried.

"No, you can't have her!" his companion laughed. "At any rate I can't get her for you. This model is too far away." The letters around the edge read BERENIKÊS BASILISSÊS, "of Berenice Queen." "Haven't you seen one of these before? The coinage of Cyrene already has a certain fame. It's known that she poses for them herself—knows no better, or has nothing better to do."

"Well, have you thought about it?" asked his father.
"And what, may I ask, has happened to your hair? You look as if a gryphon tried to snatch you by it. Or have you been the loser in a beerhouse brawl?"

"Yes," said Tryphon, pretending to hear only the first question, "I am ready to obey you—or almost so. But I've asked and
found out more about this namesake of my sister. It's said that
she is under the thumb of demagogues, rabble-rousers. Surely
these can't be matters that your spies have not found out?"

"Oh, demagogues and rabble-rousers. Don't worry about
them," said the king. "In these lands that we have brought into
the new world order, we have to have policies shaped for our
Greek and our indigenous subjects. For the Egyptians we have to
be gods. For Naucratis, since it is an old Greek outpost, we let it
pretend to be still an independent republic, and the same for
Ptolemais, our new Greek foundation half way up the river. And
even Alexandria: we allow it the fiction that it is a Greek state of
its own, separate from Egypt, though we rule Egypt from it. It
makes no practical difference. Democracy is a pleasant romance
like the other romances of the past, Pandora or the Wooden
Horse or the Golden Age. We shall find ways of living, as it were,
with those demagogues. What other rumors have you heard
about her?"

"That she swims in pools; rides a horse, wearing something
like the pantaloons of the Persians. She is trying to learn one of
the languages of the Berber tribes."

"Ladies have to have hobbies."

"It may not be possible to bring her away from her rustic
kingdom except by force."

"I think we shall manage to get her here. If you are not still
afraid of her? She's just a spirited girl. Will you not like that?"

"I would like it, except that—I suspect she is not likely to be
a virgin."

"On that point we do not yet have authoritative information.
Some say she is so pleasingly formed that it is hardly likely;
others, that she is so slow, or so interested in other matters, that
at the age of twenty-six she still is. —But," added the old cynic,
"does it entirely matter? As I intimated to you before, a woman
is one thing and a wife is another. An advantage in a foreign
princess like this is that you have not seen her and therefore
cannot be in love with her."

To this his son said nothing.

His father, mildly concerned to be understood, explained:
"Love is an exploitable weakness. It would not matter if *she* were
to come to love *you*."

(Who could justify falling in love with a face on a coin? And yet he felt the gold-and-silver image of Berenice transplanted into his heart.)

"Shall I be sent to show myself to her?"

"With all respect, I think it would be better for us to keep you here in reserve. (It is a little chafing that we have to think about stratagems; in the time of her father the Libyarch we would not have had to trouble about persuading the girl herself.) Your sister might be the one we could trust to make a reassuring first impression."

"Berenice!—but she is away in Antioch with her husband and child!"

"No, she is on her way here for her first state visit, and to show me my grandson. She will enjoy an extension of her holiday to Cyrene. And she will be able to find out for you more about the Libyan Berenice (personal aspects such as the one you mentioned) than you would for yourself."

Uncle Callimachus

The Court of the Pool was now the Hall of the People. It had been roofed over; the pool was floored over, and the water that had filled it, from one of Cyrene's many springs, had to find another way down through the city. The bronze doors had been carted off and melted down for other use, so that the People might freely enter, never again fearing to be shut into their Hall by a tyrant and massacred.

The People, who had the right to enter in council, were all those slave-owning and land-owning heads of families who could claim to be born in one of the five cities or their territories. This liberal law even included slave-owning and land-owning women, so as to embrace Berenice.

When it became known that a motion of ostracism had been lodged against Berenice herself, the whole of Cyrene both laughed and swore in indignation. What citizen had dared to do this? How could he expect, after the quick defeat of his impudent motion, to hold up his head in Cyrene ever again?

But it became known that he would not have to. He had come

from Egypt and would go back there; yet because he had been born in Cyrene of an old Cyrenean family and still owned a piece of land and a house, which he rented to his nephew, he could claim full citizenship. He was that Callimachus, son of Battus, who had left many years ago to study in Athens and was now an eminent old man among the many scholars in Alexandria.

The Cyreneans would have to abide by the law they had themselves made, modeled on the custom of Athens.

The way it had worked, back in the great days of Athens, was that once a year the assembly considered whether it was time to "apply ostracism." What this meant was: Did people have a feeling that anybody among them was becoming too powerful, too noisy, too admired? (They didn't have to say who it was they had in mind.) If the vote was Yes, then a public Ostracism was held in the agora, the marketplace. On that occasion, every citizen had in his hand an ostracon, a shard of a broken pot—a common potsherd like any of those used for the writing of notes and lists and accounts and messages. On his ostracon each man wrote, if he wished, with pen and ink if he had brought them or with the point of his knife, a name. He could write the name of any one citizen he considered was becoming too big for his boots. The ostraca were counted, and if there was a man whose name appeared on six thousand of them, he went into exile for ten years. His property and sometimes his family waited for him to come back; and when he came back he was a chastened and better democrat. Or not.

In this way (so hoped those who had suggested the system) there would never again arise a tyrant like Hippias, of whom the city had managed to rid itself. It worked, though mistakes were made. The Athenians nearly ostracized Themistocles, who had saved them from the Persians, and did ostracize Aristeides the Just, famous for his honesty and moderation.

This fine old institution was almost a parable for democracy: "The Athenians so trust the common man that they give him a chance to banish his leaders!" Having its flaws, it had fallen into disuse in Athens; but Cyrene had seen that it was worth reviving, if reformed. Potential tyrants may loom at any time, so ostracism could be proposed by a citizen at any time; then, as in Athens, the assembly voted on whether actually to hold it. In Athens there had been no pre-announced person to be voted on—hence the deep surprise that the grave Aristeides must have felt—and no formal debate; but in Cyrene the proposing citizen had to name the name of the candidate for ostracism, and the debate that followed—not among the whole population, but in the assembly—ended in the scratching on the ostraca. Callimachus son of Battus— "Callimachus of Alexandria," people were contemptuously calling him—had come back here and proposed the name of the queen, presumably for a joke; and the assembly, anticipating entertainment, had voted to let the debate proceed.

Callimachus had been virtually ostracized himself as he walked cheerily through the streets. But now he sat at table in the small house of his sister Megatima on the edge of the town. She and her husband Stasenor, a retired officer of the royal guard, were old and quiet; quiet also was Hero, the younger Callimachus's wife, who served supper to them, there being no servant other than the man the elder Callimachus had brought with him.

"I would oppose you if I could, uncle," said his nephew.

"But you can't because you don't own your house. You should finish your book and present it with a dedication to a royal person—it will have to be the king of Egypt, since he, besides being the richest, rules the most islands. Then you will be able to make some money, and buy the house from me."

"Why don't you give it to me? You are prosperous now."

"All right, I will. I'm planning to do so, after this is over. If, that is, you don't share in my unpopularity and have to leave! I'm glad to see you married at last, and I don't like to see the two of you having to live with your mother, so I should give you the means to buy another house too. I have to say that I am prosperous because I have been busy: I have written many books—many, many!"

"Yes. All short ones."

"Whereas you are writing your versified history, which you will never finish. As you know, I don't see much use for epics in our modern age. I'm glad the subject of your epic is not *On Continents!* Still, you would never finish it even if it were *On Small Islands*, or *On Lighthouses*. —No, please, nephew, don't take me seriously!"

Uncle Callimachus was shorter and broader than his nephew. His hair and eyebrows, though mostly white, were still tinged with a bronzy orange; his eyebrows were like two pointy leaves of willow or wild cherry, applied to his mildly tanned and shiny face above eyes usually crinkled in a mirth for which he alone saw the reason.

Callimachus the younger did his best to clear the gloom from his face and feel no hurt from his uncle. "Yes," he said, "you are a joker. But do allow me to point out that you too had to start humbly. In Alexandria you were for years a mere schoolteacher, until you were older than I am now. That's how you had to start. And I too am a teacher. I shall progress—"

"You are teaching children in a school? You didn't tell me that in your letters."

"No, I mean that I am chief teacher to the queen. I teach her history, but I also recruit and direct those whom she wants to teach her such crafts as archery and medicine."

"Ho, indeed! You are the head of a little Museion, an academy! And do you not get a royal stipend for that?"

"Well, I do get a stipend—not a large one."

"Don't tell me it's honorary work, though honorable! But never mind, Callimachus, I won't go back on my intention to stop charging you rent for your house. Salaries earned in Egypt are higher than what your charming patron can pay. Tell me, among the laws that you've been devising here—not you, but your land-owning citizens—you've even passed a law against us calling each other 'Uncle' and 'Nephew', haven't you?"

"Nonsense, uncle, you've got it wrong. What that law is aimed at is the stupid custom of naming sons after their grandfathers, and younger sons after their fathers. It is now illegal to do that, in Cyrene. You cannot re-use a name unless it is at least five degrees of kinship removed. I myself suggested the law—I was able to do so, before the rest of the laws had been fixed."

"And you suggested it, of course, because you are a story-teller?"

"Precisely; you understand, because you too are a writer of books. It's a nuisance that you and I have to keep calling each other 'Uncle' and 'Nephew' rather than, say, Callimachus and Herophilus, because we bear the same name. How much worse it is that we have to specify, when we talk of the kings of Syria, which 'Seleucus' or which 'Antiochus' we mean; or of the kings of Macedon, which 'Antigonus' or which 'Demetrius', or of the older line, which 'Philip' and which 'Alexander'—we have to call them by nicknames, Antigonus the One-Eyed, or 'the Antigonus who was born at Gonni'—"

"The one I like best," interrupted his uncle, "is Antigonus Doson, 'he who is always about to give' though he never quite gives. How nimble our Greek language is!"

"We should," said his nephew severely, "respect the example of Homer (even you, who don't like epics): in the Iliad we find only two heroes—Great Ajax and Little Ajax—who have to share a name; and that, I think, is the exception that shows the need for the rule: it's as if Homer made a joke of it (there could hardly be two men who are more different). As for Egypt, where 'Ptolemy' has become such a sacred title that not only every father, son, and grandfather, but every brother—"

"Come to Egypt and tell it to the Ptolemies! You might even persuade them that writing their history is going to be difficult. But if we make parents scratch their heads to find names for their offspring, I'm afraid they'll invent silly ones, or just pick them out of the Iliad. Still, I wish you luck, Callimachus, in your *beautiful battle*" (that was what their name meant) "if you'll wish me luck in mine. Meanwhile, you have your problem with you in the form of the other Berenice, don't you? Does your rule extend to women? Do you resent her presence?—do you wish she'd change her name to Hypsipyle?"

Callimachus (the younger) was one of those humbly in love with his pupil and queen—for him one Berenice was enough—and he glared silently at his uncle.

The misplaced heart

The Berenice whom, because of her marriage, people called Berenice Syra, the Syrian, had already been in Cyrene for nearly a month. She was expected back in Alexandria, where her child was being pampered, and then in Antioch, but she had not yet spoken of leaving.

She was shorter, darker, and bustier than her cousin Berenice Libyca and was seven years older. She had a long slender white nose of perfect regularity, at which her cousin stared. As for her own impression of her Libyan cousin, it was that she was *rain-washed*.

"You have come here, haven't you," said Berenice, "so as to tell your father and brother what I am like. And to tell me what your brother is like, and you haven't yet told me. Probably you will say he is excellent."

"No young man is good—all young men are bad. All men are bad, but particularly young men. They are the ones that make trouble. (Trouble is blamed on Pandora—by men.) But for a young man he is not so bad. I have a feeling he would obey you. He even used to obey me, when we were children. Then he would remember that I was his sister; but then a bit later he would be obeying me again. I think he would certainly fall into obeying you."

"But what does he look like?"

"Like me."

Berenice, seeing that she would continue to get more out of her cousin by waiting for inadvertent anecdotes—which looked like confirming her surmise that the brother was not for her—asked instead: "And what shall you say to them about me?"

"That you are beautiful."

"Don't tell me that—it's the kind of thing courtiers say. When I see myself in the bronze, I see nothing out of the ordinary; I find myself no better to look at than my maid Polymela. And," she added reflectively, "my previous suitor did not admire me."

"Well, I can tell you openly just what I will say. I will tell them that you seem very fresh of body, and that you seem to want to learn everything. Those are the things I observe about you."

Berenice flushed—and felt that she had perspired, and was not fresh of body. She turned her eyes away from Berenice's stare, and said: "Why do you say such things?"

"We all wear light clothes, in comparison with the hot ways the Libyans and Syrians wrap themselves, and it seems to me that—"

"No more of my flesh shows than is customary!" said Berenice. (It occurred to her to fear—as she had sometimes done when running or riding—that her clothes were not firmly fastened, and to wish she had not on this warm day chosen a chiton with such deep openings below the arms.)

"No," replied the Syrian soothingly, "it was just a fancy. Perhaps it's because I've heard of your swimming in pools and streams. Or perhaps it's because there is no rain in Egypt. (Your Green Mountain robs the rain before it can reach Egypt.) In Egypt the native girls who dance at feasts wear shifts that you can see their bodies through, or nothing at all, and sometimes they seem quite pretty, and yet they don't seem as clean as you. —Is it true that you have tutors in music and medicine and philosophy?"

"I read about those things, and I did ask for some lessons in music, but did not do well in it."

"And medicine, have you really learnt something of that?"

"I have had no chance to dissect bodies, but I asked for a physician to give me one lesson—about the body—and after that I read Hippocrates and Theophrastus."

"So you know which side the heart is on, and so forth?"

"Of course. And that it is not shaped the way they draw it, like the silphium seed. But what is the harm in all this? It's true I want to read more of Aristotle, and understand how the world works. Everyone would like to know more, if they had the opportunity, but instead they have to work for their bread."

"If you're so curious for knowledge you should come to Alexandria. Men there are finding things out all the time. There's one called Heron who's made a device for measuring heat—and a machine that moves by steam, and a way of finding the size of a triangle. And there's Eratosthenes, who was born here at Cyrene and made his way to Alexandria like so many others—he's made something called a 'sieve', I don't know whether it's a machine or what, it finds numbers that can't be divided by other numbers; and there's a man calling himself Ptolemy, one of those who borrow the kings' name, he's explained how the stars move in circles. And Euclid, who has drawn up all the rules of measuring—"

"What I would like to find out about next is the names of the plants I see. For this I'll have to find a peasant woman as a teacher. Why do you talk, anyway, about all this? Is your brother like-minded?"

"I hope he is" (he may have to be, thought his sister). "But I ask because I am interested myself. You will be able to tell me about the Cyrenaic school of philosophers, having been taught about them—taught perhaps by one of them."

"No, they are called Cyrenaic because their founder Aristippus and his daughter Arete were of Cyrene, and several of them did live here, but none do now—all gone to Alexandria, I suppose. So it is from my reading that I know about them. You don't really wish to be told about them?"

"Yes, I do, so as" (added in a low voice that Berenice in her enthusiasm did not notice) "to see you talking."

"Their doctrine is perverse," said the Libyan eagerly. She was sitting with her cousin at a window of the upper palace, and with the sun falling from the east she looked like a candle. "They say that we cannot be sure that anything exists outside ourselves— no, that's not quite it: they say that we can know that other things exist, that I, for instance, can know that you exist, but only because you have an effect on me. That is, the sight of you reaches my eyes, and I therefore know of your existence, but you are somewhere outside me, and I can't really know that you are real; for me, you are just the eidolon on my eyes, which are the exposed part of my soul. I can be sure of what I *think* I know about you, but I cannot know anything more; I cannot know, for instance, what you perceive and think; I can only know that you are telling me things, but they could be things I make up to have an imaginary you telling me; I cannot know whether there is really a you that perceives me, or that perceives anything else, as I perceive you. It's a farfetched doctrine, like all the philosophers' doctrines; sometimes I think that that's all the philosophers do, they try to think of something that is perverse in a new way. That's come to be the way they amuse us. And"; she paused, only for breath. Her cousin, lest she stop, asked: "And?"

"And then, supposing they find that some other school of philosophers has arrived at a similar fiction about the world, they try to reassert their originality by drawing different conclusions from it—for, you know, the groundwork of philosophy is metaphysics, and then ethics is built on that: the Cyrenaics have this metaphysics (or do I mean epistemology?) that all we can know is a mirage on our eyes, but so do some other schools; so they feel they must find not the ethical conclusion we expect, but some different one, to surprise us. And their conclusion is that we should all be selfish, and ensure our own pleasure. Because that's all we really know, what arrives at our senses and gives us pain or pleasure, and so at every moment all I should bother about doing is making sure that the moment is a pleasurable one for me." Berenice was exhausted by her own talking. Her cousin could see something to say, but not how to say it yet.

They sat in silence for as long as it takes to breathe four times. "Didn't you say," asked the Syrian, "that the room you used to live in was even pleasanter than where you sleep now?"

"Yes, I had a room over a gate, a room that had been my mother's—but it's the gate to the public hall now, so I couldn't stay there. Get up, I'll show it to you"—Berenice sprang restlessly to her feet.

On their way they passed the neighboring rooms that had been used by servants, but they happened to meet no one, The room with door opening on the gallery of the public hall, and window looking north over the city—the room where Demetrius had loved and died—had been stripped of its fine furnishings, and contained only an assembly of chests. Entering behind her cousin, Syrian Berenice noticed that the door had a bolt, and slid it, which Libyan Berenice did not notice. She was busy noticing that the floor, chests, and empty shelves had become dusty.

"You must have been sad to quit this room."

"Yes, I liked the view. But the floor is cold, because of the air underneath."

"What's in all these boxes?"

"Public records in those, I think, and unwanted gifts. Rugs— the ones my mother spread on the floor. Because the floor is cold, as I said."

Her cousin took the liberty of lifting a lid, to peer at the rugs. And then pulled two of them out—no, three—and, leaving the lid of that chest open, threw them over another. "Now we can sit down."

"If you like, or we could go now."

"The Cyrenaic philosophers are right."

"Why do you say so?"

"How can you know what I perceive? You cannot. Suppose that by 'red' I mean something different from what you do." She looked for red among the materials she had exposed.

"Of course we mean the same. That"—pointing at the fringe of a folded curtain— "is yellow."

"Yes, and so is your hair." (It was not: Berenice's hair was gold, which contains as many tints of brown and orange as it does of yellow. Yet it was what men loosely called *xanthos*.) "We call the same thing yellow, but do we know that we see it the same way? We cannot describe it to each other."

"Yellow is—lighter than red."

"It is so to me. But do you know that what you mean by 'lighter' is what I mean by 'lighter'?"

"I understand now what you mean. But you can't prove it to be true."

"No—and that is the thing. We can't prove it to be untrue. When I say a musical sound is higher, you too say it is higher, but you could mean what I mean when I say it is lower."

"You are a Cyrenaic, cousin Berenice!"

"Yes, I do not see the world you see. I see the world the wrong way round. My left is your right."

"But if you point left . . . Yes, I understand. You mean that it *could* be so, and we can't know. And also, it makes no difference whether it is so or not. Do you really incline to be a Cyrenaic? You've just now thought of saying it, to tease me."

"Put your hand on me, here."

"Why?"

"Sit down by me. Put your hand on me and feel my heart."

Instructed by her Syrian cousin, and sitting down on the chest beside her, Berenice found the place over "the apex of the heart," its lower tip where it presses closest to the skin. She put her hand inside the chiton, slid it gingerly over her cousin's warm flesh, found (as instructed) the little pit below the end of the breastbone. "Now move out along my lowest rib—the left one, of course." The finger pressed along the scarp that it found under the flesh, sloping downward— "Slowly. Stop there. Now up: find the space above that rib." The finger had to press up over the rib, drop into the first space—but it was a narrow space, hardly a space. "This?" "Yes. Press. Can you feel a beat yet?" "No." "No. That is not yet the right space. Move up to the next space." The finger pressed up over the next rib; into the next space. Somewhat wider and deeper. But becoming rather anxiously close under the swell of the breast. "Press. Press in. That is where you should feel the beat of my heart." Berenice pressed, but she felt no beat. Perhaps it was confused with the pulse of her own finger. She waited, keeping still, pressing. "Can you feel my heart?" "No." "But it's beating strongly." And the Syrian's heart was beating strongly; her flesh was hot and her mouth was parted. Berenice hoped that she was not to move her finger higher.

"You should feel it, that's where everyone's heart is."

"You have no heart!"

"No."

"Do you really have no heart?"

"I terrify the physicians. When I was a little girl, and had a coughing sickness, and the physician came to test me, all confident in his art, and he applied his hearing-tube—here where you're pressing—to hear my heart, he turned white!"

"Do you really have no heart?"

"Let's try on the other side—perhaps it's there."

"But it won't be, everyone's heart is on the left."

Berenice Syra said nothing, but leaned back, her eyes closing slowly like a cat's.

Berenice moved her finger across. Found again the small pit, explored along the lower scarp—the other one—above the taut flat plain of the stomach, up into the first slight valley, up into the second and deeper valley close under the mountain of the breast—and found the heart beating hard.

"You have your heart on the right!"

"Yes."

"So you are rare! Or is it incorrect after all?—it's common? We can be left-handed, we can be right-hearted?"

"No, it's rare. Hippocrates says we are only one in ten thousand. My body is the mirror of yours."

(Berenice would have withdrawn her finger, but the other Berenice put her hand over it, keeping it where it was, pressing, feeling the heart.)

"And why mightn't it be that my world is the mirror of yours? For me the whole cosmos is the other way around."

"Or it may be."

"It is. I am turned around."

"You don't know."

"I don't know by looking at your face. Your face would have the same beauty either way around."

"How did Hippocrates know? Did he press the breasts of ten thousand women?"

"I think not. Perhaps he was wrong. Which side is your heart on? You don't know." (Berenice didn't speak. Her ribs were braced, even before they had been touched.) "Let's find it."

The Syrian hand slid inside the Cyrenean chiton—did not find the heart, since its leaping is smooth and hard to feel in a well-tuned body, a body better clad in the cream of womanliness—but did not search long, soon drifting upward.

An hour later, as Berenice lay softened on a crumpled rug, the

Syrian palm searched again for her heart. "Yes, here it is, I can feel it now. It's marching like a soldier after a victory. Do you want to feel it?" "No, I'm sleeping." "We must remember to search for it after you've been working. After you've been swimming in a pool, or wrestling with me."

Queen Berenice's Rule

"Berenice daughter of Magas, though we admire her beauty, courage, and innocent wisdom—"

Already there was a disposition to hiss Callimachus down, but the president of the assembly, who this month was Gorgo of Taucheira, pointed to the Tongue, the sign of the right to speech, which she had put into his hands.

"Berenice, daughter of Magas," Callimachus son of Battus began again, "much as we love you for your beauty, courage, and innocent wisdom, you must leave us, and you will understand why. You have endangered us and yourself."

Since he had chosen to speak as if to her, and she was behind him, he had to speak with his head half turned. "You affronted the king of Macedon by killing his brother—"

"Half-brother," interrupted several voices.

"—and taking possession of more than a dozen of his ships and a whole regiment of his troops. None of which or of whom you returned. It had to be done, but it has consequences. He has since then been occupied in his struggle with the king of Epirus. You don't know," he said, now turning to the rest of the assembly, "because you don't have the spies that the Ptolemy has, that Antigonus is now ready to turn again in this direction. He has a hundred and ninety more ships. Do you want Cyrene to burn?"

The citizens were for a moment silenced, even though they were not completely surprised. This had been one of the possibilities mentioned in the conversations among them as they came in and took their places on the circle of five benches. The pentagon of benches represented the five cities of the Pentapolis, and on each city's bench sat the three delegates it had sent this month. A line of guards, holding truncheons—really the leather handles of whips with their lashes removed—stood to keep the other members of the public to the outer half of the hall, where they could hear but not speak.

The momentary silence was less a confounded than a glowering silence, soon breaking into angry cacophony. It was joined, to Gorgo's displeasure, by calls from the non-speaking half of the hall, and it took her some time to quell. By the customary rule there should at this juncture be one counter-speaker, but there were twenty.

Callimachus's neighbors were trying to grab the Tongue from him. (It was really a helmet from the armory, an ancient helmet of the type called Boeotian, with no chin, only a descending nosepiece between the cheekpieces; it was popularly known as the Tongue either because its nosepiece looked like a tongue or because it was easier, if set on the head, to speak through than the Corinthian type. But speakers were not expected actually to set it on their heads. Its long straight nose reminded Berenice of her cousin's.) Gorgo rose from her place, went across the ring, took the Tongue, and held it out toward Berenice. She was sitting on a separated small throne, at the point nearest to the foot of the staircase, and one would have said that she looked pale, though the paleness was in her manner rather than her color. She merely made a motion that was a shake of the head that turned into an uncertain nod.

Gorgo went back to her own place and overcame the babble by shouting: "The Queen's Rule, the Queen's Rule!" She had a seconder for the Queen's Rule, and they voted for it, because though it was not really necessary they knew from experience that they enjoyed it. The rule, which Berenice had herself suggested on one of the occasions when debate got out of hand, was simple. The usual crisscross of speakers was suspended, and the Tongue passed in strict order around the circle, like the sun around the sky.

So first it was the turn of Gnamptus of Cyrene, sitting to the left of the previous speaker, that is, of Callimachus. He said:

"I think—I think the king of Macedon will come and strike us anyway, if he so decides. Whether or not our queen is here. As he will see it, we have shared in her—in her action. In her responsibility." He ceased, with admirable brevity, and passed the Tongue on.

"Yes," said the first of the representatives of Apollonia. "Or, for that matter, the king of Egypt might. He might think it is time to repossess Cyrenaica. Either could choose to lift their hands against us, whether or not they have a pretext."

"Or," said the next—he was Amyntas, one of the Macedonians of the new settlement of Darnis, but Darnis had to count as being in the territory of Apollonia— "or they could come against us together, in collusion. These kings need only their calculations; they need no pretext, as a republic does, when they come against a republic."

"Let them remember Irasa!" came a growl from the back of the onlooking crowd.

The black voice was that of Aondas the chiliarch, who should not have spoken. Gorgo rebuked him and the many who agreed with him by laughing and cheering; she had to call again for silence and a strict return to Queen Berenice's Rule. The Tongue passed on to the next speakers. But most of them—unless they passed, which they were allowed to do by saying merely "*Sigaô*, I am silent"—voiced much the same defiance as Aondas, if in more flowery terms. "Will we be any safer against our enemies if our queen deserts us?" said one of them. "We will be less so. They will find their pretexts anyway. We will be better off with Berenice Doryphoros to lead us, Berenice of the Spear, as Alexander led the van of his host against the Persians, as Hippolyta led the Amazons" and so on.

"And," said a Euhesperidean from the west, "where is she to go?"

"Are you asking me, neighbor?" said his neighbor. "*I* don't know."

The next but one was impatiently awaiting his turn to answer that question:

"We know well that she has nowhere to go but Egypt."

He left that as if it needed no further comment. And it received none, for a while: each man, and the two women— Gorgo herself, and her friend Cleite also of Taucheira—preferred to think rather than speak; "*Sigaô.*" (Some muttered the full formula, "I am silent for now but not for ever." They expected the turn to go around at least one more time before this day's debate ended.)

The turn passed on until it came to Thrasybulus, Cyrene's other representative of the day. He was the one who had been waiting his chance most impatiently of all, because he was the very last in the circle that had started from Callimachus, and because he was one of those who like the sound of their own voices (commonly voices less enjoyed by others). He had already several times tried to jump in and been told by Gorgo: "Please wait your turn, Thrasybulus. You are not the only one with things saved up to say." (Berenice's strictly-circular Rule is simple to follow, yet there are always those who jump in and break it. The citizens did not obey it quite so politely for Gorgo as they had for Berenice herself.)

"Yes, Egypt," said Thrasybulus. "We are being asked to give our Berenice to Egypt. She was, before, to have married the son of the Ptolemy; that son was a degenerate creature that died; now she will be made to marry another son of the Ptolemy, who will be degenerate in some other way. (We are all Greeks here, we can speak our minds.) Do you know what that family is like? Ptolemy son of Ptolemy—the Ptolemy who is still king there—"

"We do not tell stories when it is our turn," said Gorgo.

"You may invert your sandglass," said Thrasybulus. "You know the rule says that we are to say what we like and to be brief if we can but to speak more lengthily if we have to, subject to the sandglass: I am to stop at the turn of the sandglass, if anyone objects, or go on, if no one does."

"Start your story then, though everyone knows it."

"Perhaps everyone does, but perhaps it will do them good to hear it retold, since it will help them to make up their minds. If not, they may stop me. —This second Ptolemy, who is called Philadelphus, sister-lover—"

"I object," said Callimachus.

"Callimachus does not live here, he lives in Egypt. So of course he knows the story," said Thrasybulus; and after a short argument he was allowed to go on. "This second Ptolemy, who is called Philadelphus, sister-lover, as if it is a title of honor, and who is now old—he married, oh, forty years ago, the daughter of Lysimachus of Thrace. And old Lysimachus married the sister of Ptolemy. And they were both called by the same name, these women: Arsinoe the Egyptian and Arsinoe Thrassa, the Thracian. Arsinoe and Arsinoe, though only one of them was of 'raised-up mind'. After a while that one, Arsinoe the Egyptian, came back from Thrace, because her old husband was dead. The story of what had happened before she came back is even worse, but too much for what concerns us now. She came back to Egypt, where she was older than her brother and her brother's wife, who had

already given him children. Yet she wormed her mind into that
of her brother, until she persuaded him that his wife was treacherous and had to be put away. And he put away his wife—sent
her to a place far up the Nile, where she had to live out the rest
of her life. And Egyptian Arsinoe took her place: married her
own full brother.

"The Egyptians are used to such customs in their rulers, have
been used to them all the way back to their gods Isis and Osiris,
but for the Greeks it was too much. Poor Sotades the mischie-
vous poet, for calling incest what it was, ended at the bottom of
the sea in a lead coffin. Nobody thinks that Ptolemy and his sister
were real spouses. All she wanted was the power, and for the six
or seven years until she died she had it, and her brother-husband
sat back smiling while she had laws written and cities founded
and canals dug and the Lighthouse built and the Museum filled,
and sent out explorers and drove out the foreign moneychangers
and in general busied herself like no king before her in any
land . . .   But she and her brother must have tried it once—"

The sand had run through, and Gorgo looked around, but no
one raised a hand to put a stop to the story, and she turned the
glass over.

"And they produced that child who was born the way he was
because his parents were the Theoi Philadelphoi, the Sibling-
Loving Gods. For him the children of the other Arsinoe were put
aside. His mother would have had him be the next King Ptolemy,
and also would have had for him our Berenice; they betrothed
him to her when she was no more than fourteen and he no more
than six; but he died.

"This is the family into which you would send our Berenice?
For that is what will happen to her if she goes to Egypt. She will
have to marry the other Arsinoe's son Ptolemy, the one they nick-
name Tryphon, the Spoilt."

Thrasybulus sat back, as if all that needed saying was said.
"Now I defer to my (since I have to call him so) *neighbor*, my
fellow citizen, Callimachus who calls himself son of Battus, as if
he is a true old Cyrenean. He who in Egypt, where he actually
lives, is a distinguished *Court Flatterer*, and in that role was the
composer of the funerary ode for Arsinoe Philadelph when she
relieved the world of her presence—I mean, when she went on
to become a goddess of the invisible kind. Oh, and also he had

composed the famous ode *Arsinoês Gamos* for her incestuous marriage."

Thrasybulus, ending his speech, pushed the Tongue aside— pushed it to Callimachus—with a "Pshaw" gesture.

Callimachus accepted it and said: "Yes, thank you. And thank you, Thrasybulus, for describing what a royal family is like—the family to which your queen belongs, Berenice first cousin to Ptolemy. I join you in hoping that she continues to allow you your Republic here, and does not call in her relatives to reassert—"

The hissing threatened again; he abandoned this futile attempt to turn the tide, but tried another tactic: "The Rule says, I believe, that a question of information may be asked across the circle, after which the turn returns to the questioner and goes on?"

"That's right," said Gorgo.

Callimachus asked his question, not across the circle, but to Berenice, who was behind him—but she was an honorary member of the circle; her position had never been made unambiguous, under her own Rule. "Do you, madam, love this country of yours?—and" (Callimachus asked the two parts of his question in one, lest he get no second chance) "would you be better able to protect it from here or from the throne of Alexandria?"

Berenice again looked back at him wide-eyed as if she were asking a question of her own.

And the Tongue passed on a second time to Gnamptus. But neither Gnamptus nor anybody had much more to say, except for the usual kind of tiresome person who when asked "And Callias, do you want to say any more?" replies "No . . . Only that" and then burbles on. The turn came around again to Gorgo herself, who said: "I propose that we now end Queen Berenice's Rule" (she meant the circling of the Tongue) "and proceed to the vote of ostracism, unless anyone has any more to say; those who have not spoken?" None of those did, but Thrasybulus raised his hand; he wanted to hear his own voice one more time.

"Yes, I will add one more thing," he said: "don't be fools, people of Cyrene and the other towns. It seemed to me that a few of you were quiet and showed in your faces that you were faintly impressed by what former-citizen Callimachus said. It isn't always that democracy leads to the right result; if you give fools a choice, they will make a fools' choice. I hasten to add that you are not all fools, friends, and I trust you not to be. Remem-

ber the story of Aristeides the Just: as they stood in the agora
marking their ostraca, an ignorant Athenian, one who could not
read or write and had never before bothered his head with politics, so that he did not know Aristeides, stood beside Aristeides
and asked him to write for him on his ostracon. 'What name
shall I write for you, citizen?' 'The name of Aristeides.' 'I will,'
said Aristeides, 'but let me ask you, what harm has Aristeides ever
done you?' 'None, but I'm sick of hearing him called Aristeides
the Just.' So Aristeides wrote his own name, and so did too many
fools, and he had to go into exile. Well, you know that story too.
Berenice is our own Aristeides. Let's go on, citizen Gorgo."

It took a squad of servants to bring out the ostraca, quills, and
bottles containing ink that had been ground and watered in the
kitchen. Callimachus, as he received his ostracon, glanced
around behind him at Berenice: she, in her little throne at the
foot of the stair, was aloof from the circle of her subjects. Callimachus tried to crack his ostracon on his knee. It wouldn't
break; he tried again, smacking it on the edge of the bench, and
it broke in halves, with a few crumbs. He turned and offered one
half to Berenice. Those who observed this fatuous little display
of loyalty did not (especially as Berenice accepted it) care to
interfere with it.

By the Cyrenean version of Ostracism, only one name was to
be written or none, and so, as it would otherwise be obvious who
was writing the name and who was not, the practice was that
everyone wrote something: either the name, or "OUDEIS"—
"Nobody." So they all crouched over the ostraca on their laps and
there were the small scratchy sounds of the writing. Callimachus, after quickly writing, handed his quill—still with some
ink in it—back to Berenice. Then the ostraca were allowed to
dry, then turned over, and gathered up and counted.

All had OUDEIS written on them, except for two. Onto those
two ostraca, even though they were the smallest, had been fitted
the longer word.

Whose daughter?

Once, three days after her mother's confinement in the scriptorium, Berenice had visited, to take what she intended as a kindly look at the conditions of work. There sat the fallen queen, bowed over her desk, which was a shaky table with four gryphon legs. She looked like Queen Cassiopeia chained to her throne and condemned (for her sin against her daughter) to whirl forever around the Pole Star.

Glancing down at where her mother's hands were crawling over the paper like spiders, Berenice noticed that the script was stabbed, angular. There were some peculiarities (not enough to render the copies useless): the final sigmas had no tails, they looked like *c*, as if Apama—never hitherto much accustomed to writing—could not be bothered to waste another moment on them: *Zeuc* instead of *Zeus*. —Apama looked up with resentful impatience. Since then Berenice had not cared, or dared, to make what her mother would consider a visit of inspection.

Now that she was to depart, she went into the room where Callimachus son of Stasenor was sitting before the few familiar bookshelves; he was seeming to read but perhaps meditating, his hand touching the shore of that toy of his, his model island. The island was not Ithaca nor Delos nor Tenedos, nor Lemnos where the Argonauts romped and Philoctetes was marooned, but an imaginary isle in the shape of a small chair, a doll's chair, draped over with plaster, and painted to represent forested slopes, a peak, glens, rocky headlands, a sea-eagle cliff, a cave, a cove with a beach. This toy, which had been made for Callimachus by a whimsical order of her father, she found strangely touching, and she touched it, laying her hand beside his. She made her request: "Could a half dozen books be spared for me to take along?"

He laughed drily and said: "You are going to find yourself living in the midst of the Library of Alexandria, the greatest in the world. Everything we have here will certainly be there."

"Yes, but—I won't be living in the midst of it, surely?—won't be able to step from my quarters into a little room like this." She imagined a few scrolls in a niche near her bedside.

"I'll pick some out for you."

She could have answered "Let me choose them for myself." But she guessed he wanted time to search out some of which he had duplicates, and give her those. He brought them to her next day, wrapped in a large leather parcel: a few of the lyric poets, a heavy dose of the tragedies of Euripides—the *Alcestis*, *Medea*, *Bacchae*, and *Trojan Women*—and for comic relief the *Frogs*,

Cloudcuckooland, and *Lysistrata* of Aristophanes. It was a generous handful. She had hoped for Herodotus and Homer and Plato and Aristotle—but they were in too many volumes.

"Thank you, Callimachus. These are second copies—I hope?"

"Yes, they are," he admitted. And to make light of it he added: "And I'm not charging you a deposit! Did you know how King Ptolemy Philadelphus acquired Aeschylus and Aristotle and all the rest for his Library?"

"No, I don't think you've told me that story."

"The Athenians agreed, after much persuasion, to lend the originals for copying; they let his ship take the precious manuscripts of Homer and Pindar and Aeschylus and Sophocles and Euripides and all the rest, just for copying, and he had to leave fifteen talents of gold as surety—enough to buy a fleet! And when he'd had copies made, he sent those back: the copies! The Athenians fumed and protested, but they had to be content with the copies and the fifteen talents (with which, it strikes me, they might almost have bought enough ships to raid Alexandria and get their books back). All so that he could keep those first editions for his Library, where" (Callimachus the Younger sighed) "you'll be able to touch them."

Having seen to the inclusion of the books in the belongings that were being crated for her, she forced herself to a farewell visit to her mother. She went again from the outer gallery into the library, from the back of which a door opened on a passage, and one of the doors in the other side of this passage was that of her mother's cell. On the floor outside sat a bulky old man. His back was propped against the wall, his knees drawn up, his arms around them and his bearded head asleep on top of them. It was Phravartes, the Persian, the one retainer Apama still had, who had come with her from Syria. Still as faithful to her as a dog, he spent every day here, jealous to protect her from further harm.

It occurred to Berenice that she should ask the old chamberlain's permission before pushing the door, but his eyes were shut and she left him undisturbed. She entered the small room where her mother lived and toiled. Some light fell from a west window, but all day two candles were needed to write by. It seemed to Berenice that her mother's eyes were red, her neck bent, and her black hair beginning to gray from stooping over the scrolls.

"Mother," said Berenice, "I am leaving for Egypt and I fear I shall not see you again."

Apama was aware of her daughter in the corner of her eye but she did not look up or pause in her scribing. Berenice found herself forced to say the rest of what she had to say in one gust.

"I have forgiven your offence. It was not such a great offence as I once thought. You can cease this work and live in a better room—your former room if you wish. You will not have power again—the power is with others now—but you will be looked after, I have arranged it."

Apama, still without looking up, replied in a prompt cold stream, like juice shooting from a bitten fruit:

"I wish to continue this work. I am good at it. Have you found a single mistake? If you have found a mistake you may order me to stop, not otherwise. I have finished the *Iliad*, all twenty-four scrolls, and I am now copying *The Sack of Troy*. When I have finished the Troy cycle (I may omit *The Homeward Returns*, I don't care about them) I shall go on to the Thebes cycle. We shall have at least two copies of everything in this library—every heroic book. I enjoy these tales. Particularly the *Iliad*, I shall copy it again. There are no heroes like these any more. But watch out for the next sun-haired Achilles you meet—he'll cast a quicker spear than you do. Stay in the moonlight, don't go in the sun" (the old queen raved)— "that is my curse on you. Goodbye, Berenice daughter of a loser and a whore."

"What do you mean?" Berenice cried out.

"Do you really think you are my daughter?" exclaimed Apama, turning full-on to her. Berenice was struck by the straight sides of her mother's face. "You are an urchin, a bastard, whom I brought here from Syria as a kindness. You would have otherwise been left to die." The words were the more terrible because the voice had been lowered. "Look at your hair."

Berenice did not look at her own hair, she stared back at her mother.

"Your hair is yellow. Mine is black. Magas was fat. You are not."

"What are you saying, mother?"

"Do you think I would mate with a glutton, a bumpkin? I would mate with heroes."

"Mother, what are you saying?"

"You are the sister of the man you killed." Apama essayed to get to her feet, but she was too stiff and she sank back. "You are the twin sister of the man you killed. The unarmed man you killed. Demetrius the Besieger had mistresses wherever he went. In his last years, in Antioch, a luxurious captive, allowed by Seleucus to drink and debauch himself to death—"

Berenice looked now at her hair, out of the tail of her eye, and it seemed to squirm and leer at her.

She turned and tore open the door, not even noticing the old man who had been dozing outside. Once more she ran through the library, along the arcade, down the stair, through the garden, into the lower palace, into the kitchen. She looked wildly around; kitchen women paused their work in consternation. She seized a carving knife, ducked her head sideways and caught with her left hand the long golden mass, stooped and began to chop. The first blow only wrenched her head and pained her left temple—damn the knife, it wasn't sharp—would she have to beg a whetstone too?—she began again, sawing.

Phravartes came puffing into the room behind her. "Madam! Stop, please stop!"

She didn't pause, lifted the knife to try another blow.

"I was here!" he uttered in his thick Greek— "I was here when your mother was carrying you and when you were born. Demetrius Besieger had been dead ten years. I know not why my mistress said it!"

The colossus

Uncle Callimachus had arrived from Egypt by the weary overland way, but now, concerned to get a prompt departure from the shore of Cyrenaica, he wheedled a passage on the *Phorminx*.

The *Phorminx* was a huge galleon of the kind being built these days at Alexandria. In the modest harbor of Apollonia its three sails and three decks loomed over the ships that had sufficed for centuries, the squat round merchantmen and the slim warships; beside it they looked like canoes. Callimachus and other freeborn passengers had hammocks below deck. His servant, Obdas, had to sleep with a motley set of others on the tarred canvas over the hatch that covered the hold. Since the

Ptolemies could afford to send the ship on a mission of nothing but carrying Berenice Syra out and both Berenices back, the hold contained no cargo, only provisions and a ballast of sand; but a small strongroom had been made between the timbers to contain the ingots that were Berenice Libyca's dowry, together with some sweet-smelling crates of precious Cyrenaican silphium.

The queens had the grand cabin at the stern, under the poop deck. In a small space outside their door slept half-Libyan Polymela, who had chosen her mistress's service over her husband.

The voyage should have taken only two weeks. Instead of the following winds of spring there were summer breezes from the land, to which the sails had to be angled, but there was an eastward current, and the ship could make three or four knots without rowing. Callimachus rushed to and fro along the rail of the deck, exclaiming about the details of the coast and the forest-clad mountainside behind it and enjoying the amusement of the sailors, confirmation of his self-image of childlike curiosity. Here and there another sail or two showed far off on the sun-filled hallways of the sea. After the end of a long first day the anchors, bow and stern, were dropped in the dark off Darnis. But the next day, after passing the Headland of the Figs, where the coast retreated into the bay of Aziris, the ship was thirty or forty miles out.

The tideless sea was so flat that there seemed no motion, forward or up-and-down. There was just the slight uncertainty, when a foot was put down, of where it would meet solid. The sun came down like a sword through the breeze. Callimachus had now joined his servant, sitting cross-legged on the tarpaulin hatch-cover in the shade of a sail, and was writing on a parchment on his lap. Unexpectedly he vomited his lunch onto it. The sea had not been without an insidious rolling. The seasickness, after this fleeting visit, flew away like a bird.

He got up to wash himself at a pail and then go in search of a sailor—the sailors were slaves of several races, including Greeks, with officers over them who were mostly skilled Phoenicians—and asked how he could find the captain. "The *kubernêtês*," said the sailor, "is Crato of Lampsacus."

"Not the helmsman, the captain," said Callimachus.

From the man's scornful look he had to learn that *kubernêtês*, helmsman, governor, was nowadays the title of the master, not the mere hand who held the tiller.

The master, whom Callimachus found inspecting the mending
of a mast-wedge, could hardly be missed: he was a big man with
a few white curls on various parts of his skull, small mouth and
eyes pursed in a small weatherbeaten smile. Callimachus ingra-
tiated himself, remarking: "You know all this coast well, no
doubt."

"Yes."

"I know it only from Scylax."

"Scylax?"

"The book, the *Periplous*, the 'Circumnavigation', by Scylax,
it's been out for many a year now. You don't have it in your ship's
library?"

"This ship has no library."

"I'll be glad to give you a copy when we reach Alexandria. It's
an invaluable handbook. It tells you all the anchorages, the distances between them, whether you can find water and wood. I
had thought it was a standard aid these days. But I suppose you
have it all in your head."

"Enough. I get along without the *Odyssey*, either, or the *Argonautica*."

Callimachus stiffened at the sarcasm and the mention of these
popular fantasies of exploration, of which he hated the second
even more than the first. He came to what he wanted to ask.

"I notice that we are now out of sight of land—have been for
some time. We won't be putting into some port at night?"

"No, we shall sail," replied the captain.

"And that is safe?"

"Certainly, out here, as long as I can see the stars."

So the ship kept on through the dark.

There was a small port-hole on the starboard side, and as
Berenice lay she watched gleam after gleam going by on the
ceiling—slowly, but twice as fast as the ship, and not backward
but forward. The ship's lanterns (which had hoods over them so
as not to compete with the stars) were shining down on the side-
wake, and as each raft of white foam went by it sent its lantern-
tinged reflection in, like a lamp passing in a street.

The cabin was largely filled by a bed for a king and a bed for
a queen, with a curtain between them. Berenice, after their
servant girls had left them, wanted to take down the curtain and
shove the beds together, but her cousin advised caution, and one
bed was large enough for them. The floor and the bed sloped

forward. In the night this mattered; while her cousin slept, Berenice at every pitch of the ship slipped footward, out of her cousin's arms, and slept little.

The Syrian had explained to her: "No, you cannot go to Antioch with me. I am in danger there."

"In danger, why?"

"Antiochus had a wife before me. She gave him a child, but he put her away, because she made a scandal of herself with a sculptor. Or so they say; who knows whether it was true? Perhaps the real reason was to clear the way for him to marry the princess of Egypt. Perhaps he was not sure how true it was: he did no worse to her than send her off to live in Ephesus."

"What was her name?" asked Berenice.

"Her name is Laodice. She is a strong woman. She is stronger than he is. Really that end of his kingdom is now her queendom. Which is dangerous in itself, because it is not far from Thrace and Macedon and all the others we have to be wary of. Laodice has a party, she and her son, whom she still wishes to make king. They will try to kill me and my little son."

"I shall come with you! If your husband can't defend you I will!"

Berenice Syra smiled and pretended to be frightened of her. "Yes, you are a warrior! They say you won your battle with nothing more than a little wound to your chin. But no, I know what to do, I have a party too. It's harder to move if you have someone who must move along with you."

"Harder to suffer—that is what you mean—harder to suffer if you have someone who might be hurt along with you."

"That too. You must stay in Egypt. We can hope to visit each other. You must stay in Egypt and marry my brother."

"How can I love a husband after you?"

"He is my brother, you can imagine that he is me."

"But he won't be you. He won't feel like you."

"Turn over and let me teach you a way."

Berenice turned over and the Syrian lay curled tightly behind her, shaped to her.

"You can easily teach him to love to love you this way. You will not have to face him. This part of your form is lovely. Men can easily be made to think that they are specially favored. And you can teach him to make love to you—this way."

"You feel like another of my selves," said Berenice. "You feel like my self, clinging to me."

On the fourth day, while Callimachus reckoned they were still off the hard desert known as the Marmarica—Marble-Land—a wind sprang from half-ahead: Eurus, the southeastern wind, the sirocco, the ghibli. A yellowness, that became a brownness, grew from the southern horizon, and advanced over the sea, and came to be all about them. The sun smeared, spread, and dimmed, like a lamp reflected in hammered bronze. Sand—the scouring of the Marmarica. Sand got in the eyes of those on the deck; those who could, went below; but sand sought them. "The gods think we need more ballast!" joked the sailors. The sails were furled, the rudders were lowered to their fullest to help the keel withstand the wind's pressing, the men (with bandages around their eyes and mouths) were set to the oars, but still the ship made leeway. They were losing Africa. Africa was repelling them. When darkness again came on, Berenice, who had never before been farther on a boat than along the coast to Taucheira, was lost in a world without shores or light; she hung between a watery gulf that went down forever and a sandcloud that went up forever; she was too terrified to sleep. How could old Battus have crossed all this sea? But then the thought came to her that the god of the ship had resolved to drive her to Syria, and she slept.

The sun shone again, they were out of the paws of the sand, the men were sweeping drifts of it from the deck, but the wind was still severe from the south.

Obdas, sitting on the tarpaulin, watched a mountain crystallize out of the sky and hang over the far horizon. After a while, three mountains.

"What is that land?" he asked his master.

"Land? Ah, I see it! Crete!"

The distant peaks grew shoulders until they joined into one range.

"You see, Obdas, that their feet are still invisible. The bases of the mountains are hidden below the horizon. That proves that the sea is not flat, it curves. The world is round, as our astronomers say."

"Round? How do you mean, sir, like a dish?"

"No, like a ball. If we were to sail on this way in a straight line, after many thousand stadia we would come back up behind ourselves."

"That's a good joke! Tell me another!"

"Indeed I believe some of our mathematicians have tried to measure the roundness by using the dipping of stars or lighthouses below the horizon. I wonder, could they use mountains like this?—I must suggest it to Eratosthenes." But he saw that Obdas was not understanding.

"It's just the mist," said Obdas. And indeed the lower forests of the Cretan mountains were whitish, because a cream of mist lay on the sea.

As they came nearer, the mist thickened to a fog. The captain changed his mind about trying to put in at Phaestus or Lebena. The Cretan coast had become invisible, but it seemed all the nearer: its craggy bulk could almost be felt through the fog. Some of the passengers imagined they could see it as a shadow, a darkening inside the fog. They imagined rocks, the mechanical giant Talos running along the clifftops hurling stones to keep ships off, as he had done for the old emperor of Crete in legend. The captain now had to think only of the dangers of striking rock. The full complement of rowers was put to work, three men standing to an oar at each of the oar-windows in the middle deck, the leather window-covers taken off.

Callimachus sought out Captain Crato again and asked him: "Which way are we heading?"

"East."

"But how do we know, in this fog?"

"The current is from the east on this side of the sea, so we keep our bow to it."

"Ah. Then where are we heading for?"

"Rhodes."

"Rhodes! I do not wish to go to Rhodes!"

"It is not a matter of your wish, sir. We shall be lucky if we reach Rhodes, and if we reach no farther. First we must hope to get clear of Crete and then not to strike the rocks of Casos or Carpathos. Then we must hope not to overshoot Rhodes—which is friendly to us—and make landfall in Lycia—which is at present, like much of that coast, in the hands of Laodice, former queen of Syria, unfriendly to us."

Callimachus turned and stumped away.

"Why is your master scared of landing at Rhodes?" a sailor asked Obdas.

"I don't know," said the servant, "maybe he owes a debt there. I'll ask him and if it's something else I'll tell you the story."

Berenice had taken to sleeping well, lulled by the ship. She slept until sunshine poured in at the porthole, and then, sensing an excitement above, she threw her peplos over her head, shot her feet into her sandals, clambered the companion way and joined the people at the rail.

Fog still embedded the ship, but the fog had become a carpet: it had a top, not far above their heads, among the masts. Through it they could, like fish looking up out of a pool, see the blue sky. And ahead, above the fog, stood a god.

A god, of incredible size and beauty. He was of dusky-yellow bronze, which meeting the sun's full light flashed in shades and facets of rosy gold. From his head sprang seven rays. His eyes were caves whose gaze was levelled far above the puny ship. Over his left shoulder lay the bronze folds of a robe, leaving the rest of his splendor naked. His right arm was lifted, straight toward the risen sun, as if lifting it into sight.

"The Colossus!" Berenice breathed.

How high was he?—she couldn't tell—he was painted on the sky—it could be that he stood beyond the world's edge.

The ship (which, she felt, ought to halt and drop to its knees) kept on toward the vast god. He mounted and mounted into the sky. Humbly the huge ship crept in under his uplifted arm. He swelled on toward the zenith, tilting back; into sight came his bronze nudity down to his feet, and then the plinth, the size of a castle, that he stood on.

"Or—but," she murmured to her cousin, "I see no lighthouse in his head. And I was told that he stands astride the harbor mouth?"

"That is a Barbarian tale! Do you think that Chares, a Greek, a pupil of Lysippus, would have sculpted such a thing?—would have made Greeks sail under his bollocks?"

Slowly the *Phorminx* glided in past Helios, the Sun—he whose image had been raised by the Rhodians, at the cost of twelve years' labor, in thanksgiving for the lifting of Demetrius's siege—and still Berenice gazed up along the seventy cubits of his rippling stature.

"Is it not wrong to be so large? *Mêden agan*— 'Nothing in excess.'"

"Not if in proportion," said her cousin. "Not only the largest figure ever made, but the most perfect. Does he not," she added wickedly, "make you gladder about marrying a man?"

On the way out

A day was needed to provision the ship, but they stayed five more, Berenice Syra being in no hurry to leave. "This is a refreshing place," she said.

The free Rhodians were a cheerful and hospitable people. They could have been called sunny, like the god who stood over them. They invited everyone to come ashore and see the sights of their city on the tip of the leaf-shaped island, and their invitation was accepted by all but Callimachus. He had pleaded with Berenice: "Persuade your cousin to have us sail on to the Carian mainland instead. To Cnidus—it's more interesting, in my opinion. And to Halicarnassus: I have a dear friend there, who was a student with me in Athens."

"What is his name?"

"Heracleitus. He has twice visited me in Egypt, and I have never visited him, and I fear I shall not see him again."

"Well, perhaps we shall have time to sail there next," said Berenice. And they went ashore without Callimachus.

Prosperous Rhodians, ship captains or merchants, competed for the honor of opening their homes to the guests. The two Berenices stayed in a house that was full of children, who were not particularly respectful and dragged the queens into their games. The town's several plazas had broad steps descending into them from alleys or markets or theatres on hillsides, and on these open-air stairs many of the citizens spent their days eating and talking. An eye raised from any of the plazas beheld the mighty statue, though it could not be said to look down on the town, since it faced out to sea—an attitude that made of Helios himself a Rhodian citizen.

And the visitors were taken out on pony carts to the three old villages, Lindus and Cameirus and Ialysus, that had banded together to found Rhodes town; and along the country lanes.

"That is our mountain Attabyrus, from which you can see the peaks of Crete on clear days, and in the other direction Asia. — And this is the quarry from which we took the rock to fill the statue's legs. *All* the rock from this quarry went to fill his legs!"

"So he isn't all of bronze?"

"There isn't that much bronze in the world! And if he was all of bronze, he would sink to Hades instead of rising to heaven. We used all the metal from the war engines Demetrius left here, three hundred tons of bronze, but that wasn't enough and we had to buy up the world's trade of tin for a year to mix with copper to make more bronze, and tin is dear because it comes from Britannia, and the Phoenicians at Cadiz have the monopoly on it. It cost Rhodes so much that the people voted not to do it, until we heard that Demetrius had managed to get the kingship of Macedon back that his father had lost, so then Rhodes voted to do it and spite him, though more likely it made him laugh. —No, only the statue's legs are filled with rock, to keep him stable. The rest of him is empty, but for the ladder that takes you up to the eyes, so if you were to hit his chest with a hammer (you'd have to be riding on a bird) he'd ring like a bell.

"—And this is the cliff from which they say Chares threw himself, because he realized he had misplanned the joint in the shoulder and the arm would one day fall. It's a lie: Chares died in his boat while he was fishing down there, and the statue will never fall.

"—And this is the hill where Demetrius used to park Helepolis, 'city-taker', his hugest siege engine, that looked down on us like a four-storey house and was impervious to arrows."

Berenice—who still at times caught herself thinking of Demetrius Poliorcetes as her father—almost hung her head.

"Yes, and this," said the guide, "is the wreck of a house that we keep this way to show the power of the stones those engines of his lobbed at us. There's the stone that did it, down in the hole, look at the size of it! He had catapults that threw things like this thirty yards. Demetrius was called 'Poliorcetes' before he had a go at us, you know: we were just the last city he besieged and the one he most wanted to take and the first he *couldn't*. He delighted in inventing war engines, and bigger ships, with more sails (he was the first to think of adding the second sail) and more banks of rowers, and room for armies on board.

"—And this is the spot where we used to meet with him during the siege, and arrange truces, and discuss the offers of mediation that came from Thrace or Sparta.

"—And this is where we and the Macedonians used to meet and get back our prisoners, paying (so as to be fair, in case there were more on one side than the other) ten *mna* for a free man and five for a slave.

"—And this is the quay where our hundred hostages got on the ship to go and live in Ephesus; that was the only point we conceded when the siege ended. And those hostages made good use of their time and came back married, some of them, and richer than when they started.

"—And these are the gates of our navy yard, but we aren't allowed to take even you in there. Everyone would like to know the secrets of Rhodian shipbuilding.

"—And these houses are Ialysus, not much of a place now because the new city has swallowed it. Demetrius was going to burn it and make space for his artillery, but we sent and asked him not to do that, because the great painting for the temple was still there in the painter's studio. The painter was still in his house, working away at it. So Demetrius sent us back his answer: 'I would rather defile the tombs of my ancestors than molest the painter and his holy picture.'"

"It seems to me," said Berenice Syra, "that you Rhodians are almost fond of your Besieger."

"He was a monster really," said the guide, "he came against us with three hundred and seventy-five ships and more troops than there were men, women, and children in the island, and bombarded us for twenty long months. But you're right, sixty years softens the memory—softens the blows of the rocks! We find him funny because he failed. We beat `im! He's had the luck to be remembered more as just a naughty lad than as a warmonger. He killed a lot of us, and yet you'll find even Rhodians who when they hear his name smile, because what they first remember is stories like 'I met it on the way out.'"

"What story is that?" asked Berenice, but seeing she hadn't heard it the man wouldn't tell it, and she had to get it from her cousin later.

"Oh, it's about him when he was young, and his father, the

One-Eyed Antigonus. They were good friends (unlike most father kings and prince sons) and old Antigonus tolerated his idling and pleasure-seeking ways, knowing he would work hard when he had to. Antigonus heard that the boy was sick, so he went to his bedroom, and passed a girl hurrying the other way. 'Hello, father,' said Demetrius, sitting up in bed, 'I'm better now, I just got rid of a fever.' 'I know,' said his father, 'I met it on the way out.'"

Berenice laughed at the story, slowly.

Her cousin stroked the golden hair and said: "You might have lost this, if you'd been a Rhodian maiden then. Another story that I've heard and that the guide didn't tell us! The women gave their hair for bowstrings."

Further pre-marital digression

At length Berenice Syra answered Captain Crato's question with "Yes—tomorrow," and the *Phorminx* was made ready to resume its voyage. The passengers left their hospitable lodgings with the citizens of Rhodes, came back aboard and watched the ropes being unhitched from the bollards.

Callimachus joined them at the rail, and the Syrian queen demanded of him: "Why did you never go ashore? I should have expected you, a man of letters, to take an interest in such a place."

"It's an island," said Callimachus, trying to laugh it off; "I delegate the description of it to my nephew and the interminable *History of Islands* that he is composing."

"Don't you believe it," piped up one of the sailors coiling the ropes. "His servant's told me the story: this old man is quite a bantam cock. There's a man on Rhodes who'd like to kill him, for driving him out of Egypt."

"Oho, Master Callimachus, you're a brawler!"

Callimachus colored, but decided he didn't mind the image of a bantam cock, so long as the story be told in the right way.

"Only a literary brawler, madam! Much as I might like to trade fisticuffs or worse with some people, I am confined by the dignity of my profession and perhaps now also my age to the more elevated modes of insult."

"Yes, like your *Ibis!*" said Berenice eagerly. "We had a copy of that in our library—you sent it—it gave your nephew a problem, he didn't want it on the shelves, but while he was wondering where to hide it I took a look at it." And she was about to say how it had made her laugh, but decided to keep that for her cousin in private.

"You are remarkable, my lady," said Callimachus, gazing at her. "Do you always get to the matter before it has been spoken? The *Ibis* was indeed the man in question: Apollonius is his name; another scribbler. I made fun of him as that sacred but filthy long-legged bird, which stands in the rivers and drainage-channels and consumes the garbage. That was the last and knockout blow in our quarrel, and as soon as it was published and circulating in Alexandria he could endure to live there no longer—couldn't hold up his head in our literary circles—and he removed himself to Rhodes. And since then he has lived here, calling himself Apollonius Rhodius, as if he never lived anywhere else."

"I rather wish we had looked him up," said Berenice Syra. "Does he still stand in sewer channels and eat garbage?"

"What he does is produce garbage. He wastes parchment and the letters of the alphabet and readers' time spinning out long old stories, stale fantasies such as the saga of the Argonauts—"

"Yes, his *Argonautica!*" said Berenice. "My mother loved it and so did I; isn't it the best telling of that adventure story? And the verse is not too bad. And it's nothing like as long as the *Iliad.*"

"No, but it's longer than it need be. Why should we dwell on the improbable doings of toughs who lived, if they ever did live, a thousand years ago? We are in modern times now. It's strange—and shouldn't have to be—that I, now old, understand what is needed in modern times, while people like my nephew and Apollonius Ibis, though young (comparatively), would have us live in a past age. —Rather than an epic in antique dialect about Jason and Medea and the Golden Fleece, I would prefer a short and perfect verse about the—ah—merits, and exploits, of a Berenice. Why," said Callimachus, "I'll compose one on the spot." And he proceeded to recite, with hesitations and modulations as if thinking it out for the first time, a verse that he had spent the past two days polishing:

tessares hai Kharites: poti gar mia tai trisi tênais
arti poteplasthê   kêti muroisi notei:
euaiôn en pasin arizalos Berenika,
has ater oud' autai   tai Kharites Kharites.

Four are the Graces: one besides those three
Just now is formed, is still with perfumes moist:
Blest and among all envied, Berenika!
Without whom even Graces are not Graces.

Berenice flushed; not with pleasure, but with anxiety, because he had forgotten that another Berenice was present. But to her relief Berenice Syra seemed as delighted with the tribute to her cousin as anybody. After smirking at the applause, "Let's tighten it," he went on—

There are four Graces, not just three,
For one is only now created:
Queen Berenice! It is she,
The Grace for whom the Graces waited.

To the poet's annoyance, in the middle of line three he and his audience lurched and had to clutch at the ship's side: it had left the quay and was rolling into the first wave.

As they cleared the inner harbor, a black quadrireme went by, a warship of the fastest kind, going in. They were not looking at it but taking their last eyefuls of the Colossus, and Berenice Syra was coaxing the elderly poet to agree that this was the most beautiful form ever shaped by human hands.

"It used to be held," said Callimachus, "that sculpture of the male is the summit of art, but I think that has changed, and so— although there is no way of agreeing on such a thing—it is now said that the most beautiful is the Aphrodite of Cnidus."

"Cnidus—not far from here, I believe! And is she gigantic too, being a goddess?"

"No, she is the size of a living woman. In fact she was modeled on a living woman, the sculptor's mistress."

"Who must have been not only real but well-built?"

"A sculptor can improve on nature, but yes—so much so that, according to the popular fancy, the goddess herself was jealous. Or, to put it another way, the goddess herself must have been the model:

Hê Kupris tên Kuprin eni Knidô eipen idousa,
Pheu, pheu, pou gumnên   eide me Praxitelês?

Said the Cyprian when she saw the Cyprian in Cnidus:
"Praxiteles, oh where   did you see me bare?"

—an epigram by somebody, not me."

The ship was coming out past the cape at the tip of Rhodes, and turning to starboard, since it would have to keep at a distance from the coast and make for Cyprus. And then they would take another week or two to work around by the eastern end of the sea, touching at Tyre and Joppa, all in friendly hands, eventually to reach Alexandria.

But Berenice Syra summoned the captain, who had been told to take orders from her unless they were too unreasonable.

"Have you heard whether Cnidus is in the possession of Laodice?" she asked him.

"No," replied captain Crato, "the ports—Halicarnassus and Miletus too—remain as free as if they were islands."

"Then is there any reason why we should not call there?—Cnidus?"

"None except that it is in the opposite direction from where we are bound."

"Not too far, though? Can we see it from here?"

"Hmm. No, hidden by Syme. That's Syme," he said, pointing sternward with his chin at a distant outrambling of the coast. "Twenty miles there, another twenty to Cnidus."

"Not far!—let's extend our holiday to Cnidus!" said the queen.

And so the ship had to go about—northwest, directly away from Egypt. Callimachus had hoped for this because he hoped to go on and visit his old friend in Halicarnassus, the next Greek city along this jagged Carian coast.

They had more time to waste on the swinging couches that had been placed for them on the shady mid-deck, as the sparkling sea went by under a now sunny sky. "Tell us more about the Cnidian Aphrodite," said Berenice Syra. "The story of the sculptor's model is a good one. Was she a local beauty?—a Greek or a Carian?"

"She was from Athens—had been brought over by Praxiteles, and was, I'm afraid, a courtesan, a rather celebrated one: Phryne."

"So the sculptor may have called her his mistress but so may not a few others?"

"Morals vary from place to place and time to time," replied Callimachus primly. "It was not Cnidus that originally commis-

sioned the statue but Cos, which is the next island past Cnidus.
But when the citizens of Cos found that Praxiteles had carved her
naked they wouldn't have her in their temple, and he had to
carve her over again with her clothes on.   But the Cnidians
smartly bought the original, and there she stands in the state in
which she was born from the sea."

"And that," said Berenice Syra, "is why tourists like us go to
Cnidus."

"They go to gawp at the Aphrodite, but when they get there
they find there's much else; Cnidus followed up on its coup, it
collects statues, it's like a sculpture-park; there are statues of ath-
letes and children and sheep and of men of letters.   And Cnidus
is pretty well known for its vintage too, and its medical school,
and for Eudoxus the astronomer."   And meanwhile as they were
beginning to cross a gulf that reached inland, aiming to pass the
promontory of Syme, he saw that his listeners were becoming
drowsy. The conversation was pleasant, up to a point, it sent his
mind back to those (though it was so inferior to those) he had
revelled in, so many years ago, with Heracleitus: it is good to be
able to talk of civilized things, better, for sure, if the minds are
equal and can raise each other into philosophy, like eagles
soaring from Olympus; he would rather be again a learner than
this teacher he had become narrowed into being. But he had to
give these half-drowsers one last bit of information for the afternoon, before the chance passed:

"Ah, now we can see that Syme is an island. From here it looks
larger than I had thought—I'm sure my nephew in his *Book of
Islands* describes it as 'Little Syme.' Nobody ever remembers
Syme except for that bit in the Iliad— 'Nireus from Syme brought
three shapely ships, Nireus the most beautiful man of all that
came to Troy, but weak he was and few the men he led.' Which
touches on—"

Everyone had stood up and was trying to look back past the
sail. The black warship had reappeared astern, was coming
swiftly up on them.

Like a shark beside a whale the quadrireme drew alongside,
and a sailor hailed. A boat was lowered and a squad of men
crowded into it and came across. They were soldiers, and three
self-important officials, and the warship's master, whose head
was the first to appear as he came vigorously up the ladder that
had been hooked for him over the rail.

"I should have recognized you," he said, "but I thought you were just another fine Rhodian. But they told me at the dock you were the *Phorminx*."

"And what's your message?" asked Captain Crato.

The other captain stood aside to let the officials finish their slower clamber up the ladder, deploy themselves on the deck, and recover their breath. Then, "Our message," said the proudest of them, drawing himself up like a pouter pigeon: "Ptolemy is dead—King Ptolemy Philadelphus—and Ptolemy his son is king, third king of the name. His camel-riders returned from Cyrene with the news that you had left, and then from Paraetonion with the news of the sandstorm that must have blown you off course, and he sent us out to find you—sent us and nineteen other ships, to Crete, to Greece, to Cyprus, to Sicily, even to Carthage and the Libyan Tripolis. To find his bride, Berenice of Cyrene. And also Berenice his sister."

So they transferred from the *Phorminx* to the *Moira*. And only four dawns later Berenice, on deck before the sun, saw the stars fade but one rise at the far line of the sea. What could that star be?—it must be Canopus, the great star of the south, that guides travelers in the desert, but that we of the middle lands see only once a year. But slowly the star instead of dimming grew brighter as the sun did; grew shoulders and a trunk, like the mountains of Crete; stood upward into the day. It was not a star but a mirror. It was the mirror in the head of another wonder of this world, four times taller than the Colossus of Rhodes, towering like a crack in the sky: the Pharos, the lighthouse of Alexandria.

Berenice to Berenice

Dearest cousin (wrote Berenice), I am glad of the chance to send you a freer letter. I can't help hoping that your husband's mission to Ephesus will last a little longer than he intends. It is still early in the year for travel, so I suppose he has gone by land. But are there not other dangers for him? If he goes there, he must know what he is doing. It is generous of him to visit his other son and restore some harmony—or it is generous of you to believe so.

I love you. And I love your little son almost as much as I love you. He reminded me of the mouse I once kept in my room and protected from my mother. If that is what a Seleucid is like, I am philo-Seleucid. I find it impossible to think that he will one day be king of Syria. I want to conceive a child like him.

Since you left with him I've not been myself. Perhaps that's for the good—my self is not the best. The Berenice your brother loves is not me. It seems he loves me. He told me he loved me before he even saw me, which is not possible. So I would think his love is a mirage, but he has a man, a hanger-on called Iphthri, who tells me all about him. He says that Tryphon has greatly changed (besides getting crowned and having to pass his days like a king). He says that Tryphon was not the kind to be faithful, but has learned that all that is foolishness, and is enslaved (as he says) to me. I fear it cannot last. He surely cannot see that it is you, not him, I love; but won't he see the coolness in me? But Iphthri sees it and says it is useful.

Your brother jokes and calls me Tryphaena; now he's calling me Leaena, lioness; I tell him he'd better get used to calling me Berenice. He is endearingly clumsy, I've twice saved him from stumbling over things. I'm growing to like him rather well. At the ceremony of the Ecpyria I had to wear the "trailing robe" of the Trojan women, and to walk down the temple steps in front of him, and I knew he would tread on it, and he did.

I had thought that marriage might be companionship. When one is alone one piles up matters that one would like to talk about with a friend. My mother did not let me talk with her—she never even told me about the changes in my body. The girls in Cyrene had to be in awe of me, though I did nothing to make them so. Once, when we went on an excursion into the country and bathed in a pool together, they were merry and friendly and told me secrets; but soon after that, when it was impressed on them that I had become a queen, they were more closed off from me than before. So your intimacy, for that too short time, was a heaven. Our hole in the ship is the heaven I picture when I am trying to sleep.

And while you were still here, and I was newly married to your brother, it seemed that he might in some degree be a continuation of you. And he was; he not only talked fondly with me, he almost fawned on me. We had no secrets from each other, except you. If he was downcast about some matter, he told me why, and when we had talked about it he brightened and thanked me. But that has changed; I have noticed it in the last few days. He is gloomy but pretends not to be, so it is a secret. When I saw him today I noticed a line on his forehead, between his eyebrows. He is too young for that. I thought of sitting on his lap, smoothing the line with my finger, and warning him not to frown. But I have to prepare the way first. I will build back our talkingness.

Enough of these things which I did not wish to talk of in the letter your husband might read.

When you told me that the city of Alexandria is the largest in the world, I imagined it as like two or three Cyrenes, but it is infinite! And it was all not here, only two generations ago. Alexandria is larger than the world, and (I knew it from the moment I saw the Pharos) every thing in Alexandria is larger than that thing elsewhere. I am a stranger in this ocean of modernity. With you I did not go out of the Brucheion quarter, and I thought that was the city, but it is only the royal quarter! Now I have been taken farther, but the city still has no end. There is the sea on one side—I can look at it from my window—and on the other side I have been taken as far as the shore of Mareotis, the lake that stretches away inland. I was taken in a litter. I dislike being carried in a litter (almost as much as I dislike having kohl painted on my eyelids and henna on my feet), yet I would have been wearied to walk so far. Yet they say this is the short dimension: the city stretches like a long field between sea and lake; in the other directions, east and west, it goes on, and for all I know has no end. I certainly have not yet seen either of its ends, though they say that somewhere far off there is an end—a wall, a gate, country.

I tell you about the city where you were born! But you may like to know how it appears through my eyes, so that you may be amused at how wrong I am. The land is too flat and too hot, the streets too wide, the buildings too large, and all separated because of the law that no house may be built nearer than a yard to the next. Can it be true that there are four hundred theatres, three thousand palaces, four thousand public baths, twelve thousand fruit shops? The police are called Medzae, I don't know why; they used to be Nubians but now they are Idumaeans; the soldiers are Judaeans. There are forty thousand Judaeans living in the Brucheion, and the favorite plays in the theatres are the

"Tragedies of Ezekiel," which are scenes from their holy book. We were taken to see one of them: the "theatre" was not a proper theatre like the one where you and I saw the *Oresteia* or like my own great theatre set into the mountainside of Cyrene, but a mere room in a house, and not a very salubrious one. They said the "tragedy" would show the ancestors of the Judaeans escaping from Egypt across the Red Sea, which dried up for them. But instead they impudently treated us to two playlets—one about an Egyptian wife who was scorned by a Judaean and accused him of raping her, and another even more indecent about a Judaean who had to marry his brother's wife—they called that one "The Threshing-Floor of Onan."

We have dogs in the streets of Cyrene but nowhere near so many monkeys and cats, and it's as you say, the Copts, though they despise the dogs and laugh at the monkeys, stop and bow to any cat that goes stalking by! Once I saw them killing a dog that had killed a cat.

And we have been taken to the temple where gods hang from the ceiling by "magnetism"; and we all of course revisited the city's midpoint, the Soma, as they call it, the Body, Alexander's great round tomb where he lies preserved in honey—or is it the Sema, the Sign?—I can't remember all they told us about it. The mourning for your father the Theos Philadelphos ended and his coffin has been placed there, alongside his wife the Thea Philadelphos, and his father the Theos Soter and his mother the Thea Soteira, and alongside Alexander himself. The first dead Ptolemy and his dead consort are called the Savior Gods, the second dead Ptolemy and his dead consort are called the Sibling-Loving Gods—I wonder what kind of gods your brother and I will be called?

And whether there will be any more Gods or Ptolemies. I have not been able to be made pregnant, though yesterday I thought I was.

Dear cousin (wrote Berenice Syra), why have you not written to me? Don't you still love me? If my brave woman Cusaba is able to climb out of the city and bring this to you, show it to my brother, in case my message sent by a man has not reached him. There is little time. Antiochus is dead—the fool—in Ephesus, Laodice has proclaimed her son King and come out of Anatolia with forces larger than ours, I am shut up in Antioch.

Throne and balcony

Berenice found her husband slacking in his chair that looked out on the parade ground. There were thrones for him in every comfortless room of his palace, and this counted as a throne, though it was placed in a passage opposite to a balcony and was shaped like a box, into which he could almost disappear. There were guards standing at the end of the passage; Berenice, brushing past them, ordered them aside with a gesture so that they would be out of earshot. Ptolemy sat leaning back, his right foot advanced, his hands on his lap, his head bent forward. When he noticed her approach he raised one hand to touch his head, as if shielding himself from her.

"Perhaps you should lead my army," he said as she unrolled the letter.

Berenice felt herself constituted of anger from head to foot; she could not remember a time when she had not been.

"You must lead your army," she said; "I will look after Egypt for you." Then suddenly: "So you know about this?"

"I've known for—eight days."

"Then why haven't you already set out?"

"You think it simple—it's the most complicated undertaking in the world. Winter is not over, it would be dangerous to trust most of the army to ships. We have to go by land, and places with names like Mageddon and Hazor and Cades are not secured, Philistia and most of Phoenicia are ours but the inland is not— Judaea and Hollow Syria—despite all our Judaean soldiery. Our forces are almost ready, we have had to raise mercenaries, I am having to order the 'state loans' as it's called when the rich are required to scrape together extra taxes; lists have to be made of those citizens who can afford to raise a 'ship'—the number of men to fill one. If we don't secure early booty in Syria, we will soon be unable to pay the army."

"It is indeed a care for you," said Berenice. "And I have been kept in the dark about everything."

"And I have to decide what forces to leave at home in case the Macedonians take advantage of our absence—or the Nubians— or the Cyreneans! Or the Copts, who have plenty to resent—or in case all goes badly for me in Syria. And then, Alexandria and Naucratis and Ptolemais cannot simply be ordered to furnish their regiments, they are jealous of their status as our 'allies' not subjects, they have to go through motions in their own assemblies, Alexandria is particularly touchy, they will comply but it takes time, and the moon is to suffer eclipse on the middle night of this month, which is the night after next. The priests will know from the sight of it whether our enterprise is to be fortunate. All this, I'm afraid, has to be done. I, too, would rather not wait—but the waiting coincided anyway with the time we needed for all this preparation. I hope we shall be ready to start on the morning after."

"After what?"

"After the eclipse, in two days' time."

"We shall be too late!"

"No. I have taken my step to ensure that there is time. I have sent a large gift in gold, by sea, to Aribazus, satrap of Cilicia. I can't tell you how many talents, I don't at the moment remember, but it will be enough. Cilicia lies across all the routes from the rest of Anatolia into Syria. All he has to do is bar the passes of the Taurus. And if Laodice tries to come by sea—which she will not, it's too early in the year—a few ships can easily stop a fleet as it tries to round in single line the dangerous capes of Lycia and along the coast they call Rough Cilicia. To clinch it I have promised Aribazus, after she is dealt with, the satrapy of Lydia also, the richest province of Anatolia; he can have it himself or in gift to his son. I have been told what the man is like."

If Lydia is Anatolia's richest province, Berenice wanted to say, and Anatolia is still Laodice's, what is to prevent her from sending her own bribe? But Ptolemy looked expectant of appreciation for his clever move. And anyway:

"Look at this," she said, showing her own letter. "'I am besieged in Antioch'—already."

"So she told me too. But she exaggerates. I have had more recent information. Laodice has not yet left Ephesus; it is only her paid people in Syria who tried to raise trouble and they have been beaten off; they are not many, Berenice is loved." He sat up and smiled at her. "You found me in a moment of despair."

"It was despair for your sister?"

"Yes, and for this task."

"Husband," said Berenice, "it is a Colossus of a task, but I would expect you in some degree to relish it—to seize on it. Even if you aren't anxious to save your sister—and your nephew, who should become king of Syria for you. I've been told that

Perdiccas dreamed, and Antigonus dreamed, and many others dreamed, of remaking the empire of Alexander; and here you have a better chance than any of them did: you have one of its halves and now the other half is asking you to take it. Don't you want to emulate Alexander—and all those forebears and predecessors of yours who became 'great' by conquering? I've read the *History of Egypt* written for us by that priest, Manetho: those past kings were always going a-conquering into Syria, and coming back and boasting about it. The records of their victories and captives and spoils were carved in the temples . . ."

"Yes," he said. "I think their records were mostly lies, except that they did indeed make a lot of widows."

He was sitting up straight, but she was standing close in front of him. This throne had no pedestal, she was framed by the sky in the opening behind her, whose light fell on his upturned face; it was almost as if he was kneeling and pleading with her. He found, as often, that he was uneasy with her in front of him; he would rather have her beside him. The first time he had seen her face-to-face, he had immediately thought: she is not quite as I expected from the profile on the coin—she is squarer. Not that it should matter—and it doesn't.

"You are *bearer of victory*," he said.

"You are *warlike*," she replied.

"Unfortunately, it is not true of me, whereas it is of you. You have killed a man, you have ruled a country for nine years; I have done neither. My father scorned me in favor of a—"

"And my mother scorned me," said Berenice. "Go to war and save your sister. I shall love you if you do that."

"I will. I swear it by all the gods. But one needs strength."

"Strength?—it's your soldiers who will have to strike the blows. You have only to order them about."

"That's what needs strength. I'm strengthless in that I haven't been brought up to know what to say. Even when a builder speaks with me, I don't know how to impress him and dismiss him. How shall I dominate a general? —Forget what I said. Sit on my knee, Berenice."

She moved uncertainly toward him, and noticed that they were not alone: on the other side of him crouched a small distorted figure.

It was a stunted man, with wide lopsided bare torso of an unhealthy white-blotched cream-brown, and white-gray hair sticking several ways in untidy spikes. It was Ptolemy's clown, a dwarf whom he called (because he couldn't pronounce the Egyptic name) Coptolemy.

Berenice had seen a dwarf, in the market at Euhesperides, but that was long ago, and she was repelled.

"He shouldn't be here really. Nor should you. I'm waiting for the notables who are to stand beside me when I review the troops out there, which will be at the stroke of the *tocca*—I'll send him away before they see him."

"Send him away now, I don't like him listening to us."

"He doesn't matter. He understands no Greek."

"Then what is he for? You understand no Coptic."

"Nonetheless he amuses me. Sometimes it's good to have someone to talk to who understands nothing you may feel like saying. He agrees with me on that! I laugh at the stories he tells me in his gibberish. Besides, he's a wonderful mimic, and he can stand on his head."

The dwarf, seeming to understand something, shuffled away backward, hid behind the throne.

She put him from her mind and perched on her man's left knee. "Unclasp your hair. Why do you keep it hidden?"

"So that everyone doesn't stare at it."

"I want them to! I want to." As she reached her arm behind her, he stroked its underside. (He preferred the soft underbelly of her arm to its strong upper side.) Then dived his hand into the river of her hair as it bathed his thigh.

"I would know this river if I saw a ripple of it."

She fingered the thin chain of gold links that passed around his neck and disappeared inside his shirt. She knew that what dangled from it was that eight-drachma coin which he pretended had made him fall in love with her.

"Who was the artisan who stared at your face? I'm jealous of him!"

"His name was Sandrogon—"

"You even know his name! Wasn't he just a tinker?"

"He was a journeyman painter—they called him *Planêtês*, wanderer—he'd come from Sicily or somewhere. He made the drawing with charcoal, and the mint made the carving from it, and the mould from the carving."

"Were you short of artists in Cyrene?"

"I think he offered to make his drawing free."

"And then sold it for more, in the market!"

"Perhaps; who knows? Does it matter?"

"Sold it to one your worshippers!"

"Hush."

"He drew your cheeks . . ."

His hand began a gesture toward her head, and she flinched; but his three middle fingertips touched her brow and stroked downward.

"You must not frown, my darling (or else you must take this ribbon off your hair also and let it fall forward). You have the beginning of two lines descending here."

She smiled and said: "Is that so? And you have a line there— a single one." Too late, she saw that now, coming second, it seemed like a retort instead of another gentleness.

"So," he said, "I have a single line on my forehead and you have a pair? Ah—d'you know what they represent?"

"No, what?"

"My line represents the Nile, beside which I should stay, and your lines represent the two rivers of Syria, the Leontes and the Orontes, where you should go conquering. Or even better, the two great rivers of the east, Euphrates and Tigris!"

"No," said Berenice. "If I have two lines there, they make me like that little animal that Egyptian people worship in the streets—the cat. I've noticed that cats have two lines there."

"Yes, they do! But the lines are made of fur."

"I'm a cat, and cats are goddesses in Egypt! And I should stay here and give you a kitten."

Berenice miaowed at her husband, and they laughed and she ran away.

He slumped back into much the same posture as when she had found him, still smiling at first, and then thinking: "What did she mean? She so much wants to bear my child that she's already imagining . . . Or is there a sign today and she's forgotten to tell me?"

Sounds of reed trumpets and shouts and clanks began to come from the parade ground. He failed to notice them until the gong struck for the hour after noon—at which he got to his feet so hastily that the blood rushed from his head. He hurried forward onto his balcony. He had been reviewing the troops at this hour for several days. He had reviewed the contingents from Sais and Busiris and Bubastis and Sebennytus and Mendes in the Delta,

from Heliopolis and Memphis and Leontopolis and Crocodilopo-
lis, and yesterday had come the most remote, from ancient
Thebes far up the river. To tell the truth, most of these levies
from the Egyptian towns were symbolic; if the war were won, it
would be by the professionals, the hard Libyans and Nubians who
were kept in barracks, the Judaeans, Macedonian settlers and
mercenaries from Greece. Today, and finally, it was the turn of
the Alexandrians themselves—a motley force drawn from a city
that contained all these elements—along with the police who
were to maintain order in the capital, and (a block of men almost
as numerous) the priests of the royal cults. The priests were
present in order to consecrate the expedition to its other object
(which seemed to some more important than saving the king's
sister): the quest to recapture the sacred trophies of Egypt that
had been carried off into Asia by past conquerors.

As Ptolemy stepped forward to the balcony's edge, there came
another sound—behind him—and he turned. The notables who
were to stand beside him at this final review were coming up a
stair, and leading them by a long way was Sylcon, the Dioecetes
or "Housekeeper," who hated to waste time and who with his
long legs took stairsteps three at a time. Though he was not unex-
pected—he was the factotum who really undertook most of the
complicated cares that the king had complained about—he was
always a startling sight, this man, Sylcon, with his extraordinary
height and his shiny blackness, and his strong knowledge of all
and only the few words to be said; and, still a little dizzy, Ptolemy
took an inadvertent half-step backward.

The dwarf darted from behind the throne, lunged, seized
Ptolemy's robe to save him, but was a moment too late. The
balcony's rail broke; king and dwarf fell over the edge toward
death.

The sun god's hair

For the chief priest of the Savior Gods, and all the other priests
who stood on the parade ground with him, the sight augured
very badly for the expedition—or did it? The two figures turned
over in the air—an arm whirled out like the scythe of a chariot-

wheel—and the king, having fallen onto the cobbles on top of the dwarf, was taken up almost unhurt. This augured perhaps well.

Berenice did not see her busy husband or know of his accident (his ludicrous but harmless accident) until the next afternoon, when he came to her, conversed for a while, and said: "Everything is ready. At last I have nothing more to do."

"Then you should rest. Sit down," said Berenice, herself rising restlessly to her feet. She had been sitting most of the day—as she found herself now doing throughout most of her days. At times when she felt like issuing outside and jumping on her horse, she had had instead to sit still and pat the head of a cat. The cat had opened its eyes and seemed to say:

> The business of the cat is sleep.

Or perhaps

> I know you wish that I could smile.

"Yes," said Ptolemy. "I think we should lose ourselves in some pleasant entertainment, for this last little time that we have. A company of players has offered us a performance that they say they have perfected for us—they say it will be amusing and even amorous, but I think it will be another of those silly Judaean plays, and for it we would have to go to their theatre—they have their scenery, they say they can't bring it here—so instead I have ordered some musicians. They are black people from an island far to the south, they are said to be lively and soothing."

"I would like to go to both!" said Berenice (amusing and amorous; lively and soothing)— "I would like to go to the theatre."

"Very well, we shall. They are doing it in the daytime for us. We shall be carried there."

They walked down a stair and along a corridor toward the litter, followed by the usual courtiers and bodyguards. The one who customarily kept closest was a small man in a gray cloak, called the Mnemon, the "Rememberer." His job was to whisper the names and titles of other officials discreetly in the ear of the king if he seemed to have forgotten them. But on this occasion Ptolemy moved a pace or two ahead, then made sure to give a few signs as of wincing, quickly suppressed. He was in two minds, not wanting to let his wife know of the foolishness of his fall— but wanting to let her know of its amazingness, and that he was hale enough to have survived it. Accordingly she asked him: "Is something giving you pain?"

"Yes," he said, slowing so as to walk again beside her and just in front of the Mnemon, "I fell from a balcony yesterday! It broke under me."

"You fell from the balcony! Are none of your bones broken?"

"No. Shaken a little, but nothing broken except this thumbnail that I'm hiding! Don't mention it to the priests, they will say I have to be whole to lead the army!"

They got into the litter and she began to ask him more about it, but he talked instead of the Council of Advisors, whom he was leaving to help her in the administration of Egypt.

The litter, carried high on its poles over the shoulders of eight shaven-headed slaves, did not take them far—not inland to the Judaean district where most of the theatres were to be found, but down by the Little Harbor into alleys that, though close under the Palace, were a warren of brothels and eatinghouses, in the shadows of high stark warehouses; human canyons and crevices, which had evidently escaped the not-less-than-a-yard-apart regulation, and among which night seemed to be settling prematurely. When, closely surrounded by the column of their attendants, the royal pair descended some steps and entered at a door, they were not sure which kind of establishment it was the door of. The front room was a small gymnasium, where several muscular Egyptians lay in the air, prostrate over small wooden boards, which they gripped as they writhed in curious exercises. They jumped up, seized their boards, and retreated to stand shyly at the side of the room. The Greek owner of this establishment, by name Polycleides, welcomed the party in some surprise and led them on. A crooked corridor passed openings that looked like the back rooms of the brothels, but the space they came into was part of a warehouse.

From a small room at its back a few steps descended into this space, but chairs were brought and placed at the steps' top, where king and queen could look over the top of an audience which, apprised of their arrival, became quiet. The space was lamp-lit at the end serving as the stage. They saw that the scenery was indeed too heavy to be easily moved. There was a mountain, and a stuffed lion, and a temple roof supported by two massive pillars.

The play was certainly a Greek version, or mockery, of one of the "Tragedies of Ezekiel." Helios, the God of the Sun, appeared, though he had a Judaean name, something like Shimshon. His golden hair had been stiffened with grease so as to radiate from his head in long conical spikes—no, it was not his own hair, it was a great wig that sprang upward from his mask. He fought the forces of darkness, the horde of the Philistians or Palaestinians; laughing in triumph, he mowed them down in heaps, wielding only the jawbone of an ass. But the heaped bodies crept off the stage, and returned to fight as new waves of Philistians, among whom the tall Sun went whirling and reaping and laughing again; but now they sent their wicked woman, Dalila, who was acidly beautiful and also rather tall. (Ptolemy felt that she was somewhat miscast: a small-bodied imp of a temptress would have been better. He did not mention this thought to Berenice, who was not as short, light, pliant, *manageable* as the wenches he had favored before he acquired his beloved Queen.) And Dalila seduced the Sun Hero and wheedled from him the secret of his strength, which was his sun-ray hair. And as he subsided from love into sleep (sinking behind something that could have been a rock, a pillow, or a tombstone) she brought shears and gingerly cut it off, his spiky halo, and brandished it aloft; and the enemies came creeping back and swamped over him and captured him, and put out his eyes—Berenice ducked her head and shut her own eyes at the captive's howl and the horror of the sight, though she knew it was only a clever operation on the actor's mask. And the blind Sun was imprisoned among his taunting enemies, carousing in the temple of their own barbarous god, a Fish; but the Sun's treacherous lover, pitying him and repenting of what she had done, lopped off her own black hair. This had the effect of transferring her own strength—such as it was, apparently not negligible—to him; and in a final endeavor the eyeless giant rose and stretched out his arms and felt for the pillars and hugged them, and (being not really as substantial as they looked) they crumpled toward him, and the pasteboard roof fell fatally on the whole cast of characters.

Except for Dalila, off the scene at the time. For the wonderful thing about the play, perhaps its point, was that the Sun God and Dalila were the same actor!

So cleverly that the audience was slow to realize it, the man and the woman who seduced and cajoled him had never been visible at the same instant; and when you did realize it, you had to laugh with admiration at the slick alacrity with which the man slipped from sight—sometimes behind one of the pillars—and the woman replaced him. You might think you had seen them embrace, but you had not; a censor might think he had seen indecent contact, but he could not have done. The play was this one double-actor and the supporting swarm of enemies who went crouching and snarling around him. As a man, he was a tall figure, young, strikingly athletic, clad only in a loincloth, displaying torso and legs of oiled gold. His voice was a gaily strained scream, almost as high as the perfect falsetto into which he relaxed as a woman. As a woman, he—or she?—or offstage assistants—had clapped onto him not only a different mask but a stole of black netting that included breasts (and disclosed their white sides and red tips through its mesh); a heavy swollen-hipped skirt embroidered with upside-down pictures in violent colors, swirling around the bare feet; a broad tight waistband, bluegreen and shiny like seaweed; a wig that included a pert headdress; and, when there was time, a jangling necklace. Bits of this costume, clapped on at speed, sometimes forgivably slipped. And by what illusion of stagecraft could it be that the actor as woman seemed shorter, whiter, older than the man, and of a different though also alluring shape? The Dalila mask was a face, sweet, sharp, pointy, shifty; her lashes were long and her cheeks bore not a red but a black spot. The Man mask was flat and blank, so that (as the raucous witty words poured from behind it) it came to seem horrible, even before it received its only features, the bloodied eyes.

The actor had to be a man—a man's body being a woman's with a subtraction (and with an addition, unstated by apparel). Could these two bodies really be the same? Berenice fell to studying it. They were, yet they had nothing in common. No part was visible in both guises, except the hands and feet and glimpses of the neck and ankles; short of some birthmark or deformity, what betrayal could there be in those? And then she realized that the Dalila face was *not* a mask: it was his face. It was his face, painted, and over which while shedding all else but the breech-clout he clapped the Sun God mask. Even in the face, painted and held only in grotesque expressions, there was little chance of seeing something that could be recognized again. The actor had perfect control of both his bodies and of his Dalila face—but for one unconscious mannerism, that expressed perhaps a demonic relish: Dalila bit the right end of her lower lip, and a scene or two later she did it again.

The players (except Dalila, who no longer existed) rose from the ruins to acknowledge their applause, and Ptolemy genially indicated that they were to be paid. "And—the female too, where is she?"

Berenice turned her head to see whether he was serious; everyone else was more polite. The Sun God said nothing, so the character dressed as a Fish—he had been the leader and also the god of the Philistines, and the director of the company—said that she had had to hurry away.

"Well, so must we," said the king, beaming; "is she taken sick?—give another stater for her." He got to his feet, and Berenice said: "Do you have no other question for them?—I have."

"We must go, Hontiphas worries that we shall be late." Hontiphas was a gray-haired counsellor who had not been enjoying the play. "The play was long, the moon will have risen."

They started out the way they had come, but politely one of the troupe informed them that they had been brought in by a laborious back passage (so as not to see the scene-preparations); behind the stage was the door that opened into a more respectable street, almost under the palace wall. As they made for it, Berenice hung back, and turning she caught the actor before he could sidle away. He kept his distance and, when she said "Take off your mask," he simply did not. Nor did she insist; she had a feeling that she did not want to be drilled by his eyes.

"Is that how it works?" she asked, and became confused—she should have given herself a moment to frame her question; but when she began again— "The hair—cutting off the woman's hair"—he understood and framed it for her: "Does the woman's cutting off her hair give her strength to her husband?" He did not speak in his stage scream, but not in his own voice either, or perhaps the mask muffled it.

"Yes, is that so?—is that what is believed?"

His laugh was merrily unmuffled, but muffledly again he replied: "Yes; but not quite in the way we showed. We have to observe the decencies." He bowed to her, and withdrew with such a swift step that she half expected him to reappear as Dalila. She had to rejoin her entourage and leave.

The missed eclipse

Coming out, they were dazzled by the full moon, already high enough to pour its brilliance into the dark street. They faced an arc of ragged figures, each throwing a moon-shadow toward them—beggars who had learned of their presence. Even through moon-shadow, the hope-against-hope could be seen in a child's ravaged face. They were soon cleared away by the "wasps"—the yellow-tunicked police. Berenice, turning and looking back at the door from which she had emerged, saw that the painted sign over it said:

ASCALON

That was the name of a place on the coast of the Philistines, but why was it written here?

She would have asked, but Hontiphas was already explaining about the celestial event. "It is to be viewed from the temple that is being built for the Theos Philadelphos," he said, referring to the late king. "Other priesthoods have argued for the honor, but the very act of choosing the temple of Ares in order to witness this phenomenon and announce its meaning will seem to presume war, or if Demeter or Hestia, then peace; or if the Serapeion, then an Egyptian cult will have been favored over the Olympians. And so on. To avoid all jealousies, I suggested the new temple. It has the advantage of being as yet no more than an open space."

Berenice hoped that there would first be time for them to return to their quarters, eat something, relieve their bowels.

While the party stood waiting for their litters to be brought around to them at a trot, Ptolemy, seeking for remarks about the play, compared it somehow to the story of Cassandra, who became able to prophesy after the snakes licked her ear but whose prophecies were not believed after . . . No, that would not work: perhaps the giant Antaeus, son of Mother Earth, whose strength was refreshed every time his wrestling opponent threw him to the ground . . .

The high wall facing them across the street was the wall of a garden called the Menagerie of Sarmas, containing oryxes and an elephant and peacocks—one of which let out a startling and doleful cry. Above the wall poked trees, and the climbing moon

was not yet free of them. Berenice thought it already had a
strange look.

"Is it already suffering eclipse?" she asked.

"No," Hontiphas assured her, "the priests tell us that eclipses
happen in the middle of the night, when the moon is highest."

"There is—I thought it looked as if there was smoke on it."

"Perhaps the gardener had a bonfire."

It was the middle night of the Macedonian month of Loeus (called
Munychion by the Athenians), the first month of spring.

All waited. The king and his family and courtiers and priests
were up on the paving of what was to be the temple's platform,
raised by three steps from the middle of the sacred precinct, the
temenos. Along the sides of this space lay stacks of marble tiles,
cedar beams for supporting them, sections of Doric columns,
blocks already cut to their triangular and quadrilateral shapes and
waiting to be carved and fitted into the temple's pediment. The
rest of the enclosure, three steps below, was filled by the crowd.

The circular moon cruised slowly toward the top of the sky,
growing only brighter. Chairs and stools had been brought for
those on the platform. Still their necks grew tired of craning
upward; the necks of the standers much more so. All were cold.
Berenice raised her arms behind her head and laced her fingers
within her hair—not ashamed to expose her armpits, which the
barberess had recently waxed. But a maidservant threw a shawl
around her. Her eyes widened to fill themselves with the moon,
until its brightness began to seem as overbearing as that of the
sun; she shut her eyes, but still let her head rest back on her
hands, appearing to gaze, and passing in and out of reluctant
sleep. She remembered the song she had sung to the lute in
Irasa—

> *Deduke men a selanna*
> *kai Plêiades, mesai de*
> *nuktes . . .*

"Well, while we are waiting," said the king, "what is that star
above the moon?"

The one who had to field the question was Mnesimus, chief
priest of the cult of the Theos Soter, the Savior God, that is, the
king's grandfather; he was sitting closest, being the senior priest
present, since the chief priest of Alexander was in bed and said
to be near death. Mnesimus in turn asked one of his acolytes

what constellation the moon was now in, and received the answer: "The Virgin."

"Yes," said Mnesimus, "so that star must be the one called the Spike of Wheat, which is held in the hand of the Virgin; who was Persephone, daughter of Demeter. Some say it is not a Spike of Wheat but the handle of a Broom that she holds."

"And those two stars, higher up again?"

"Ah, if the moon is in the Virgin today, it will have been in the Lion yesterday, so one of those stars will be the Heart of the Lion. The brighter one, I'm sure, since it looks somewhat red, like a heart."

"The Lion! I see neither a Virgin nor a Lion. Is he large or small? And what are those little stars down there?"

"We do look at the stars," said the priest, "but before dawn, at the beginning of each decan of ten days, to watch for the heliacal risings of those that mark the festivals of the year; now they are unfamiliar for me—they are in different places. I shall have to refer you to the astronomers."

"If you will excuse me," said the acolyte, "the bright red star is the planet of Ares, which moves. The white star with which it is almost in conjunction is the Heart of the Lion."

"The planet of Ares! Then this is surely a sign about war?"

"Yes, but I believe it is for the omen-takers to decide what kind of a sign, after the eclipse has been seen. It is a doubtful sign, since the planet was in opposition two months ago and is now stationary—"

"You seem to know more about it than the chief priest, young man."

"He and I," said Mnesimus, "know about the meanings of the greater stars; we leave the cataloguing of the little ones, which are without significance, to the astronomers."

The learned men formed a body standing at a respectful distance on the terrace. They were the researchers, teachers, and students who lived and worked in the Museion, whose libraries and cloisters and dormitories rambled through so much of the palace quarter. Many of them were from Samos, Halicarnassus, Abdera, Corinth, Syracuse—all over the Greek-speaking world— since nowadays scholars gravitated less to informal old Athens than to brash Alexandria. Among them stood Callimachus, with the twinkle of eye that meant he was hoping to catch a glance of acknowledgment from Berenice. At the head of this scholarly platoon was the President of the Museion: none other than Eratosthenes of Cyrene. He could very likely have answered the question, since he knew almost everything: he was not only literary critic, chronologer, historian, musicologist, mythographer, and poet, but mathematician, geometer, geographer, and, in a sense, an astronomer: he had recently set himself to measure the size of the Earth. (Despite all this he had an approachable, a genial face.) Nevertheless he thought it safer, or perhaps generous, to call forward one of the specialists, named Elthys, who was more sure than himself of knowing the stars' names.

"So," said the king, "is that star indeed the heart of the Lion?"

"Yes, your majesty."

"And is there no picture of the Lion? I had understood that the stars are arranged in pictures."

"If I may ask your majesty to turn your chair—to your majesty's right. Now you will see the star not above the moon but to its right, which is as it should be."

"As it should be?"

"Yes, because now the picture of the Lion is level. He is trotting rightward, as if away from the moon."

And the king and all his courtiers saw it: a Lion—huge! Suddenly the temple, the city, the nation, seemed small, like a mouse looking up at a cat.

Berenice breathed deep, as did the Lion she saw. He stood as if on a mountain edge, his shoulders braced.

"Yes, yes," said her husband, "his head—his legs—his chest— with his great Heart in it!"

"Yes," said the astronomer, perhaps unwisely adding information too soon, "some also call that star the *Basiliskos*, the Little King."

"I should have thought that one name for a star is enough; there do not seem to be so many stars."

"That is because the moon is now spreading its glare across the sky."

"Do you mean that the moon has eaten the stars?"

"One could say that. There are stars that we can't see now— there are for instance some fuzzy little stars in the space north of the Virgin that make a tuft for the Lion's tail, or, some say, a lock of Ariadne's hair (though why Ariadne I don't know—her hair played no part of her story); I know where they are, though I can't see them now. The moon hides them—as the sun hides all the stars in the day."

"Stars in the day! Surely there are no stars in the day."

Elthys was at a loss, but Berenice said: "I have read the *Phaenomena* of Aratus, I will explain to my lord later."

And another hour passed. All the spectators had had to turn gradually: the moon, climbing from the east, had reached the south.

A few late-arriving scholars appeared from the street (they made their way through the crowd and climbed the steps to join the others and whisper to Eratosthenes), but they were the exception: most of the movement was in the opposite direction: the crowd was dwindling as people slipped away by ones and twos. And murmurs began, and then audible calls:

"There is no eclipse!"

King Ptolemy turned his gaze—though saying nothing, because he did not yet know whether to be consternated, glad, angry, or amused—on priest Mnesimus.

"In old times," the priest burst out, "before there were *scientists*, men beheld the eclipses when they happened; we did not know when the gods would send them, but we saw them and drew the knowledge from them that the gods intended. Now we defer to the *scientists*, who tell us when eclipses will happen— and are wrong."

The king turned again to the chief scientist, who was concluding his muttered conversation with the late-arriving scholars. "Who told us there would be an eclipse, Eratosthenes?"

"It is in the tables," replied Eratosthenes. "But I am competent in some parts of astronomy and not all; I will call on a colleague—"

"Is there so much to astronomy that it takes more than one man to know the parts of it?" said the king, with a witty glance upward at the few stars in the moon-bleached sky.

"The science of eclipses is a large branch in itself, and Conon of Samos is our authority on it. He is writing a whole book about it. He has been pressing on me since yesterday noon that the tables—which he had a hand in drawing up—may not be fully accurate. The tables—"

"So, not fully accurate!" interrupted the king; and Mnesimus, and the other priests following him, were ready to stand up and show their displeasure as soon as the king did.

"The tables," continued Eratosthenes imperturbably, "show the eclipse at midnight, but Conon points out that the tables say that only because it is as good a guess as any. The tables don't precisely know—nor does he, but he knows somewhat better. I pondered the consequences of believing him and urging a change in the court's plans, and being wrong—or not doing so, and being wrong; and before sundown I sought out Conon again to ask him some more—but I could not find him. And he has only just arrived here, rather breathless." And as Conon of Samos came forward, perspiring despite the cold night, king and priests wondered: did this man find the eclipse somewhere else?—in a ditch, maybe?

Conon was one of the younger of the scholars now residing in the Museion, yet he had a beard (uncommon since Alexander set the fashion for shavenness); it was a narrow black beard ringing a small face with eyes strangely far apart, as if used for judging distances.

"Approach, Conon. Are you indeed an authority on eclipses?"

"I am a student of them," said Conon. "Also of comets."

"Well, explain what has gone wrong with this eclipse."

Conon glanced up at the moon, and then over to where it had risen half a night ago, and said:

"The tables announce an eclipse for this day, and they are right. It is marvelous to be able to predict the day on which an eclipse will happen; it is even more subtle to be able to say at what hour."

"Eclipses of the moon happen in the middle of the night," said the priest flatly. "Those of the sun happen in the middle of the day—there was one six years ago, which we all saw—and eclipses of the moon happen in the middle of the night, when the moon is opposite to the sun. I saw one when I was young."

"If that was always so," said Conon, "they would happen only for one side of this round Earth and not the others."

"And who tells the tables?"

"The Babylonians—"

"Haugh! The Babylonians!"

"The Babylonian star-clerks, for half a thousand years, have kept their lists of eclipses that they saw. And Thales of Miletus, three and a half centuries ago, was the first to discover—if the Babylonians themselves did not, which I think they did—that

there is a kind of music in these numbers. There are eclipses in
many years, perhaps in every year, if we could be in every part
of the world to see them. But for each eclipse—each eclipse of
the sun, or of the moon—there comes another such eclipse, fifty-
four years and one month later—six hundred and sixty-nine
cycles of the moon. That is what you find if you pore over the
lists of the Babylonians."

"So"—it was Berenice who asked— "there was an eclipse
fifty—how many did you say—"

"We call it the Exeligmos, this span of time. Fifty-four years
and a month. But no, it's even subtler than that. No one noticed
an eclipse an exeligmos ago, or if they did they were perhaps in
India, and did not write it down. But the matter is more subtle
yet," he said, ignoring the yawns of part of his after-midnight
audience. "These eclipses that follow each other are like a braid
of long strands, and they interweave with each other, and it is
from the spacings of them in time that we understood, when we
made these tables, that there would be a strand that starts with
the eclipse of tonight."

"There was no eclipse tonight," said more than one.

"Yes, there was, and I watched it. And so did these, my students." He turned and waved a hand at three eager boys—no,
two boys and a chubby girl—who hung back, in the pack of
scholars but almost panting to detach themselves and come
forward. Conon brought forward one of them, who presented
the drawing he had made with charcoal on a piece of plaster-
whitened papyrus.

There was a horizontal line, and two circles, one above the
line and the other below; each had a small smudge at the left.

"I found it was most likely," said Conon, "though by no means
sure, that here in Alexandria the eclipse would begin to happen
about the time the moon was rising, opposite to the setting sun.
It might even be before the moon had risen for us, in which case
there would be for us only a part of an eclipse, or none; or, if at
moonrise or not long after, there would be an eclipse to see, but
low on the horizon. And in that case, here in the city you would
not see it even if I persuaded you to come here at the right time:
it would be hidden by the city. And what if I was wrong, even
by only a little? But I was determined to see whether I was right.

"I and these three bright youngsters hurried across the city to
the canal. It's a long way, we hired a man with a mule cart. Since

the canal lies along the south side of the city, we could from a bridge look along it and see the moon rising. And we could see its reflection in the flat water, as you can see in Philenor's drawing—see the fact twice over."

He took the shaky drawing from Philenor and swung it before them, tapping the smudge on the left—on the left of each of the moons, the upper one and the one reflected in the canal. "This is the shadow of the earth, just beginning to touch the moon. This eclipse began to happen *exactly* as the moon rose across Alexandria's horizon."

Then Andreus's drawing, done more than half an hour later. The moon had departed upward and rightward, so that there was now no canal or reflection; the horizontal line now was a scribble including reeds and a hut; it represented the strip of land between the canal and the lake. The smudge had moved somewhat higher up the left side of the moon, and had deepened to an arc, biting nearly a quarter of the way across the moon's circle—and Andreus had rubbed it in vigorously with his charcoal.

"Was it really so black?" Berenice asked the lad, and eagerly he replied: "Yes, and it was red too—I mean it was a sort of brown—black and red as well—but I had no red color to color it with."

"And see its round edge," said Conon; "it is round but not so round as the moon—it is part of a larger circle. It is the shadow of this great round earth that we live on."

"And there is gray too," said Andreus; "see, I used my charcoal

lightly and rubbed it with my fingers here—it was very thin gray—it was the shadow of the air around the earth!"

Conon opened his mouth to correct this explanation of the pale gray spreading over the moon outside the sharp reddish-black, but decided not to.

"This was the greatest moment of the eclipse," he said. "The shadow did not go on to cover more of the moon—it shrank—Theonida, show your drawing."

The moon as drawn by the third student was a much smaller circle, but that was because it was at the top of her paper, with the horizontal line of Lake Mareotis at the bottom. And the smudge on the moon had shrunk to a mere touch at the upper left. With still a suggestion of the ghostly shading on the rest.

"That was the end of the eclipse. And then," said Conon, "we hurried here, but it was an hour and a half after sunset and we could get no mule driver and had to run as much of the way as we could."

Priest Mnesimus sat back on his chair, hands on knees with thumbs outward. "You say you saw it. A complicated story. No one else saw it."

"You think we are lying. There will be others in the town who will be found tomorrow to say that they saw it."

"They are not lying," said Berenice.

Her husband turned to her and asked: "Why do you say that?"

"It was what I saw too, among the treetops. I saw it just as the girl drew it. I saw it at that time."

There was a silence, after which: "Then," said another priest, "the omen-takers will proceed to tell us what this signifies for the king and the war."

"Yes," said another— "in the morning. They must first pray and make the sacrifices and ask Apollo. The darkness covered only the west of the moon, is that correct?"

"The north," said Conon.

"And will those who live to the north have seen it?"

"Those who live to the north and especially the east are more likely to, yes."

Many had an inkling of what the omen-takers would decide to say—that the south remained blessed with light while those to the north and east were smitten with darkness, or that those who had seen the moon wounded were marked down by the gods to stumble and fail and those who had escaped the sight were safe—though for the moon to suffer eclipse in the house of the Virgin, the daughter of Demeter, might mean a failure of the wheat harvest—but for now they were concerned to get to bed.

Berenice and Ptolemy went to bed. Nobody had said: "You missed the eclipse, you and your whole court, by looking too late—does this have a meaning?"—Berenice did not say it either. Unlike their parents, they usually slept in one bed, but not on this night touching. Not only was it long after the midnight of a night that was to be short, but the play they had seen had not been in any pleasant sense amorous.

To war

The Canopic Street, widest of Alexandria's wide streets, bristled with noise. Spectators filled the tall colonnades that lined both sides; others had scrambled to the colonnades' roofs, and farther back, where great houses peered above the colonnades, yet more spectators filled the balconies and the open-sided top storeys. Yellow-jacketed police with their staves strove to keep clear the paved width of the street itself, but the crowd closed in before and after. Along the street came marching the strength of Egypt. These were only three ceremonial regiments—the main force had departed by water, in troop ships along the canal—yet the regiments shook the street and seemed mightier than all of Agamemnon's host. The noise reverberated from colonnade to colonnade: the crowds shouted, and the troops shouting their marching songs tried by shouting louder to overtop the crowds. The spectators were the more numerous, and their excitement noisier, with just a tinge of mockery, because the start had been later than intended: it was already almost noon.

The regiments passed through the city wall by the main eastern opening, the Sun Gate, more often called the Canopic. In the front went a golden chariot—really a long quadriga or four-horse cart, from whose back stood a sort of menorah bearing the crowns of the Two Egypts and the smaller crowns of Cyrene, Nubia, Cyprus, Crete, and lesser dependencies. In front of this stood two slaves holding ostrich-feather fans to shade a throne, on which Berenice rode with Ptolemy, though she would go only as far as Canopus town. Canopus, inside the Nile's westernmost mouth, was the port older than Alexandria, named (Greeks said) for Canopus, ancient helmsman, or for the star of the south on which he steered. (Or, said others, for *kônôps*, cone-face, the mosquito.)

By now she knew that even beyond the gate she would not find open country, as outside a gate of Cyrene: instead there spread suburbs, the first of them called Eleusis though it was nothing like holy Eleusis in Greece. To the left of the road was a jumble of poor dwellings, some made with driftwood from the sea, interspersed with patches of rubbish-strewn sand; to the right, gaudily luxurious hostelries lined the bank of the canal. Some of these had names, Theatês, The Spectator, Thallos, The Young Shoot; over one of them the sign read cryptically Amphoterô, Either Kind. On through Eleusis the marchers marched, but the royal party paused for refreshment at an airy pavilion. It was a tent-like roof of reed bundles on a forest of palm-trunk columns, and you could see through its cool brown shade to the glitter of sun on the canal.

The reason for honoring this establishment by pausing at it was that it was opposite to the mouth of another canal, which here turned off southward. It ran away toward inner Egypt, a wide trench dug by thousands of hands with mattocks and baskets; one of its banks bore a firm towpath but the other was marshy, thick with bulrushes and papyrus sedges. It was the branch canal that brought to Alexandria its fresh Nile-water (or water as fresh as Alexandria would get). Fourteen miles inland along this canal was a pontoon bridge at which barges had to stop and pay their tariffs, whether bringing goods from Egypt to Alexandria or the other way around; and a hundred miles up was the head of the Delta, where the two greatest branches of the Nile split. The troop ships, having passed from the Eunostus Harbor into the canal, were to come along and turn here and go by this long but easier route, and descend the easternmost branch to Pelusium, there to begin the land march into Palestine. That way, the troops could eat and sleep on the ships, and begin only outside Egypt to batten on the land and camp on the ground.

So at this canal junction the king could review the ships' passage too. But it happened that the ships had started at dawn and made better speed and had already turned the corner and disappeared into the haze of the flat landscape. Oars, poles, and rudders had left the water full of upchurned mud, but now on this bluebrown surface—which moved only slowly seaward—all that floated was one papyrus-bundle canoe. On it stood a boy, with head shaven except for the "sidelock of youth"; he held a throwing-stick carved in the shape of a snake, and peered in among the reeds for ducks to bring down. Beside him a young girl, wearing nothing but a lace of beads around her waist, crouched to pluck a lotus flower.

They were in another world, oblivious of the floating army that had passed and of the throng of courtiers that had flowed into the space overlooking them. Nor did any of these appear to give them any attention, except Berenice, who before taking her place at the table stood for a few moments looking.

Turning and finding an Egyptian servitor at hand, she said: "There is a heron that seems to stand on the boy's wrist."

"Yes, tied there for a decoy."

"And there is a cat on the boat!"

"Yes, to run and fetch a bird that is hit."

"Will a cat then jump in among those reeds?—will she agree to swim?"

The man shrugged.

"And has she let herself be trained to bring her prey?"

The man shrugged again.

At which moment four ducks burst into the air. The boy folded his arm back to throw. Berenice turned away.

She took her seat. Nearest in strict order were the Advisors, royal relatives, and various other distinguished people; Iphthri did not rank among them, though in the procession he had been one of those riding nearby. Next to her sat the silent dignitary called the Dioecetes. She noticed Callimachus, farther off though as near to her as he could get.

"My lord Sylcon," she said to the Dioecetes, "may I ask you to let me talk with Callimachus? I believe he once lived in this town."

The Dioecetes got up and courteously exchanged his place with the lesser man. Others pretended not to be shocked; and Berenice told herself: "It matters what people think of me. I have been brought up in a lesser court than these Ptolemies who have been bred as gods. But even the gods have their reputations to consider." These uneasy reflections flitted through her as the tall black shape moved away; and indeed she wondered whether she would have preferred his company, despite his silence.

To Callimachus she said: "You can tell me about Eleusis, can you not?"

"Eleusis is the city of Demeter's Mysteries, which no one can tell about except those who—"

"I am not referring to *the* Eleusis, as you must know; I am asking you about this place in Egypt, this Eleusis where we sit. I believe you once lived in it."

"Yes, this is Eleusis the tawdry, where I was a schoolmaster after I first came to Egypt, forty years ago."

"And your students still speak highly of you."

"No, those will be the civilized students, the willing, to whom I became a teacher later—in Alexandria, after I was rescued from here. After I came to the attention of Arsinoe. Four long years I tried to teach the rudiments to the sons of butchers and sweepers, until some poem of mine became heard of in the city, and I was brought to the Museion, like a bedraggled songbird bought in the market and given a garden to live in. Your parents-in-law were lovers of culture—both of them, though I considered Arsinoe to be my patroness. That is why I can never hear words spoken or snickered against them."

"Did we pass your school?—or the house you lived in?"

"No, they are not on the highway. They were—over there some way."

"As we passed those very splendid houses just now, or houses with plenty of colors and curious decorations—there was one that appeared to be a sort of theatre opening on the canal—I noticed my husband and his former companion Iphthri exchanging what looked like smirking glances." (Her husband, sitting on the other side of her, was turned another way and talking; nevertheless he might have heard her.)

Callimachus politely waited for her to say more; but, that seeming to be the question, he replied: "Eleusis—yes. Let's say that it is not a place to be enjoyed if you are a schoolmaster and poor."

"So what is it that one can obtain in those houses?"

"What is it one can obtain?"

"Yes."

"Oh—anything. Anything you want. —But let me add that Eleusis is insignificant; it is squalid but dull, it is just the begin-

ning of what they call the 'Canopic life'. From here along the
coast to Canopus itself—well, you could say, the noise at night
grows longer and merrier."

"Oh, so shall I—"

"—But not, of course—it will be in abeyance during the
king's progress."

Berenice was a little disappointed that she could not expect to
be kept awake by revelry.

And Callimachus was annoyed with himself. He might look
kindly on cultured compliments and even dalliance, but he did
not like squalor and sordor. He could, instead of hinting at the
"anythings" to be obtained in "those houses," have told her
merely and truthfully that in them you could drink the fine wines
grown around the lake, or, if you could not afford those, the wine
from Antiphrae, so bad that it was said to be mixed with sea-
water.

Conversation lapsed, and Berenice's attention dwelt vaguely
on the men with vast fans who tried to drive away the flies that
infiltrated the pavilion from the town on one side and the canal
on the other, and even the sparrows that flew through. Then the
dancers filed in and spread into a space among the columns. A
girl stood playing a deep Egyptian harp that was taller than
herself, and in front of her the others drifted in patterns; some
shook rattles, but so cautiously that they merely clicked. All
wore long loose dresses of white linen so fine that even the
distant light from outside the pavilion shone through, and the
tapering lines of the bodies were clear. It seemed to Berenice as
piquant as anything that might happen in "those houses." Why
should she and her husband be shown this?—was its purpose to
erect men's sinews for the war? But only one was naked. She
was naked except for a girdle of small cowrie shells, which
tinkled as she moved—they had copper beads inside them—and
her body was shaved. Cowrie shells look like half-closed eyes and
avert the Evil Eye, but these tinkling shells seemed made to draw
the eye, the licking eye. She was not bold, but danced among the
others, with the same half-walking motions, if anything less confident; surely she would have preferred to hide herself. Or did
she, being Egyptian, care not at all that she was defended by no
clothes? It was the nakedness of just *one* that seemed acute, so
that Berenice's temples beat. Was something to happen to this
girl after the dance?—was there among the watchers someone

who had a claim on her? Yet again, no one showed visible interest.

The dancers dissolved away into the room they had come from, the company rose, and they went on, through a Greek district called Nicopolis, "city of victory," and an Egyptian one called Little Taposeiris, each with its dusty markets and local temples but few signs of the hedonism that was supposedly to climax at Canopus. Even Canopus, when they reached it, would be sober: it had had to be cleared of the pleasure boats that lined the banks, because it was there, next morning, that Ptolemy and his more select followers were to go aboard the sea-going fleet and sail for Ascalon in Palestine.

The road now ran along what had become not much more than a ribbon of land between beach and canal, with a ragged belt of palms and among them the nests of penury and opulence in odd alternation: fishers' and scavengers' huts, and country houses.

"Who are the rich farmers," Berenice asked, "that build these houses? I see no fields behind them."

"Officials, I suppose," replied her husband. "The money with which they build derives from us." He turned to ask Sylcon in the carriage behind: "Whose house is that?"

"Ico, nomarch of Sebennytus," replied the Housekeeper briefly.

"How can he govern Sebennytus if he lives here?" asked Berenice.

"Oh," said Ptolemy, "I suppose he has a house in Sebennytus too."

Even in what seemed to be deserted stretches, spectators came crowding to the road as if sprouting from between the bushes. The tail of the third regiment could be seen ahead, and the riders began to come up with it. But about here the road rose slightly onto a crust of tawny rock, which slanted out to a headland. The headland was called Zephyrion, for Zephyrus, the western wind which it collected by thus hooking into the sea. On it stood clustered palms and, out beyond them, something silhouetted against the gray-purple of the low eastern sky, and picked out by warm light from the sun declining in the west. The shape suggested a ship: high stern, and at the bow a strange jagged projection, like a flight of birds.

Temple on the headland

A side-road turned off toward the headland, and though narrower than the earthen main road—hardly wider than the chariot wheels—it was paved with pink slabs, and had mint and asters planted along its edges. A small crowd, with expectant faces, stood on both its corners, like human gateposts. But the procession pressed on past them, to their disappointment and also that of Berenice.

"Are we not to visit the temple?" she asked.

"We are too late for that now."

"I wish we would. How much farther is it to Canopus?—only a *skhoinos*, and the sun hasn't set; we can still lie there tonight."

Her husband found nothing to say.

"You don't like it because you don't like to think of your stepmother," she said. "But it's Aphrodite's temple too. I want to go there. —I'd rather go off the road for a while than stay in the dust of all those heels!"

"Then we shall!" he said, and gave the order.

But it was not easy to turn the cortege and go back to the fork in the road. Gaily Berenice tried to seize the reins from the driver; all three laughed—Berenice, the king, and the driver—and the result was that the four horses swerved off the beaten road and began to stumble toward the headland over ground dotted with stones and dry plants. The twenty carriages behind came to a halt, and after some moments of confusion the voice of the Dioecetes was heard, telling them which were to go on and which to go back and around in order to ensure the safety and comfort of their monarch.

"That man," said Ptolemy— "I wish I didn't have to leave him here."

"Oh, don't be jealous of him!"

"I think he could manage the army better than my generals can—that's what I mean." As she knew; her light jest had fallen on unlight ears.

The chariot's tall but slender wheels were not meant for rough ground; they stuck on a tussock. Berenice slid down and began to walk, but soon repented of it, and let the chariot get moving and take her up again. They regained the pink-paved way, as it reached the edge of the sea, and came around the palm grove and again into view of the small temple.

It was a blatant fusion of Egyptian and Greek. The propy-
laeum, the gate, was a pair of slope-sided flat-topped rectangular
towers of the solid Egyptian kind, miniatures of the great
entrance pylons of the houses of the gods at Heliopolis or
Thebes. Then came the lighter body of the temple, but though it
had a pitched tiled roof in the Greek style it had no flanking
colonnades: it was stripped to the original core of a temple, the
naos, the shrine. That was why the whole was called the
"*naïskos*," the little shrine, of Aphrodite-Arsinoe. And from the
seaward end of the roof arose that carved extravagance, which
was indeed a flock of birds. Aphrodite, goddess of desire, on her
dainty chariot, drawn by a great white swan, its marble neck outstretched, its white wings like sails. And above and behind the
swan, also on sculptured reins, a pair of turtle-doves and a flock
of Aphrodite's other birds, the lecherous and fast-breeding little
sparrows. The marble sparrows were as large as doves, the doves
as swans, the swan as a camel. All sloped into the sky, in the act
of bursting into flight over the sea, aiming for where?—for
Cyprus, Aphrodite's birthplace, where she was born of the foam
and came gliding ashore to bring love to the world.

The little crowd that had been at the junction now came
walking—some of them skipping—back along the pink-paved
pathway and reappeared behind the chariot. They were servants
and children from the hamlet that was hidden in the thicket
beside the temple. But Eunyle herself, priestess of Aphrodite-
Arsinoe, stood on the temple steps, flanked by six acolytes,
waiting to greet her visitors. The acolytes were shy, except for
one who, at sight of so many well-dressed men, managed to
convey a writhing simper through her modest garment. The
priestess wore a silver-gray dress that ended below her breasts
with a tight band that held them up, and, above, a system of
silver-gray strings, scattered with small jewels, that appeared to
clothe her breasts and shoulders but did not. Her eyes were star-
tlingly outlined with kohl, and tight black tubular coils of hair
hung beside her neck.

More discreetly off to the side of the temple stood a squad of
soldiers, who had apparently been posted to protect it and were
billeted in the hamlet. And, a surprising detail that Berenice
would have liked to ask about: a cart was being loaded with bird-
cages—they looked like large boxes, but an agitated burbling
came from inside them.

But the party went into the temple and made the expected sacrifice of harmless corn, figs, and whey to the goddess, who despite her softness is able to stir up wars and sway their outcome. In the temple's innermost recess, the *adyton*, unenterable except by the priestess, touched only at noon by a shaft of sun falling through a transparent alabaster tile, stood the statue, which was of Aphrodite draped. In fact it was a reasonable representation of the elder Arsinoe as she might have been before she went away as a bride to Thrace. The sculptor had done his best to make a desirable Aphrodite while not getting absurdly far from the hooked nose and bulbous chin that Arsinoe and her brother had inherited from the first Ptolemy; and indeed, seen from the front, these features were not too prominent. This little temple was the monument to the love that Ptolemy Philadelphus had claimed to feel, and perhaps did feel, for the strong-minded sister who came home to be his queen.

His son (who was his son by his earlier queen) hurried the ceremony along and was impatient to get out of the temple and finish the day's journey.

But Berenice said to the priestess: "I want somewhere to lie down for a space."

Ptolemy peered anxiously at his wife's face. She had not paled, but she was perspiring. The day, the first day of spring, seemed to be getting warmer as it ended. They were led down steps at the right of the shrine to a room that was in the temple's foundations. It was a room such that Ptolemy thought: Had she known of this?—but she had not. It was cooler than the shrine but also brighter, as long as the day lasted. One side of it was open toward the sea: it had a knee-height wall, on which stood two Cretan pillars, with a way between them, so that one could step out onto a stone terrace. From it a meadow of thick soft grass, lush but scythed to a handspan in height, sloped quickly down between two walls to the beach. The room was furnished with a couch, two small tables, a mirror, candles, a marble basin, floor-rugs woven with Phoenician designs, a folded blanket on the couch, a picture that might have been of Heracles ravishing a not-unwilling Auge in a temple; and there were doors to two smaller cells, one at each side. Ptolemy did not ask the room's purpose; perhaps it belonged to the priestess, though it seemed too orderly and bare of smaller personal oddments.

Berenice went to the doorway that looked out on the sea. And

turning leftward she saw the orange sun on the sea horizon, back
past Alexandria, even back past Libya. A movement vertically
overhead caused her to glance up: a flight of real pigeons, if she
was not mistaken, had dashed inward from the sky. They had
disappeared—if indeed they were real and not suggested to her
mind by the statuary doves on the roof—and now all that was to
be seen was the outstretched head and neck of the sculpted
swan, outlined against the sky and catching on one side the
orange-gold from the west. Even as she stared, the glow was
chased upward by the gray-blue of night.

Servants came, carrying a second couch, an oil lamp from
which to light the candles, sweet cakes and fruit and wine, and
vases of water, and then they left.

Ptolemy took his cup of wine from the small table it stood on,
gulped most of it hurriedly, turned to hold out Berenice's to her,
but she was already lying on her couch, her cheek on the cushion
at the head of it. So he sat on the foot of his. She looked across
at this man who loved her with respect, but without the foolishness of passion. She patted her couch, and he came over and sat
beside her, upright.

"You have not made love to me before leaving for another
country," said Berenice.

He stroked what he could of her hair, which she had loosened
so that it lay deployed beside her on the hard cylindrical cushion.
On their wedding night he had made a speech to her: "Your hair
is a meadow of Elysion."

"I would—but we are expected in Canopus. And you are
unwell."

"I am not unwell. I am not unwell."

Why do his hands not praise me as did hers?

Why does she try to feel between my ribs?

He raised himself on his elbow and said: "We must go. Do you
feel able to, now?"

"I want to stay here. Please go on without me. I would rather
part with you here."

"Yes, I shall have to." He stood up, washed himself and
dressed not too quickly—but quite quickly. He had to draw on
first an unaccustomed garment, the stiff chariot-corset that he

would wear till the end of the war. Before going he said: "I am afraid that you will . . ."

"That I will what?"

"That you will forget me."

"What nonsense!" said Berenice, sitting up. "Are you mad?"

In this moment he looked like anything but a king.

"You mean you are afraid that while you're away, if it's a long time, I will forget our love and look about me at other men. But that will never be. I have only ever loved, and will only ever love, your sister and you."

"I know."

Berenice was alarmed that he did know.

"Yes," he said, "I do know about the two of you, and that it was more than the love of sisters or cousins. She told me. Don't be distressed. She told me because we are friends, my sister and I, and also because she saw the need to explain something to me for your sake."

"I see." Berenice Syra had explained to her brother why his bride, though virgin, might not appear so. She knew the language of passion more fluently than her brother did, despite the kitchen girls and street girls and village girls of his youth.

Berenice! At the thought of her, Berenice suddenly bowed her head, reaching up one hand to cover her wet eyes and the other to him. He sat down again for a moment to weep with her for the sister who might die.

"I shall save her," he said, standing up. "To that I swear. — And you will swear?"

"Swear what?"

"To be faithful."

"Fool!" she said, leaping up— "why do you return to that? I have answered you."

"If you are unfaithful, I shall have the man killed!"

"Of course you will! You are a king and can have anyone killed for sneezing. Swear yourself, swear yourself, you are the one who needs to."

He backed off from her fury, looking a fool indeed; bowed his head and said: "Forgive me. You don't know how much I love you."

They did their best to repair it, sitting down together in silence and embracing. He reached again for her winecup and brought it to her lips; but she took only a sip, so he drank it himself.

Then, tipsy, he said to her: "I'm suddenly not young. I'm already thinking it will be unbearable for either of us to die before the other. —How can I be strong?"

"Be strong? I don't know!" she said, laughing. "You are quite strong."

"But not for war," he said, almost mumbling; "not like Sylcon the Housekeeper."

"He's not your general, you forget! —But if you want to be like him, I suppose, strong-silent-stiff, you could try pressing your shoulders back!"

"What d'you mean? I'm round-shouldered, I slouch?"

"No, no; you asked me. So I thought around for a suggestion."

"Yes," said Ptolemy, heroically repressing his renewed jealousy of the Housekeeper, "a good one—there—you're right! It makes me breathe deeper! Will you do it too?"

"Perhaps—if I remember."

"Ah—every time I remember about you, it will make me heave air in and see the world better!" And he left, saying that he would send the servants to see to any of her needs.

When the servants came, she had thought of a few things to ask them for, and then sent them away, saying she was comfortable and would sleep. They departed, and she stepped out between the columns.

Nothing was happening in the world. The sea was holding its breath, awaiting her permission to chafe the shore with its smallest wave. There were two clouds in the sky, one gray, the other higher and still white. The zephyr, the western breeze, came along the sea from Cyrenaica, faint, but it cooled her face.

Why had she given that answer to her husband?—who had perhaps expected something such as "Sacrifice to Zeus" or "Touch the earth, like Antaeus." And was she not herself weak in this flat country? She straightened her own back, and felt the sea air lighten her chest as the mountain air had done in Cyrene.

She was still naked, except for her anklets—chains of little silver links with dangling stars that tickled her heels. She waded down through the grass, lay on the narrow strip of firm sand, and rolled into the water. It was not as warm as she expected—but soon it felt warm. At first she didn't mean to let her hair get wet, but when it did she laughed and went on rolling until she was submerged.

She stilled herself in alarm: something broke her horizon.

Figures, one sitting, one standing. They were on a wooden boat: a young man digging with a paddle, his brown body nearly black in the twilight, and behind him a priest, standing and holding his arms outstretched so as to make of his white robe a sail, which collected the slight breeze. And behind him again, in the boat's stern, a pile of something—netting?—with white glints in it. They were not far away, a hundred yards out, but they passed eastward and around the cape, without noticing her head.

She stumbled out of the water and, walking up the little lawn, saw one more bird fly in through a hole in the northern pediment of the temple. She could make out that there were several holes in the stonework; the space in the temple's roof was a columbarium, a pigeon-loft. She returned into the chamber, dried herself lightly with the blanket, wrapped herself in it and lay down. For an hour she could not sleep, and guessed that it was because of the absence of Polymela. She was accustomed to having her maid asleep in the outer chamber.

She thought about her cousin, soon to be rescued. Or, better, driven back to Egypt along with the rescuer. Not till morning, when she would have to return to Alexandria, did her mind turn to her task of governing Egypt.

The strider

For the first several days Berenice woke early in fear of what was expected of her. To have played at ruling Cyrene hardly helped. Then she began to wake late from boredom. It seemed there would be no more actions in life—nothing but pompous routines—yet a whole capital was watching her in judgment, and she had not even her husband to share the gaze.

Everywhere she went one pair of close-together eyes gazed at her—those of the Mnemon, the gray little man who had dogged Ptolemy's footsteps, discreetly prompting him with the names and functions of the many personages he had to encounter and re-encounter and whose faces and marks of office he could not be expected to remember. Berenice remembered them easily. In any case most of them passed before and around her like figures

painted on a wall; there were only five to whom she was
expected to pay any attention, her Council of Advisors.

The Council of Advisors was headed by the topmost of all officials, called the Dioecetes, the "Housekeeper." Strictly, it was for
Berenice to preside at their meetings, and this conscientious man
always deferred to her; but as she had no particular business to
bring, and he had armfuls, he took the lead, always studiously
maintaining his deference. He had so many documents—official
material on scrolls of parchment, petitions and memoranda of his
own on ostraca—that they had to be carried in a box by his clerk,
a small red-haired Greek, who kept quiet and wrote notes and
was the only other person present beside the other four Advisors.

These were old men brought out of retirement, highly experienced and with large volumes of intelligence. To Berenice's surprise they did not include the mild, waggish, but somewhat
eager-to-please man she still thought of as Uncle Callimachus.
She had assumed that he, who had been sent to woo her from
Cyrene, was one of the most prominent men in the kingdom. He
was esteemed as the most accomplished living poet and most
industrious of scholars, the informal leader of the literary com-
munity. But not the formal leader; he worked in the king's
Library, but was not even the Chief Librarian. He was smiled at
more than respected. He was not officer material. Nevertheless
she was inclined to let him continue as her own personal
Advisor. He could sometimes even advise her in improvised
verse, like the Delphic oracle.

The Advisors spent some hours with her each day. As these
hours began to shorten, she saw that her Advisors looked indul-
gently on her but expected to govern Egypt for her rather than
with her. Once, she was in the anteroom of the council chamber
before they heard her approaching, and from the light murmur
of a few undeciphered syllables she sensed the bantering cyni-
cism of all males (except the Dioecetes) when they get together.

Below them was the vast system of officials, and having first
interviewed the most important of them, the secretary of the
royal correspondence, she hit on the idea of filling her time by
summoning the rest, or at least the topmost echelon, one by one,
so as to acquaint herself with their names and duties: the
nomarchs who governed the nearer provinces, the chief priests,
the inspector of banks and markets. And the *Eklogistês* or finan-
cial overseer (a short man with a busy little cough and calves like

bubbles); and the *Idiologos*, "special agent," who had to look into unclaimed properties; and the inspector of canals and drains—a truly important official, who had also to ensure that the water sold by water-sellers had been properly distilled; but as she listened to him she couldn't help remembering Callimachus's lampoon of the man he called the "Ibis."

As each official arrived for his appointment in Berenice's reception room, the Mnemon, at her elbow, murmured the expert murmur on which he prided himself, with lips that did not appear to move. His expert and often unnecessary murmur irritated her. "This is Magnes, son of Lampron, overseer of the mint—"

"No, it is not," burst out Berenice, "I saw him yesterday, and this is Neander, Guardian of the Tombs, who waited his turn but did not get it. I Remember better than you do, Rememberer! You are dismissed. A woman can do her own remembering. I do not need you. Your office is abolished."

Appalled and mortified, the Mnemon left her, never to return. She felt a pang of penitence, but it was outweighed by the load of impatience she had suffered. Callimachus was present and suggested quietly to her that it might not be wise to abolish traditional offices, but she dismissed him too—for the moment— and turned still flashing eyes on the Guardian of the Tombs, who had come from ancient Memphis where he had his headquarters.

Like all the others, he assured her, with a mixture of smugness and obsequiousness, that all was well in his department. The tombs and mastabas and pyramids of the royal god-ancestors, of Ramesses and Tuthmosis and Sesostris and Cheops and all the others, stretching back to Menes and the beginnings of time, were safe in his tutelage—safer indeed than back in the times when a native-born Egyptian held the post he now held. It might have been, in the past, that gangs of looters stole in the night to the Valley of the Kings and tunneled into tombs and came out loaded with gold, leaving the rest of the grave-offerings and the paintings and inscriptions smashed and the embalmed bodies of the kings and queens to crumble into dust, "but any greedy peasant who considers such a crime nowadays knows that he will be caught by my officers and hanged by the heels."

On an impulse Berenice said: "Escort me to the Great Pyramids. I have been shown their tops in the distance, but no one has explained them to me."

A trace of reluctance crossed the Guardian's well-fed face, but he had to arrange it.

So, four evenings later, Berenice was lodged in Memphis itself, first of all cities, founded by Menes the first of all kings; and she was shown its great old temple, first of all temples, the Hi Ku Ptah— "the house of the soul of Hephaestus," the interpreter translated it; "they call the god Hephaestus by their name Ptah."

"Say it again."

"Hi Ku Ptah."

"It sounds a little like Aiguptos—Egypt!"

"That is what it is," said the interpreter; "this is where Egypt began. The temple is the house of Ptah; so the city is the house of Ptah; so the land is the house of Ptah."

"Hi Ku Ptah! Ai Gu Ptos!" said Berenice delightedly. "Did you know that, Guardian? Say it: Hi Ku Ptah."

"Eigou Pheta . . . Pethas . . ."

"If you can say *Ptolemaios*, you ought to be able to say *Ptah*. It's the god Hephaestus in Egyptic."

"The god who founded the world," said the interpreter in a low voice.

In the morning a line of pony-carts, with the Guardian's in front to lead the queen's, went trotting northward out of Memphis town. The road ran through fields; a village; fields; a village; fields, seamed by their irrigation ditches. Across many fields to the left there rose, parallel to the river, the cliff-line of the desert's edge, and pricking above it nine miles northwest could be seen the triangular points of the three Pyramids, which Berenice had already glimpsed far off from the boat.

In the villages, people hid behind the corners of their small houses, or made their obeisances if caught in the open; in the fields, peasants looked up from their work to stare. There were curiosities of rural life for Berenice to see—things without the importance of the Pyramids. A man held down a large wooden comb with one foot while tugging flax through it to tear off the heads, and his wife sat on the ground and rolled the flax on her thigh to rove it into strings for weaving. It was the Egyptian month Pharmouthi, second of the four months of Shemu, the Drought. Though it was far before midsummer—it was the time we call April—the heat was already heavy, and a canopy over the queen protected her head. The lifegiving flood of last midsummer had long ago shrunk off the fields and out of most of the ditches, and the ground was hard and the *stooping classes* (as Berenice had heard her mother call them) were beginning the labors of the harvest.

On went the retinue along the straight road of Egypt. Far to the left was the line of the cliffs, somewhere to the right the river in its trench four fathoms below the land, and beyond it the other line of cliffs. Egypt is a canyon across the desert, through it flowing the Nile that filled it with soil and life. But for little beings crawling along the road it was wide: the farthest-off that could be seen, rippling along slightly above the green of fields and palms, was those dry lines of cliffs. They told, if listened to, of the desert of which they were the face.

Ahead on the dusty road appeared a small cloud of people. There was something strange about them, and when they drew near enough it could be seen that what was strange was the lanky young man whom they surrounded. He was walking in an unnatural manner: determined, jerking, almost stopping at the end of each stride, as if his legs were logs—thighs pulling at each other, like those of one hurrying on mud and afraid to slip. Behind him, and watching him attentively, rode a man on a donkey. Around them, like flies they had collected in the villages, buzzed a number of curious men and jeering boys. There was also an ambling policeman, with club ready to drive the boys off if they threw stones.

When these people perceived who it was they were meeting, they scampered aside from the road to stand respectfully— except for the jerky walker, who was looking down at his toes: only after another two strides did he sense that he was alone, whereupon he halted abruptly at the end of a stride and stood where he was, one foot a yard in front of the other. Berenice saw with astonishment that his ankles were chained together. A copper chain ran from one ankle to the other. It was fixed to each ankle by a copper clasp, over an anklet of cloth to prevent chafing. His sandals were more like boots and had woollen socks inside. The rest of his brown skin was mostly bare, and he was sweating. The jerkiness of his walking had been caused by taking strides as long as the chain would allow, so that each foot had to stop when the chain snapped straight.

"The queen wishes to know what the strider is doing," said the Guardian to the clerk on the donkey. "Is he a prisoner?"

"Certainly not," replied the clerk, "he is well enough paid. I and he are measuring the distance from Letopolis to Memphis, if it please you."

"How—you are measuring—what for?—who told you to?" Berenice stammered.

"I don't know who has commanded it," said the clerk; "only that we know where to go (after all, Memphis is four miles wide): we must stride exactly to the temple of Khnum, the corner of it nearest the river, and then I have to report the number. The number of his paces. It isn't easy, I have just had to write 'Eight thousand eight hundred and one' on my tablet because you interrupted us."

"I crave your pardon," said Berenice, to the Guardian's slight disgust.

"Yes," concluded the clerk, "he is to make every one of his paces the same, if he can—the length of his chain, which has been measured for him. I mean, it has twenty-two copper links, which seemed to be his stride. I have to report that too. —He is not finding it easy, as you see. He has not done this work before."

"To whom do you have to report the number?"

"To the scribe Pem in the nomarch's office."

Berenice, then, to find out what this was about, would have to ask the scribe Pem, when they got back to Memphis. (But she forgot to.)

Seeing that the earnest strider was still standing like a triangle in the middle of the road with one foot a yard ahead of the other, endeavoring to keep his balance—like a flat picture on the wall of a tomb—she bade him go on with his striding. He re-began carefully—restraining his arms as if afraid they would swing him too far—while her own cart resumed its journey. And in half a mile they met a second strider with his clerk and policeman and spectators, acting as a check to the measurements of the first. This strider was a short, cheerful black-skinned fellow who made the action look as fluent as a dance: his chain (which had only nineteen copper links) seemed a plaything rather than a hindrance, so well were his bouncy strides adapted to it, and he even grinned at the queen. He too, and his clerk and his soldier,

knew no more than that they had to report their strides to the
clerk Pem in Memphis.

The Vigorous Peasant

Where the queen's party came abreast of the Pyramids there was
a crossroads, in a cluster of houses; they turned left into the road
that ran toward Pyramids and desert. At this corner started a
long mud-brick wall, on their right, surrounding some rich man's
garden. The wall was ten feet high, but there was a gateway in
it, or rather a temporary gap made by taking down a section of
it, and as Berenice was carried past she saw something and told
her driver to stop. He brought the pony to a halt as soon as he
could and made to turn it, but she got out, telling him to stay
where he was, and walked the few paces back. Meanwhile the
Guardian's driver had proceeded unaware; the following carts,
full of the queen's attendants, almost piled up on hers, but she
motioned them to go past and wait ahead. So she was alone as
she peeped in at the gateway.

The activity she had noticed was not important, merely interesting: it was a team of workers moving some material. A large
sloppy heap, rosy in color, sat in the gateway, where it had been
delivered on perhaps an earlier day and mixed in the last few
minutes: it was gravel and sand and lime and water. Beside it
stood a tall old man, holding the very long handle of a shovel;
and, to help him lift gobs of the dense material from the pile, a
rope, attached to the handle close to the blade, was gripped by
no fewer than four men. All wore nothing but tightly wrapped
loincloths.

Another man came running: he had across his shoulders a
yoke, from each end of which dangled a copper pan. He presented one of these pans; the team of rope-pullers pulled, the
shovel-handler pivoted the shovel, the shovel stabbed into the hill
of mortar and rose under a mass of it and turned over in the air
and slapped the load onto the pan. The pan-holder then presented the other pan, and it was loaded likewise. He ran off with
it to where it was needed by other workers who were laying
blocks somewhere within the compound.

Berenice had noticed merely a sparkle of activity—a flash from the shovel, arms yanking a rope, pans swinging on chains above bare running feet; at any time in any street of Alexandria a hundred such inexplicable bustles might be in progress—but she felt like understanding this one. The workers had not yet noticed her (standing aslant from the gateway) and she did not want them to. But as she watched the activity it caught fire. It was the man with the pans. He was a short stocky sunburnt curly-haired young peasant. Having delivered his two panfuls to the builders, he returned, not walking but running, not just to the dome of mortar but around it. He arrived with a shout; stamped down his right foot; bent at the waist and knees, right knee forward; planted his right elbow on his right thigh; presented the right pan almost at his shoulder-level. The shovel, already above it, turned over and delivered the load; the pan, under the thud of mortar, sank (an inch); dramatically he staggered, steadied, and shouted "Raa'!" (It was the name of a god.) That pan was full; he straightened and then, instead of just turning a quarter-turn leftward, twirled completely around rightward, before stamping down his left foot and, with mirror-actions of the other side of his body, presenting the left pan. *"Raa'!"*

With both pans full, he ran off between the fig trees to the builders, shot the mortar to where it was needed, returned by running all around the pile, rearrived with a shout and a stamp of his right foot, just in time to maintain the beat: the next shovelful arrived just as he did—the shovel-holder and the rope-pullers were freed from need to pause in their swings. He was speeding the pace with the accents of his shouts; they intensified to a chant. The old shovel-holder and the four rope-pullers grinned and joined in. (One of them was clearly the vigorous peasant's father: gray head but the same blunt face, stolider.) All six were shouting the sharp shouts in unison; it had become a holy shanty, and steadily it speeded.

Berenice thought: I did not know people could work so fast. (Egyptians are lethargic—that's what everyone says. The land is so hot. There are sicknesses in the molten air and the fetid water that eat away their life-force. They squat against walls in the bits of shade, unable to rouse themselves to do anything.)

They noticed her, and she hoped they noticed her admiration, but if so it made no difference to their actions or their faces, both already stretched to the full. She wondered how long men could

work at such a rate, and moved off without finding out. She
stepped back onto the cart; the Guardian of the Tombs had
returned to wait for her, and they went on. The road began to
rise, running up a causeway across the last of the green plain,
aiming at the high crusty edge of the desert. Looking down from
the causeway, she saw hovels among the fields. She said to her
driver, since there was no one else to say it to: "One of those may
be the hovel where the Vigorous Peasant lives."

To her surprise, because she had hardly spoken a previous
word to him and assumed he only knew such words of Greek as
"Stop" and "Wait" and "Go on," he said: "'The Eloquent Peasant',
madam, that is the name of the story."

"What story?"

"I thought you were referring to 'The Eloquent Peasant'. It is
an Egyptic novel."

From which Berenice learned that the Egyptians had novels.

The driver had time to tell her a bit of it before they arrived at
the Pyramids.

The sloping road attained to the high edge, and the view opened
into the desert. When Egyptians die, they go west, like the
setting sun: their bodies (if they are kings) to be interred in
chambers of the rock with mortuary temples carved into the
cliffs, or even in pyramids on the tableland above; their souls
traveling out into the Western Desert, conducted by Jackal
Anubis into the halls of the afterworld. On the visible plane, the
souls that traverse the infinite desert are sparse bands of Libyans
and caravans of traders between the oases. Of which one was
the far-off island of Berenice's birth.

She gazed angrily at the greatest of the Pyramids—gazed up
the immense stair of stone that climbed dizzily to the distant sky.
It looked higher than it was wide, a stair too steep and with steps
too huge to climb, yet boys were scrambling far away up it.

Of the Seven Wonders of the World—the *theamata*, the
things that should be seen—this was the third she had seen, and
the largest, oldest, and ugliest. "It is the highest structure ever
made," said the Guardian, "higher than the Hanging Gardens of
Babylon—four hundred and eighty feet. How do I know?—
because a Greek measured it, Thales of Miletus. He came here
three hundred years ago and the Egyptians asked him to find the
height of the Pyramid by the same sort of magic with which he

had predicted harvests and eclipses. So the first thing he did was to lie on the ground, and have them make marks at his foot and head. Then he stood there until the time of day when his shadow reached exactly to the mark for the top of his head, and had them mark where the tip of the pyramid's shadow fell on the ground; and it was there, commemorated by that stone, which we call the stone of Thales. Only just outside the pyramid's foot; four hundred and eighty feet from its middle. That's how he measured it!"

"You tell me this story," said Berenice, "to show me that a Greek can look after the pyramid better than an Egyptian can?"

"Oh, I would not—" began the Guardian modestly.

"It is a ruin."

So many of the myriad fine white slabs of the outer casing had been lost—presumably to the sand-laden winds of the desert—that the inner Pyramid was shrugging itself free, like a snaggled thing crawling out of its smooth skin. The inner Pyramid was a stack of two million stone cubes, and though each of these cubes was of intimidating size—chest-height on a side—they were brown and rough, and the dark patches of them emerging from under the once-perfect casing made the whole pile look like something under attack by gigantic moths.

"People have, in the past," said the Guardian of the Tombs, "robbed too much of the limestone casing."

"They destroy it?"

"They take, or they used to take, the slabs to add to their houses, the slabs being beautiful."

"And will there be work to restore the Pyramids to their beauty?"

"There will be, if the king grants us money to do it."

"These Pyramids are stumpy ruins," said Berenice, and as she looked about her on the dusty ground she saw that they were surrounded by donkey-dung and pedlars selling trinkets.

"No one knows how they were built," said the Guardian, hoping to escape into his lecture on their history. "The blocks must be so heavy that not even one could have been moved except by a thousand men under the lash of a mighty ruler. The Egyptians will tell you that they were flown to their places by the mind of Imophis, the magician; the simpler say, and I think rightly, that only gods could have handled them. A mathemati-

cian of Syracuse, Archimedes, has shown that with levers of sufficient length—"

"I know the power that built the Pyramids," said Berenice,
thinking of the energy of the peasant, and turning away.

The pedlars were standing silent and subdued behind their
stalls. She walked over to one of them and looked down at what
he was offering.

"Whose portrait is that?" she asked, about a carving set into a
brooch.

"King Apophis," he said, giggling. He was a boy who rolled
his eyes about and twitched.

"A king!"

"A thousand kings, there are!"

"And how did you get it?"

"It came from his tomb!"

"From his tomb! You didn't get it from there, I suppose?"

"No, my uncle!"

"But—your uncle doesn't rob tombs? There is death for that."

The boy grinned and made the bribe-sign on his palm.

Berenice returned to the Guardian and said: "These Pyramids,
they are the center of your responsibility?"

"Yes, since they are themselves tombs of kings. They are the
tombs of three great kings from very long ago. More of your historians—the scholars of Alexandria and Athens—come here to
view them than go all the way up to Thebes. There are certainly
more of these pedlars here than anywhere else."

"Perhaps you should live close by."

"I will," said the Guardian.

On the way back she had him ride on her cart, and as they
came to the gateway in the wall—from which the workmen and
the whole rosy gravelly pile had gone, leaving only a rosy trace
on the white dust—she said to him: "Someone is building a
house here, apparently of stone, so let us go in and see whether
this is an example of someone who uses slabs taken from the
Pyramids."

The poor man's face struggled, and then he went down on his
knees, on the wobbling floor of the cart, and begged her, for the
sake of his wife (who was ailing) and his children and grand-
children, to spare his life after he had resigned from his post and
paid damages.

Fortunately for him, Berenice—who had been innocent of

any expectation that he was the owner of the house—had already made herself sorry for him by speaking to him so harshly, by calling his Pyramid a stumpy ruin. She was more concerned to get to where she could wipe the dust, made messy by the man's tears, off her feet.

Short yellow cloak

Thinking about these findings, during the river journey back to Alexandria, Berenice wondered whether, after catching a corrupt official, leaving him in place might work better than executing him and replacing him with another. He had had his fright. She also concluded that instead of summoning officials to her for their interviews she would do better to make visits to them at their places of work.

This proved not possible with the next now waiting, the chief of security in the city. He was relatively junior—she had already received his superior, chief for the whole of Egypt—and he was in fact only the ninth of the appointments postponed by her trip to the Pyramids: yet, when she came back, she learned that this man, by name Sosibius, was in the audience-room. He had been there all morning. He had taken it upon himself to be punctual, even if she was not. As soon as, entering the room and assuming her place on her throne, she saw this tall young man standing with his arms folded, she suspected that he was not going to be apologetic for jumping over others or even forgiveful for being made to wait.

They were not alone: four guards stood at each of the room's two entrances. These were palace guards of hers—but they were actually subordinates of his, wearing the same uniform: the *chlamys* cloak, dyed bright yellow with saffron and having a blue band along the lower border, short enough not to conceal the knife stuck into the belt. The only differences were that Sosibius had two blue stripes, and did not carry the knife nor hold the staff with heavy club-like tip.

He came forward to the foot of the steps and made the usual obeisances to her, then explained his functions and answered her questions smartly. And when he saw that she recognized him—

though he didn't know how—he showed no sign of fear or even embarrasment. The slight narrowing of his eyes, accompanied by the slight biting of his right lower lip, suggested that he estimated her as an interesting sparring-partner.

She felt the attraction of this man, younger than herself, and was afraid of it. His powerful shape made her aware that he could snatch her up and whack her violently to the floor, though she knew he would not presume to touch her. Her questions withered; the more he showed himself expert on his job, the more she felt herself too vapidly ignorant even to find questions. But if she stumbled into silence, he might even smile over her.

"Are you Idumaean?" she asked.

He contained his laughter almost perfectly, just allowing her to see that anyone else but he would have laughed aloud. "No, madam. I am of good Theban blood. —I refer," he added, in case she was even more ignorant, "to sacred Thebes that is in Greece, not the one in this country."

He went on to explain to her: "My men are indeed mostly Idumaeans—you are right. You may have wondered why our police are called Medzae. Until a generation back they were Nubians, mostly from a fierce tribe called Medzae. But Egyptians got resentful of being policed by the men from the south who had often in the past been a terror to them, so now we recruit men of lighter skin but comparable toughness from Idumaea, which is the desert land to the south of Palestine. But the term 'Medzae' lingers on in popular (as you might say) usage. I think it is strangely effective. It sounds feminine, it sounds like a sort of drift of women—in amusing contrast with the regard in which our Medzae are actually held. A troublesome scene in an Alexandrian street can go quiet at the mere word that 'The Medzae!' are coming. It's useful."

Well, that was worth knowing. But after this she did find herself feebly silent. So she said suddenly:

"You are quite good as an amateur actor."

He smiled, and she won, this time, by not smiling back, though it was difficult.

"Have you any more questions, my *Despoina?*"

Feeling herself now in slight advantage over him, she demanded: "Do you obey the edict of Ptolemy Philadelphus by ensuring that your Medzae use no torture when interrogating?"

"Of course," replied Sosibius (a pair of words he used often).

He didn't bother to add such "of course" provisos as "Sometimes a modicum of pressure is necessary" or "Women are squeamish and Ptolemy Philadelphus had to say what his queen-sister wished, and he also issued an edict that all Greeks and Macedonians should learn Egyptic, and all citizens should learn to read."

"I know where the Cryon is but I have not yet seen it," she said. "You are at work there every day?" And realized that it was another silly question: he had already told her of the whole days he spent out with his patrols, checking their efficiency.

"On no fixed days," he replied. "I like to surprise my staff."

Which was what she had intended to do to him.

So it would be a matter of luck. She decided that the best day was tomorrow. She was at the prison at dawn, having informed no one until she descended to her carriage and told the driver, who slept beside it, to start. To her annoyance its broken wheel had not been mended; she had to order her litter-carriers to be roused instead.

The Cryon, the Cold House, stood in the Rhacotis quarter. Sometimes it was called the Prison, though it was not all prison, and the city had other prisons. The band of land, between sea and lake, that was now Alexandria had once been a strip of sand and palms and one Egyptian village, Rhacotis. That was before the coming of Alexander, who laid out the long *chlamys*, the rectangular "cloak" of his city's shape, and his two lines that crossed in the middle and were to be the widest of the wide straight streets. Brucheion and the complex of palaces were in the northeastern quarter; Rhacotis, far off in the southwest, with only the western wall beyond it and the Moon Gate and then the Necropolis, the city of the dead, was the poorest and roughest quarter and no doubt the most deserving of the headquarters of the feared Medzae.

The Cryon bulked above the low dwellings of Rhacotis. The heavy door at the street was well barred and guarded by yellow cloaks. There was no doubt that it would be opened for the queen, but it took her a fit of anger to get it opened as quickly as she wanted. She saw a central courtyard, narrow and dark between towering colonnades, and in a room left of it, to which a policeman made an ushering gesture, she saw Sosibius. He might have liked to use his skill at slipping from the scene, but could not, because he was behind a desk and a human wall of his own making: two shackled men standing before him, each held by two policemen. (She had the slightly surprised impression that the two in trouble were not common ruffians but well-to-do citizens.) He rose to his feet and greeted her suavely.

She said that she had accepted his invitation to tour the Cryon. He did not say that he had made no such invitation, but a game had begun, which she suspected she would lose.

"You must first rest," he said, "because there are stairs to climb. Indeed I can have your majesty carried up them in a litter."

"I am well rested—I can still walk," she said hotly, fancying that he had glanced at her belly: had he seen something so small that she herself had not yet seen it? She walked out of the room and turned left along the colonnade. Behind her a polite entourage followed, consisting of not quite all the men who had been standing around, since two had been quietly sent to bring the news of her presence to other departments of the building. She saw a stair that went *down*, and took it.

But that was what he designed for her to do. Before knowing it she had walked into a pleasant and quiet room, almost a bower, with a cushioned couch around the wall, a further door to a kitchen, and a view into a small sunken garden that was mostly pool (no cellars could be deep in Alexandria, with the sea only feet below). Sosibius ordered refreshment for her, unobtrusively closing the door.

And coughing. And yet she had heard it.

She stood and turned her stare on him, heat rushing into her face.

"What is that?"

"Oh, the questioning of—" He bit his right lower lip, for once so sharply that he himself noticed it; he did not like to make mistakes. "A mad prisoner," he said, "that is all."

He began to talk easily, but she tore herself away from him and his voice, snatched open the door, and now he would have had to shout to cover the scream, distant though it was. It was the howl from which the stage howl of blinded Samson had been learned.

"Go and find what Leucus is doing," Sosibius said to one of his men, "I think he is disobeying orders and must stop—run!" The yellowjacket ran past Berenice—and she ran after him, as best she could.

He disappeared from her around a corner, she panted up the

stairs where he must have gone, and rammed her fist on the door that had slammed. On the other side of it someone was dropping a latch, but fumbled it, and the door trembled and she flung it back on him, and there lay the dwarf, or what was left of him.

Sosibius arrived and explained.

"This is the slave who tried to murder your husband the King. He shall of course die, but first we must find out from him what we can. He is not of course the principal, and we know who is. Let us call that person the—let's see—the Rooster. A difficulty, which—"

"Wait," said Berenice. "I cannot bear to see this fellow—"

"Yes, let us come away," and he began to lead her out of the torture chamber.

"Bring my litter!" she yelled up into tall Sosibius's face. "Give him a draught of wine, bandage him as well as you can, then have him carried to the Thermidion!"

The Thermidion, the Warm Little House, was the smallest of Alexandria's fifty hospitals but the most special: it was inside the palace and reserved for the king.

One of the policemen laughed, then clapped his hand to his mouth.

"If he dies—" said Berenice.

There was a silence of no great length at all before Sosibius smoothly gave the orders that the queen required, along with others that she added. She sent two of her own party of servants with the litter.

Then she conducted Sosibius—not he her—back to his office near the portal of the building. He quite expected her to take the chair behind his desk, but she did not care to do that; so he had something fetched for her to sit on, a stool. She picked it up, moved it back, sat with her back to a wall, but lower than him as she faced him across his desk.

"Go on," she said.

He explained again to her, as if she was stupid. "This was the slave who tried to murder your husband, by throwing him down from the balcony, as he reviewed the Alexandrian regiment. I was among those who saw, from the parade ground; which was as well, since it was my responsibility to arrest him. I also was able to see, since I am trained to be observant, and since the balcony's parapet was a mere rail, that he was brought into the room by another, who, after bringing him in and sending him forward, stayed back during the deed, then rushed to the balcony to look down and pretend to be as horrified as the rest of us."

"And who was that?"

"As I said, let us call him for the moment the Rooster, or Cockerel if you prefer the term. I feel obliged to treat him as innocent until we have corroborated his guilt."

She got up and looked out of the doorway, setting the door open. No Medzae were listening outside; they were standing at a distance.

"Who is he?" she said.

"I had hoped not to tell you until we complete our inquiry."

"I require you to tell me."

"He is the Dioecetes, the Housekeeper of Egypt."

"You can dare to say that?"

"It will be certain when we have extracted the information from his accessory. Who is, like his master, Nubian."

So Ptolemy had not even known where his little clown came from—that he had been born in some African village far away to the south, and was among people who, Egyptians as well as Greeks, shared no language with him. Except possibly the Housekeeper, who like other black Egyptians was perfectly Egyptian in all ways but blackness.

"Sylcon is not his master; the king is."

"But our Nubian Housekeeper, it seems, was his secret master."

"So do you have a Nubian to interrogate the dwarf?"

"Yes, the gentleman you saw standing by. Many of our Nubians, though they have lived in our land a long time, still speak their own language; the dwarf is an exception in speaking it only. This is not much of a difficulty," said Sosibius, though he had had his frustrations and even suspicions about an interrogation conducted in a language he did not yet know. "A greater obstacle is the little man's stupidity and toughness of body, so that he has given as yet few trustworthy answers. As far as we can make out, he claims that he tried to *save* the king from falling. Yet he fell himself—happening to preserve your husband's life though only accidentally, as your husband will have told you."

"All he told me" (Berenice thought) "was that the balcony broke under him." But she neither wanted to hear that Ptolemy fibbed, nor to set the policeman arresting a carpenter. "So that was the reason," she said, "that the king suffered barely a scratch. And what about the dwarf?"

"Well, he too was lucky. Only one arm was broken."

"And then you began torturing him."

"Not until recently, when it was apparent that he might continue obstinate. And not extremely; he has to testify, when he is ready to do so. —It is a case of necessity, is it not?" he added. "The life of a king."

"Why should the little man throw away his life by murdering a king, whether or not he fell with him?"

"Look at him. If you were that creature, would you care whether you live or die?"

"Why would he not incriminate Sylcon and end his torture, if he knows he is going to die anyway?"

"He is an animal that does not know it is going to die."

Berenice, who had not resumed her place on the stool, now advanced and stood close in front of Sosibius's desk, a board of cedar resting on ornately carved and gilded legs.

"What does the Housekeeper himself say? Does he admit that he brought the dwarf with him?"

"He will have to, when the dwarf has admitted it, which will be soon. Or will be, if you allow us to continue questioning him. We will notify the charged party only when our information is full and we bring the charge, otherwise he will be busy trying to cover his tracks, and so I ask you not to inform him yet. I know you think it surprising that he is not aware; but my force is a disciplined one."

Berenice gazed at him.

"You say," she said, "that you saw the dwarf brought into the room by Sylcon."

"Pulled up the stairs, led into the room, pushed forward by the shoulders. It's lucky that I, besides being observant, am tall and could see what some others perhaps could not. The moment the king was dead, the Housekeeper would have been the one to give commands in the House."

She put her fingertips down on the polished surface and leaned toward him. (He had a not unpleasant odor.)

"The dwarf did not come into the room with Sylcon. He had been there with the king all along."

"Really? If you say so, your majesty. But may I inquire what

makes you think so? It is unlikely (for a state occasion), and contrary to what I observed."

"It is contrary to what you say you observed. That is because
you are a liar. I was there. Not there at the time; I had just left.
The dwarf was with my husband while I was with him."

Sosibius returned her gaze without moving a superb sinew of
his face.

"Yes, you postponed your 'interrogation' of the little man—
does he have a name, by the way, besides 'Coptolemy'?"

"His Nubian name is, I am told, Saha."

So that was the "Egyptic name" that Ptolemy could not pronounce.

"You put it off for perhaps a day. Until King Ptolemy was on
his way. He could have given you the lie."

"I hope you don't mind my observing, madam, that your
theory is rather complex. You accept the rigmarole of the dwarf
that the king stepped backward and the dwarf tried to save him?"

"Your lie is rather too simple, Police Chief Ovkorsakos. Rig-
maroles are usually the truth—or at any rate the truth is very
often a rigmarole."

"Wonderfully said! I have had that thought exactly. But the
rigmarole could be longer. Could Sylcon not have placed his tool,
the dwarf, in the king's service?"

"Could Sosibius not have placed his tool, the dwarf, in the
king's service? I shall have it found out."

"I can see that neither of us can at this stage prove our theo-
ries."

"I prove mine to my own satisfaction by knowing you did not
see what you say you saw. And I am your queen."

She removed her fingertips from the desk. "I will inform you
tomorrow of your new posting. I cannot have a liar in this position. And this time you told a stupid lie. You may have told many
cleverer lies in the course of your climb to this office. The guards
at the ends of the corridor could say what I have said, that the
dwarf was there—oh, I suppose they are in fear of you. You have
risen to a powerful position and you wished to rise to the most
powerful of all—short of king—by bringing down its present
holder; by accusing him, I suppose, of trying to rise to the position of king."

"Yes," contributed Sosibius, "and I hate him. Can you guess

why I hate him? It's the hatred of a tall man for one that is even taller!" and he laughed merrily.

But his hatred for the officeholder above him was now as nothing to his hatred of this woman. He had been careless enough to tell, for once in his life, a falsifiable lie, and she had caught him in it.

"Be in the audience room at dawn tomorrow," she said on her way out. "Wait there till I choose to remember about you."

She stalked out—then wondered how she was to get home across the length of the city. But he had already, as he followed her down the stairs, given word for another litter to be at the street door for her.

The victor

Rumor traveled fast in Alexandria, and about sundown Callimachus sought an interview with Berenice. He did not get it till the middle of the next morning; she had retired early, but had difficulty sleeping, and on rising visited the Thermidion. The only other patients there were a royal cousin and a joiner who had fallen and broken his back while working on a summerhouse for the king's garden.

The dwarf turned horrified eyes toward her. She realized that the expression derived from his pain, not from her; she wanted to ask him questions, but he would neither have understood them nor been able to speak. She went away and sat in the boxlike thronelet overlooking the parade ground. She was interrupted with a message that one of her Advisors hoped to see her. She asked which one, and was told it was Callimachus, son of Battus. He was not an Advisor, and she instead kept her next appointment, with the overseer of slaughterhouses. Later she visited the Library, which was no trouble since, though itself vast, it was within the vaster maze of the palace. Callimachus learned of her presence, and when he appeared she had the room that she was in cleared and invited him to sit.

He thanked her and said: "You and I, daughter of Magas, are Cyreneans, and can speak with each other more freely than these Alexandrians can."

"Are you here to Advise me?"

"I hope so."

"As to what?"

"Perhaps to be careful about the man called Sosibius."

"I can do what I want with him—reduce him to the ranks, have him imprisoned if I wish."

"He is a remarkable young man."

"Yes, he is quite remarkable. He takes part in bawdy performances in the squalid back rooms of slums."

"Does he indeed? Yet another talent of his!"

"He presumably belongs to a sodality for dramatics. He minces on a stage, got up as a woman."

"Are you sure it was him?"

"I'm sure it was all supposed to be a daring secret, but I penetrated his disguise. Has that gone around the gossip of Alexandria yet? He acted the part of the Forces of Light. I found him and his performance engaging to look at for a time, but soon I solved his disguise further and saw him as the Forces of Evil."

Callimachus sat back and examined his knuckles. Then he said: "You have not read my ode, *Sôsibiou Nikê*, 'Sosibius's Victory'?"

"Yes, I remember that, but it was for an Olympic victor, Sosibius of Tarentum, was it not?"

"You have it confused, I'm afraid: Sosibius of Lacedaemon was a grammarian; Sosibius the son of Dioscurides, of Alexandria—our Sosibius—was the victor. He has been three times victor: in the Isthmian Games, the Nemean Games, and the Panathenaic Games. At wrestling, running, and hurling the discus, he is better than most men alive."

Berenice was speechless.

"Or was, not long ago. He is still only twenty. The Delians issued a decree honoring him, and at Cnidus a statue of him has been erected. He is a native-born Alexandrian, and still, as you can imagine, a hero to very many Alexandrians."

"So that is why I should be careful how I handle him?"

"I don't think he runs or wrestles now (though what you have told me makes anything possible) but his accomplishments and popularity enabled him to slide easily into his next career, that of politics. He obtained the chiefship of police for the asking."

"He didn't have to train—to work his way up the ranks?"

"He applied for the post three months ago, took his place in the Cryon and, from what I have heard, learned his way around that grim establishment at once."

"Is police politics?"

"I think in his case one is intended to lead into the other."

"For him that line has now come to a stop and he will have to proceed in another direction, such as to one of the cells in his own jail."

"I"—Callimachus folded and re-folded his lips before re-beginning . . . "Alexandria is a volatile city. There have been occasions when inflamed mobs ruled it and a King Ptolemy could do nothing but retreat into his palace and wait out the excitement, and many people died. One time it was priests who caused the trouble, other times the army (whose pay was overdue or who had lost a war they considered badly handled); and there have been even more trivial sparks to the fire—a law-suit, a misunderstanding about a name, the killing of a cat."

"Why do they think cats are gods?" Berenice asked.

"Because cats don't die, or so they believe—cats go away and hide to die."

"Then why are gulls not gods?"

"I don't know. —But, as I was mentioning about Alexandria and its mobs. One time the Greeks took out their grievances on the Judaeans; another time the Egyptians massacred the Nubians."

"Massacred the Nubians—why?"

"Well, to belong to a people that supplied the police, and that once held the country in subjection, does not tend to make a dark-complexioned person popular. It was from then on that Nubians ceased to staff our police force and were replaced by Idumaeans. —In any case, you will see that a place such as Alexandria is like several kinds of tinder rubbing together, and one needs to watch out for blazes—spasms of popular madness. I can only suggest that you find work for Sosibius that will seem to everyone honorable but that will not be political."

"Inspector of Drains."

"I beg your pardon?"

"I would like to appoint him to the important position of Inspector of Drains and Sewers."

Callimachus laughed, picturing Sosibius as another long-legged Ibis, standing in the trenches of pollution. But he talked with her some more, until they sent for Hontiphas, the Advisor who knew all about recent deaths and vacancies. And then the queen sent for Sosibius, but was told that he had gone back to the Cryon, since it was after noon.

Sent for again, he presented himself as soon as could be expected and said that she had told him to "wait all morning" and he had done so. Berenice could not remember whether she had used this form or words or not.

The audience room had a high throne in which Berenice sat, and before it a group of chairs for her Advisors, though on this occasion they did not all need to be present, nor did she say anything. Indeed she felt that she could neither safely look at nor speak to Sosibius, and she told the Dioecetes to preside.

Speaking for her, therefore, Sylcon the Dioecetes informed Sosibius, son of Dioscurides, that he was not to return to the Cryon, because he had been removed from his post; and fell silent without saying any more. Then Hontiphas congratulated Sosibius on becoming Chief Priest of the Cult of Alexander.

There was a longish interval during which Sosibius did not speak. It seemed he might turn on his heel and depart. Or even strike Hontiphas, though Hontiphas, despite his fussy manner and valetudinarian habits, was a tree-like old man who did not look as if he could be easily felled: he widened upward, to the gray hairs that prickled the sides of a monumental head. But Sosibius removed his glance from Hontiphas, as if removing a finger from grease. He gazed coolly at Sylcon. Neither of them dropped their gaze: Sylcon because he was not constituted to do so, Sosibius because he stood and the other sat, and so for the first time he looked with comfort—slightly downward—into the black man's goldish eyes.

At length: "Sosibius a priest," said Sosibius ruminatively.

"It is the most exalted and powerful of priestships," said Hontiphas. ("Powerful"—the word was slightly surprising. But it meant, presumably, that the office commanded respect on the supernatural plane.)

"Sosibius is not an enthusiast of the Olympian gods, let alone the godship of Alexander." He spoke of himself as another person. It was as if there were two Sosibii, standing and considering each other. Or that was the notion suggested to Berenice. And it was because she recognized such a nature in herself: the fancy to be aware of several Berenices who took turns flitting through her.

"Do you regard Alexander as a mere mortal?" demanded Hontiphas.

"Yes. What else? He is dead. Exists no more. He was not born on Mount Olympus or from the head of Athena; he was born for Philip the Second (drunkard and womanizer), warlord of Macedon, out of Olympias (jealous spitfire), princess of Epirus. And dare it be said that he was himself a moody, intemperate megalomaniac. *'Mêden agan,'* said Aristotle, 'Nothing in excess,' but his pupil Alexander's way was *'Everything* in excess'—war, wives, wine—which was why he died at an earlier age than I intend to." Sosibius could have been Alexander (he clearly felt), if they had been born in different stations.

Poor Hontiphas could not express his shock; he frothed. Sosibius bowed deeply to the queen, then to the Dioecetes, whom he thanked emphatically for the appointment (ignoring Hontiphas). The libations were poured and drunk, the oaths pronounced, and he departed. (To make sure that his close partner, by name Agathocles, took his place behind the police desk.)

The writing on the lighthouse

Few and slow were the reports that came back of progress through Palestine. At home Berenice's attention was demanded for more trivial matters.

"*Despoina*, will you come to see the Pharos? Something strange is happening to it."

She hardly wanted to hear about the Pharos. She was beginning to feel sick in the mornings.

"Is it falling?"

"No, but a piece of it is!"

She descended and found the morning air cool, fresh, damp, so that she almost declined to step into her litter. "It never rains in Egypt!"—that was so often said, yet there had been in the night a gusty swirling rainstorm that left the southern faces of the houses dripping: it could not have come from inland—it must have come curling in from the sea over the delta and then curled out again to the sea it came from. The wide cardinal streets with their colonnades were cleansed every day, by men wasting cartloads of water drawn from the canal, but the alleys that filled the vast blocks between the streets grew every day thicker with dust and trash, which now after the shower had become flows of mud.

The company of courtiers and priests, with Berenice in her litter, descended past the Royal Harbor and the Little Harbor and made its way west along the quaysides of the Great Harbor. At the corner which was the beginning of the causeway called Heptastadion, several fishers, who had been sitting on the low sea wall, laid their poles and nets down and—rather to Berenice's disappointment—jumped up and bowed and made themselves as scarce as they could. Not so a cat, which was eating a fragment of fish. The bearers paused to set the litter down and bow to the cat—whereupon Berenice seized her chance to slip out of the litter and walk. After first offering to the cat her own prayer:

Teach me to sleep.

They entered on the Heptastadion, the causeway of seven stadia or nearly a mile, that ran out, between the Great Harbor on the right and the Eunostos, the Harbor of Good Return, on the left, toward the Pharos island. The Great Harbor had already become shallow close to the causeway, because of silt settling against it—as could be judged from the sight of a man and a horse, twenty yards out in the water and only chest deep. The man, holding the horse by its bridle, was unaware of the royal party because his back was to it and he was noisily splashing, or perhaps he was just determined not to pause in his horse-washing: he kept turning the snorting head to left then right as the horse tried to get past him and march ashore. Berenice would have liked to stop and watch this too, but everyone else paid no attention and pressed on.

They came to the island and turned rightward toward its northeast tip, where the Pharos punctured the sky. It seemed as high as the island was long, though that was not quite possible. They entered its shadow and then went in at the door of the huge square castle that made the base, and up the stairs to the court— its sides lined with statues—in which stood the square tower, twelve storeys high, with the eight-sided tower on top of that, and the round tower on top of that, and the statue of sea-god Poseidon on top of that, and the lamp in Poseidon's hand on top of that, and on top of that the chamber that contained the fire

and the mirror—the fire that by night and the mirror that by day
could be seen forty miles out at sea.

The Pharos tapered into the sky, or spread from its summit in
the sky down to its wide foot on the earth; clearly it would be
toppled by no wind or even earthquake; yet anyone who had ever
helped to lift a block of stone could hardly believe that such a
stack of them could stand without killing each other and sinking
into the earth. (Could it be true that the Pharos's foundation was
of glass? And that its blocks were jointed on the seaward side not
with mortar but with lead?)

To look up at it was to be dizzy. And across the top of the
lower stage of the tower, the square stage, was the dedication—
letters as tall as men, yet so remote that Berenice's keen eyes,
when these letters were first shown to her, had had to read them
squintingly:

TO THE SAVIOR GODS FOR THE SAFETY OF SEAFARERS

The Savior Gods: she had supposed those to be the divine twins,
Castor and Pollux, to whom sailors pray because they save ships
at the ends of storms.

"No! The Savior Gods," her cousin had explained, "are the
founders of our dynasty: my grandfather the first Ptolemy and my
grandmother (and yours) the first Berenice."

"Why are they Saviors?—who was it they saved?"

"Only the Rhodians. Ptolemy sent them enough help by sea to
make sure that Demetrius could not starve them out. Independent Rhodes was an asset to his strategic plans and a nuisance to
Macedon. So afterwards the Rhodians politely addressed him as
Sôtêr, 'Savior', and he liked it. And it's useful now for distin-
guishing one Ptolemy from another. Better 'Ptolemy Sôtêr' than
'Ptolemy son of Lagus', the Rabbit!"

"Well, their lighthouse at least is a savior, it saves seafarers."

"Not often, I think. There are few storms here, except the
desert Eurus that blows ships out to sea. I doubt a ship has been
driven on Egypt by a storm since Menelaus and his helmsman
Canopus after the Trojan War. The lighthouse, I think, is to show
the way to Alexandria and to boast."

Berenice now again gazed up the face of the lighthouse to the
political letters. They were of lead, set into the limestone, and
around the whole inscription was a projecting band of what
looked like limestone also, white against the pink granite of the
tower. It looked just like another part of the ornament, a frame;

architecture, she had sometimes thought, especially in Alexandria, was nothing but shapes added on shapes, lines and corners and mouldings and bands whether needed or not, as if to confound an artist who might try to draw it. But this band was not limestone, it was plaster. And the plaster had begun to crumble in the rainy wind! Chunks of it had fallen. And the gazers from below could see that above the line of letters there were other letters, slightly smaller: the beginning of a line:

ΣΩ . . .

Could it be again *SÔTÊR*, "Savior"? But other letters had become partly visible, farther along, the bottoms of Sigmas and a Delta:

ΣΩ . . . Σ . . . Σ . . . Δ . . .

From the parapet above, workers were already dangling on ropes, with chisels, to tidy the work of the storm.

More chunks fell. And it became:

ΣΩΣ . . . ΟΣ Ο Δ . . . ΟΥΣ ΚΝΙΔ . . .

Sôs . . . us son of D . . . ês Cnid . . .

Berenice turned away. She started to give an order, had to pause and master her throat, then gave it: "Tell them to stop the work—at once. They are to cover up those letters.   —No, destroy them." She looked around for her litter, got into it and told the bearers to take her home, at a run.

Her scalp felt tight and she undid the "mating-grasshoppers" clasp from her hair and shook it free. She ordered a bath to be poured; swallowed some of the resin of silphium that had been given to her for the nauseas she had begun to feel (though the doctors prescribed it for so many other conditions that she was not confident of its effect). The thought came back to her of a crab that had crawled, barely alive, from a cooked dish she had started to eat—or was that something from a dream? And the horror of what she had done with the spear had been returning. She lay back against a cushion, with her eyes wide open, and then determined to confront her fears.

Stepping from her bedroom into the ante-room, she was about to go out and find a guardsman to send, but instead, remembering her loosened hair, called her maid Polymela, who appeared at the door.

"Find Melas and send him—send him to the temple of

Alexander. The chief priest is to come here immediately, I have to question him."

Polymela stepped away into the corridor to the left, and within a breath the chief priest of Alexander, himself, stepped from the right, into the room.

Berenice was in the act of raising her arms to the back of her head, having realized that she had better re-braid her own hair in case her maid did not return in time.

It was as if she had fainted, had stood on the spot for an hour unconscious, then opened her eyes on this nightmare of a man.

She went white and stepped backward. Sosibius closed the door behind him (in the same motion silently sliding the bolt) and advanced on her.

She recovered slightly, got herself to a throne and sat down. It was one that was against a side wall, and after unwillingly showing him her profile she had to turn her head rightward to face him. He stood there in his usual mode, perfectly at ease, saying nothing. He bit his left lip and noticed it; it seemed to summon his senses. She did not notice it, nor the sharp knife on his left hip.

"Are you a god?" she asked.

He smiled and remained silent.

"I know you are not," she said. "You do not believe in the gods."

"I believe only in myself. And in you."

"Do not take one step nearer."

He took two, darted out his left hand, and lifted her by the thick hair on her nape. She failed to scream. He put his right hand behind her knees to carry her the rest of the way.

When he could spare both hands, he kept the hair firm with one while he sliced upward through it with the other, so that she barely felt a pull.

A few minutes later, from a dip into weakness deeper than hers, he rose and left her with: "Now a King Sosibius is in you."

Polymela came knocking on the door to tell her that the priest of Alexander had been on an errand, but Berenice did not call her in.

Later she called, and had the maid bring her a certain headdress. "It's in the wicker box," she said, "in the red cabinet." It was

made of wool mixed with a woman's hair, dark brown; it rose
high above the forehead and was parted in the middle and hung
down in front of the shoulders in thick ringlets that were knotted
together at the ends; it had protected the head of perhaps
Arsinoe from the sun.

"Hand it to me," said Berenice, stretching her hand around the
jamb of the door. (But the secret could not be long concealed
from Polymela, who had to know it before night.) Berenice
learned that two messengers awaited her: one being Callimachus,
the other from Syria.

She did not wish to receive either, though the maid added:
"Callimachus says that what he has to say will comfort you. He
dares to say he guesses that you have been disconcerted by a
mistake."

Berenice said she would listen to him tomorrow. She had
some fruit brought to her, saw no one else till the next day, and
from then on wore the scalp-hiding regalia of an Egyptian queen.
In the evening she talked quietly with Polymela, asked her what
more she knew about the bodies of women, asked her to find out
whether the barberess in Eleusis knew more. In the morning she
allowed Callimachus to see her in the ante-room, darkened by
shutters.

Full of what he had to say, he gave no sign of noticing the
change in her habitual costume. He smiled gently at her—he
seemed to have become her father—and she had a surging wish
that she could talk to him as one. But he could not resist enjoying the preamble with which he insisted on preceding his com-
forting explanation:

"May I speak to you about the inscription on the Pharos?"

"I suppose you'll have to."

"Those letters that (if I am right) gave you a shock—they have
all been revealed, because two taps of the chisel brought the rest
of the plaster away before your wishes could be conveyed up
there to the workmen. (I told Sylcon to shout, and he has voice
enough to reach the top of the Pharos, but he considered it
beneath his dignity.) Some were in fear that what would be seen
would be some terrible prophecy, that the king would die or the
Nile run dry. Others were laughing and, I'm afraid, hoping that
it would be something bawdy. Others made other incorrect
assumptions."

"And what was it, Callimachus, what was it?"

"All it is is another name. The inscription now reads:

SOSTRATUS SON OF DEXIPHANES OF CNIDUS
TO THE SAVIOR GODS, FOR THE SAFETY OF SEAFARERS

"Not . . .?"

"Yes, Callimachus, not.   To you I'm a mere frightenable woman. And who was—tell me the name again?"

"Sostratus. He was the architect. He happened to be from Cnidus in Caria, and there is a statue of him, too, there. He built lighthouses for the Coans and the Eretrians; Ptolemy Soter brought him here to build our emperor of lighthouses. He was dead and gone before our—before anybody here aged twenty was born. It would be . . ."

"It would be clever indeed for a schemer of our time to insert his name under the plaster of a monument built two generations ago."

"It certainly would. Sostratus was as clever as a mortal can be: to direct the making of this giddy mountain, the Pharos, so that it should not fall. Yet he was a mere chief artisan. In Greece or Cyrene, he might have been allowed to sign his work, but not in this land of god-kings. In his lifetime he didn't dare to make his name be seen alongside those of the Savior Gods: now we see that he put it there—not merely with theirs but above them— but covered it with thin plaster, knowing that some year, after he was gone, the plaster would weather off."

"Thank you, Callimachus. Thank you for explaining to me about Sostratus son of Dexiphanes. He knew, evidently, about stones and foundations and lead and plaster and storms. He was not to know that his name was similar to that of a scoundrel born after his time."

She seemed to look inward at herself; she was trying to remember that resolution she had once made, to impose on herself a longer pause between the event and her reaction. She said:

"I think I'm only foolish in short bursts. I shall not again be tempted to attribute magic to my enemies. I'm ready to face the news from Syria now."

"It's good news also, I've heard," said Callimachus— "though of course none of us other than yourself can tell except by rumors, which are probably founded on the expressions on couriers' faces."

Ptolemy to Berenice

My queen and goddess (wrote Ptolemy, on a small scroll of papyrus most of which has survived to this day),

Our affairs mostly prosper. I shall tell you the events of the last few days. The fuller reports are being written, and I shall correct them when there's time and they will go into the archives and be the basis of the inscriptions when we return in triumph, but for now this is my report to you, my only queen and governor!

I wrote to you from Tyre, telling you of the progress of our land forces under Anaxalcus and Alcalonus; our navies were far ahead, since our enemies have never had much of a showing on the sea. Parts of the Anatolian coast are still in their hands, but fewer now. A fellow called Aribazus—a Persian, as you can tell from his name—was Laodice's appointee in Cilicia, and he had seized a lot of money—fifteen hundred silver talents—and cached it at Soli and was going to send it to Ephesus for her—

Berenice paused in her reading. Doesn't he remember telling me about Aribazus? Those fifteen hundred talents must be Ptolemy's bribe—wasted. It's true that I have a better head for these things than he has.

—was going to send it to Ephesus for her, and it would have helped her raise more troops. But the men of Soli were having none of that—they're good men, despite their famously bad Greek—and they rose up and grabbed the silver, and my admirals Pythagoras and Aristocles sailed along the coast to Soli and gratefully accepted both the silver and the city for me. Aribazus got away, but only as far as the Cilician Gates, the pass through the Taurus range, and there some other right-thinking men caught him and cut off his head and have brought it to me.

Back at Tyre, we understood from reports like this that our enemies ahead of us were crumbling (Andragoras—I think I told you about him—had done what damage he could and taken to his heels) so we saw it was time to move on more quickly. We assembled as many ships as would be able to get into the enemy's home harbor of Seleuceia, and we went on board at the beginning of the first watch. We sailed along the coast as far as a fortress called Poseideion and anchored there about the eighth hour of that day. At dawn of the next day we sailed from there and reached Seleuceia, the port for Antioch.

The welcome we got! The people of Syria, one and all, loved their true queen and are enraged at the cruel treachery of Laodice and her son. Priests, magistrates, officers, soldiers, laborers, children, they lined the roads, with garlands around their heads, offered sacrifices of thanksgiving at every temple and at makeshift altars in the markets—I could wish you were there to be proud with me.

This was Seleuceia. The next day, leaving as many troops there as were needed to garrison it, we took as many of our other supporters as we could into a smaller number of ships, and sailed up the Orontes. The valley of the Orontes, from Seleuceia to Antioch—those who speak of its beauty are not exaggerating! It is like Greece's Vale of Tempe made larger.

As for Antioch, the reception we found there was even nobler, so much so that I could take thirty lines to list the welcoming committees, the holy images brought out from the temples, the expressions of loyalty. There was some blood on the streets and damage to the walls, since there had been hostilities in and around Antioch until the day before, but our enemies had fled— they've fled to the Anatolian mountains. I had to receive all the expressions of loyalty and take my part in the sacrifices, and as the sun was about to set I immediately went to see my Sister, and after that I had to stay up dealing with all sorts of other matters that required my attention; I've had to give all of today, too, though wearied, to audiences and councils with my advisers and generals. I, if not others, will certainly be informing you later of our decisions. Work opens before me that will make me worthy of you.

Before the last lines of this letter, Berenice burst into tears and flung it from her.

She sobbed for most of an hour, while Polymela at first touched her shoulder, then knelt and embraced her around the waist and, laying head on her lap, wept with her; then went and stood at a window.

Berenice looked up and said: "Why does he lie to me? His sister is dead. She's been killed by a man—some man, called— Andragoras. Or some other of the hairy demons called Men— some *as* or *os* or *es*."

"But Laodice—"

"Be quiet, woman! To See My Sister. Her dead body." She threw her arms around her maidservant. "His sister is dead, why doesn't he say so!"

"Because he can't bear to lose your love."

"He has lost it," shouted Berenice, striding about. "I shall go into the temple of Bast and become a priestess. —No, I shall go back to my own country. I hate cities and I hate kings."

Polymela stood by, eyes cast down, waiting for the wildness to wear off.

At length: "Send again for the chief priest of Alexander," said Berenice. Her cousin's voice seemed to tell her not to mourn, but act. "Wait," and she reached to the shelf for a stylus and a wax tablet and wrote a note and sealed it with her carnelian signet-ring.

Portrait on olivewood

"I know how to be a queen," she told herself; "I have taught myself." Planning the confrontation in the audience room, where she would be two steps above the man, and where she arrived before him, she thought how to make her height greater. There were guards, as usual, in the two doorways at the rear; she told them to stand far enough back that they were out of sight, though they could be called at a word. Then when Sosibius arrived and approached the foot of the steps and made his obeisance, she ordered him to kneel.

To her relief, without a blink he obeyed.

Even on his knees he managed to appear at ease, his body if anything more gracefully erect than if on his feet. He might have allowed the corner of his lip the merest lift on noticing her head-dress, but did not. His arms were folded across his chest, one hand holding the package he had brought.

After maintaining a long silence while looking past the top of his head, Berenice said:

"The Pharos was built before you were born—"

"Gods are not born."

"Never break in on a sentence that I am speaking. You are no immortal. You are a ruffian who will be killed when my husband arrives home."

"Why not now?"

Berenice did not say, Because I know that you still control the men you used to control.

"Perhaps I have a use for you. You were not clever enough to create an inscription before you were born, but you were quick to notice and seize an opportunity."

"Mere chance gave it to me," said Sosibius modestly.

"Yes. And what Fortune takes, she may take back."

"How true. I shall be on my guard against future rolls of the dice."

"Perhaps," said Berenice after what she hoped was a threatening pause, "perhaps it will be advantageous for me to use a clever (if otherwise despicable) man in my management of Egypt. I will shortly explain how. Now give me that."

Sosibius brought the long parcel to his front and began to unwrap the linen covering. "May I stand to hand it to you?"

She nodded, and he stood, finished the unwinding, advanced one foot onto the lower of the two steps, and stretched across the bench to offer up to her: not her hair, but a picture of it.

It was on a long ellipse of wood, a steeply diagonal slice from the trunk of an olive tree. All around, the rough bark remained, like a sloping frame. The sawn grain had been polished flat and sized with gypsum. The colors were rich thick pastes of madder and ochre and chalk and ground lapis in wax, glossy under a lake of gum-arabic varnish.

The tress looked immensely long, as long as it would look in a mirror, though it was half its real length, as in a mirror.

"You had this painting made in one day?"

"No, earlier."

Against a background of deep blue, the golden cascade flowed and rippled and folded over itself. Its filaments folded over each other, like the muscles in the current of a river, or like the lobes and shoals of sand left by the last freshets of winter in the untrodden bed of a desert stream in the first days of the dry season.

Nestled in a curve of the hair, to the left, was the glimpse of a cheek: enough to suggest a female face.

"Who painted it?"

"A pupil of Apelles." (Berenice did not ask any more about

that, fearful of hearing that the use of paints was yet another of the talents of Sosibius.)

"As you can tell," he added boringly. "Only since Apelles has there been that fifth color—that blue; only a follower of Apelles can command the price for that color."

"You may keep it. Go away and bring me what you were told to bring me."

"We may form an alliance, as you have perceived," said Sosibius— "Shall I return to the floor and kneel?"

"By all means."

He did so, but it was a mistake to let him: it had become a bit of stage business, no worse than a private game, and therefore suggesting a kind of intimacy between them. He kept his eyes level, and even this was an impertinence, since they were on her throat, if not lower. She thought, too late, that it would have been better never to let him stand: make him crawl to her, put his chin on the step, stretch out his hand from there to offer her his mocking gift.

"You think," said Berenice, "that by keeping your trophy you have power over me. Let my husband see it, and I fall. But you fall too."

"Yes. So instead we form a compact. As you have suggested. I have a certain power, as you put it, and you have the same power over me." (He did not point out, or need to, the asymmetry: that he could choose the time to make the revelation that would condemn them both.) "So we must stick together. It would be best for us to co-operate and find the reasonable ways to apportion the tasks of ruling Egypt, which is too heavy a burden for you alone. And we would continue in this amicable situation when the son who is to be born is king. I have pictured that he will be called Ptolemy Philometor, the lover of his mother."

"You speak of tasks and of apportioning them. Are they compatible with the function of the Priest of the Cult of Alexander?"

"I interpret that function broadly."

"I don't like the way you talk, Sosibius. Indeed it disgusts me. You are a boy, and you plume yourself on talking as smoothly as an old cynic."

"I'm sorry for that, I will try to be naive."

Berenice allowed herself one of the gaps of deliberate silence to which she was entitled, hoping to think better what to say next; and also to rest—everything in life was seeming to use up her force sooner.

But she had forgotten to instruct Sosibius not to break in on her silences as well as her sentences. "But we must be adults," he said as if it was still his turn to speak, "and plan how to divide our responsibilities—between yourself, and myself, and the noble Dioecetes—so that I can best help him and you. In any case you must soon delegate for a period."

"Give me back my hair."

"It will grow back."

"What you have will wither."

"It will ever remain the famous object that it is, a thing that anyone in this empire will recognize by its beauty. Would recognize, I should say: they will not have the chance, it will remain a treasure safely hidden who knows where."

"How many women are there in Egypt?"

"One hundred and fifty myriads—including little ones," he replied promptly, as if he knew.

"And do you think it likely that there are no women with hair more beautiful than mine?"

"If there are, it is black, and they are peasants, so no one has a thought for them."

"*I* have a thought for them. —You can have this picture back, anyway."

"Don't you want it? It is almost as beautiful as the original. It could be made still more so, to be sure: I would prefer to see a swan-like neck and back represented there instead of those silly stars."

"Let there be a limit to your impertinence. Take this or I will throw it," and she found that it had what might be a handle on its reverse side. A sort of multiple loop had been loosely attached to the wood by two copper staples, but could not be for hanging the picture, being vertical.

"Be careful not to break it, if you please. It's something else that I brought for you, a *skutalê*-message. Shall I show it to you?"

Disdainfully she handed back the picture, and he removed the thing and uncoiled it. It seemed at first to be a mere string. It was a strip of fawn-colored leather, not much more than a finger wide, but so long that to hold it straight he had to stretch out both arms. Ink marks were scattered along it, at least two hundred of them, but they were not letters: they were short lines, mostly straight, sloping left or right, some touching each other, and running to one or other of the strip's edges.

"You have the king's copy of the *skutalê*, there," said Sosibius, pointing. And there was, among the paraphernalia on shelves in a bay of the wall behind her, a round wooden staff, about as long as a forearm.

"May I ask you to hand it to me, or shall I step there and fetch it out?"

"Fetch it," said Berenice, keeping her eyes straight ahead as he stepped past her, so as to deny her fear that he would strike her with the stick. She was uncomfortable at the thought of his head passing above hers and looking down ironically on her wig.

He took the stave and stepped back to the floor in front of her and carefully wound the strip around it, spirally, so that one edge fitted to the other all the way along. This took some care, and he sat down cross-legged on the floor so as to handle stave and strip on his lap, and Berenice had to wait. She tried not watching him, and then watching him with a contemptuous air, and then, since he was not aware either of her eyes or of her contempt, just watching him. He stood up and, keeping his fingers around the stave's two ends so as to retain the wound strip tightly in place, held it out level so that Berenice could see the result.

The message had been written along the strip by the sender when it was wound around his copy of the *skutalê*, and then unwound for sending, so that nobody could read it; it had been stuffed into couriers' pouches like a mere jumble of string. Anybody into whose hands it had fallen would have made nothing of its little marks, unless he knew of this old method invented by the Spartans for sending secret commands to their generals in the field; and even then, he would have had to know the exact diameter to which to plane a length of wood. Rewound now, around the receiver's stave, it showed all its little marks reconnected into two lines of letters:

> ANAXALCUS, AT ANTIOCH, TO THE DIOECETES: THE KING WILL NOT
> RETURN UNTIL HE HAS AVENGED HIS SISTER. A YEAR AT LEAST, I THINK.
> DO NOT YET TELL THE QUEEN.

Berenice looked at the words and thought about them. The two little lines above the bridge of her nose slightly deepened.

"This message is for Sylcon, not you," she said.

"Yes, I have borrowed it from him."

"Be sure you return it to him before he discovers he has lent it. You already owe one debt too many."

Sosibius laughed delightedly. How he enjoyed talking with her!

"He does not know yet that he has even received it. I thought you had the right to see it before him."

But Berenice seemed already to be thinking of something else—she had sunk into a contemplation—and he realized sympathetically that she did not feel the same pleasure as he in their repartee or in the discussion of their roles in the stage-play that was the handling of Egypt. She was moving on her throne in a way that showed discomfort; was more than ready to be rid of him. "Did I forget to draw in my breath?" she was thinking. "I have not prevailed."

"You are distressed," he said, with every appearance of fellow-feeling. "Another year, at least, of a lonely task. Your Advisors are made of wood. Or of papyrus. You and I are made of flesh and soul." She said nothing, so he went on. "We do not have to go into details now. I am sure you will let me know when you are ready to discuss them. I merely put it to you that this will be—because of your presence at the head of it—no cynical arrangement. I want to see that things are done in your spirit. Egypt will be a happier land under our reforms. I shall pay attention to the hundred and fifty myriad peasant women of Egypt, and their husbands and children. You have recently seen some of the villages, I believe, and the thin men toiling in the fields, with aching backs and blistered hands and cloths over their heads to keep off the sun and the flies. We die at eighty; they die at thirty. Do you know that of what they harvest they have to give a full third to you in taxes? Do you know that the priesthoods, such as mine, own half of the ten thousand villages of Egypt, and keep all those taxes for themselves? Your predecessor did much for the public good, but I perceive that your ideals go deeper than libraries and canals and lighthouses. My part of our bargain will include the enforcement of Coptolemy's Law."

"How do you know of that? I haven't talked about my notion with anybody."

"You must have forgotten mentioning it to someone close to you. And I can learn everything. That is why I can carry out such policies for you; you simply cannot, despite your most ardent and humane intentions. And I am honest about this. I doubt we shall ever achieve a constitution for Egypt along the Cyrenaican lines, but I really will see to it that Coptolemy's Law is observed in our time—whatever it costs me in laughter, and however inconsistent my friends may think it with what they know of me. They also know, some of them to their cost, that continual surprises are to be expected of me."

"You have friends?"

"It's my word for people who have had dealings with me."

She looked at him almost dreamily. Did she purely hate him or did she add a trace of pity to the mustard of hatred?

"But do you believe me?" he said, beautifully earnest.

"I can't tell by looking at you and your lizard eyes. You're an actor and not much more. But I think you're right that I should have to leave you to do it, and myself to keeping a watch on you and finding out whether you're doing it, which I think you'll find I am able to do quite well."

"You are the perfect queen, quite possibly the first such in the world, and I mean that, too, sincerely. And how is the patient?"

"I don't know whether he will live, but his bones have been set after a fashion and he has recovered some use in his limbs."

"I'm glad to hear of it."

"Leave now, Sosibius son of Dioscurides, before you make me vomit." And, using a backhand flick, she flung the picture at his heels.

Violence among the books

I have jumped (thought Berenice) from a little country to a great one, yet am cooped in a lesser space.

She had been accustomed to walking around Cyrene unencumbered by guardians other than a companion or two; and riding her horse out through the town gates into the high farmland. That could not be done at Alexandria. She had to stay in her palace, except for excursions that were more like military campaigns. And even then, when she rode out surrounded by attendants, Polymela reproached her: "You are not as careful of your baby as you should be. And it's too hot for you"—the noon sun was now almost overhead. So she had ceased to ride out.

Only within the palace could she move with something like her old freedom. With its wide corridors, its courtyards and gardens, it was vast enough to be a world. Yet it had not cocooned her against the violence of the world outside. A spear in Cyrene, war in Syria, violation inside this palace— "I am the one" (she reproached herself) "who let all these Furies in."

"No, you are not," said Polymela. "None of them was your fault."

"The violence of my impulses lies behind them."

"How did any impulse of yours cause the war? The cause of that is Laodice."

"But what about the man?" murmured Berenice. Only with her maid did she recur to the subject—the subject of either man. "There were good things about him. Was killing him the only way? It is for that I am being punished." So Polymela knew it was *that* man she was referring to. Berenice could not now remember how she had managed to do it, could not even remember the angle at which she had held the spear. But she felt still the horror that had come with—instead of preceding and preventing—the driving of the spear, and thus she found the way to blame herself for things that followed. Another time she might say, of the other man: "There is nothing good about *him*—*he* is the one I should have speared—but I called him a god." Though she talked of these things with no one but the maid, she felt others talking with their eyes every time they looked at her.

If she had to be penned, it should at least be somewhere safe. And this was part of why she spent so much of her day in the bookish calm of the Museion. Here too, as within the rest of the palace, seeing only people she had seen the day before, she did not have to brave the eyes of people seeing her for the first time in her Egyptian wig.

"People looking at me"—it was brought in on her, as never before, that the life she had been born to was different. At her, people had always looked (she did not have the vanity to think it was because she was beautiful), and she had never cared, she had been brought up to it. But now it felt like a siege that she was helpless to escape.

The palace spread through a quarter of the city, and the Museion spread through a third of the palace—Ptolemy Soter, its founder, had granted it space, and Ptolemy Philadelphus had granted it more and had made it into more (less, grumbled the religious) than other Temples of the Muses: it was a university. Berenice knew many even of the students by name, and of the great scholars she was able to chat familiarly with the two who were generally held to be the most eminent—Callimachus and Eratosthenes—because they both, like her, were from Cyrene.

When at last someone had enough effrontery to say to her: "I am surprised that you hide your hair," it was Eratosthenes, and she was able to make the reply she had prepared: "I am tired of people looking at it. They look at it instead of at me."

She had encountered him in the great corridor, which led past the ends of the library's nine courtyards. After some more conversation she said to him: "I divert you from your duties!"

"Any man in Egypt," he replied gallantly, "if you were to deign to stop and exchange words with him, would be not just obligated but delighted."

But Eratosthenes was genuinely happy to be interrupted; in fact he was not discernibly busy, but was himself strolling the corridor of his Museion with his hands behind his back and his smile—a smile that was neither permanent nor automatic, but slightly sad and the more likable for that. His face was of the lucky kind of which Berenice instantly thought "Likable!" It was something to do with the sags under his eyes, the honest weight of his nose—but could likableness be built into the proportions of a face, did it not have to be etched by a lifetime of amiability?—and had he lived long enough for that? He was a generation younger than Callimachus. His hair was only beginning to be flecked with gray. The black of his hair wanted to be called blue, though not especially dark—not the blue-black of the abyss, *kuaneos*—nor of course the blue-green, *kuanos*, of a sea-god's hair.

"I realize," said Berenice, "that I didn't complete my plan of interviewing the principal officials of the land. I was investigating them—the inspector of drains, the Guardian of the Tombs, everyone from the Dioecetes down—so as to teach myself about the bureaucracy. But I had forgotten the Director of the Museion, perhaps because I see him every day. Would you say that your Museion is a branch of government?"

"I would," said Eratosthenes, "and the late king and queen certainly gave me to understand that they considered it so, when they invested me in this office. So do please investigate me!"

"The difficulty with that," said Berenice, "is that I can't summon you to my presence, because you are already in it, nor can I make a surprise descent on your establishment when you are not in it, because you are always in it (as am I); also that there is nothing to investigate, because you are so obviously trustworthy. I have no hard questions to ask you!"

"Really? What about the stealing of the books?"

"Oh, I know that half the library's books can be called stolen—I know the story of the cheating of the Athenians out of their classics, and the confiscating of all books that come into the port on ships. But these are white thefts—they are for the building of the best of libraries. Aren't there any other scandals?"

"Well, don't you want to ask me, or someone, why it is that I am Musarch and not my teacher, the great Callimachus?"

"Yes, I've wondered about that. Why?"

"I don't really know—perhaps you can find out for me by your investigations behind my back. I was a student under Callimachus. So was Apollonius; he and I were both Callimachus's students. He had many students, and we were all proud to study under him. At the death of Zenodotus, I certainly expected that the turn had come for our master Callimachus. But instead Apollonius gained the post. Callimachus could not abide this; he could not live and work here among the books as subordinate to the other poet who had been his pupil. You may have heard of their feud, as bitter as only a quarrel between poets can be, and that the strength of Callimachus's . . ."

"Spite? Envy?"

"The strength of Callimachus's reputation was such that it was Apollonius who retreated—got out, fled to Rhodes without even remembering to tender his resignation to the king. And then the trustees recommended me! Me, another student of Callimachus. I declined, pointed out to them, as if they couldn't see, what would happen—but it did not happen. The king appointed me, almost by force, and Callimachus seemed as pleased as everyone else and applauded me at the ceremony! Can you explain that?"

Berenice looked at him and saw that he appeared honestly puzzled.

"I have never understood it and I sometimes wonder whether I could undo it. I can only think it was because although I too dabble in poetry I hadn't composed a long 'Tale of the Argonauts', or talked as if I knew better than him about his own poetry. To this day I know that he is a scholar of higher standing than I am."

"Do you really think so? And do you and he work tolerably together?"

"Very much so. —May we sit down by this fountain?— All of us here are learned heads and creative spirits, Muse-bitten—we can't stop ourselves continually making more things on papyrus—but we go about it in different ways. I'm the kind that picks some book off a shelf, glances into it, notices something interesting, hurries off to my writing-desk to use it, putting the scroll down somewhere that I forget—or, worse, shoving it back onto the wrong shelf. I'm lucky that my great predecessor Zenodotus set up this system that we have, classifying everything under the nine Muses, arranging the authors under the twenty-four letters, and hiring us this staff of drones whom you see busy with their wheelbarrows, carrying scrolls back to their right places. I am left shamefully free to spin a poem here, a geographical treatise there. That's why they call me 'Beta': they say I'm second in every subject, first in none."

"No!"

"Yes, they do, I know—the students have told me! But Callimachus is the kind that keeps everything in order. He wants to finish every little thing perfectly, and before starting on the next. He perfects them, one after another, and proceeds to the next. And so he has done a great deal in his long life (not as much as some, such as Didymus 'Bronze-Guts', who has written four thousand books—but to more effect). And Callimachus runs the library for me in the same way. Yes, though he's not the Librarian, he doesn't mind; he's the Library Cataloguer. He's the one who has done the essential work, nine-tenths of all the work that is done here, compiling his *Pinakes*, his 'Tables', which take up a hundred and twenty scrolls—five times as many as the *Iliad!* They are the list of all the authors and books there are. All the books in the world are in this library, and they are all compressed into Callimachus's catalogue. Only because of that can researchers find the books they want to find (researchers, that is, with Callimachus-minds rather than Eratosthenes-minds). He hasn't quite written all those thousands of entries himself; he drills his army of student scribes to do it; but he is always looking over their shoulders and almost guiding their pens."

"He still works as hard as this?" Berenice was surprised, partly because Callimachus himself whenever she saw him seemed fairly affable and relaxed—if it were not for being beside Eratosthenes, one would have called him an affable and relaxed man—and partly because he was more than seventy years old.

"Yes, he does. The *Pinakes* have constantly to be revised and enlarged—whole scrolls scrapped and written again, usually as two scrolls. But Callimachus keeps working smoothly. I think he does it merely by planning his day: Callimachus, unlike my wayward self, plans his day. Oh how he plans his day!"

"That's a hint," said Berenice— "no, don't protest—that I have taken enough of your own time," and Eratosthenes got up and bowed. "You have none of your attendants with you?" he remarked.

"Surely I don't need them for safety in your library!" she replied, and went on her way in search of a book (Eratosthenes would probably not have been able to tell her which of the nine Muses to find it under).

Next afternoon she came back to ask the Musarch something else. She made first for the room he worked in, though not expecting him to be there; it was a pleasant room in a small tower, with wide board floor and wide window looking north toward the sea. At the foot of the staircase stood a janitor, holding a stave horizontally in front of himself. The sight gave Berenice a shudder of memory: the soldier with the spear. As she approached from his left, the janitor did not instantly see who she was, and made, as he turned toward her, a barring-the-way gesture with his stave—then went down on his knee to ask pardon.

"What's the matter?" said Berenice. "Is access to Master Eratosthenes forbidden?"

"Yes, your majesty—but not of course to yourself. He is not to be disturbed—but he'll have to let himself be disturbed by you."

"What's the reason? Is he ill?" (Or something more interesting?—with a female student?—with a police interrogator?)

"I don't understand exactly, your majesty; he's in his room with barley-beer and a tray of nuts and two students; he's said he's not to be disturbed all of today. They're doing a tricky work of some kind. —But I'll go up and disturb them for you."

"No, don't. Stay where you are." She walked on. Well, a chance to spy into the Library without the Librarian's guidance. Not that there was anything more to find except more of the nine

Muses—two or three more of the cloistered courtyards, with their book-bays around them, that she had not yet idled in.

She rounded a corner into the hall of Urania, the Muse of Astronomy, and almost collided with a ladder. (And beyond it, at the same instant, she saw something else surprising: a hole, dug in the middle of the couryard, and a long pole lying beside it. But there was no time to wonder about that: the collision with the ladder came first.) The nearest bay at the beginning of the left side of the cloister was not really supposed to be a book-bay, it was just a shallow architectural feature, but the books on astronomy had multiplied so much that odd spaces like this had been pressed into use; moreover, as in so many other places, shelves had been added to such a height that the shelvers could reach them only by ladder. And this shelver—a tubby girl whom Berenice thought she recognized—had set the twelve-foot ladder too close in, perhaps to leave room for those walking around the corner, more likely out of mere lack of instinctual physics; and there she was, up at the top, with a load of scrolls in one arm as she held the topmost rung with the other. "Look out!" yelled Berenice—

The fat girl, looking back over her shoulder, was on the wrong side of her center of gravity—and here she came, and the ladder with her!

Newly sharpened steel

A more cautious queen, especially one concerned for the new life in her belly, would have leaped back to safety, but Berenice, daughter of Magas, pulled in her breath and stepped to position and held up her palms stiffly above her face.

On her palms the girl's buttocks stopped—heavily. The ladder was arrested and tottered back onto the safer side of vertical; Berenice staggered, almost kept her feet—almost—had to totter away one and a half steps and crumple at knees and hips. She sprawled on the floor, her wig came off, the scrolls scattered; the girl sat, on Berenice and on one of the scrolls, which cracked open with a clean pop.

Berenice extricated herself and got to her feet, grabbing her wig in the same motion. She had a nervous hand to it as the girl, still sitting, said: "You're the queen!" but took her eyes away; she had not noticed the shorn hair—was perhaps short-sighted. "Thank you," she added grumpily, and on the second attempt got up, to make her curtsey.

"And you—you're the student of Conon the astronomer, aren't you?—Theonida?"

"No, mam. My name is Phyllis, daughter of Agacles. I study in the department of the Muse Terpsichore."

"So you study poetry—not astronomy?"

"Yes. The lyric and the dance."

"Then why—ah, you shelve books. This one is broken, I'm afraid." Berenice stepped over (rubbing a bruised hip) and picked it up. It had cracked along one of the joins between its pages, but its tab still hung across its end.

"'Eudoxus of Cnidus—On the Higher Spheres.'"

Berenice burst into reckless laughter.

The girl's face!—still grumpy—Berenice laughed again—would she have to explain?—that made it funnier still! "Fell to earth while reaching for the stars"—of course she couldn't explain. The girl managed a dutiful laugh, a grumpy laugh—could a laugh be grumpy? Suddenly Berenice was annoyed with her. "Is there a Muse of Laughter?" she asked sharply.

"Mam?"

"I was wondering where the books on humor are shelved. You have brought me close to seeing why some things make us laugh, which I think not even Aristotle succeeded in explaining. Things must come patly together—the stars and your ladder—and somebody must be hurt—in this instance, you." (She noticed that the part about her own wig did not seem to her funny in the least.) "Well, never mind. Lead on."

"Where do you want me to lead you to, *basilissa?*"

"I'm sorry—sit down, Phyllis." She guided the girl over to one of the tables out in the cloister, where the sun still slanted in. (They went widely around the hole and the fallen pole, temporarily careful of further accidents.) "Are you hurt? I was thinking of going around and about in the Library with someone who knows it, but there's really no need to walk around. Sit down beside me. You do this work and you're also a student?"

"Yes, both, like all the others. We get taught by our teachers in the morning, and in the afternoon we find books or shelve them or mend them or write labels, or paste pages together for making new scrolls, and in the evening we read and write, and have our supper all together with the scholars in the hall." Phyllis was now sitting up proudly; she didn't even have a bruised hip.

"The Museion is a fine place to work in?"

"It certainly is. We have weeks when we cook and sweep and catch the rats, but we don't mind."

"I'd like you to tell me any complaints you have. Anything you've seen that is wrong. You will be absolutely safe, I shall not—"

"Complaints, your majesty?" said Phyllis angrily. "How should I have complaints? I've been here eight months, and I still can't believe I'm not in the Elysian Fields. There are only three girls here—and I'm one of them! I was born in the poorest street in Eleusis. I had to fight for a place here against a rich girl whose father slipped a bribe to the teacher—I saw him—but I recited my *Hymn to Demeter* perfectly and the teacher took me. My father has to pay nothing, I get my food, and when I've finished I'll become a teacher myself and live the rest of my life here, reading and talking—I shall read Aristotle too—paid a salary without tax—do you know how much tax everyone outside here has to pay, even my poor father? Living here, there's always someone to talk with, it's like being still at school and playing with friends." She stood up. "I'll take you to my teacher, Copilaeus of Cos. All the teachers here (except the one) are fine."

Berenice had to hurry after her—wanting to ask about "The one?" but the girl was already in the next courtyard, and as soon as she found Copilaeus of Cos, who was on a stone bench in the cloister of Terpsichore, clipping his toenails with a small blade while reading a work by Demetrius of Phaleron—he had the scroll drooping in balanced halves over his right knee, his left heel up on the bench close in front of him, the clippings falling on the ground or on his sandal—she said: "The queen is not sure that this is the best library in the world."

Copilaeus was a wizened man whom nothing could surprise. He reintroduced his toes into his sandal, stood up and bowed.

"It is in a sense the first and only Library," he said reflectively. "It is certainly larger than all that may have been before, perhaps larger than all others put together—and I include our rivals in Pergamum. I'm not sure that largeness is all—but largeness we have. King Ptolemy Soter wanted *all* books, much as his friend

Alexander wanted *all* lands; and king Ptolemy Philadelphus did it. He sent out book-buyers to places that even Alexander's armies hadn't been to. He may have spent more money on books than on ships. It is something to have all books in the world, in all languages. Most of them are Greek, but we have here all the books of the Egyptians, the Chaldaeans, the Persians, the Judaeans, and are translating them into Greek. This is the world's memory."

"But largeness is not all?" said Berenice.

"The library that was the start of this was Aristotle's. We managed, by hook and crook, to inherit it. It was one man's collection, and he and his friends could use it. The library of the king of Pergamum is the king's library, and so were the libraries that they say the kings of the Assyrians had. But this library has open doors. Not, of course, open to the street, but into the rest of the Museion. It is for the use of us, scholars and students."

"I begin to see how lucky we are to be in it."

"Yes, we hardly know how lucky we are. Perhaps there will be an age when people will look back and think 'I would love to have been there, to see how it was in the Library of Alexandria.'"

"Why, do you think it won't last for ever?"

"Well, it may, but there are such things as mice and booklice and other misfortunes that Pandora released into the world—wars and fires and earthquakes. The kings of Assyria had a library, and Cyaxares the Mede burned it, and the Persians had a library in their palace, and Alexander burned it. Their books were of clay, so perhaps they still lie baked harder and hidden in the ruins, but our books are of papyrus. If someone who didn't care for them were to use them as kindling, they could keep the four thousand baths of Alexandria heated for five months."

"These are gloomy thoughts," said Berenice. "What were you reading?"

"It's Demetrius of Phaleron, *On Style*—perhaps it's what started me thinking gloomily. He was the poor fellow who founded this library. He was a pupil of Aristotle, but he got into politics and had to flee from Athens; he came here, and he suggested the library to king Ptolemy, but he fell out of favor and took poison. He was a literary critic, and he quotes passages from poets, and I've noticed that some of them I've never seen anywhere else. This one of Sappho:

Espere panta pherôn osa phainolis eskedas' auôs

phereis oin, phereis aiga, phereis apu materi paida—
Star of the Evening, all you bring back
that radiant Morning has scattered:
the sheep you bring back, the goat you bring back,
the child you bring back to its mother.

"Demetrius quotes it as an example of 'charming repetition', and if he hadn't done that we would never know she had written it."

"I have a copy of Sappho," said Berenice, "I thought I had seen that little poem."

"Perhaps you are right.   Fetch Sappho, Phyllis," said her teacher.

Phyllis went into the book-bay, and Berenice turned and peered after her, anxious that there should be no ladder. But this bay had no more than five shelves up its walls, and Phyllis began to rummage among the scrolls in the division marked with a Sigma. Copilaeus turned and watched her ironically.

"There are too many under Sigma," she muttered. "Simonides, Stesichorus, Semonides of Samos . . .   They should be sorted Sigma-Alpha, Sigma-Iota, as well."

"There aren't as many of them as that," said Copilaeus, and winking at Berenice he said: "It's reassuring, isn't it, when a girl can't find Sappho?   —Phyllis," he said, "you forget something I told you: Sappho spelled her own name with a Psi: Psappho."

Phyllis went to the Psi section and found Sappho, shelved in this pedantic way.

Sappho was opened across the scholar's lap, with Berenice holding the beginning of the scroll as the rest was unrolled, and they scanned through, much quicker than Berenice could read: Copilaeus was one of those who could take in a page at a glance. They came to the last short poem and Copilaeus let the scroll roll itself back up. "Not there," he said, and sent Phyllis with Sappho back to her shelf. Berenice said: "Why did you say it's good when a girl can't find Sappho?"

"Impure," he said, "is what they called her; a 'tribad'. Impure! Her lyre is the purest that ever played. I'm glad for my colleagues that most of them have risen above worrying about whatever she may have done with her body and have almost worshipped her. She lived so long ago—almost as far back as Homer. They didn't mind her Lesbian dialect—they weren't prejudiced against dialects as now, when everyone wants to speak just one kind of Greek. Of course there are some who sneer at her; Porphyrio calls her 'Masculine Sappho'; he expected only men to write poetry. He says she was ugly, dark-complexioned, small; according to Socrates she was beautiful, but I think he meant the beauty of her lyrics." (Phyllis had come back and was listening.) "The poets of her time, Alcaeus and Anacreon and Archilochus and Hipponax, admired her so much that people think they all loved her. Solon after hearing one of her songs said 'Teach me it so I can die.' Antipater of Sidon called her the Muse on Earth, reproached the Fates for not making her immortal. Someone else (I forget who) said 'No day will ever dawn that does not speak the name of Sappho.' They're always quoting her for her 'Sapphic' metres, and the plectrum and the *pêctis* lyre that she invented, and the Mixolydian mode, the most moving kind of music; and for points of grammar, and just points of excellence. Dionysius of Halicarnassus uses her as the example of the 'smooth, soft, musically fitted' use of words. And she says more than the words say. Did you notice that last epigram?—Phyllis, bring Sappho back."

Sappho was brought back, and unrolled to her last poem, or at any rate the last in this scroll: "Sappho's," it was headed, "Written on an Urn."

> *Timados hade konis, tan dê pro gamoio thanousan*
>   *dexato Phersephonas   kuaneos thalamos:*
> *has kai apophthimenas pasai neothagi sidarô*
>   *halikes himertan   kratos ethento koman.*

The dust of Timas, this. She died
Before she could become a bride.
The dark house of Persephone received her.
With newly-sharpened steel the girls
Cut from their heads the lovely curls,
Each proving how the loss of Timas grieved her.

"You see," said the scholar, "how she makes words work twice. 'The blue-black bridal chamber of Persephone received her'—that is of course the underworld, but it is also the House of the Virgin, one of the Houses in the sky—the constellation of the Virgin, who was Persephone, who before she was taken down to be queen of the underworld was called Koré, the Maiden. Sappho is telling us that poor young Timas died when the sun was in the sign of Virgo."

"Well, perhaps so," said Berenice, uncomfortably—still wondering whether her own shortened hair had been noticed.

The width of the world

She rose to her feet. The literary discussion had been long
enough and she had ceased to enjoy this scholar and his over-
teacherly conversation. He bowed to her and, since the girl
Phyllis went away with the queen, he had to replace the books
on the shelves himself; later he found the scrolls that she had left
scattered on the floor, muttered angrily, and loaded them back in
the wheelbarrow.

Phyllis stuck with the queen, anxious to be seen in her
company as they made their way down the length of the library.
But the cloisters, earlier busy with readers, were now surprisingly empty, even though the midsummer sun had not yet left the
tops of their walls. The nine cloisters lay down a slight northward slope, so that the wide narthex or connecting corridor that
ran past their ends descended from the level of each cloister to
the next—not by steps, but by a ramp, for the sake of the wheelbarrows in which books were moved. The library had been laid
out on this plan at the order of Ptolemy Soter, and since fully
seven of the nine Muses represented branches of poetry—Calliope of the epic, Melpomene of tragedy, and so on—librarian
Zenodotus had had trouble forcing into them the mass of books,
which he more practically divided into Prose of various kinds,
and Poetry. And after that, as the collection grew, even the nine
cloisters had not been enough, and storage rooms, as well as
offices, had been added to the left of the corridor, and finally a
"Daughter Library" for citizens to use, out in the town on the Serapeion hill. There were, among the left-of-corridor departments,
locked rooms for books and pictures too indecent to be viewed
by any but the king or the chief librarian; and rooms that did not
contain books or pictures at all, but curiosities—gigantic bones
found in the desert, shells coiled like rams' horns, Nubian carv-
ings, treasures that looked as if they might have come (if anyone
had asked) from the tombs of kings older than the Ptolemies.

The library's topmost cloister belonged to Calliope, Muse of
the epic, not, as might have been expected, to Urania of astronomy; she lay next down. As Berenice and her dogged companion
descended the corridor, they saw a small crowd on its lowest
level: that was where everyone had gone. They had gathered in
front of two young students, one of whom (Philenor) was jabbing
his finger at a square board held up by the other (Theonida);

something was marked or pinned on it which—since they were facing away from her—Berenice could not see.

The students had made some announcement and were excitedly trying to answer questions. "No, *two hundred* and fifty-two thousand! . . . No, not diameter—circumference! . . . How?—well, let's begin again—hold it up, Theonida—this is the well, or, as we should say, let this be the well, and let this be the pole, and this is the sunlight, falling straight down the hole, and this is another ray parallel to the other one, so this is the shadow of the pole . . ."

The listeners, a not uncultivated group, were not scoffing, but were divided between the perplexed and the skeptical. "Why Syene? . . . Would another well do? . . . How does he know how far? . . . Is the well as deep as the pole? . . . The pole couldn't be that high! . . ."

A man, issuing from an open door at the corridor's side, strode up behind Theonida, removed the board from her hand, and said brusquely: "Don't trouble trying to explain it to these. I will explain it in writing, in my own time. —Well, for now I will explain it adequately. Since *this* is perpendicular to the circle, and *this* is parallel to *this*, then *this* angle is equal to *this* angle; hence if this angle is known—which it is from the relation of *this* to this—and *this* distance is known, then this distance must be to the whole circumference as this angle is to the circle; hence the circumference is known. That is it, in brief. You must excuse me, we've been working all day and I deserve my supper."

Berenice, seeing him from the back, did not see him as the amiable Eratosthenes until one of "these" interjected: "At least, Eratosthenes, show your diagram to those behind you." And Eratosthenes, sensing what was meant, turned, bowed, and made as gracefully as he could the transition to the Eratosthenes who addressed his superiors.

"Queen Berenice," he said, "will certainly understand. May I explain what we have discovered?"

"Please do," she replied without moving nearer.

"I have determined, your majesty, the size of the world. It is two hundred and fifty-two thousand stadia around."

Berenice did not say anything, though her lips parted slightly; the mouth of the girl Phyllis, standing behind her, dropped wide enough to show her tongue.

He repeated: "Two hundred and fifty-two thousand stadia! At last we know this, which has never till now been known. The size of this thing we live on!"—he stamped his foot on it. "This will shine among the intellectual achievements for which your and your husband's reign will be for ever celebrated." Still holding the board in one hand, he was holding out his half-circled arms as if to embrace the whole round world, as if that was the way he had measured it—an unfortunate gesture that made her wonder whether he had noticed her own growing girth.

"I can understand your pride," she said. "I would certainly like you to explain this discovery."

"I shall be honored if you will appoint a time!"

"Well, my curiosity is as much stirred as that of these people, and I should like you to explain it a little more fully, for them as well as for me."

"With pleasure!" exclaimed Eratosthenes, without further thought of his supper. "How to begin?"

He gazed at his diagram, which showed a large circle, a hole sticking into it, a pole sticking out of it nearby, an arrow pointing straight down the hole, a parallel arrow pointing from the top of the pole to intersect the circle.

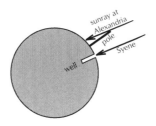

"I learned," he said, "that there is at Syene a deep well down which, on one day in the year and one day only, the sun at noon shines all the way to the bottom. I'd like to say I learned of this from some traveler stepping off the boat, but I learned it from one or other of the pamphlets I was browsing. Was it just a travelers' anecdote, a mere curiosity even if true? I realized that it means more (if true). It means that on that one day, which has to be the day of mid-summer, when the sun climbs farthest north in the sky, it is in the zenith—that is, overhead—at Syene. Which must be the northernmost place where it can be overhead.

"I thought about it, and I drew myself a sketch like this one.

"I had to wait, till after the midsummer of last year, to receive from Syene the report I had asked for, and it's true. (I could have made the journey to Syene, you will say, but I would rather not, especially at midsummer—you feel how much hotter it is here than in Greece, and at Syene the sun really is overhead.) There is such a well, on an island in the river, and the sun does at midsummer shine down it. For several noons it touches the water at the bottom, but on that one day its full circle fits the circle of the water. Then I had twelve months to carry out my measurement, and to wait till the midsummer day of this year, which was yesterday, to make the final measurement.

"From Alexandria here at the north end of Egypt, it's a straight line south to Syene at the south end of Egypt. How lucky that the land of Egypt is a linear land, north-south. It's the easiest country in the world to survey, it's the only land whose population has been counted, you could measure it with a string (though that's not, of course, how I measured it).

"I had to wait till the next year's day of summer solstice, which was yesterday, and I measured the noon shadow of that pole that you may have noticed I planted in the courtyard of Urania. When I say I, I mean that I and these two students of mine did the digging and measuring and calculating. If the sun were to pass overhead here, the shadow of the pole would shrink to nothing at noon—and the world would be flat. But at noon the pole still had, as we knew it would, a short shadow. The world is round. My pole is ten cubits high, and we measured the shadow as one cubit and twenty-six hundredths of a cubit, and made our calculation from that—and our calculation matched what we had already measured more easily: we had marked the end of the shadow, and taken the pole out of its hole and laid it on the ground at a right-angle to where the shadow had been, and stretched a string from the end of the shadow to the end of the pole; and yes, the angle between the string and the pole was seven degrees *and one fifth* of a degree. And that means that the sun was seven degrees and one fifth of a degree from being overhead. (That, as it happens, is one fiftieth of a full circle.) So the distance all around the world must be to the distance from here to Syene as three hundred and sixty degrees are to seven degrees and a fifth."

He paused and looked around at the listeners; clearly he

thought they now had all they needed to do the calculation them-selves. Nodding encouragingly, he said: "Seven and a fifth degrees to three hundred and sixty degrees is five thousand and forty stadia to: *two hundred and fifty-two thousand stadia!* That's the answer! That's the circumference of the world!"

Two hundred and fifty-two thousand stadia.

"How beautiful," exclaimed Eratosthenes of Cyrene, "how beautiful to know how vast it is! And seven and one-fifth degrees is one fiftieth of the circle of three hundred and sixty degrees, so the way from here to Syene, the whole length of Egypt, is just one fiftieth of the way around the world! The vastness and the beauty reward us for all the work we have been doing all yesterday and today, these two and I, putting together all those figures to fix that one necessary figure that made it possible—that makes it just as possible for you, by pure thought, to find it all out—the distance from here to Syene."

"But," said Berenice, "did you tell us that—and how you knew it—how many was it?—from here to Syene?"

"Oh!" said Eratosthenes, "I apologize: yes, the essential figure, I did mention it but I forgot to lay stress on it: it's—"

"It's known to be five thousand stadia," said a professor of geography. "He used that."

"No," said Eratosthenes, "if I had just used 'what people know', I would have made the world two thousand stadia too small. From here to Syene is five thousand *and forty* stadia. Exactly. That's the essential figure. That and the angle, here at Alexandria, are all we need. With them you could have per-formed the calculation yourselves."

"And how did you know that?" asked another professor— "you say you had already measured it, the distance to Syene—how? How did you find it out more exactly than 'what people know'— if you did? Did you stretch a string? Did you crawl along it with a cubit-stick?"

"I sent chained walkers."

"Chained walkers . . ."

"Yes, men walking all the stages of the way, counting their paces, with chains between their ankles. It's their reports we've been putting together, and correcting for their different strides, and comparing with the Record Office surveys and all their tri-angles so as to correct for all the bends in the road. I did have to pay nearly a talent out of the Museion's budget. But wasn't it worth it for finding out how large the world is?"

Berenice, at least, thought it was worth it. A ball two hundred and fifty-two thousand stadia around. She had learned that great fact, and another—the difference between a view downward and a view upward.

"I am afraid there is some great error," said the professor of geography. "Your world is three or four times too large."

"Why do you think that?" demanded Musarch Eratosthenes, a hint of his haughtiness returning.

"We know," said the professor, "that the Pillars of Heracles are near the end of the world in one direction, and that Alexander when he marched to India marched almost to the end in the other direction, and those are both no more than thirty thousand stadia away."

"You have not yet learned," said Eratosthenes, "the difference between 'what men know' and what I know. There is much beyond those 'ends of the world'. The outer ocean must be wide, wider than all lands put together, or perhaps there are even lands beyond it. Alexander would be disheartened to know how much more remained to be conquered."

Letter on Sappho

When Berenice regained the solitude of her bedroom she took Sappho from the little closet in the wall and looked for the "Timas" lament. Sappho she quite often dipped into, but didn't read through—Sappho was not to be read through: after reading a poem of hers one lingered and mused. In this copy too the poem was the last in the scroll. That she hadn't read it there was perhaps because it was 'Written by Sappho on an urn' and she didn't care to read epitaphs written on funerary urns; it seemed like a death at the end of Sappho's manuscript.

> With newly-sharpened steel the girls
> Cut from their heads . . .

She let Sappho roll up—then opened her again, realizing that she had noticed something. Yes:

> *Timadoc hade konic . . .*

The handwriting had improved with long practice, but it still had something of the stabbed, impatient look—and the tailless sigmas. Apama had not gladly copied anything but epics and heroics. She would not have copied Sappho—but it seemed she had. Berenice laughed: was her mother talking to her?

The scroll had not been filled: there was a handspan's length blank at the end. She fetched her scissors and was about to cut this off, but then moved her scissors leftward and made the cut, carefully, before the poem. On the blank space she wrote to her husband:

"I have understood the truth. The gods did not allow you to save your sister.

"I grieve for her. She was as dear to me as my self. I have shorn my hair for her, as was once the custom for such a friend. I shall forgive you in time. Perhaps I shall have overcome my grief by the time my hair grows back. Perhaps you should not return until then." She reconsidered the last sentence and in some panic drew a line through it. But she had written it, the piece of the Sappho scroll could not be spoiled and thrown away for nothing, she did not go in search of other papyrus on which to rewrite the letter.

It was enough, it gave her relief, she took off her Egyptian wig and let her nape-hair show. It had recovered a little of its length and some of its softness.

Polymela said: "Are you no longer afraid that your husband will hear of it?"

"No; it will be explained by a message I have sent him. It was the custom in the time of Sappho and her friends that if a beloved one of them died, they would cut their hair in mourning. So this is what I have done for Berenice, and I have told him of it." She smiled at her maid, from whom there was no need to conceal anything. Polymela (she told herself) knows as much as I do—she knows about what happened between me and my cousin, and what happened between me and that devil—and she is almost as clever as I am at intuiting the implications.

"But what will other people think?"

"You may tell them the same, and so shall I. May not a Berenice violently mourn a Berenice who is her cousin and her husband's sister?"

"But what if the man who has taken it from you lets it be seen?"

"He can't, because it would destroy him as well as me. He will keep it hidden somewhere."

"Then what did he think he gained by taking it?"

"He did it to hurt me, principally. That is the nature of him and his act, to hurt—not body but spirit. He did not draw blood—I didn't even feel what he did with his knife as he did it. But you are right: though his every act is malicious, it is also part of some plan. He thinks that I have to live in fear because some word of it will come to the king and it will seem I have *some* lover. But I have forestalled that now."

"But perhaps he has hidden it somewhere else."

"Else than what?—what does it matter where? We don't know where he has hidden it. I don't care if he has even defiled it; it's no longer part of me. He has it in his house, or under the Tomb of Alexander—if he has not burnt it. Where else?"

"Why, perhaps in the house of someone else. Someone else who might be blamed."

Berenice blenched. In the house of someone else whom he might thereby ruin.

The question for the oracle

The Dioecetes—but how was she to warn him? What could she tell him that would not compromise herself?

He came to see her on business almost every day, briefly. Also, he and the other Advisors had their regular meetings with her four times a month, on the day before each quarter-phase of the moon. Though there were only five Advisors they were divided into three cliques (one consisting of the Dioecetes alone), so it was likely that they got together less formally among themselves. And they had also to convene whenever there came a message addressed especially to them from their king in the distant fields of war.

Half a month might pass without such special dispatches, but at other times they were frequent and even trivial, and it was with disguised annoyance that Sylcon had to interrupt his work, and Hontiphas to rise from his couch and be carried to the palace, so as to waste an hour considering Ptolemy Tryphon's remarks on Syrian food or complaints about his camp bed.

Yet these letters suggested that campaigning was changing Ptolemy from the rather feckless young man he had been. In his traveling tent (a system of equipment that had to be loaded on a cart drawn by twelve oxen) he still lived in luxury compared with the life of his soldiers, yet war was hardening him. He allowed himself to express sometimes the disgust for slaughter and destruction, sometimes the lust for further conquest, often even the boastfulness of the old conquering Thothmeses and Ramesseses—as if he had heard of these various attitudes, like costumes worn by other kings, and in his juvenile way was still deciding which of them he fancied. His skin had browned—even the scratchy words of the letters somehow suggested it. He had seen more both of the sun by day and of the stars by night.

When one of his sealed messages came for the Advisors, it was the Dioecetes who received and opened it, and then read it aloud, having notified the other four to attend, and Berenice. But she was not so constrained by duty, and she received separate letters from her husband, so she ceased to be present at all such meetings, telling the Dioecetes: "Inform me if it is a matter that concerns me."

Now came something of a different kind, and he sent word to her that it contained news and a request. So she came and listened.

"We are at Thapsacus on the Euphrates" (Ptolemy wrote). "The House of Seleucus will never rise again; its scion is on the far Anatolian coast, clinging with his last few followers; his mother has killed herself, and I can ignore him. I have received the homage of the governors of Nisibis and Dura, and indications of goodwill from others yet farther beyond the river, even into Babylonia and Persia. A delegation from Bactria has invited me to possess myself of it—"

"Bactria!" exclaimed the advisor Artemidorus. "If he goes conquering all the way to Bactria he'll be five years away, even if he marches at the speed of Alexander."

"The message is not finished," said Sylcon, and he read on:

"It is open to me to go forward. I wish to be sure whether I should embark on this vast project. Will my expectations be fulfilled? And is all sound behind me? It depends on the gods. Ask the best of Oracles. The answer is to be carried directly from the Oracle, not to you but speedily to me. I must know whether by proceeding I would build or destroy an empire."

An astounding message! But Berenice said nothing. She had already received her letter, in which Ptolemy begged her not to forget him if he should be away another year in Asia.

The other Advisors nodded sagely. The king needed encouragement from on high. He had demanded the advice of Apollo. "He is saying," said Artemidorus, "that he could remake the empire of Alexander—"

"Or destroy his own," said Hontiphas, completing the sentence exactly as Artemidorus would have completed it. They all knew the story of the most disastrously misunderstood of the Delphic oracle's answers:

> If you attack the Persians, you will destroy a mighty empire.

Croesus had attacked Persia, and the empire he had destroyed was his own.

"I shall appoint an envoy today," said Sylcon, "and he shall start for Delphi tomorrow, with appropriate gifts."

"No," said Hontiphas: "if it could be done as simply as that, the king would have sent an envoy from his camp. You do not understand the requirements of religion, and the weight that it gives. Hundreds of questioners come to the oracle, and those that come with religious sanction are heard before those that come from a tailor asking whether he is to buy more cloth, or even a general in a camp. You are obliged to call to us the chief priests. They must frame the king's question in the best terms and choose appropriate gifts and the envoy and instruct and purify him."

With impatience Sylcon had to agree. "We shall adjourn, then," he said, "and resume today, at the hour after noon, with the chief priests present—that is, those of the royal cults. Not of the rest" (he meant the Olympians, Demeter and Hermes and Dionysus and the others who had temples in Alexandria, as well as the Egyptian deities). "This is an imperial matter, and between three priests there may be quite enough wrangling. Shall you be present, *despoina?*"

Here, if ever, was a moment for Berenice's royal pause. The chief priest of the cult of Alexander was Sosibius. Did she want to be in a room with him and others?

"I shall come if I come," she said. And she did not. Priests and Advisors could be left to appoint an envoy.

Promptly at the hour after noon Sosibius, wearing a leopard skin over his left shoulder, entered the council chamber. He now as a chief priest had to trail a bevy of lesser priests, whom he could do without, and he left them outside the door. His manner was modest, and he glided to a place close to the influential Advisor Calerno, who had been born in Crete.

Some waiting had to be done for the other two priests. The doorway of the council chamber was guarded by a young officer who stood at attention with his spear planted beside him and his thighs tapering above polished greaves. Sosibius, in conversation with Calerno, caught the Advisor's eye, and remarked in an undertone:

"No me importaría morir entre las columnas de ese tiemplo."

He didn't really whisper in Spanish, but in Calerno's native Cretan dialect, indicating that he knew it, as well as the Advisor's predilections. *"I wouldn't mind dying between the pillars of that temple!"* Calerno smiled in tentative understanding.

The priests of the Savior Gods and Sibling-Loving Gods arrived, Sylcon again read out the letter, and Hontiphas explained what was needed: the priests must appoint and train a messenger, who would sail with a suitable entourage to Delphi.

"And how long will that take?" asked Sosibius, as if he didn't know.

"The selection and preparation of the envoy?" said Hontiphas— "only as long as it takes the three of you to decide and to do it."

"We can select the envoy today; I mean, how long will the mission take? Forty days, a hundred?"

"Why, it depends whether the ship sails to Corinth or Athens—that is, to Cenchreae or Peiraeus, the ports of Corinth and Athens, and then whether they ride overland or take another boat from the other side of the Isthmus to Cirrha, and go up from there to Delphi; or whether they sail around the Peloponnese. And then on how close their arrival is to the seventh day of the month, when Apollo gives answers; and then as to the return, or rather the voyage to Seleuceia, so as to—"

"Have we no oracle in Egypt?" asked Sosibius.

"Delphic Apollo is clearly meant," said the high priest of the Sibling-Loving Gods.

"Perhaps, but what was said, if I remember, was 'the best of oracles.' And I also remember the story that Croesus, before asking his fatal question, considered many other famous oracles to whom he might send it, and one of them was Zeus Ammon of Siwa."

"That is correct," said Hontiphas. "He sent of course to Apollo of Delphi, and also to Apollo of Abae, Zeus of Dodona, Amphia-raus of Oropus, Trophonius of Lebadeia, Apollo of Didyma (or, as some say, Branchidae), even to Zeus Ammon of Siwa, over this side of the sea; and all of them failed the test that Croesus set them, except Apollo of Delphi. Only Apollo's oracle of Delphi correctly answered the Lydian king's test question, which was: 'What is king Croesus doing at this moment, a hundred days after he sent his envoy to bring this question to you?' Only Apollo of Delphi knew the answer, which was an unlikely one: Croesus— richest king that ever lived though he was—was at that moment cooking himself a lamb and tortoise stew."

"Yes," said Sosibius— "remarkable!" (And he was the only one to laugh aloud at the remarkable little story, though he had heard it as many times as the others had.) "Remarkable indeed. A lamb and tortoise stew! Who would have thought of that? Delphic Apollo passed that amusing little test, and then failed in the great question itself. He caused Croesus to attack the Per-sians, and Croesus ended by being cooked himself, on a burning pyre. The gods" (here Sosibius niftily theorized) "did this to punish Croesus for not keeping to the oracles of his own land. He should have asked Apollo of Didyma, on his doorstep. (And if he had, he might have got his answer in six days instead of a hundred, and had more chance of outmarching rumors and taking the Persians by surprise. I might mention that Apollo of Delphi, also, was punished, for his own deceptive answer. His temple burned the next year.)"

Hontiphas cleared his throat in preparation for what to think at the idea of a god or his oracle being "punished."

"We should," said Sosibius, "ask our own Zeus Ammon of Siwa. If I wish to find out which ear I shall be scratching a hundred days from now, I shall ask Delphic Apollo; if I wish to find out whether I shall succeed in conquering the world, I shall ask Zeus Ammon of Siwa."

A thoughtful silence fell, into which Sosibius dropped his clincher:

"As did he whose priest I have the honor to be: Alexander. With somewhat more success than Croesus."

Alexander (as every schoolboy knew), right after mastering Egypt, had had himself led west into the desert to the oasis of Siwa and the temple of Ammon, mightiest of Egyptian gods, whom he identified with Zeus, whose son he was ceremonially declared to be, and from whom he received his mission to march to the ends of the world.

"Ammon and Alexander," said Leophon, an Advisor who till now had said nothing. "Their priesthoods are closely connected?"

"Indeed," said Hontiphas, who knew all about this kind of thing, "Alexander is assigned to the same *hiera phratria*, holy clan, as Ammon; but within it Ammon of Karnak is over all, and Ammon of Siwa is regarded as the father of the god Alexander, who in life was adopted by him as son."

"Well, so that is all right," said Leophon. "The priesthood of Siwa will take no orders from that of Alexander."

"An oracle takes no orders but from a god—I wonder what you are suspecting?"

Sylcon did not give much weight to the theology, but he said: "It would be speedier."

"The only caution I would add," said Sosibius as if remembering something, "is that it's such a primitive oracle—doesn't allow writing, I think?"

"Yes," said Hontiphas, "the custom of Siwa is still as it once was at Delphi: neither the question nor the answer may be written. They have to be carried in the questioner's head."

"That should not matter," said the Dioecetes— "may make things speedier. No document to prepare—just be sure the envoy has a good memory."

"Well, we can find such," said Calerno, "I suggest that Sosibius take care of that" (Sosibius, ex-policeman) "and he can be instructed by the priests, while we attend to assembling his retinue and the necessary gifts—that smart young officer over there could captain the escort, why not?—and they can be on their way tomorrow. A week along the coast to Paraetonion and a week in along the trail to the oasis, and a week back, and another two or three on the sea—he can be in Syria inside a month and a half."

Nubian laughter

There was no lack of opportunity to encounter the Dioecetes. He had so much business about the palace, and dispatched so much of it himself because this was quicker than sending clerks, that when passing within the queen's sight for the fifth time in the day he might even abbreviate the courtesies and press rapidly on. He knew the precise order in which to do things, and had the *finding* stride of someone bent on getting to the next task: he lengthened his stride like a racing walker by throwing hip after leg; if there were steps to descend and corners to turn—or obstacles to evade, as when careless servants had left a chair or a bedpan in the passageway (over every one of which her husband Ptolemy would have tripped, then wasted time in cursing it)— Sylcon achieved it in the minimum number of elastic foot-aimings. Rounding a turn in a stair, he pivoted one hand on the knob of the banister to gain speed. His swiftness was distinct from the fussily hurried gait of officials anxious to seem busy— and from the effortless movements of Sosibius, whether busy or not.

It did not so often bring Sylcon to where Berenice could actually talk with him. But some time the next day he came to her about another matter, and when that was approved and he was bowing out she remembered to ask him what had been done about the mission to the oracle. He replied that an envoy had been appointed and was on his way to Siwa.

"To Siwa? Not to Delphi?"

"Siwa was suggested by the priest Sosibius, as nearer. And he and Calerno also undertook the instruction of the envoy."

"Instruction?—as to what?"

"As to what to say and how to conduct himself, no doubt, and what will be expected of him at the shrine."

"Not, I hope, as to how to change the terms of the question— or of the answer."

"No, why should that be?"

"I don't know—but: Lord Sylcon, it is time for me to speak with you of something."

He waited respectfully.

"But not here," she said. "Is there a place where we can talk and be sure of not being overheard?"

"Is that not so here?"

She was sitting on a broad soft stool in what she called the Maroon Room, which had walls of this deep color with a frieze of lake fishes; a woman, whom she had just dismissed, had been painting daisies on her toenails. The room was a cool one with no windows, but opened, down two wide steps, onto a courtyard in which servants could be seen passing to and fro.

"I would like to think so," she said. "But the other day I was told something I had said in private, by somebody I had certainly not said it to." And here she would very much have liked to say: "I shall visit you in your house. There, surely, we should be private."

By visiting the Dioecetes at home, she might accomplish two things at once: have her confidential talk with him—warn him about Sosibius—and also have a chance of guessing where in his house something might be hidden without his knowledge.

And so she could not help saying: "I think of visiting you in one of your houses." When he listed his houses, she would have to guess the likeliest, probably the one where he kept his family, and most often slept.

"I have only one house."

"I'm quite surprised at that! I know that Calerno has at least two in the city and two in the country; and Artemidorus told me he owns eighteen villages and has a house overlooking each."

"Well, I have one, and it is quite a simple one. But I gladly invite you to it."

But self-preservation prevailed. That the queen had been in the black Sylcon's house would certainly become known. That she had not only visited and been entertained there, but had left her attendants in an outer room and withdrawn with him into an inner one for an hour of secret business, would not escape his servants and would spread beyond his walls—and then if Ptolemy ever was given cause to suspect her, this would seem certain confirmation.

"You are right after all," she said. "I am too cautious. We can talk here, of course. There is no one within earshot."

"Is your dwarf then deaf?"

"Oh, him!" she laughed— "not deaf, as far as I know, but he understands no Greek."

The dwarf, still limping, and scarred, and unable to straighten his right arm, and somewhat more bent over at the belly, and lacking hunks of his hair and two of his fingernails, and one eye forever closed, but otherwise nearly his old ungainly self, now spent his whole days not far from Berenice, so long as she remained in her palace. If not, he contented himself with hanging around her Libyan maid Polymela instead, and letting her be the one to chatter into his uncomprehending ears.

Sylcon turned his gaze on the dwarf, and suddenly directed at him a few strange syllables. And the dwarf spoke some words back. They sounded to Berenice like *"malanaka-tashaharaka-tamasklaka"*, and the two talked in this clacking manner—a short clatter of sounds from the Dioecetes and a short splatter back from the dwarf and another burst from the Dioecetes (a staccato burst—his syllables came out more hesitantly than the dwarf's) and then a longer gabble from the dwarf—at which the Dioecetes, normally so tall and staid, suddenly tipped his head back and gave himself to an orgy of laughter.

The dwarf too presumably uttered a laugh, though it was hard to find in the maze of his face; and Berenice could not help laughing, silently: not at the joke, of which she had no inkling, but at the contrast between the two of them: the stunted being, like a human beetle, and the long slender upright glossy black rod of a Dioecetes, for all she knew the tallest man in Egypt, his height slightly decapitated but his dignity increased by the ring of gray hair around the bald summit of his head.

He sobered and said: "His name is Saha."

"Yes." She did not confess that she still called her dwarf by the clownish name of Coptolemy, as her husband had done.

"He comes from the land of Kush, as my ancestor did—the land you call Nubia. He was born in a miserable village only a day's walk from Napata, from which my ancestor came five hundred years ago in the time of Pharaoh Piankhi, who was himself Nubian. —The dwarf is of no consequence, as you say. Let him stay." And the Dioecetes asked forgiveness for his levity, and made himself ready to listen to what the queen had to tell him.

She heard herself saying, as if echoing what Callimachus had once said to her: "I want to warn you about the man Sosibius."

Sylcon waited for more of her warning, and she said: "He is an evil young man. It would be a mistake to trust him, at any time."

"Why?" asked Sylcon simply.

She could not tell him, or anyone, of her chief evidence. But there was something she could tell him.

"Supposing a message comes from Syria, in a secret form—a *skutalê*-message, no less, intended for you—say, from Anaxalcus, the general. Would it be brought to you here or at your house?"

"I have arranged that such messages are brought to me at my house. If I am not there, the courier waits until I am."

"Is that because you do not entirely trust . . . But never mind. A message of that kind, for example, telling you that the king 'will not return until he has avenged his sister—a year at least.' A message that ended: 'Do not tell the queen.'"

Sylcon stared stonily in front of him. "Yes," he said, "that was a message for me. After deciphering it I destroyed it, and I had thought no one but I had seen it."

"That I learned of its contents doesn't matter any more, since now we know that the king may be away not one year more but five. What matters is that Sosibius brought it and showed it to me. This must then have been before you saw it, and indeed he said so, and said that he would return it to wherever he had removed it from. Which would, then, have been from your house, or from the courier who was trusted to carry it to you alone?"

"It would, and I understand your advice as to the Priest of Alexander. Thank you, my *basilissa*."

Her advice was accepted—the matter apparently ended— almost more quickly than she had hoped. Was the Dioecetes not going to ask why Sosibius had shown her that message?—or talk of what it revealed about the resources Sosibius still had despite no longer sitting in the office of the chief of police?—was he not even going to voice indignation that his own house might have been pilfered, or his courier suborned or murdered?

"Are you not going to ask me more?" she said.

"Yes, madam. I ask you to tell me whatever more you wish."

"Well, then, I tell you what Sosibius aims at. He aims to supplant you."

"Is that what he says?"

"He says that he aims to assist you, but I believe that what he means to do is to supplant you." (And she remembered earlier words of Sosibius: *"Yes, and I hate him!"*) "And perhaps he sees himself in the end supplanting me and the king my husband."

"These are grave charges. Why would he give a hint of such aims to you?"

"He argues that, if I accept what he calls his co-operation, he can help me to govern Egypt in a style that would suit my desires."

At this the Housekeeper's manner of pausing, of preserving silence in expectation of more, became even more polite.

Berenice felt herself reddening as she said: "My desires are rather unformed, but I think of them as starting from what I call Coptolemy's Law. It's foolish, you'll think at first. Coptolemy is this dwarf—that's the kind of a name he had until I found out that he is really called, as you say, Sa Aa. I'll find something different to call my law. But it is just that no one, henceforth, shall be hanged by the heels."

"Was that one of the things that were done to Saha—Coptolemy?"

"You know then that he was tortured?"

The Housekeeper's expression said that he could see this by seeing the condition of the dwarf—whom he had seen before, as a whole dwarf, in the king's company. But he said: "Yes. And that he was spared because of your intercession."

"And do you know what he had been accused of?"

"Of trying to kill the king."

"And—" But Sylcon, it seemed to her, did no better than reserve judgment on whether the dwarf was innocent; if asked, he would say only that what she said, he would accept.

"And of being used by you to murder the king." —She didn't say it. It would push his skepticism to the surface.

"I don't know whether it was one of the things done to him," she said. "Ask him. He's alive. But I have learned that it is done to some prisoners until they are dead. It must be the worst of all possible deaths. —Is it?"

"No."

"That it is done is something I cannot bear."

"There are harder deaths for treason to the king, and hardest for threatening the order of the world by treason against the gods."

"I don't want to hear of them. There shall be no more of this, nor anything worse than it."

"So you would abolish it, and those?"

"Yes."

"And Sosibius asks you to believe that if he had wide power he would help you to make this change in the law?"

"Yes, and more of the kind."

Sylcon did not need to say: "Is that likely?" His silence said it.

"What is a ruler for?" Berenice asked suddenly— "What is a ruler for, but to work good?"

Sylcon looked as if he either had nothing to say to this, or far too much to begin to say.

"I would not need Sosibius, Lord Sylcon, if you would . . ."

He was standing before her all this time, as far off as he respectfully could, because he hoped not to be looking down too steeply on his queen. She was still sitting on her broad soft stool, playing with a piece of green thread in the edge of her garment. He had come to look with approval on her adoption of the Egyptian headdress, but the Maroon Room did not do well for her color. Nor did it impress him as a pleasing room in itself; why were yellow fishes swimming in a sea the color of stale blood? He wished that the custom were still as it had been in the times of the Persian rule over Egypt, when a courtier not only had to come barefoot into the presence of a monarch, but could not stand before a monarch, let alone look down on a monarch. He now turned his head aside for a moment. When he was ready he faced her and said:

"I have lived in the land of Egypt for five hundred years—that is, my family has—and we are Egyptian, even though we have married among our own people and kept speaking our own language in our houses. I uphold the way of Egypt. I have to, it is my function to maintain the *oikos*, the house; that is, the land. My father held a post in the administration of the nome of Abydos, as did I to begin with; I worked and was selected for higher work. Egypt is changeless and should be as it always has been. Libyans, Nubians, Hyksos, Sea-People, Assyrians, Persians have at times burst in and ruled Egypt, but mostly they learned to continue in the way of Egypt, and this has been true of Pharaoh Ptolemy Soter and Pharaoh Ptolemy Philadelphus (under whom I was honored to advance). They have upheld the gods and the customs that maintain order in Egypt and the world. Egypt is a land of plenty, but there are some bad years, and there will always be some hunger here and there, and we will administer in the ways we know. Another of the things that will never change is that there will be criminals, hence prisons and punishments, and there are Egyptian laws relating to them.

"Nevertheless, if you wish and command me to, I will confer

with others, experts, on what can be done about instituting Coptolemy's Law. Even before the return of the king your husband."

Berenice looked up at him.

But when Sosibius learned that she had turned away from him
and to the Dioecetes to do this—

What a web I am caught in! she thought. She said: "Wait till I
have thought about it some more."

The Dioecetes bowed. He had a look compounded of readi-
ness to depart and uneasiness, and said: "So, then, I am to maintain a watchful attitude toward the priest Sosibius?" It was as if
he said, So that's all you really have to tell me?

"What do you know of his successor in the post he had
before?" Berenice asked, remembering that this was another
investigation she had not made.

"That's Agathocles—who used to be one of his officers. He is
unlikely to be in any sort of league with Sosibius," replied Sylcon:
"he was, I believe, his defeated wrestling rival at the Panathenaic
Games."

Berenice laughed (slightly). The Dioecetes again bowed, and
before leaving spoke once more to Saha the dwarf, then said surprisingly:

"May I take him sometimes to visit my children? He would
amuse them."

The horned magician

Faithful to the court style of a century ago, the Dioecetes withdrew by walking backwards, turning around only when he
reached the exit of the room and had to descend the two steps to
the courtyard. This caused Berenice to notice, even more, his
back, and to marvel at its board-like flatness: his spine must be as
straight as a pole, and his shoulders like a cross-tree. Though he
was tall, it was his bearing that made him appear even taller.

She had the impression that he went away to send her a
weapon against Sosibius, though he had nothing to do with it.
He crossed paths in the courtyard with Hontiphas, the Advisor
for religious affairs, who exchanged brief courtesies with him

and then came before Berenice, flourishing a piece of rag on which had been scrawled these letters:

THE TRAGICOMOEDIA OF
NECTANEBO
PUBLISH IT NOT IN ASCALON

"What is this, Hontiphas?"

"It is a handbill: a handbill for a scurrilous performance! It was handed out in the street, not to me but to one of my servants, by some grinning fellow—"

"Ascalon, wasn't that the name of the house where we were taken to see that silly play?"

"It was."

"The play about the Sun God of the Judaeans?"

"Yes, that was the place, it's where these fellows who call themselves the 'Philistines' put on their low entertainments. Ascalon is the name of some place along the coast in Palestine."

"I know, but 'Publish it not in Ascalon'—what does that mean?"

"That is their way of announcing it; they mean to say that they *will* publish it, that is, perform it, forbidden though it ought to be, and that is the place to go and see it."

"Ah! They mean 'Psst, this is a secret for you, this is where to go'?" said Berenice, laughing. There crossed her mind a crazy image of another way to advertize: a poster pasted on the flat back of the Dioecetes.

"Yes, that is what they mean—it's no real secret: it's their usual dive. It's where they will flaunt their debaucheries this very evening before such dregs as care to go and pay their drachmae for such vulgarity. It is a low place of entertainment, almost a bawdyhouse. Whoever recommended us to venture there that other time should have known better."

"So shall you go to this performance?" asked Berenice.

"Certainly not, or at least with reluctance, because it should be looked into. This performance, on top of being no doubt as scabrous as that other, will be illegal—sacrilegious."

"How do you know?"

"From its title, which can only refer to the slanderous story that goes among the Egyptians, that Alexander was really a bastard, an Egyptian."

"Alexander really an Egyptian!"

"Yes, they pretend that his real father was Pharaoh Nectanebo."

The ensuing pause seemed to Hontiphas a sign that the seriousness of the sacrilege was making itself manifest to the queen. What she was really calculating was its implication for herself.

"Can actors," she asked, "be arrested for slandering the god Alexander in this way?—slandering him and his parentage?"

"Yes, under the law of the first year of Ptolemy Soter's satrapy, confirmed by a law of the first year of his declared kingship. I believe the law even mentions this particular damned fiction."

"And imprisoned, or what?"

"They would be tried, and the gravity and circumstances be weighed by the high court of Alexandria, on which you as representative of the king would be entitled to sit."

"So you will witness this play, then, to see whether it is indeed sacrilegious?"

"I would do so only with reluctance, as I said. Could you not—"

"I certainly understand your repugnance to the place," said Berenice. She felt at least as much—but more determination to use the opportunity. "Very well." She stopped for thought—distracted by the image of Sosibius caught not only capering below the dignity of his office but insulting the very god-hero of whom he was now supposed to be the priest. He might not be one of the actors this time. But he had been so much the whole company on that other occasion that it was hard to see what they would do without him. And the chance had to be taken.

"If you will not go, then I will," she said. "But it cannot be conspicuously. Do their performances always begin about sundown?"

"Yes, I believe—"

"Then there's not much time. Send for Polycleides—wasn't that his name?—the man of the gymnasium, to guide us there. Don't tell him what it's about, *at all*; have him brought here, very quickly, under guard, with no explanation. In the same way, send for six of the Medzae—do you think that will be enough?"

"I suggest ten," said Hontiphas.

"Have them brought to me here from the Cryon, immediately, without any explanation whatever to themselves or to their superior. And finally: will this performance offend Egyptian sensibilities also? —You don't know. Have the chief priest of any of their temples brought to me in the same way, only he'll have to be one who understands Greek."

Hontiphas, driven out by the queen, hurried. And just before sundown, Polycleides found himself forced to lead this party—the queen, ten police, four of the queen's own guards, and Mentuophis priest of Har-Apis (Berenice was beginning to understand the blendings of Egyptian gods)—to the same back-street entrance of his gymnasium.

From there they went through as far as the small room that overlooked the theatre from the rear. Berenice stepped in front, and held out her arm to stop them there, where they were in darkness and unnoticed from the stage. They had to stand, and could barely see over the heads of the crowd in the warehouse-like space—a crowd of men and not a few women, most also standing and a few at the front squatting, and none behaving decorously.

The "Tragicomoedia of Nectanebo" had already started, but nothing much had been missed: it was all slapstick and short squawking speeches of which at first Berenice could grasp little; the audience grasped more, though some of them were scarcely paying attention. Their heads prevented her from seeing the actors from the chests down, until a growing roar among the back of the audience persuaded the front of the audience to squat.

The drama did not pretend to be a "Tragedy of Ezekiel": not the Judaeans, this time, but the Egyptians were the people whose story was being mocked. The tall masked actor, with the voice disguised in falsetto and the superb and largely bare body that she knew too well, now represented Nectanebo, last native Pharaoh of Egypt—last of a thousand Pharaohs. As before, he towered over crouching foes, who swarmed around him clad now not in the clinging fish-scale armor of the Philistines but in the soft caps and massive beards and flapping robes and effeminate trousers and upcurled slippers of the Persians—as if Persians would really wear such cartoon costumes into battle.

This time the demeanor of the masked actor was less exultant, more resigned to coming fate. (Berenice hoped it was not to be another mutilation.) The battle went against this last of a thousand Pharaohs; there was to be for Egypt another of its ages of adversity. His head sprouted horns, heavy and curling (they were slapped onto him in one of the moments when he disappeared behind a pillar): into him had come the soul of Ammon, Ram God of the Egyptians. But his horns did not avail to thrust back his enemies, who drove him down the river and off the land. It was a wordy play, more was done with such lines as "Ammon, live within me!" or "Oh, I have nowhere to go but the sea!" than with trying to show the sea or tipping him into it. But in the "sea" (composed of flutter-robed human waves) he did swim, using a curious wild overarm motion.

And the Ram swims across the sea to Europe; staggers ashore in Macedon, and sets up shop as a wandering magician from Egypt. (Berenice glanced aside at the Egyptian priest. "Are we to let them tell this lie?" she was prepared to murmur. But far from being scandalized, he was smiling broadly.) Strollers along the sea front (some of them not bothering to change out of their Persian garments) laugh at the tricks of the mountebank with the goat horns, buy trinkets and nostrums from him; he counts his pennies, becomes more cocky, goes up to the court of Pella and finds employment with King Philip. King Philip (a crude man— jokes about his smelliness—a reference to Demosthenes, the Athenian orator, who when told that "Philip has died!" retorted "Impossible—we would smell him from here")—while King Philip busies himself out on his parade ground, training his phalanx, his new kind of army, and then while King Philip is away subduing Greece, in preparation for the world-overturning attack on Persia, the magician with his brazen tricks entertains Queen Olympias instead, until she backs into her bedroom, delighted as his full Rammishness arises in following her.

Berenice observed that the actor, despite all the opportunities for extravagant clowning in his Ram-Magician role, was lazy in it; it seemed he had become somewhat bored with his male self, he put more into Olympias. As Olympias he was lush, loud, brilliantly colored (again the costume had to be clapped onto him in moments as he withdrew from sight): Olympias the arch-tigress (as Apama would have said), who had perhaps in real life been a tigress only in the ferocity with which she defended the rights of her son against his drunken father. Olympias wore not a tigress's head (perhaps they hadn't been able to find one) but a lioness's above her own startling face. For Berenice it was fascinating to notice, since she was alert in advance, the devices: the short wall at the back of the stage, behind one end of which Nectanebo disappeared and from the other end of which sprang Olympias;

there was a revolving platform with a bed on it, and a curtain that
could be drawn along one side. On the bed Olympias crouched
on all fours, like the cat she was, her breasts grouped, her eyes
burning: it was amusing to be tricked out of noticing that
Nectanebo was not actually in view in the moment when he was
being lured, nor Olympias in the moment when she was being
sucked to her. (In the absorption of watching for the tricks,
Berenice forgot to watch for the telltale biting of the right lower
lip.)

Seeing what was coming, Berenice glanced at the priest
again—how would he take this lie? But she saw that to him it
was no lie: it was the myth that comforted Egypt. It was a per-
version of the great political act of Alexander, when he first
arrived in Egypt and made pilgrimage to Siwa and had himself
ceremonially adopted as the son of Ammon, and thus made Egypt
his. —And (the end of the play was rather rushed, so much
stagetime having been consumed in conjuring tricks and foot-
work designed to keep the audience guessing whether ramgod
Nectanebo was or was not in view at the same time as strident
Olympias, and whether either of them might be in view at the
time they coupled) there quickly springs from her (in the shape
of the same actor) her son Alexander, Lord of the Two Horns, and
he takes over his father's army and returns as savior king—
ousting the slippershod Persians—to Egypt: as is his right as
Pharaoh Nectanebo's secret son, Alexander Pharaoh, son of
Nectanebo, son of Ammon.

Applause, some of it ironic, in which priest Mentuophis
joined so noisily that Berenice nervously smacked her hand down
over his. Nectanebo-Ammon-magician-Alexander bowed, surrounded by the rest of the company—the Persians, and King
Philip, now grinning and holding a cuckold's horn to his head,
but not of course Olympias. —But suddenly, to Berenice's shock,
Olympias ran back onto the stage.

So she had been a different actor after all! So that was the
game, the game for the spectators: come to see the "Philistines"
and guess whether the two-roles-one-actor feat was part of the
play this time or not.

And was it also part of the game, and Sosibius's own risky
game, that only his own "Philistines" as yet knew who he was?—
the audience came each time hoping to see him unmasked in the
role of himself? Berenice imagined them some evening rushing

the stage to unmask him—the whirling jawbone or ram's horn as he fended them off and mowed them down . . . They had redoubled their applause for the painted lady, Olympias. The applause's style and the calls mixed with it ("Hey, Bilistiche, you forgot to show us your *gumnaix!*") made plain that this was a tigress lady well known in the bordellos of Alexandria.

Now it was time. The yellow-cloaked squad, to whom Berenice had already given their orders, stepped smartly out of the little back room and waded forward through the crowd, on whom fell a hush (not with complete suddenness but rather like a load of bricks tumbling off a cart and settling). Six of the Medzae positioned themselves to block the exits; the other four made for Sosibius. They halted a couple of paces from him, and Berenice said (she had no need to raise her voice in the silence): "Take your mask off."

From something in the hesitancy, rather than the slowness, of the movement with which he raised his hand to the mask, she already felt a qualm: the Sosibian way would have been either to refuse, or to do it with defiant disdain. He took it off. And was not Sosibius.

Like him. But like isn't enough.

Berenice was staggered into silence, but no one else was. A laugh went up, the four policemen ringing the man stepped forward grinning; one of them clapped him on the shoulder.

Silence was restored out of politeness to the queen. "Who are you?" she said.

His own answer ("Agathocles, son of Teon") was unnecessary, so many had already answered for him: "It's Agathocles!"

"Put him under arrest for impiety," said Berenice, and turned away, the spirit gone from her. She hastily answered someone's question as to where they were to take him and what should be done next day, and sought the door, not turning her head even for a moment to see how seriously her order was being taken by the police chief's grinning subordinates. Nor would she inquire into the matter next day. The Medzae would probably play at jailing their chief for a night. They were still Sosibius's. Alexandria was a fruit full of maggots from skin to skin.

Eucus

She had to go out by the devious way to the back entrance, because that was where the litter this time was waiting. But on coming to the street, she was impatient of the litter and strode ahead, and her people had to follow. She knew the way around back to the palace. In these dense streets other lights and sounds of the night now sprang like mushrooms in leafmould. She passed, on her right, a building whose two windows, wide and low, were open into a long room blazing with too many braziers. In the room a woman was singing. As she sang she moved to and fro near the windows so that she could be seen sometimes through one, sometimes the other. Deeper inside were people, making their own noise, few of them looking her way. The song was an archaic melody that everyone knew, that came from far back in time and perhaps from the mountains of Macedon, a sadness over faithless love ("But first it bended and then it broke And so did my false love to me"—like that, but not that), but she was a paid artist who went beyond it, and within the next and the next strophe it stretched and rose. She was a strumpet, unlistened to by a tavern crowd, but to Berenice she was an actress in a play, outpouring more intensity than the whole company of the Philistines. The singer was seen at the left window; she wandered behind the intervening bit of wall, appeared at the right window, the nearer to the house's corner (where an alley disappeared into the darkness), and her voice came out with searing passion—piercing the more because for a moment she faced outward to the listener in the street whom she could not see:

> No, no, no, no, I will not sleep
> But still for Eucus I will weep!

The walls and the singer were black against the lamplight. Whether she was black or white, eighteen or eighty, Berenice could not tell, but she knew that Eucus had been lost to death and not betrayal. She hurried on. *I should do nothing but weep for Berenice Syra.* She came to her senses: no, I should love the one given to me to love. I will. Even though he is a king. She strode on, oblivious for once of the obedient, the followers always dogging her. Until they diffidently caught up with her and told her she was going the wrong way. She was two blocks farther off than she had started. She turned and began to trudge anxiously through streets that were not now noisy or sordid, merely too long. It had become like one of those usual dreams in which she gained back to little Cyrene but it became vast as she tried to find her way home across its multiplying slope. But she clung to the dream, as one does; shuddered away from letting it be superseded by the litter. How bleak the world without either of them.

Siwa

After seven long dry days, one of the travelers could bear the monotony of the horizon no more and burst out: "There is no oasis! We have missed it! You are leading us into eternal desert, we shall never find an oasis!"

"It is ahead," replied the guide.

"How do you know? We could have missed it!"

"No, it is very broad."

"But how did anyone discover it? Why would anyone go seeking so long into this waste?"

Besides Cleon the envoy, who was being pulled in a donkey-cart, and Gylippus the soldier in command of his escort, who was walking, there were several merchants. Their servants and baggage and the rest of the escort followed with camels half a mile behind, setting up a separate dust-cloud, which drifted back toward the distant sea. The guide and the other Siwans rode donkeys.

"When the army of Cambyses the Persian tried to find the place," said an Egyptian, "they were led by the flight of birds. And look up!" Against the sky they saw a stork on its way south.

"Yes," said another, "and the army of Cambyses was lost in the desert and never seen again. They are all somewhere under the sand."

The Siwan guide remained silent. The oasis had existed before the rest of the world—it had been a planet, a diskworld on the waters—and his people had always dwelt in it.

In the afternoon of the eighth day, the barren ground broke into separate crags, between which the track wound down and down. "I should think," remarked Gylippus, "we're lower than the sea by now!"

"We are, so they say," said a Phoenician, "though I don't know how they know."

Through the gateway of the last two crags, the caravan emerged onto a vast flat floor. It was a plain very unlike the desert above, being thick with palm-groves. This lower sea, this sea of bristly green (in which there were the smaller seas of salty lakes, though the palms hid them), stretched out of sight to left and right. But three miles ahead in the middle of the plain rose an island-like mountain, with a dun-colored city on its slopes and a temple covering its summit. Beyond it could be seen the line of the opposite escarpment.

The road, straight and white, shot out into the plain. On either side ran ditches, oozing and scummy (water underlay the ground, the oasis had too much of it). Beyond the ditches stood the ranks of palms, and from the green shadows came voices floating: laborers, singing palm-songs to their beloved trees in the Siwi language. Each song, as it ceased, was answered by another from somewhere else.

From far off among the trees the tones were soft; but when a song came from near at hand, it was answered battlingly or even interrupted by a song from the other side of the road. There was some rivalry between the Siwans of east and west.

As the road approached the city, the camels were led off leftward to a warehouse outside, because they would not be able to get through the gate. "It was built for donkeys," said the guide. The visitors were impressed neither by the wall, which was of dried mud, nor the gate, called *In-Xal*, so small that they had to stoop through it, nor the dark narrow passage within. The air inside this dense mud-pile of a city felt cold after the baking air of the desert and the stifling air of the plain. And the first thing seen, before the eyes adjusted, was a fire, burning low in a grate set into the passage's left side. Next to it was a mud bench on which a man in a black robe lounged with his cheek propped on his hand. His duties, of which he was negligent, were to guard the gate and to keep the fire alive day and night. It seemed to the newcomers that the fire was needed to warm the city's air, but it was for the women to come to for a flame if their own cooking fires went out. There was a pile of palm ribs and date husks, for rubbing to make sparks if this fire itself died; which it nearly had, so a woman was doing Black Robe's duty for him: kneeling, she was fanning the embers with a flap of her skirt, while other women waited with the palm-bundle torches they had brought. They drew their blue veils up and looked over them at the strangers.

The passage turned a corner to the right and opened into a space wide enough for the sun to come in. Against a wall leaned a shed, a structure of poles roofed with palm fronds. Day was not yet ended, and on each of the two mud benches inside this shelter sat a row of old men, the heads of Siwa's families. Most were asleep, the rest were engaged in arguments with each other, but one, turning his head to look at Gylippus's military tunic, said something which the guide translated:

"Want a girl for the night?—No?—A boy?" Gylippus, having been instructed in the temptations he must resist in order to bring himself and his mission safely to the oracle, declined. There was one other oracle-seeker, but he was ignored; he was only a miller who had come to ask how he could save himself from bankruptcy by getting the debt a rich customer disdained to pay.

The party still included the donkeys that had been ridden all the way from the sea, and as they pressed on along the narrow alleys and met loaded donkeys, these had to be forced backward or led aside into the forecourts of houses, before anyone could pass. The lane ended suddenly in a yard surrounded by palm-trunk pillars. The other oracle-seeker and the merchants were led off by touts to find accommodation, the envoy and his escort were settled in the suite reserved for royalty, and after supper the envoy went up alone to the room reserved for him in a tower.

Coming down in the morning he found Gylippus at a table with bread and ale, who said to him: "You do not look well rested!"

"No, it was too hot up there."

"Well, in Egypt we have it as hot, don't we? It's cooler down here."

"For me it cannot be too cool. I was born in Phrygia, in the mountains. If it's too hot I'm miserable whether I'm dreaming or waking—though mostly there's only one choice: lying awake hour after hour and remembering."

"Ha! What's all this stuff you remember?"

"I remember everyone, every word, the evil stories I've heard,

the springs when I was happy, every twist of the Gordian
Knot—"

"What is the Gordian Knot?"

"It hangs in the temple, in two halves. Gordius tied his oxcart
to the altar with a complicated knot and prophesied that
whoever untied it would possess the world. Nobody could see
how to do it—you couldn't even see any rope-ends to begin
with—but Alexander, when he came through Phrygia, they told
him about it and he just slashed it with his sword. So they say.
Anyway there it hangs, in two halves, either side of the altar, and
I can remember every detail of the inside of it, like a cut-open
cabbage."

Gylippus laughed and took their conversation into some other
direction, but Cleon was muttering soundlessly to himself: "I can
remember being delivered from my mother. I can remember the
number of steps I've ever climbed. All the words ever spoken to
me. One sleepy mistake, in a life twice as long as hers . . ."

There were no portentous delays as at Delphi, for a phase of
the moon or a month when the god was present; there was
merely waiting for the hour before sundown. In mid-morning
someone told Gylippus: "Hey, like to come along and see a fight?
It's a Day of Siwa: the East families are having another of their
quarrels with the West families. East says West offered you one
of our women." "Oh, I—!" "Don't worry about it. It's just the
pretext, we have a lot of other grievances to settle."

Gylippus jumped up and went along, and as they made their
way to the secret south gate and the stony field outside it his new
East-Siwi friend said, "You're a fine fellow, we'll be glad of your
help." "Oh, I'm to join in, am I?" —In short, Gylippus came back
with not much time to spare before sunset, pleased with himself,
with a swollen ear and a bruise in its purple stage on his temple.
To his disappointment he learned that he was not to go up to the
oracle: envoy Cleon had to go by himself.

A priest came for him and led up devious alleys that curled to
the eastern side of the rock. The caskets of gifts had already been
accepted, dedicated, and stowed in the temple treasury. The
temple was silhouetted against the staring light in the west, so
that the god was both inside his temple and it inside him:
Ammon here was worshipped as the setting sun. His residence
was a tube-like tower that rose in the middle of the western end,
and in which he descended to meet his questioners. A broad

flight of steps led up into the temple itself, but the envoy did not have to ascend it: there was a low doorway in the north side of it, and he had to stoop and go down smaller steps into darkness. He wanted to keep his hand on the priest's shoulder, and, after some steps, did so. The stair wound down into the rock. Like all travelers he had lost at least one useful article at some stop in his journey; it was a gray woollen waistcoat, he had thought he wouldn't need it, but began to wish for it. Gleams played on the walls from somewhere down ahead, but the air became cold— even his sandalled feet felt the coldness of the steps—and he was shivering before he reached the bottom and found himself in a lighted space and at the brink of a lake.

It filled the passage ahead, whose ceiling sloped down as it went away into the darkness, as if it would lower to the water. But the water close before his feet glistened under steady light, which came from openings on either side: the openings were windows into other rock-cut rooms, and someone had set oil lamps on the ledges, where they shone through grills of metallic threads. Where this fractured light lay on the water, it seemed to pick out beautiful ripples—strange ripples, that did not move, and lay straight, in nets that met at angles. And Cleon was seized with the conviction that what he was looking at was not water but ice. He absolutely remembered striations like this, in the frozen water of a Phrygian lake—no, not a lake, but a wheelbarrow that had filled with rain and been left outside on a freezing night. Would he have to walk forward on this ice? He made to kneel and touch it with a finger, to find whether it was a mere film, or a slab. And to see if he could see how far down the black water went under it.

But just as he made to kneel, another kind of light, riotous and ruddy, was born ahead: somewhere, braziers had been lit. And there appeared on the lake a terrifying vision: in the middle of the burst of flickering crackling light, something hung, head down.

A monstrous figure, dark; and the lowest part of it was flanked by two dark masses: horns. Ammon. He had descended to his audience chamber at the far end of the passage. He could not be seen directly because of the dipping of the ceiling: this was his reflection in the icy mirror.

"Say your question," whispered the priest.

The envoy began to speak—but the priest scolded him:

"Quieter!" His small voice would be magnified as it boomed along the mirror of the ice. In which, too, the god could see him.

He lowered his question almost to a mutter. The god boomed back—and the god did not restrain his voice. Huge syllables thundered around the shivering envoy, so that he could not help raising his hands to defend his ears. The syllables were not even in the Siwi language he had heard, but in an age-older form of it; and they seemed painfully beautiful. There were only fourteen or fifteen syllables; the last two or three died away together over a longer time than the whole poem had taken. Then there was a long silence while the envoy shivered and the priest thought.

And then began to speak the meaning of the oracle in Greek. But the envoy kept his shivering hands to his ears. He did not want to hear the words. They were not loud like the god's, yet he could not keep them out of his ears, but he fought to shut them out of his brain; he needed these words not to mingle with the words that were already in his memory.

Still led by the priest, he went back up the dark stair. Afraid of toppling back, he kept a hand out to touch a step ahead—the stairway being steep, it was as much as the sixth step ahead. Longing for sunshine, he emerged into night. Then it was the turn of the miller to go down to the oracle.

Next day, as they began the return to the sea, Cleon described to Gylippus some of his experience. "But Alexander," he said—"I can scarcely believe that he was treated like that—could get no nearer than that to Zeus-Ammon, who was supposed to be his god-father!"

"Oh, I've heard," said Gylippus, "that Alexander just waded through."

ove in cage

Berenice was the first to learn that the army was already on its way home. A woman of startling appearance arrived in Alexandria, with her own guard of a few armed men, whom she had to leave outside when she was admitted to the queen's presence.

"I know you," said Berenice, "you are the priestess from Cape Zephyrion?"

"Yes, your majesty," replied Eunyle. "And I am also the custodian of the pigeon post. This message has been received, it is marked for you, and so I've brought it to you myself."

"The pigeon post—what is that?"

"The rock pigeons, which I keep and feed in my dovecote, and train to come home—only I in this country know how to do it, though in Babylon it's a well known art; there is no better way of sending messages. I was asked by the army to offer my pigeons, had to let forty be taken—you saw them being loaded." And Berenice remembered the boxes stacked on the cart, and the burbling that came from inside them.

"But till now," the priestess babbled on, "the rascals haven't sent back even one, no doubt forgot about them, and I was ready to curse king and army if they neglected my pigeons and let them die. But at last they've sent this one, whose name is Anthermes; I was going to let him rest first and feed, but I could see that he hadn't flown very far—I expected him to have come from Babylon or Bactria, but he's as fresh as if he's only flown from Ascalon or Raphia—so I've brought him straight to you." Then the priestess recollected that she hadn't brought her beloved pigeon himself, only the tiny tube, a section of cane, that had been tied to his right leg, and she handed it to Berenice.

Each end of the tube was stopped with a bit of wax that bore the king's seal—only a fraction of it, there was not room for more, but it was enough for recognition. She broke the wax, and found that the tube seemed filled by a tight white spiral of papyrus, of only one thickness, not like the cross-laid paper of books. She struggled to extract it, and Eunyle showed her how, getting a purchase with her long fingernail on the innermost corner of the coil, then turning the tube so that the coil tightened and shrank. In this way Berenice managed to get it out; it recurled, and she carried it to a table and stood a vase on one end of it while she forced it out flat. It spread only as large as one of her fingers, and on it she read:

21 BOEDROMION, BE WHERE YOU LAST SAW ME

She let it roll up, and walked away. Then, turning back to where this little thing projected from under the vase like a toenail, she tilted the vase up and back so that the papyrus coil rolled into hiding under its foot; and walked over to a chair and sat down.

She said presently to Eunyle: "You must expect me at your temple three days from now. Have that room again ready for us."

"The king is returning?" said the priestess, and burst into congratulations about the joy that awaited his wife and Egypt, but Berenice was not so sure.

The news came by riders the next day. The main body of the army was as yet no nearer than Raphia on the borders of Palestine, but at the third quarter of the month Boedromion, the month of "running with a shout to help," which the Macedonians called Hyperberetaeus and the Egyptians called Thoth's month, two immense companies were to meet: the army returning triumphally from Asia, and the welcoming procession from Alexandria, led by music, dancers, and the ceremonially-borne statues of the gods. At the front of the army—half a day ahead—would march Alexandria's own regiment. It had this honor because it was bearing home to Egypt her sacred relics. The Alexandrian troops, more than half of whom were Judaeans, had been sent on an advance excursion from Thapsacus into Mesopotamia and claimed to have pushed at least as far as Babylon, of which they said they had special knowledge, some of their ancestors once having been exiles there; and at Babylon they found and seized these treasures that had been carried off long ago by the Persians—by mad Cambyses when he conquered and looted Egypt: the double crown of Ahmose, the images of lioness-headed Sekhmet and crocodile-god Sobk and Min with his upright phallus and Khnum surrounded by the people he creates from the mud of the Nile, the sarcophagi of bulls and cats and other sacred animals, the robe that Ramesses had worn when he received the submission of the Hittites, the sacred books—even the Egyptian artisans whom Cambyses had taken away to work on the palaces of Susa and Persepolis (or at any rate their descendants). Along with the floats bearing these trophies rode a swarthy man and woman dressed in turbans, supposed to be Sandracottus emperor of India and his consort Sandracotta; also a man with slant eyes and yellowish skin that had been treated with pastes to make it look yellower, a platoon of rather small elephants, some bears and panthers and strange birds and a pair of tigers, not even in a cage but led in a strong yoke. The show made, in short, a loud apparent declaration that Babylonia, Persia itself, and lands yet nearer to the dawn had been brought under the Ptolemaic yoke. No matter that, a few days later, soldiers would mention to their families that little of it came from farther east than Syria.

It was said that the king himself would be coming at the head of the Alexandrians, in order to be the first to enter Egypt and receive the congratulations of his officials and his queen.

Berenice had to arrive at the Cape of the West Wind in the evening of the twentieth day of Boedromion. She was welcomed by a lavishly smiling Eunyle, and found the room under the temple's seaward end now sumptuously prepared, for two. In one of the little chambers at the side was a bed for her handmaid, but there was no room for other attendants—they were taken away, presumably to be billeted in the village.

What else was different? The picture. Instead of the pale sweep of Auge's naked side, the golden flow of Berenice's hair. The sight of it added a layer to her fear. She wanted—but did not want—to ask the priestess who had brought it.

She had little to do but gaze at the picture of her stolen hair, and revisit thoughts already too much visited. She almost wished to call for Sosibius. Could there be time even now to close the bargain? He had one thing to get, she had two: her hair, and Coptolemy's Law. If he were to grant only one, which would she take?—her own safety, or the death of torture?

Of course it was too late, and it was her husband who would appear. She could not stop herself from imagining their meeting. She was too good at it for her own comfort. It might be that when word came that the army was approaching, she would go out, see him on his horse at the head of the Alexandrians, he would leap down, they would embrace, and her fear would be imaginary. More likely was that he would confront her furiously and contemptuously. More likely again, she saw him halting several paces off from her, herself trying to smile, hoping to begin the gesture of opening her arms toward him, he looks mournfully at her: "Are you guilty?" She rehearsed her "Of what?" She envied the Dioecetes for the startled candor of the "Of what?" with which he would be able to answer, if indeed he did not simply maintain a silence of dignified amazement.

With Polymela she went down to the water's edge to look along the coast at the sun as it set—again, on the sea to the right of the city—but she did not bother to rise when the girl, doing the same at sunrise, came back and prattled about something she had seen in the sky. "It was a sign of something!" "Yes, of rain, maybe!" said Berenice wearily, "what else are clouds signs of?" She got rid of the morning by dozing. The afternoon was so quiet that life seemed to have come again to a standstill. The only sound was the shifting of the waves—until there came a crop of raised voices from somewhere at the front of the temple.

Berenice stirred herself: she did not want to miss any of the pageantry of the troops' arrival, if that was what it was. She went to the door—and found it bolted on its other side. She went out onto the small lawn. There was a gate in the right-hand wall—but it too was barred on the other side. She pictured herself having to climb over the wall, or wading out into the water to pass its end. She went back through the room and hammered her fists on the door. It was opened by Sosibius.

The Lady's shining tress

She might have fallen back shrieking, but by now she was merely sickened. Enough of this evil magic. "I'm tired of you," she said. "Go away."

He was again wearing the yellow of the Medzae—the yellow with three blue bands.

"'By whose orders'," he said, "'am I confined here?'—that is what you want to ask." He was kind enough not to mimic her voice, of which he would certainly have been capable. "By mine. The king your husband, incidental to learning that the Dioecetes is his rival, has learned that the Dioecetes took the precaution of removing me from my post. So he sent orders that I was to be reinstated, or rather (so that my comrade Agathocles doesn't have to lose his new rank) I am raised to the even more useful post of commander of the Medzae of all Egypt. (With a hint of yet further advancement if . . .) He sent for me to meet him at Canopus—my second personal interview with him: he called me for a conference at his camp last month. I come fresh from his presence. He could not publicly order you to stay here, which would (if you are innocent) require some explaining; so he arranged for me to see to it privately."

Berenice walked off and sat down on her bed.

Sosibius closed the door behind him and leaned back against it with folded arms.

She should get up and go and stand in the outer doorway, with the daylight behind her. To stay where she was, wasn't it an invitation to a second rape? But she did not want to move. And she knew that he was utterly cold toward her.

"The army, then," he said, "is at Canopus? (you wish to ask). Some of it; it is straggling in; when it collects itself it will, I am told, make the triumphal parade into Alexandria, led by Alexandria's own regiment, tomorrow or the day after.

"And Ptolemy is also at Canopus? (you wish further to ask). No, he is in advance of everybody. He left Canopus, escorted by me and a company I provided; we have come riding along the highway, and I have stopped by, with his permission, to visit you and inform you of all this with the tact for which I am known; after which I will make haste to catch up with him. He is on his way into the city, feeling that he needs to be the first to know the truth, to be present when it is found out, so that he doesn't have to take the police's word for it."

"How can he do that—"

"It might seem cruel, but (as he explained to me himself) it would pain him to see you before this is done. Imagine the stiffness and sadness of the meeting if you are as yet under suspicion. Of course it will be a different matter when—or if—you are cleared and he can make a new beginning and celebrate with you a joyful reunion."

"How can he go ahead like that?—that's what I mean, as you know. I don't believe it. How could he, returning from half a year's war, ride into his capital, which is waiting to turn out in jubilation—how can he ride in by himself, without his army that has conquered Asia for him?"

"He is not, as I pointed out, quite by himself—"

"No, he will be accompanied by you. Is that what Alexandria is to greet and congratulate? You and a parcel of your yellow-jacketed thugs."

"Of whom he at present appears to be one."

"Oh . . ."

"You should see him—you too might hardly recognize him! No one here has for a while seen his thinning pate without the covering of crown, or ceremonial headdress, or helmet, or broad-brimmed *petasos* against the sun; even so, his face is well browned by his campaigning. You could take him for an Idu-maean nomad! So all he had to do back here in Egypt—he and a companion of his, who also, it seems, once went on incognito jaunts with him—was to put on this uniform. The eyes of anyone catching a glimpse of yellow-and-blue in the street go to the uniform, not to the face—the uniform, and perhaps the trun-cheon held in the hand. And I suggested that he make a habit of holding the top of his cloak across his mouth, as if against the dust—his chin being, I have to say, the only memorable feature of his countenance.

"Yes, the two of them, he and his sidekick, have become tem-porary Medzae. They are acting in a little play, are they not? Thus they will be able to witness the examination (which may be a rather invasive examination) of the Housekeeper's house, indeed will be able to take part in it—will have to take part in it. I told my men these two had been transferred from Naucratis. They had to put up with a bit of the usual ragging, I'm afraid, which your husband's raffish friend seemed better able to deal with.

"But I do admire your husband. He is not only browned but hardened. He has survived at least two attempts on his life by assassins sent by his enemies. He has only once tripped over a tent's guy-rope. He will make a good husband to his next wife. I wonder which city he will send you to for your retirement? What a shame, by the way, that he will not be founding cities called 'Berenice', like all those 'Arsinoes' that his father founded.

"There is of course the danger that he will have you killed, rather than risk the birth of a black child. If so, I hope he orders poisoning, rather than one of the more inhumane methods that have been known of. But I shall do my very best to deflect him from that. I shall convince him that the black seed was sown too late. And then, when a white child is born, even if lacking a bulbous chin, I believe he will (even if with a gulp) recognize and elevate our son, as his first-legitimate-born; he will be more honorable in this respect than his father was."

"Stop talking," said Berenice. "You've come here to gloat over me and glory in the new heights you think you are climbing, before you go to Hell. Go there now. I don't care for any of it. I shall probably never know how you managed to plant the false seed in Ptolemy's mind without incriminating yourself, nor do I care to know that either."

"I?" cried Sosibius. "You give me too much credit! It was the Oracle."

He advanced—but only to the middle of the room; and made an absurdly sweeping gesture around it.

"Antioch! Antioch on the Orontes, the capital of our fallen enemies, seized recently by the god Ptolemy, your husband (who is now, by the way, being called Ptolemy Tryphon no more, but Ptolemy Euergetes, the Worker of Good, for bringing home the sacred relics of Egypt, so long ago stolen away by the Persians). Antioch: I have never been in that great city, but I see it—"

"Another of your charades," said Berenice. "Spare me. Just tell me what you have to tell me."

"It is my way—I can't help it. Surely so much less dull for you? Let us enliven what otherwise might be unpleasant."

She shut her eyes; then thought she had better keep them open, though keeping him only at the edge of her field of vision.

"Don't fear any more rough handling from me," he said. "I respect our child."

She said nothing, though she felt the fury bulking larger in her than the child.

He resumed his charade.

"Well—king Ptolemy, in his bivouac—his quarters in the palace of the Seleucids. He receives a missive from his faithful queen." Sosibius unrolled in the air an imaginary letter.

"'Words from my love! Written, I see, on—what is this?—written on the endpaper of a scroll of Sappho. "The dark house of Persephone received her . . ." How interesting.'"

At close range his histrionics were even more distasteful: the letter-waving, the jaw-stretching and eyebrow-lifting, the contrapposto posing of his consciously admirable body.

"'Her hair!—that supernal hair of hers! She has cut it off! In mourning for her sister-in-law, she says! Alas, I must be in mourning for her hair! Do I deserve this? She is angry with me, she says, because of my sister's death—but she may forgive me, in time, she says—perhaps by the time her hair re-grows, she says . . . I should perhaps not come back till then—she says. (She regrets saying this—scratches it out—yet lets me see it.)'"

Sosibius gave a little laugh; glanced at his victim, as expecting her to ask him to explain why he laughed; she did not, but he explained anyway. "It occurred to me to imagine what picture went through the king's head when he read of this. Perhaps he too laughed, realizing that the lopped tress of hair he was seeing was black! The hair of that actress, Dalila! And her man got strength when she cut her hair, and yes (the king thinks), I have grown stronger. I'm a conqueror now!

"But the fleeting and paltry image of the black hair (on whichever part of the body) is of course brushed away by the long golden flow in which he has so often laced his fingers. No Dalila would tempt him more than fleetingly these days! There might be for him, as for his men, a bounty of Syrian women— 'But I live now only to worship Berenice.'

"(Yes, it's true. They're even laughing at him for that. What a doting husband you are losing.)

"A week passes and he is encamped at, perhaps, Aleppo or Beroea, when there comes another letter, longer, made of minor remarks, but ending:

"'And I am pregnant. Your grandparents are called the Savior Gods, your parents are called the Sibling-Loving Gods; I wonder what kind of gods you and I will be called, and this fourth Ptolemy that is already kicking nastily inside me.'"

Berenice's impotent fury flushed into her face. "Do you think you can get away with reading my letters? My letters to him?"

"I hope you have the opportunity to tell him about it and be believed," said Sosibius, slightly bowing. "Anyway, you now know what kind of gods you will be called: the Euergetae, the Do-Gooding Gods—your husband and you (or whoever is his next queen).

"But now Thapsacus: Thapsacus on the bank of the great river Euphrates; the damaged but extensive palace of the Seleucid governor, now occupied by your husband the king. Here it is that he must cross the river if he is to march onward, eastward, and conquer further lands; and here he awaits the advice of the Oracle, for which he has sent. And there may be something else for which he waits: a letter from his love that shall say: 'My hair is grown.' Meaning that she has got over her anger and grief and would welcome him home. If that were to come, he would perhaps ignore whatever any Oracle may say about marching on away eastward.

"It does not come. But the Oracle's answer comes." And Sosibius began one of his quick-change routines: hopping from one spot on the floor to another, so that (only without changing his costume) he was Ptolemy, and was Cleon, the envoy who brought the answer. Now there is no imaginary piece of papyrus: the envoy has had to memorize the gnomic answer:

"Thus spoke the Oracle" (assuming a creakily portentous voice intended to be that of the Oracle coming through the nervously self-important throat of the envoy)—

> Time to regress; the Lady's shining tress,
> From her house swept, is in a keeper's kept
> —The lady harnessed by the lord of darkness;
> Time to return, if you would see what's born.

"Thus," said Sosibius, "spoke Zeus-Ammon of Siwa."

Berenice stared in front of her—stared at the foot of the door into the side-chamber where her maid had slept.

"What do you make of that?" She remained expressionless, so he resumed his expressive charade.

He jumped two yards and spun around sunwise and was Ptolemy. "'Say it again, fellow.'" He jumped two yards back and spun around countersunwise and was the envoy, who repeated:

> Time to regress; the Lady's shining tress,
> From her house swept, is in a keeper's kept . . .

Back to his Ptolemy position. "'A tress!' says Ptolemy— 'a house and another house—a lady—taken by a lord of darkness!—what can all this mean? This is no answer to the question I sent. How can this tell me what will happen if I march east? I am afraid that oracles, as usual, send "words wiser than a man can understand"—*sophôter' ê kat' andra sumbalein epê*, as Euripides has it.'

"And perhaps he asks his generals who stand around, but no one ventures a guess. At length he thinks of asking the bearer of the message, who says humbly 'It is not for me to say.' But it occurs to the king to press him: 'Well, have you not been thinking about it all these days, during your long journey here, bearing it in your head?' And so the good Cleon is forced to admit: 'Well, sire, I suppose I have, and—I would think, sire, that the tress might be your lady queen's celebrated hair.'

"'Of course!' pipes up one or other of the generals— 'Even the common people call her Berenice Eucomos, she of the fine hair.'

"'You could be right', says the king; 'but I asked nothing about that. She is behind me, Asia is before me. Kept in a house— ' He becomes wary. Is it public knowledge that she has cut it off?

"Evidently it is. 'Some say', says someone else, 'that she has had a disease.' 'No,' says another, 'they are saying she has dedicated it for a vow—hung it in a temple, but that may be—only what they say. Perhaps one of the small temples within the Brucheion, or that *naïskos* on Cape Zephyrion— '

"'You may leave me', says the king abruptly. — 'I will think about it later, there are other things to do now.' And the messenger and everyone withdraw.

"A house within a well-kept house. The house of the Dioecetes, the Housekeeper of Egypt.

"It suddenly is not a difficult riddle to solve. All is not sound in Egypt behind him. The Oracle has answered the second part of the question—that now overriding the first. He had better return. A warning has been sent from a source he cannot suspect—from Zeus, no less. His queen has so well used her broom of bright hair for the dark-faced Housekeeper that it is now a keepsake in his house, and the child she is to bear may be born with the face of the Aethiopians, the Burnt-Face People.

"What a dreadful mistake, is it not?"

As Berenice did not answer, he continued: "I so admire the fortitude with which you receive this."

"Who is Creon?"

"Cleon, you mean? Don't you remember him? Your husband didn't remember him, but I thought you would."

"They are common names, I remember several of both."

"Well, this was a Cleon who was qualified for this mission by happening to possess an excellent memory. A memory that you underestimated. He had to memorize not only the question to be asked of the Oracle, but the Oracle's precise reply, couched in the convoluted form that is expected of Oracles. In fact his memory is so good that he memorized it even before he heard it."

The Mnemon.

"Ah, I see you know the one I mean. I expect you are reflecting that (a principle I have myself learned) it is not wise to offend a person, even quite an insignificant person, unless you crush that person completely."

"So he memorized it before he heard it, did he, you liar?"

"Well, before he heard it from the Oracle. Of course he may also have memorized whatever it was that the Oracle said. Which could even have been the same—you never know what miracles of coincidence the gods are capable of! Unfortunately we shall never know what the Oracle actually said, because I was not interested in finding it out from the little Mnemon before the memory died with him."

"So you've already had your tool silenced?"

Sosibius looked modest.

"And where is Sylcon? Is he too being kept under duress?"

"'Sylcon'—you say the name so fondly! Probably not far from here."

"Ptolemy will believe none of this," she said.

"What, not believe the pronouncement of the infallible Oracle!—of Zeus? He has to believe it, and has done so, I am sorry to say."

"It could mean a dozen things."

"Such as?"

"I shall have it found out, from Siwa, what the Oracle really said, before you had your doggerel substituted."

"Yes, it would be of some academic interest to know. Perhaps Babylon and Bactria have reason to be glad that no more war is sent their way. Perhaps the Oracle said something like 'Cross the river and you will reach to the end of the world.' —Ah, that would have been a fine prophecy, wouldn't it? (what clever ideas I have!)—just the right oracular style, with opposite possible meanings! Unfortunately you may not be in a position to send and find out, because before then something else will have been found, which will cast a shadow on yourself along with the respected Dioecetes, and, I'm afraid, set limits to your movements."

"You really think that everything will turn on the finding of this one poor scrap of false evidence?"

"No, your Lock of Hair, treasured and no doubt frequently kissed by dear Sylcon, is a powerful unit of evidence, but it is only the key by which to unlock his house. Other will be found along with it."

"I see. Other things forged and planted by you. Letters from Syria—from me . . ."

"How quick you are! I would have employed you as a detective. But life works out sadly different from our hopes." He mimed pity (inclined head, drooping mouth), and said: "A last suggestion, by which you might yet preserve yourself. Tell him that the Dioecetes raped you."

"Go away!" she said hoarsely, rising to her feet.

"I will, I will!" (miming fright)— "I must indeed leave you, because the king and his company have already passed, and I am expected to be in the city and assist in the search."

"I'm sure you will know exactly where to look."

"I do have to confess that I know the undersides of Alexandria's houses well—I have quite enjoyed qualifying myself to be Inspector of Drains, the job to which I know you wished to appoint me. I shall stand back, though, and let others do the finding. In fact, it's not altogether a bad thing that I shall now be somewhat late: probably they will already have found it without me."

"Yes, you wouldn't want to take credit, would you?"

"No; on the other hand I must be in time to save them from giving up if the ingenuity of the hiding-place defeats them—to guide them with a suggestion, if necessary. So I beg you to excuse me; I underestimated the time we would spend enjoying our conversation."

He bowed and turned to leave. This exposed his back to the door from the side-chamber, and Polymela, who had with quiet effort broken a pair of scissors into its two halves to make of one half a dagger, rushed out and stabbed him.

The blade went into his left shoulder and met bone. She had struck as hard as hatred could, but not with a low enough aim or a long enough weapon. It was good to hear him yowl with pain, but not good to see him whirl and catch his assailant by her wrist and send a blow of the side of his other hand to her hip.

She fell writhing and crying, and he said: "Good, now you will have to choose between looking after her and—doing whatever else you might think of doing. To you, little woman: remember next time to strike under the ribs, and upward." And he was gone.

Berenice knelt, in a storm of tears, trying to help Polymela's leg back into joint.

Sargane

Sosibius bolted the door behind him, ran up the steps and along the side-aisle of the temple to the front, where the men left to guard it were hanging around. He smiled to see their gaping mouths: he was as upright and relaxed as usual, his wound betrayed only by the blood that had spattered over his cloak. Every one of them remembered the story of Berenice and her spear.

"Strip!" he said gaily to the youngest of them. And he took off his own bloodied cloak and the tunic under it, called for a jug of water with which to wash his shoulder, put on the other's tunic but rolled it down to his belt, to roll up later when the bleeding ceased; and kept his cloak in his hand, also to don later, since it was the sign of the Medzae authority.

He looked around and said: "Where's Sargane?" Sargane was his horse, whom he affected to love better than any man.

"She's around the corner—they're mending her shoe. She's thrown a shoe." He hadn't noticed.

He strode to where a group of men was trying to hold the mare still and get her hoof up and re-nail the shoe.

"What are you bungling, you fools?—where's the farrier?"

"Ain't no farrier here. Nowt but girls and children and fishers in this place."

"Give me that." He seized hammer and hoof so hard that the unhappy horse was for a moment still from shock; drove the nail in—it missed the hoof wall and went into the quick and the shrieking horse jumped away, her braided mane flying. He grabbed the rein, held it struggling; "Run into the village for another horse. Go!"

It took them a while to come back and say: "No horses here. Only donkeys." One who happened to be behind him let himself grin at the idea of Sosibius on a donkey.

He leapt onto Sargane; what did a shoe matter, why did a horse need it for fourteen miles? What she needed was a strong hand—and she had it: she had now been injured by him twice: for a joke he had had her tail docked. Half way along the pink-paved mint-bordered path, Sargane sank on her knee.

He slid from her and abandoned her with a kick, took the cloak over his left arm, shook his sandals off and snatched them up with the fingers of the same hand, and set out running. Along the path to the highway, and off along it, he went with easy strides. He was good at distances as well as the dash and looked forward to the pleasant exercise of overtaking his squad, who would be riding at no more than a jog-trot.

People near the gates of farms stood and watched this athlete loping past. His left arm, carrying the cloak and sandals, was clasped to his waist for ease; his right arm swung all the more. But after a while, his left shoulder troubling him, he clasped his right hand to that—which made running, with neither arm to swing, less easy. His shoulders turned from side to side with a will of their own, causing his heels to strike the road with something of a twist.

His mind ran faster (obscuring the distance, as well as any pain), picturing the move he had made: one move cleared the two between himself and the King. Yes, let's invent a game, in which the player moves his *adversary's* pieces, making them cancel out each other. I'll be the new Palamedes, who in legend invented all games . . .

Suddenly he sat down by the roadside. His head swam, the wound had not dried, the blood was trickling to his waist. Should he use his cloak to stanch it? To his disgust he was on the verge of fainting. He put his head down between his knees.

After a lapse of whose length he was uncertain, a kindly peasant, coming by with a cart pulled by a mule, offered him a ride. Not altogether glad, because of the ambling pace, Sosibius accepted. Clambering in, he found the cart's floor covered by heaps of cucumber and garlic, and distastefully shoved himself a sitting-space, keeping his head bowed, hoping to be hidden by the sides. Could he clothe his shoulders yet? His sweat chilled him, it was the last evening of summer, the sun was already too low to fill the cart. He pulled the tunic up, put on the cloak, blood and all. The driver stopped to chat with an even older man.

"I can pay you," said Sosibius, "if you hurry. Ten staters."

The peasant hadn't asked for money, but his children needed it, and the rich young man's plight was evident. He thrashed the mule, which thereupon stood still. Another thrash—it backed up a pace. After some persuasion in Egyptic it consented to move again, and the cart rumbled on at the same rate.

Sosibius saw two horses in a field, tethered to stumps by long lines. He jumped down, scared the mule into a ditch where the cart stuck out of the way, hurdled the prickly-pear hedge, slashed the rope of the tall dappled mare with his knife, and using his knees and the rope as a rein he made her jump the hedge and launch into a gallop.

The gallop declined after half a mile into a fast trot. The sun, now very low, was glaring in the eyes of horse and man. It set before they came to the suburbs, and began to be replaced by the glow of Alexandria, its night-dazzle—Alexandria, it was said, was brighter by night than by day; and as they approached the Canopus Gate (the gate that was called the Sun Gate) he noticed over it—over the northern quarters, to the right of where the sun had sunk—what seemed like a flame: a far thin towering flame or the sunlit smoke from that flame, curving rightward as in a gentle breeze, of a dusky white against the graying blue of the low sky. The smoke, if it was a smoke, was far back, at the other end of the city, where the Nubian quarter was. Had his stupid men set the Housekeeper's house on fire?   As he passed in through the gate the ghostly impression was obliterated by the rushlights in the streets.

The game of Robbers

Sylcon had not come home the previous evening, so nothing had been done about sending the dwarf back to the palace; and for the first time he had been allowed to stay in the house overnight. He curled on a mat in a corner of the courtyard, along with one of the domestic cats. He still wondered why his fellow Nubian, who did not worship these animals, even tolerated them in his own house.   The servants were so disciplined that there was scarcely a crumb to sustain a mouse. And Housekeeper and cat were opposed in nature: the most smoothly busy of beings, the most smoothly un-busy.

In the morning he was lying there with his eye open, and the cooks gave him some dates for breakfast.

The children were used to him by now, teased him only occasionally and sometimes took what he said quite seriously. They liked being able to say things about him to each other that he wouldn't understand, in Greek and Egyptic.   Each of them had three names, Nubian, Egyptic, Greek—the elder girl was Utpala, Seshen, Nymphaea, "Waterlily"—and he made up names for them in other languages of his own invention, and they made up rude names for him.   His imitations of their dignified father and argumentative mother and the impudent but doting servants had them in fits of laughter; more wonderful still was how he could mimic statesmen and scholars while knowing only from their tones and motions what the things they said might mean. He had the sidelong jokiness of the poet Callimachus down pat, the inability of the Chief Librarian to keep his eyes down to the level of your own, the imposing craftiness of someone called Sosibius and his mannerism with his lower lip, the wide eyes and impulsive movements of Queen Berenice, the luckless movements of the king.

"Why aren't you as black as us?" the girl had asked him.

"It depends on the tribe," was his answer. (But the grayness of his face had more to do with his own condition; the blackness of theirs, with the purity of their family.)

In the afternoon their mother gave them time to play with him again. The elder girl, tired of games with string or pebbles and stories about cats and mice and crickets, said to him: "Do you know how to play Senat?"

"Of course he doesn't," said her little sister. "You have to play that with Dad."

"Well, he looks as old as Dad."

"But he won't know Senat."

"I can teach him. Do you want to play Senat," she said to the dwarf, "or Tau, the game of Robbers?"

"Tau."

She brought out the board, which could be set up like a little table by folding out four legs ending in the shapes of goats' hooves. She set it in the middle of the courtyard, they squatted down either side of it, and she shook the pieces out of the drawer under it. She arrayed her army of thirty black Policemen on their alternating squares, and he, copying her, did the same with his thirty white Robbers. She told him the rules of the game, which (like Senat and all other games) had been invented by the god Thoth— "You move a man one square, any direction, or he can jump over another man, and if you get a man on each side of one of mine, you've captured it—you put it in your bag."

The two armies of little clay obelisks started off on each side of the board, separated by the two empty rows in the middle; they advanced and mingled with each other, and pieces began to be taken. She was impatient with him for playing slowly. Her little brother, squatting beside them, stretched his hand in and tried to move pieces and the girl batted him away. He said: "Can I have these ones you've put on the ground?"

"No."

"Why are you putting them on the ground?—you said to put them in the bag!"

"I like to see how many I've captured," she said smugly. "I'm the Lion and he's the Goat!" The Lion in the story wins the game and eats the Goat.

"One time," said Saha, "it was the Goat who beat the Lion and ate him." And he invented a fantastic version in which the Goat led the Lion along by letting him jump over piece after piece until he fell into a trap. At which the two smaller children clapped and wanted over again the story about the Lion's tricking by the Hyena (the Lion sits down to eat his Antelope supper, the Hyena points to a cooking-fire—it's really the setting sun—the Lion goes off to fetch it, comes back an hour later complaining "It went down into the ground!—Where's my supper?" and the Hyena, licking her chops and picking her teeth, says "It went down into the ground").

While the dwarf used time with this story, the cat came pacing lightly past, rubbed its muzzle against a corner of the board, and sat down as if to listen. It hooked a paw in an experimental pat at one of the pieces (Saha's pieces, captured from him by the girl). The girl warned the cat off, but a moment later it was playing with the pieces, beginning to scatter them. So Saha put out his hand to shoo it; and it swatted him with opened claws. It did not draw blood, but from then on a place on his hand itched. He felt his reputation betrayed—felt that the children who could have been thinking "Even animals take to him!" were thinking "Even animals scorn him." The cat was gray, with muffled tones of orange, and face made unsymmetrical by a black patch under one side of its mouth. He had thought this cat-face acceptable, like that of a plain but amiable girl; now he thought it evil.

"Come on, Saha!" said the girl, "it's your move."

She had an advancing wall of three pieces, shoulder-to-shoulder as if defying anyone to surround them. He stretched out his misshapen hand—not the hand with the fingernails missing, on which he was sitting—and slowly took up one of his pieces, and lifted it over another to a square where it was between the advancing three and a single piece behind them.

"Hey, you can't put yourself into a captured place!" said the girl, flushing.

"Yes, you can," said her sister, "you told us that rule, you've been doing it yourself."

All three of her men were captured simultaneously—no, four! It was a feat that had never been achieved in any game of Tau. She and the dwarf were level.

"I'm tired of Tau now," she said, tipping the men off the board. Her little sister and brother mocked her as she went off to read a book, and they stayed playing knuckle-games and stick-games with Saha; he taught them a drumming game in which the sticks were tossed from hand to hand, to a chant about monkeys making a bridge over the crocodiles in the Nile. Then they wanted another game of hide-and-seek.

Wearily Saha hoisted himself to his feet. He would have to hobble from room to room, and up the stairs.

How he wished for the times when he would have been able to catch these children by the heels and swing them, screaming with thrill, in circles till landing them softly on a cushion; to toss them in the air and catch them, or teach them to stand on their heads or roll like hoops. Now the strength was not in his arms and chest, and he could use only what was in his head and the poor words of his one language.

When he couldn't find the children anywhere else, he climbed painfully up the second stair. The house was higher than the others in the Nubian quarter only in that it had, like fine houses in the middle of the city, a shade-shelter roof. Above the flat clay roof was a light roof of poles, admitting dapples of sun and supported all around by palm-trunk-shaped columns, up some of which vines grew from pots standing on the ledge outside the balustrade. The family could go up there on the hottest days and sit in the shade with cool air moving through, and could see down into a marketplace, and another family's courtyard and, not far away to the north, the Eunostus Harbor, toward which ran shining slivers of a channel. The Nubians had become confined to the northwestern quarter, just about the farthest spot in Egypt from their southern homeland. And it was in this northwestern district that the great canal along the southern side, having hooked around the city's end, emerged in the harbor, and also threw off a multitude of side-channels, which ran partly in tunnels under the streets or were tapped by wells.

The dwarf could see that there was no one on the roof either, though he pretended to look behind chairs and jars. But one of the columns on the western side cast a bit more of a shadow than it should. He went quietly to the balustrade, put his head over, and said to the little girl, who was standing on the outside ledge and clinging to the column:

"Please don't hide here. If you fall I will be killed too."

She consented to let him help her climb back over the balustrade, giggling, and calling out something in the eternal tune of mocking children ("Laa laa le-laa laa! Laa laa le-laa laa!") but in one of the languages he confessed to not knowing. Whereupon he went, in even greater trepidation, to one of the columns on the northern side and reached around and, before the little boy could giggle or squirm, took his arm in a tight grip and pulled him gently in.

"You understand Greek!" said the little girl— "You lied, telling us you don't!"

"My turn to hide," he said.

"Yes! We'll stay up here and you run and hide! We'll count to forty—we'll count in Egyptic, because it's quickest. *Wa, senu, khemt, fedu* ... "

Saha hobbled away down the stairs; and then down the lower stairs, into the courtyard. He hurried, but not desperately, he knew they usually got mixed up around "seventeen." He hoped to find a good enough hiding-place so that he could rest for a while. There were plenty of places to hide in this cluttered house, even though it had only four main rooms around the courtyard on each level. The women grinding grain in the court-yard and the men cooking in the kitchen grinned at him. There was the well-top, and beside it the filtering-box, filled with layers of sand and fig-bark, for purifying water drawn up from the underground channel; he could have hidden under that, but two servants were busy at it, one pouring jugfuls of water in, the other sucking on a pipe to pull the water through. One of the rooms had two planks X-wise across its doorway, indicating that it should not be entered, because it was being redecorated: the old plaster had been scrubbed, and the floor had been tiled. Saha ducked under the planks and ventured into the bare room, and had time to read a name scrawled on the wall—

SNOSTRI

—before a big workman came after him: "Not allowed in there till the tiles are grouted."

"Who's Snostri?"

"Me. Plasterers always sign their names on the wall before they put the plaster over it. They should have left the tiles till after the plastering, but the wife changed her mind and wants maroon walls, with pheasants painted on." And the plasterer lifted the dwarf out by his armpits.

So where should he hide? No time left now; he fell back on the place where he had last hidden—the children wouldn't think he would do that, or they might think of it straight away, and either way they would be pleased. There was a cluster of jars taller than himself, standing in the corner between the staircase and a wall; he crept in among them and sat hugging his knees; from some angles he wasn't hidden at all. The children came running down the stairs—they could, if they had thought of it, have looked down on the top of his head; they ran to and fro around him; they had forgotten where he hid yesterday. Looking along the wall beside him, he saw the little boy come running and throw himself flat and make as if to wriggle through the gap under the door of a closet. The doorway, near the courtyard's corner, was low and narrow; a thick but ill-fitting timber had been re-used to close it—perhaps on purpose to make this look like the most unimportant of closets.

"Don't!—we can't go in there, it's Dad's safe-room, it's locked anyway."

"I'm going to hide in it next time, I can slide under!"

"You'll never dare!"

"I did once!"

"Liar! Anyway, he couldn't."

"He could, he's so small."

"Not small enough. —He must be upstairs after all." And they ran away.

Saha came cautiously out on his hands and knees, looked around—and set himself to insert the bits of his body, bit by mangled bit, under that locked door.

He did it feet first; that way it was even harder—he had to pull himself along the ground instead of pushing, and could not feel what was coming—but the head end of him, if caught, could explain that he was only playing a game.

Now his chest was in (by puffing his lungs flat), and his shoulders. He turned his head sideways and pulled on.

His head stuck.

His feet had already met the opposite wall.

He had to twist his body over, bend his knees. And soon they too met an obstacle, the left side of the space inside, while his heels were against the right side. If he had been any longer he would not have been able to fold himself short enough. Saha was the only key that could open this door.

An agonized minute later, with a new scrape-bruise all down his left cheek and ear and temple, he was inside the little room.

Gradually the light from the gap under the door made the interior discernible to his one good eye. The left side, against which his knees had stopped, carried three shelves. On them, some scrolls and small boxes, money.

He raised himself to sit with his back against the other wall and stayed there, resting, feeling his scraped cheek. If only he could see like a cat. He screwed up his good eye, waited for it to adapt to the meagre light that came from under the door, and fixed it on the objects on the shelves, making them emerge out of the grayness, one by one.

The bang of a door flung back—screaming—a chair thrown over!

Heavy voices; the mother yelling back, upbraiding the intruders. More crashes: the men had clubs and axes, they were smashing chests and wardrobe doors and the larger vessels. They sensed that the Dioecetes had already fallen and this trumped-up game—a bitterer game of hide-and-seek—was a piece of his humiliation. Another scream; the children.

"Where's your father's safe-room?"

The girl answering stoutly: "I don't know. What does it mean? He doesn't have one."

They seized her and held a knife-point to her throat.

The mother still held out, but the little boy: "Don't hurt her! It's there, there it is!"

The heavy steps came over: a club smashed at the door. It was too thick to break; an axe tried to get splits going in it; many smashes later it was ready to be wrenched from its lock and hinges.

Leucus, ducking his head through the doorway, strode into

the little room, another of the Medzae behind him. They began, moderating now their roughness, to sort through the things on the shelves.

Alabaster lid

The dwarf had been saved by the cat, which chased a mouse under the door and across the room. Or, no, it was the mouse that did the saving. It disappeared at the foot of the wall. The cat, making inappropriately pretty whimpers, froze at the foot of the wall, trembling in frustration.

Saha crawled over and the cat, hissing, dashed around him and fled the way it had come. He found the fingerhold under the foot of the wall, through which the mouse had scampered. This lowest block of the wall was the only one that did not have a filling of dust in all the joints around it. He pushed his forefinger into the slight crevice—a misfit between the block and the floor it rested on—that had saved the mouse; felt a touch of oil. He tried to lift, pull left, pull right; nothing happened. He pulled his finger out—it was stuck despite the oil, he had to pull a bit harder. At this the block granted the hint of a tremble. He pressed the spread fingers of both hands against the stone; pushed to the left; and with the slight purchase of this friction the stone began to move. It was a thin, smooth slab. He got it rumbling along; a stain of oil oozed from under it.

It stopped when it had half moved out of the way. The gap was not much more than a handspan wide, knee-high.

He put a hand cautiously through, into the blank darkness. There could be a cobra inside. He felt the smooth top and sharp edge of a step. He turned and, again feet-first, bit by bit he put his body through. The top step shifted disconcertingly; it must be broken, it threatened to shift away under him; he arched himself over it, got his feet down on the next, got his shoulders and head through, rose to a sitting-position, went on down.

Each step was a lighter gray; the last two seemed almost in daylight, though they were still in a tunnel, and beyond them was the gleam of water, in a wider tunnel. Below the tenth step, a narrow stone pavement: a small quay. Beside it lay a boat, of the

kind called *ambatch* because made of the wood of that tree. It
was hitched to two posts, and the rope at the right—the
upstream end, the stern—was tight, the other slacker, ready to
be cast off, so that the bow of the boat nosed outward. Its floor
was tightly and neatly stacked with boxes; three side-to-side
spaces open between the stacks, enough for legs, the stacks
acting as seats. This was the escape prepared by the Housekeeper for his family in case of another massacre of Nubians.

The water moved here a little faster than in the great canal. All
the way from the Ethiopian mountains, the Nile—receiving no
more rain—flowed smaller; at Letopolis it began to split, into the
branches of the Delta; every channel into which it redivided
flowed smaller and slower again. But this channel, like the other
braids under the Nubian quarter, had picked up some haste, as if
drawn by something: which it was, because not many hundred
yards ahead it came to the top of a stone incline, down which it
slid to debouch into the Eunostus Harbor; otherwise, the slight
tides of the sea would have brought salt water into it. The end of
the tunnel could be seen, and the light of the dimming day over
the harbor.

The dwarf clambered into the boat and fumbled at its contents. The boxes were all exactly uniform, all nailed shut, except
for one that lay under the stern seat; he felt inside that, but there
were only a few small scrolls and clay tablets and other scraps of
writing-material. He pulled out one that had a cylindrical shape;
it had a seal, which he could not read; he broke it; there was only
another letter inside. There were two short oars, and a few loose
tools. He pawed over the boxes, whereas (he remembered) he
had not touched those in the safe-room but had only gazed at
them. Would Sylcon allow his wife a key to the safe-room?—or
rather (he tried to imagine) would Sosibius think that Sylcon
would allow his wife a key to the safe-room? He looked around
him; fancied that in the stonework of the tunnel's side there were
formations like crannies, ledges, on which something might be
stowed; for a moment, that there was a recess like a shrine in the
jut of rock where the little quay ended.

It wasn't here. It was in the safe-room after all. With limbs
speeded by panic, he set himself to clamber back up the steps.
As he came to the top, the light from the courtyard under the
safe-room door came so bright into his eyes that it was like a

sunrise—even though the sun by now had set and the courtyard light was mostly the hectic light of torches.

And that loose top step—

It was not a step: it was a coffin, a child-size casket. Its flat top, whose glassy smoothness and perfect edge he had noticed without remembering noticing, was a lid, of diorite perhaps or of alabaster, translucent if there had been light. The rest was rougher to the fingertips—granite—but not rough in shape: it was carved, his fingers felt the exquisite details but could not tell whether they were the leaves of plants or the scales of animals. Or the drapery and curls of human figures. Did the lid slide in grooves? No, it had knobs at its back corners that fell into slots, hinging it, as it was lifted.

What was inside was soft to the touch, and even in this darkest place it faintly glowed. A ribbon clenched it at the end where it had been cut.

Set here, perhaps earlier this same day, where Sylcon would come only occasionally, but where he could be imagined coming occasionally to worship.

This casket should be set adrift in the sea, like the infant Perseus by his mother, set adrift for ever—but the dwarf knew he could not lift it and get it down the steps; he lifted out the tress and started away; he would let the channel and the sea take it as it was. —Then came the crash from inside the house, the screams, the abrupt voices of the Medzae. Frantically he turned (he had to lay his prize around his neck to get both hands free) and hoisted the sarcophagus; tried to fill with it the gap in the wall; it wouldn't stand on its end; he wrenched the lid, one of the little knobs cracked off, then he realized that he needed only to lift the other out of its slot, he stood the lid at a slant inside the box so that its end propped the top of the box up, slammed the heel of his hand against the bottom so as to jam this hasty block in place, and slithered away down the steps.

Sosibius stopped the horse abruptly by putting a hand over her eyes, slid down without caring where she went, strolled into the house, and the first thing that the periphery of his vision noticed was a slope curiously silhouetted against the orange sky above: the shade-shelter roof had collapsed on one corner, because one of its propping pillars had been knocked away. He saw that his men were still roaming around the house, smashing vases and cabinets and flinging mats aside, driving little crowds of terrified servants from courtyard to kitchen and back to courtyard, but they were doing it listlessly, compounding chaos as if as a matter of duty.   Of the two new recruits, the curly-haired one was among those still showing some zest for the rough game; the other was among those who had come to a standstill—he was standing back and watching gloomily.   He had done a bit of searching at first, got his hand stuck in a drawer, been laughed at for his ineptness. Also observing, with folded arms and a white gown, was the Advisor Calerno, whom Sosibius had notified of the proceedings and who might have been considered a sufficient witness, but on whom Ptolemy had preferred not to rely. One and all turned and stared at Sosibius.

"Well?"

Since he didn't say anything about his uniform, which was now red-yellow-blue, they didn't care to ask him. No doubt he would later tell them the story of some exploit. He let them give him their negative report.

"I see. So there was no safe-room?" he said with his back to it.

"Yes—over there—looked there first, of course, but no luck, that's why we're prodding everywhere else. May have to take the whole place down like you said."

"Yes, you may."   He strolled over, peered in through the smashed door of the safe-room; stepped inside and pretended to take a look around it, at the cracked-open boxes and scattered papers. For those few moments inside the safe-room, he actually had his eyes shut. He was re-living the pleasure he had had in finding this hiding-place, and pre-living the pleasure of the moment that was to come. Then:

"Where's Leucus?" he said, putting his head out. (He had wondered whether to take Leucus into his confidence over this trick, as so many others; but it had been important enough to handle by himself.)   "Leucus, my dear, come back inside here. Where are your eyes? Can't you see that that block at the back is false?" And as he guided Leucus in for a better look, he observed that the block was falser than it should be.

"Give—" He began again with clearer throat. "Give me that." He seized the pick and hit the underside of this casket that was posing as a block. Though it would, as he could see, tumble away at a touch, and though he had paid for its exquisite making, he hit it hard with the end of the pick, so that it went away down the steps in three pieces. "See, you fools?—go down there. No, I'll go" and he went onto his knees, got through, and went down, feeling around with his hands for what, as he soon knew, wasn't there. He got up to a crouch, went on down, stumbling over the broken pieces of alabaster, kicking them before him. The boat was gone.

As he came back up, he experienced difficulty in painting his usual mask of commanding serenity over his inner grimness. The world had been all contemptible, except for the bright castle inside himself; now that too was invaded by despair. He noticed now the bloodstain (not his own, that had dried on his shoulder) on the threshold of the safe-room. He found his men, his police force, in some bafflement as they tried to handle a squall of two small children.

"Where's Saha? You've taken him away! You've hidden him!"

"We shall leave," said Sosibius; "there has been—"

"Where's Saha? Where's Cop—"

"Silence!" Nobody had ever heard Sosibius bawlingly lose his temper, and the children were almost as amazed as the Medzae were cowed.

"We shall leave now," he resumed sweetly; "the matter is not yet resolved, but we shall certainly . . ." He did not know what to say we should certainly.

"We shall go back to Canopus," said the clumsy Naucratian recruit with the thinning hair.

"This is King Ptolemaeus Euergetes," said Sosibius, and after two beats the men went down on their knees.

"What shall we do, sire?" asked Sosibius.

"I don't know. Go to your houses for now."

Some time, at which Sosibius helplessly chafed, was consumed in settling matters, before Ptolemy turned to the street door, Sosibius having detailed four men to accompany him, find horses and escort him to the Cryon, where rooms could be assigned for his use during the night without the populace learning that he had been in the town; and they would ride with him back to Canopus before dawn.

After they had gone, Sosibius seized three others in one double armful and bundled them to the door. Outside was full dark. "Get yourselves to the Eunostus Harbor. Commandeer a launch, and look for a small boat with a dwarf rowing it. It won't have got far, you'll find it. You had better." But they didn't.

White night

Ptolemy received a supper in a surprisingly pleasant part of the Cryon. Surprising also was to find the Cryon served by an abundance of Egyptian servants (who all, unknown to him, had to live outside the walls of the city). They heated a bath for him, such as his senior officers (but few of the other ranks) were enjoying at Canopus. He enjoyed it lengthily, then lay on a comfortable bed and went to sleep.

He woke soon, though the time seemed to him an uncertain time in the middle of the night. He was picturing the collapsed roof of the trashed house. It was like many a scene of war, but it was the house of the Dioecetes. He would order it to be repaired—pay for the building of a new house. He began to feel perversely uneasy that the room he lay in, though pleasant, was in the basement of the Cryon; why was it not on the roof? He curled on his right side in hope of returning to sleep—yet, even curled, pressed his shoulders back; it helped even in this.

In the second or third month away, he had begun remembering to press his shoulders back; and felt at once that the breath came cooler into his chest and that he smiled. When he remembered—even though he could not remember all the time, could not become fixed in ramrod shape like the Dioecetes, who did not have to remember—it still seemed to help, whether in fighting or speaking or merely walking or even sleeping. He felt that he appeared taller, and that men respected him.

This time the result was not to bring sleep but bring him to his feet. He threw on the same tunic and yellow *chlamys*—it was all he had here—and went out and up the stair to the courtyard. Medzae were still about, and they snapped to attention.

"I wish to speak to the superintendent."

He expected to be told that the superintendent had gone home, but they took him to the office, where he was greeted by Agathocles, whom he told: "I want Sosibius fetched back here. There is a question I must ask him."

"I am afraid," said Agathocles, "that Sosibius went down to the port. I have a notion he is on a ship."

"On a ship! Why? Have him fetched. Ships can't leave in the night."

"It may have done. But of course I will send—"

"A ship to where?"

"To Side in Pamphylia, I believe. He has accepted an offer of employment from Seleucus."

Ptolemy received this insulting information with narrowed eyes and lips.

"Being without a wife," added Agathocles, "he has not much in the way of household possession—"

"Has something frightened him?" asked the king, not expecting an answer, but Agathocles said:

"Perhaps the comet!"

"Comet, what comet?"

"That is why the people are out in the streets," said Agathocles; "there is a certain amount of alarm. It will soon die down, the thing is not seen any more, it disappeared soon after the sun did."

Ptolemy stood for a few moments, and then said: "I shall return to my residence. Have a coach fetched." He longed for his own home in the palace—and he longed for Berenice, though she would not be there.

He found himself in a closed carriage escorted through the streets by no fewer than thirty marching Medzae—even though, inside the carriage, and dressed like them in the yellow-and-blue, he would not be recognized, would be taken by the crowds for no more than a police officer. And there certainly were restive people in the streets. Could they have heard not only about the comet but about the bits of intelligence he had himself received from Syria?

No, it was not yet known here, and would not be known for several months, that the power of the Seleucids was not at an end. Seleucus the Second, son of Antiochus the Second, still had an army in the province of Pontus; his brother Antiochus Hierax was at Ancyra in the middle of Anatolia; it had even been reported that their mother Laodice was not dead. If Egypt wished to hold its Asiatic acquisitions it might have to go campaigning again next year.

Nobody yet in Alexandria was troubling about this, and the triumphal return of the army would not be spoiled. It was only a comet that might spark a riot.

Ptolemy had the carriage bring him to an inner courtyard, he surprised only a few of his servants with his presence, and prepared again for bed. He had had to learn, over the past six months, to stay awake during councils after battle (for which the

trick of the straight shoulders and deep breath helped him) and
to sleep in spite of the violences of yesterday and the fears of
tomorrow. Most of "Laodice's War," as people were calling it—
the third of the wars that had been fought between the Ptolemies
and the Seleucids—had consisted of mere feints that sent
Laodice's supporters into retreat; when, almost by accident, the
troops engaged, the skirmishes had been of archers and cavalry;
but one night, with an eyeful of hand-to-hand fighting in his
brain—men glimpsed through the gateway of an orchard outside
a village, tussling horribly, in unfair knots, two against one, one
against three, weapons chopping among flesh, a man down and
being stabbed, a large man on his knees shrieking as a sword
went down his back, another on the ground only half dead as . . .
That night the sights of the day had taken long hours to turn into
nightmares; after that he had somehow hardened himself to it.
More of the worries were about where these thousands of men
were to eat and excrete. Now he looked at his bed with serious
longing, but then he knew he would not sleep. He put on clothes
of his own, and made his way to the living-quarters of the scholars of the Museion. Everything was quiet there; he forbore to
knock on doors and find out where the apartment of Eratosthenes was and have him roused. He went down a stair and on
along the main corridor of the library, to the hall of Urania,
though telling himself it was foolish to expect an astronomer to
be reading Urania's books at night, just because her courtyard
was open to the stars. But there was a lamp on one of the tables
in the cloister: a small plump student was bent shortsightedly
over a scroll. He approached, and had to clear his throat to make
her aware of his presence. She got to her feet.

"You are up late, wearying your eyes," he said. "Are you studying the comet?"

"I have heard about it, but I am studying—I am studying many
matters," said Theonida, flustered, "because I am to be examined
about them tomorrow."

"I think it was Lycon," said the king, "who was mentioned as
being the authority on comets."

"Conon, perhaps?"

"Yes—that was the name."

The girl hurried off to find Conon. And in time Conon of
Samos appeared, still tying his belt and smoothing the fringe of
black beard that encircled his face, and rubbing his wide-apart

eyes. He did not see why he should conceal from the king that he had been catching up on sleep.

"Conon! You have not been up observing the *komêtês*, the hairy star?"

"I have, your majesty, but it is not to be seen in the middle of the night," said Conon. "Only in the evening and the morning."

"It's causing a panic, they told me."

"Yes, ignorant people think it means something. I shall be giving a lecture tomorrow, explaining it rationally."

"I'm glad to know that. You may give me a first hearing of your lecture."

"I shall be honored," said Conon, "to give it to such an exalted audience of one. And to be apparently among the first to welcome your majesty home."

"Pardon me, Conon! You have not only been roused in the night, but roused by someone you supposed to be in another country. Someone of a less scientific spirit might take me for a ghost."

Conon was tempted to tell the king that he looked like neither a ghost nor a god. He overcame the temptation by beginning his lecture:

"This comet—"

"Why is it called that?"

"You may not have ever seen one?"

"I think not."

"No, because the last great one, according to the books, was forty years ago. When I was a child in Samos my father took me out in the night and showed me one; all I remember is that even to my young eyes it looked almost as small as a star. But the Babylonians kept records of them, and said they looked like brooms."

"Not like hair?"

"Like hair, brooms, whips, scimitars—who knows what they really are? They look like soft stars with hair trailing from them, and they move—they move slowly past the stars. They appear from somewhere, and disappear. As for this one, it seems to be a great one. If you were here the evening before last, you might have heard those who had noticed it telling the others 'A piece of the sun broke off!' Someone came running and telling me. But I had already been watching it for five days, as have the country people who are up before dawn. Haven't your troops been seeing it?"

"I'm afraid the troops have taken to sleeping later, in their march home."

"And not taking much interest in what the night sentries may have told them, I suppose. Well, after the first morning when someone came and told me about it, I started getting up early and going on the roof to look for it. I couldn't see it the first time; my eyes aren't as sharp as those of a peasant. Next morning I was just able to see it; it was a bit higher, but still lying nearly flat on the horizon to the right of the sun. It's come up from the south; it must have been frightening the Ethiopians. It's climbing higher and standing up straighter; it was in the constellation of the Crow and has climbed into the Virgin."

"The Virgin. But that is where the moon was when we were watching for it to be eclipsed?"

"Yes, that was half a year ago. That was the beginning of spring and the sun was then in the Fishes, about to move into the Ram, and the full moon opposite to it in the Virgin, about to move into the Scales. Now we are at the beginning of autumn and the sun is on the opposite side, in the House of the Virgin."

"And the comet with it?"

"Yes, passing northward across the Virgin's body. (The Sun is at the Virgin's feet, and the comet is crossing her head. And the planet of Aphrodite, by the way, is at her waist.) Now it's passed across the path of the sun—it's in the Virgin's breast—and beginning to show itself in the evening, and people think it has sprung out of the sun. I saw it this evening. Nothing but the sun was to be seen until the sun went down. As the sky began to dim the comet's hair appeared, and many more people must have seen it. It was low over the sea, to the right of the city, north of west. Only its broom could be seen—the end of its hair. Probably not everyone has seen it even yet, but that won't stop them getting excited. I watched it until it went down too low and the stars began to appear, and then I thought about it some more and drew myself diagrams, and then I went to bed."

"So I shall have to wait till next evening to see it?"

"No, I think it can still be seen in the morning as well as the evening, for at least one more day."

"How can that be?—seen in the evening and the morning too?"

"Well, being above the sun and bright—it goes down with the sun and will come up with the sun. But at a different angle, because—well, because the sun goes down in the evening *that* way, and comes up in the morning *that* way. If I just had a tablet—"

Student Theonida, who had been sitting at her table listening instead of persisting with her homework, sprang up and brought him a wax tablet, and the astronomer sketched on it, explaining what he thought would happen in the pre-dawn sky, and answering questions.

"If it keeps moving the same way, it will climb on *so*," he said, "into this space that doesn't have a name—the Lion's tail, though it's really in the House of the Virgin, being north of it . . ."

"How many watches of the night are left?"

It was a safe guess that half the night was left, but Conon looked up at the stars that were crossing the opening of the courtyard above them—the stars opposite to the sun: the Ram, the Flying Horse, Queen Cassiopeia—and made a show of estimating it.

House beyond the world

Ptolemy Tryphon returned to his quarters, sat for a while on the edge of his bed with his head bowed, arms crossed on knees. He looked up at an angle, eyes unseeing the wall he was looking at, moved his night-lamp about, made gestures, trying to keep fixed in his mind the sketchy celestial forms that had been described to him. Once more he put on the yellow cloak, taking some clothes of his own in a bundle, and went out and found a horse. He stole out of his own palace like a thief, and rode the fourteen miles to Zephyrion. The people he saw in the streets and the few in the suburb and along the open road kept out of his way. In the hamlet on the headland no one was to be seen, and he sought around for somewhere to hitch the horse. The only thing he could find was a thick deformed twig of a thorn bush that had been trimmed. Then he went into the temple and down the steps.

He expected to slide the bolt of the door softly back, but it was not fastened. He came quietly into the room. But Berenice was not on the bed.

He felt around in the dark to make sure, looked in the side chambers, even went out into the little garden by the sea and looked from side to side.

He dropped his bundle of clothes in the room, went back out of the temple and stumbled around in the hamlet, and beat on a door. A frightened woman, roused from sleep, led him to the priestess Eunyle's house. When she opened her door to him and saw the yellow of the Medzae, she set her face grimly. She had in her hand a sprig of silphium, and steam rose from a towel that was over her forearm.

"I am Ptolemy, son of Ptolemy," he said.

She waited for a moment before making her obeisance to him. "Where is my wife?"

"She is helping me tend a patient."

"May I come in and help too?"

"No more help is needed, the patient is well." She turned away and in a moment Berenice came to the door. She looked into Ptolemy's face, stepped out into the dark with him and shut the door behind her.

He looked at her white loose dress, belted high under her breasts so as to cascade over her shape, and said: "Does our child still kick nastily inside you?"

"Often."

He knelt and kissed her feet. "Forgive me, I mistrusted you because of a mistake."

After a moment, still kneeling, he had to repeat: "Will you forgive me?"

"My hair is somewhat grown," she said.

He stood up and felt it, behind her head. It had grown by the width of three fingers and covered most of her neck.

He kissed her.

"I can leave here now," she said, "my maid is sleeping. She had an altercation with another policeman, and got hurt."

He looked down at his yellow cloak and laughed. "So you haven't been sleeping?"

"No."

"We'll go back into the temple of Aphrodite and sleep into the day. But first I must show you the reason for my mistake, if I can." He was scared that he wouldn't succeed in this, or would miss the chance: with eyes now used to the dark, he thought the sky had already begun to pale. "Where's the other side of this headland?—I'll find a way." He took her by the hand and hurried in among the trees. Before long the two of them, hand in hand, were blundering about, lost in the night and stumbling on roots. Ptolemy threw back his shoulders, but it didn't help him find the way.

Eunyle came behind them, holding a shawl which she handed to Berenice. She told them: "There is a path, about five steps to your right," then went back where she had come from.

They found the thread of a path and trod cautiously down it. It opened onto a beach, tucked into the end of the curving bay that came from the Canopus mouth. Here there was a clear view of the eastern horizon: sea to the left and land to the right. A boat—made of wood but of simple design, without keel or thwarts—had been pulled up by its handle-like stern so that it was lodged on the sand. Toward the stern was a heap of netting. He helped her in, and there was room for them to recline against the heap if he half-turned toward her and laid one arm around her shoulders. They wriggled around a bit, because the net was not quite as soft as it looked, and being a cast-net it had little hard things—shells—sewn into it as weights.

It was, as six months ago, the season when the sun went down most steeply into the sea, exactly in the west, and came up most steeply out of the Delta and Asia beyond, exactly in the east. The sky was a rich throbbing blue, but still the blue of night. It was cloudless except for one wisp near the horizon. There remained more than an hour to dawn, and plenty of stars in the sky. The scatter of them along the Milky Way passed overhead, a glittering bridge from Egypt into the northern sea. In front there were fewer, but high hung the sharply horned moon (a few days before new).

"The star close by the moon—it's the Heart of the Lion again. And below that, the Virgin stands straight up, though she doesn't have many stars, and her only bright one—the Spike of Wheat— is still down below the horizon, where the sun is."

"Indeed, Tryphon, you've learnt a lot that I don't remember you knowing! You've been learning it out there in your life in the camps!"

"No, I usually had at least a tent over my head. It's Conon the astronomer who's coached me in this, and I'm trying to remember, so as to show it to you."

"Why?"

"You know that I sent and asked for an oracle to tell me whether I should stay longer away, and keep warring?"

"Yes, I had to know that."

"And do you know what answer the oracle sent me?"

"What answer"—asked Berenice— "did the oracle send you?"

"It was this," and he repeated it:

> Time to regress; the Lady's shining tress,
> From her house swept, is in another kept
> —The lady harnessed by the lord of darkness;
> Time to return, if you would see what's born.

"That is hard to understand," said Berenice.

"Yes, and I didn't understand it rightly until helped by what Conon told me. It was telling me to return home for the winter, when the season for campaigning is over, and when the child is to be born. Sound advice, don't you think?"

"Certainly, and rather obvious."

"But Oracles never tell their meaning directly; they wrap it up, so that we'll be in awe of them, and sometimes misunderstand them. 'The lady who was harnessed by the lord of darkness'— who is that?"

"Who is it?"

"Why, Persephone, whom we also call Coré, the Maiden, who was seized by Hades and taken down to be his queen in the underworld. The starry Virgin is her picture in the sky. The House of the Virgin is the house of the sky where the sun now is, at the end of summer—the time to come home."

"So we shall lie here and watch the Virgin appear, with the sun in her?"

"Yes, and something else."

They lay in the boat, whose bow was lifted by occasional ripples. The texture of the sky seemed to have grown minutely brighter, either because their eyes were more used to it, or because light was really creeping in, the beginning of the long suspense before sunrise.

Berenice said: "I'm a little cold, in spite of the shawl. What else are we waiting to see?"

"A comet, a long-haired star, which some people have been seeing before dawn for several days."

"And why do we want to see it?"

"'From her house swept.' Wait and see."

They waited. The sky seemed unchanging, even the one thin

cloud unmoving. She said: "I'm told that you are no longer
Ptolemy Tryphon now but Euergetes, the Good-Doer."

"That was a decision of the priests, because of the bringing
back to Egypt of the relics."

She postponed suggesting that there might be better ways of
earning the title. She wondered whether he would tell her for
himself what his suspicions had been; and whether there would
ever be a time when she too could tell him the truth. And
whether there were truths about himself that it was not usual for
a man to tell.

"No, I must explain now," he said, "in case that cloud stays in
the way and we don't get to see the comet. If I'm remembering
right, it should come up *there*. It's in the body of Virgo and its
hair will sweep upward over her. And then, according to Conon,
the next day or two, it will move in that direction, out of Virgo
into that dark space. 'The Lady's shining tress' is the comet—
sweeping from her House into another House of the sky (that
doesn't have a name), where perhaps it will be lost."

"And you thought the poem referred to my hair?"

"Yes! We can still say it does! A beautiful conceit. We can
have Callimachus write us a ridiculous poem about how your hair
became a comet and was swept into the stars. —What did you
do with it?"

Of the many answers she had tried to think of for this anticipated question—about burning it in accordance with another
Sapphic poem, throwing it away when it became ugly, destroying
it to make sure it transferred her strength to him—she felt herself
driven back on the lamest: "I don't know. I've forgotten where I
put it. It's not important. It may be dust by now. I'll find it some
time."

Then suddenly she was rescued by remembering the story
about how King Ptolemy Philadelphus got the Athenians' best
books from them.

"Did you go into our room?—in the temple?"

"Yes, I looked for you there."

"And you saw the picture?"

"Picture?—no. I was groping in the dark to find you. What
picture?"

"The picture of my hair. It was painted for me—they persuaded me to have a picture made—it's a gift for you."

"Thank you! But the gift I want is the original!"

"But that's what happened: the artist took it away to paint it and sent the picture and never came back—never came back for his payment."

"Ah! And was he your friend Sandrogon the Wanderer? Did you send all the way to Cyrene or Sicily for him?"

"You remember that name, do you? No, his name was—I've forgotten. It doesn't matter."

"He's probably left the country and is selling it in Athens!" said Ptolemy merrily. "He'll get a high price for it! Queen Berenice's Hair! Who was he? Let him have it, I'll send no ship after him. The painting shall hang in the temple and we'll hang Callimachus's poem under it. —All we want now is to see your heavenly hair, the comet."

Callimachus when she last saw him had been a sad man. He had received news that his friend in Caria was dead. He would not be ready yet to compose his silly poem.

They were silent and watched on. But the sky had certainly begun to pale.

"I'm afraid we may not see it. If only that cloud would drift along!"

"But we know it's there?"

"Yes, perhaps we can see it tomorrow. —Or we'll see it this evening. But I wanted to see it now."

There were no more stars to gaze at. They gazed at the cloud that insisted on loitering in just the wrong place, and had even become taller, though more translucent as the sky brightened. It rose in a long pale swath, dusted with gold as if by the coming sun—it was like electrum, the "child of silver and gold." It broadened upward and curved gently to the right, as if a sea breeze was pressing it, but it refused to move. It was a strange and beautiful cloud, but Ptolemy cursed it. He took his arm from around her neck and began to get up. His clumsy motion gave the boat a push, so that it went shallowly afloat. He prepared to put his foot in the water and pull the boat back, so that they could get out.

"That cloud," said Berenice— "I think it is not a cloud."

Ptolemy's foot punched down into the water and he lurched, trying to regain his balance and slew himself around to stare.

The sweep of gold was the hair of her comet, a form so vast that it already towered above the horizon, while its starlike body

eipe tis, Hêrakleite, teon moron, es de me dakru
  êgagen, emnêsthên   d' hossakis amphoteroi
hêlion en leskhê katedusamen; alla su men pou,
  xein' Halikarnêseu,   tetrapalai spodiê:
hai de teai zôousin aêdones, hêsin ho pantôn
  harpaktês Aidês   ouk epi kheira balei.

They told me, Heraclitus,   they told me you were dead,
They brought me bitter news to hear and bitter tears to shed.
I wept as I remembered   how often you and I
Had tired the sun with talking   and sent him down the sky.
And now that you are lying,   my dear old Carian guest,
A handful of grey ashes,   long, long ago at rest,
Still are your pleasant voices,   your nightingales, awake,
For death he taketh all away, but them he cannot take.

—Poem in elegiac couplets from the *Epigrams* of Callimachus (the elder). Translation by William Johnson Cory (1823-1892) in his *Ionica* (written in 1850, published in 1858).

Berenikê daughter of Magas　　　*circa 273-220* B.C.
Dêmêtrios ho Kalos son of Dêmêtrios Poliorkêtês
　　　　　　　　　　　circa 285-256 B.C.
Ptolemaios III Euergetês son of Ptolemaios II Philadelphos
　　　　　　　　　　　circa 280-221 B.C.
Kallimakhos son of Battos　　　*circa 305-240* B.C.
partial eclipse of the moon　　*246* B.C., *March 18*

had yet to rise. (And after it would come Venus and then the sun.)

The long-haired star stood beyond the world's edge. Colossus, Pharos, Pyramid, they were as grains of sand at its feet. And over the next days it would sweep slowly north, to dwindle and disappear and seem to leave that little tuft of stars as its trace.

Made in the USA
Charleston, SC
13 December 2015